Two Hundred Brand New Shiny Cadillacs

A Novel

Immigrant Worlds & Texts

Other Titles in the Series:

Memoirs of a Jewish District Attorney from Soviet Ukraine, by Mikhail Goldis, edited and translated by Marat Grinberg

Nabokov on the Heights: New Studies from Boston College, edited by Maxim D. Shrayer

Hyam Plutzik and the Mosaic of Time, edited by Victoria Aarons, Holli Levitsky, and Hilene F. Lanzbaum

"An exhilarating journey through the turbulent dawn of post-Soviet Russia. The gleaming Cadillacs of the title, the unforgettable characters from New York and Moscow, swirl before the reader's eyes like the dazzling, ever-shifting fractals of a kaleidoscope. A masterwork of narrative brilliance."

—***Jose Manuel Prieto,***
author of *Encyclopedia of a Life in Russia*

"A frolicking ride of a novel, full of excitement and stunning insights at every twist and turn."

—***Lara Vapnyar,***
author of *Divide Me by Zero*

"Ah yes, the great Russian realist tradition of Tolstoy and Chekhov sped right up to the present moment . . . Ooops! Wrong doorway. Pavel Lembersky has swept all the cards together and reshuffled the deck for us. Whether it's twelve chairs or two hundred Cadillacs, the ride has begun. Gogol opened the stable door, Bulgakov changed the horses to wildcats, and now it's time for further antics on the living page. Let excess and exuberance reign. Whether the scenery's from Moscow or Boca Raton, the real and irreal will swap their masks at whatever pace they please. All these irregularities of expectation come from close to the bone when the writer's raised up from late-Soviet Russia into another world and has seen the kingdoms fall. This is not some ingenious offhand po-mo jape from the land of the lucky. Its multiplex cargo comes straight from a true joker's heart to you. I wish this book the happiest of landings."

—***Rafi Zabor,***
author of *The Bear Comes Home*
(winner of PEN/Faulkner Award for Fiction)

Two Hundred Brand New Shiny Cadillacs

A Novel

Pavel
Lembersky

BOSTON
2025

Library of Congress Cataloging-in-Publication Data

Names: Lemberskiĭ, Pavel, 1956- author.
Title: Two hundred brand new shiny Cadillacs : a novel / Pavel Lembersky.
Other titles: 200 brand new shiny Cadillacs
Description: Boston : Academic Studies Press, 2025. | Series: Immigrant worlds & texts
Identifiers: LCCN 2025012880 (print) | LCCN 2025012881 (ebook) | ISBN 9798887197555 (hardback) | ISBN 9798897830206 (paperback) | ISBN 9798887197562 (adobe pdf) | ISBN 9798887197579 (epub)
Subjects: LCGFT: Novels.
Classification: LCC PS3612.E4544 T96 2025 (print) | LCC PS3612.E4544 (ebook) | DDC 813/.6--dc23/eng/20250510
LC record available at https://lccn.loc.gov/2025012880
LC ebook record available at https://lccn.loc.gov/2025012881

ISBN 9798887197555 (hardback)
ISBN 9798897830206 (paperback)
ISBN 9798887197562 (adobe pdf)
ISBN 9798887197579 (epub)

Book design by Lapiz Business Solutions
Cover design by Lily Balasanova
Author's photo by Igor Dashevskiy (back cover)

Published by Cherry Orchard Books, an imprint of Academic Studies Press
1007 Chestnut Street
Newton, MA 02464, USA
press@academicstudiespress.com
www.academicstudiespress.com

In loving memory of my cousin
Valery Semenovsky (1952–2024),
theatre historian and playwright

"Does that mean," I said in some bewilderment, "that we must eat again of the tree of knowledge in order to return to the state of innocence?"

"Of course," he said, "but that's the final chapter in the history of the world."

—Heinrich von Kleist, "On the Marionette Theatre"*

---

* Translated from German by Idris Parry.

Contents

PROLOGUE

The Boca Raton Recluse

Has Mr. Davis disappeared without a trace, Mrs. Teal?

Nope, no trace.

Do you know if he was of sound mind when last seen leaving his Algonquin Hotel suite midtown Manhattan?

As sound as he'd ever been. We spoke two days before.

Were the police or the press properly notified?

Yes. Yes.

How conclusive was the police report?

How conclusive is anything, Mark?

Yes, Mrs. Teal, but do I need to tell you that what we have on our hands is the disappearance of an American filmmaker of considerable renown, a director whose genre-bending musical comedies, courtroom dramas, crime mysteries, etc. made the AFI top 100 and garnered a few important national and European awards, including the Golden Globe and two Oscar nominations?

And let's not forget that British something or other.

Was Mr. Davis ever a member of the Communist Party?

You kidding me? Coming from where he—where we came from, what we've been through? Wouldn't be caught dead. Was lucky not to get blacklisted. What Communist Party?

I'm sorry, Mrs. Teal. My questions may sometimes lack finesse, but the book research is a project long on assumptions and short on tact.

Whatever.

Shall we talk about his first film, the breakthrough silent *The Wild Ass's Skin*?

The Skin was not his first one, Mark. A two-reeler called *A Flat* was.

Do you remember what it was about?

More or less. It featured a fidgety young fellow behind the wheel of a roadster. The man, played by Gregory himself, runs over a beer bottle, gets a flat, pulls over by the side of the road, takes out a pump from his trunk, and tries to put air in the tire. Only it works exactly the opposite way. The tire gets more deflated with every push of the pump until it's completely flat, and also, the car is getting deflated along with it, now looking like a mattress with two flat doors. The man tries to get inside the automobile, only he's lying on the mattress instead, tossing and turning spastically. Then, wouldn't you know it, a cop shows up and writes out a ticket, not for speeding. For sleeping at the wheel! As the cop walks away, the man follows him on the sly and pulls the button from his uniform. Now, the cop is shrinking too, until his flat figure is lying flat on the sidewalk. Then, by degrees, the street, the city, the US, the Western hemisphere, and the Eastern hemisphere, the universe itself undergo a drastic scaling down through deflation. Sort of the Big Bang in reverse. And that before the Big Bang theory even gained traction! Talk about serendipity. Talk about art imitating science. How does it end? The man in a straw hat holds the entire universe in his hand, now the size of a hanky. It actually *is* his hanky, the universe is; then he blows his nose into it, folds it up, and sticks it back inside his hip pocket. Then flags down a cab with a "Flat rate" sign on its door. Not bad for a twenty-three-year-old first timer, eh?

Not bad? I think it's great! And funny. And the theme of shrinking is already there, too! Doesn't it recur in *The Wild Ass's Skin*?

It sure does, Mark. Greg's thinking was precisely that. Things are just too big, too numerous, too bloated. His take on life, his philosophy.

But how did he handle the shrinking scenes, the Earth, the universe?

Animation, Mark. Animation was his thing. Kind of a pioneering approach for its time. His stand-up was innovative, too, by the bye.

I bet it was! How one advances from stand-up to movies is a whole different enchilada, Mrs. Teal!

A sixty-four-thousand-dollar question, Mark. How does one skip ahead from stand-up, a very American, very Jewish genre, to screen writing and then directing? Why Jewish, you ask? Why not? Haha. But seriously, in stand-up, you pile up one-liners to reach a crescendo. That's how Greg explained it to me anyway. In a motion picture, there's got to be plot twists. Say, a missing person turns out to be not so missing. Women posing as men as they are wont to do in Shakespeare . . . The stuff of comedy. What Greg did in *The Scoundrel,* his second one, if memory serves, he had a man posing as a woman pretending to be a man. A double loop required by the plot. But what is a plot? A way of working out the auteur's quirks. And like so many things, it starts with a joke, a one-liner-type premise, from a "let's suppose," from a "what if" . . . A man has to hide for fear of being exposed by the husband of a woman whose favor he seeks. But the husband is in on the fact that his wife's lady friend is a man. So "she" turns into a plumber on the double. A plumber who, of course, is all thumbs, can't even fix the leak—a comedy, and obviously, not a particularly sophisticated one. Truth is, I fell in with the artsy crowd at the time and started law school, so I was hanging out with bright college boys and avant-garde artists and filmmakers. Does Maya Deren's name ring a bell? I knew it would, bet you know your film history! I don't want to drop too many names at this juncture, but a number of poets, soon to be well regarded, were a part of our circle, too. So, I wasn't particularly thrilled by Greg's early efforts to make it in the industry one way or another. By then, he'd also got hitched to his Irish girlfriend Caitlin, a freckled beauty with a thick blond mane of hair who was expecting his child, so he had to think of fending for his new family. The eventual transition to the talkies was not too big a deal for him. Didn't take long to figure that no acting was in the stars for Greg, as his accent was still pronounced at the time. So, he focused on directing. Made a couple of musicals, which were okay, and minor successes, too. But, in all honesty, he was no Busby Berkeley, and neither did he ever claim to be. Maybe because his chorus girls were mostly second-rate and not too leggy, or his leading man, though tall, dark, and handsome, and a capable tap dancer, was just unable to sing while waltzing. I mean, he was audibly short of breath in every other scene. Some assistant editor clown called the picture *The Wheezing Waltzer*, though the actual title was *The Wizard of Waltz*. They even had to use two stand-ins for the lead, which pushed the modest budget over the limit and caused Greg's first major falling out with studio heads. Then, he did a few Depression-era comedies that went a long way to establishing his reputation. I'm referring to, first and foremost, *His Bride's Dowry*, *Nobody's Child*, and *What Martha Knew*. I believe he was the only American director ever to eventually be given the green light to do a remake of his own movie some forty years later. *What Martha Knew* with what's her name in the lead. Jessica, Jessica . . . Did you see it? I think you should! But perhaps it's enough for today . . . Of course, it's a shorthand, rambling preview of coming attractions, but at least you have something to show for your second week on the job. Let's continue next time, shall we?

Absolutely, Mrs. Teal! And believe me, it was awesome. Take my word for it.

Then I thanked Mrs. Teal for her time, turned off the recorder, patted the perennially sleepy Honoré D. on his big brown head, closed the door behind me, got into my rented Nissan, and reached my hotel in twenty minutes.

Once in my cell on the third floor, I fixed a quick avocado and alfalfa sprouts multigrain abomination, poured myself a glass of Pinot Grigio from a bottle that Marge, a receptionist who sported ochre cat-eye glasses and bows in her curly hair always kept cold for me in the fridge downstairs, and started transcribing the above dialog.

***

Do correct me if I'm wrong, because more often than not, I am, but I think it is right about here that you'd probably want to know how come by the end of last month, I checked into a three star hotel featuring a drained in-ground pool in downtown Boca Raton, FL, where I spend my nights filling pages upon pages with someone else's life story, mentally chained to the rickety writing desk by the window like some myopic circus animal, a defunct fridge next to the plywood wardrobe that has seen better days, and a mini bar locked upon my request. Truth be told, by now, I could have sprung for something more accommodating, even borderline fancy, but you know how it is with old habits: they die hard. And though I can't complain about the pay (3K per page, money wired to my bank account upon weekly delivery, complain I could: after all, it is my money that is being disbursed to me in such a roundabout and delayed fashion), yet the question remains: How come a tolerably intelligent, adequately educated programmer in his early '30s, with all due humility, an ace at rollback data management, got involved in transcribing hours upon hours of interviews with one Rosalyn Teal, a legally blind feisty ninety-two-year-old lady who inhabits a spacious if somewhat cluttered three-bedroom Spanish colonial with her guide dog chocolate Labrador Retriever Honoré D., an interviewee whose main subject is the turbulent life and times of her older brother, Mr. Gregory Davis, a Ukrainian-born Hollywood director gone missing for ten years at the time of this writing? Who could blame you for asking? Now and then, I can't resist mentally scratching my head, either. Mostly on weekends when, for diversion's sake, I take a long meandering ride through Boca in my rented silver Nissan Presea, palm fronds swaying in front of the white hotel facades, the docked boats bobbing placidly in the bay, the partied-out young women in little black dresses tossing their cookies onto the cobblestone driveways next to stretch limos with their tinted windows rolled up. Then I drive to the FedEx office downtown, deserted this time of day, park the rental in the sprawling lot, and fax one week's worth of transcripts, averaging about thirty-five pages, to St. Petersburg, the original one, the one on the Neva River, not its distant Floridan relation.

So, what brought me to Boca? . . . because I still have a feeling I'm getting ahead of myself—if for no other reason than a part of me is admittedly sluggish—though my initial plan was to begin at the beginning. That is, stick to the chain of events, however tangled, that had led up to my catching the red-eye to Moscow three months ago, chancing upon the punk princess Tasha Tschelicheva in a packed nightclub with throbbing walls and fog effects that commingled with real cigarette smoke and took forever to clear and only then deal with my taking on the Boca Raton Assignment on Tasha's film scholar aunt's behalf. I reluctantly choose to refer to it as "an assignment" since I've already been paid the retainer and two installments, so I can't really call it a shakedown, though initially it seemed like one. However, things being what they are, the said assignment helped me to navigate some hot water back in Moscow and ultimately get in touch with Mrs. Teal, the widowed Boca retiree with whom I have managed to strike up an unlikely rapport bordering on affection. However, starting from the start was never my forte or MO. You start from the start, and a whole can of worms pops right open, the little crawly bastards' multiple hearts beating in under-rehearsed unison. Just how far back do we go anyway? Granted, the Big Bang or Original Sin may be overkill, but wouldn't the latest *Star Wars* sequel be too recent? Are the amorous granddads bringing daffodils to their bashful grandma fiancées a few old countries back an absolute must? Only if they contribute to a good fleshed-out story with enduring characters and a memorable finale.

Be that as it may, here, in a nutshell, though in more detail than ever revealed to Tasha or anyone else, is the story of what brought me to Boca via Moscow where, as luck would have it, I witnessed the attempted coup of October '93, met the golden-haired punk princess Tasha T., and hired two bodyguards who did their best to collect the money I was owed by my so-called business partner Vik Z-sky, only their efforts weren't entirely successful. I mean, what kind of success is paying the ultimate price for it, even if the job is well executed? In my book, it ain't any.

As for the sequence of events featuring the events' emcees, for this is the title I like to accord to my significant others, past and present, it is as follows: breaking up with my vivacious slim-limbed doppelgänger Lilly K. in San Francisco; then, after a spell of celibacy, trying to bed the brown-eyed, vanilla-skinned, dyed-in-the-wool Deadhead Kristen Morse whose dimples and tiny birthmark in the left corner of her chapped lips made me temporarily lose sleep right around finals. Talk about bad timing and hyper-fixations. I followed Kristen to New York, where she had hightailed pursuing a career in independent film and where I thought it expedient to start seeking employment in the burgeoning field of computer programming. The two prongs of the quest achieved almost simultaneously, the latter made the much-needed inflow of steady income a palpable reality. The former tangentially resulted in a two-week stint as a PA for a fly-by-night film production company that employed Kristen as script girl so I could be next to my nomadic lover 24/7 before my job kicked in. The breakup with Kristen, gone location scouting someplace outside Toronto with Bungo, a stoner gaffer turned writer-director, where she stayed through the entire shoot, plus one year of postproduction was followed by my sizzling affair with a recently separated Albanian co-worker almost twice my age and half my girth, the swish of her patterned skirts accentuated by the flash of her chiseled calves driving the entire IT department's male contingent up the wall by the cooler on our floor and in the cafeteria. And it was Vjollca, my vaguely menacing paramour, who put me in touch with the beady-eyed Russian businessman Vik Z-sky, a compact middle-aged man beset by nasal hair issues who was visiting New York with his handsome Oxford-educated daughter, Alena of frosty smile and perfectly done nails, and Vik Z-sky's associate, a sinewy gent with a slight stammer who answered to Vodovozkind—an encounter that changed my life in more ways than one. Was it Vjollca's stab at retaliation for my manifested wavering vis-à-vis the question of tying the proverbial knot, I will never know; for Vjollca, as I found out towards the end of my Moscow sojourn, is no longer among the living. The car accident on the Henry Hudson Parkway near the Ninety-Sixth St. exit after one too many double apple mojitos at a coworker's birthday bash in Washington Heights turned poor Vjollca's upper body into one extra-large airbag wrapped kofte, very rare. I'm neither sadistic by nature nor am I, one should hope, being unnecessarily flippant. It's just that we didn't part on the best of terms, Vjollca and myself. Stuff happens.

Enlisting my father's fresh-off-the-boat septuagenarian college buddy Uncle Shura Tiraspolsky's expertise in dealing with your garden variety Russian gangsters, for that's exactly who Vik Z-sky and his retinue were, seems in retrospect poor judgment at its most flagrant on Dad's part. Not only was the well-meaning and chain-smoking Uncle Shura a little hard of hearing, but he was also given to sporadic snoozing fits during business lunches with Vik Z-sky and co in the legendary Russian Tea Room and other choice midtown eating establishments—and precisely what kind of signal would that proclivity likely send our overseas "partners"? A wheezing signal, a lightly snoring signal, an occasional drooling-over-the-profiterole signal, anything but the requisite signal of robust vitality and forward direction expected from a rookie member of the American business community. But my laissez-faire dad just wanted to offer help by proxy and without as much as sullying his wizened little hands, particularly in matters of iffy financial returns, whether immediate or long-term. He also deemed it detrimental to business to take half a day off from the daily grind at his Neider Laundromat Emporium on Emmons in Sheepshead Bay and waste his precious time meeting God knows who to discuss the particulars of acquiring God knows what within the shortest time frame possible. Or was it because the business contact came from his ne'er-do-well prodigal offspring just back from a five-year stay in California and thus was not to be taken even semi-seriously? But look, Dad, I'm doing okay now, really. At long last, gainfully employed. Those undergrad programming courses sure came in handy. Just looking to make an extra buck. You have a problem with that?

As it quickly transpired, the mob trio came to town seeking to acquire two hundred brand new Cadillacs for the newly opened markets in Russia—nothing to sneeze at, if you ask me. Shipping was specified as "by air." Shipping where? Vik Z-sky wasn't too explicit on the cargo's final destination. Moscow initially. Though with that kind of stock, you could conceivably open a dealership on a planet in Alpha Centauri and thrive there, too. Where did these guys hail from? Also Moscow, where else? Though Vik Z-sky himself did speak Russian with a trace of an accent that was hard to pin down, but hinted vaguely at ties to Central Asia, a land where magic fields are supposedly overgrown with fragrant joy flowers. Why would anyone want to buy two hundred Caddies in one fell swoop? Simple: they had the dough, and the market was hungry for it. So how come Dad didn't want to give Vik Z-sky and co the light of day even after I ran the numbers by him? Hard to say, like so many things with my impulsive dad, including his recent divorce from Mom and shacking up with a lissome contemporary art curator from Bryansk, whom he helped set up a gallery space on the Lower East Side, an arrangement wherein he was footing the storefront rent while the poker-faced Tatiana was busy maintaining the discursive relevance of the project and overseeing the engagement with the radical left in Latin America. Was Dad too busy feeling rejuvenated in her illuminating company in the privacy of his two-bedroom Upper West Side condo to even consider getting involved in his son's side venture? Or was he too proud to entertain the thought that there might be new opportunities within the country he had chosen to slam the door shut on long ago? "Just tell those crazy Russkies we can get the cars for them wholesale and cheaper than in Detroit, too!" he blurted out, chewing on the stinky Cohiba in his oak-paneled Sheepshead Bay office as he waved the entire thing off. Semi-serious turned out to be pretty damn serious by my or anybody's lights. The one-thousand-dollar commission per vehicle offered by Vik Z-sky amounted to how much? That's right: two hundred thousand. That was roughly my programming annual take-home multiplied by six. Six years of languishing in front of the monitor staring at the little green dancing characters on a small black screen till I'm blind, making sure the rollback procedure works smoothly as a baby's bottom should the system abend and the code revert to the pre-crash point with all the data intact . . .

The only snag is I never got to collect the fee. True, I had enough wits about me to ask for a ten percent retainer upfront, which the entrepreneurial visitors paid me in cash upon closing the deal with the Potamkin Cadillacs flagship store on Eleventh Ave. And I did my bit getting the dandelion-haired salesman with a beatific set of pearly whites and paisley suspenders to knock off 750 dollars per. And I did see to it that shiny Eldorados, Sevilles, DeVilles, and Fleetwoods were delivered to JFK by four eight-wheelers in a timely fashion (it took three days and countless cab rides back and forth to the airport). And I was there by the freight dock at the crack of dawn, a lukewarm white-and-blue cup of coffee in hand, Alena the leggy Oxfordian fashionista in shit-brown suede pumps along with Vik Z-sky's henchmen Vodovozkind by my side, the latter, by the way, seriously beginning to rub me up the wrong way demanding to know how come I chose to live in the cardboard paradise surrounded by false smiles and no theatre or music until I just had to tell him in plain Russian to shut the fuck up and let me do my job, i.e., supervise the loading of merchandise onto cargo planes and sign the papers to the tune of five thousand dollars per vehicle prepaid in cash by Alena Z-sky.

However, on the morning of payday, the day when a bit of proverbial laughing on my way to Citibank was finally supposed to take place, it turned out that Alena the ice queen, Vik Z-sky, and Vodovozkind checked out of their Avenue of the Americas Sheraton suite one hour before our scheduled appointment. Guess what? Feeling fucked over is not something I am wired to deal with calmly. Sue me, but it keeps gnawing away at me day and night. Call me fussy, call me a staunch believer in fair pay for fair work, but, as a matter of principle, I quietly quit my programming job (save for hitting Vjollca for Z-sky's whereabouts in Russia—to no avail), then took out just enough money from my savings account to cover the airfare to Moscow plus two months' living expenses, all gung-ho about tracking down the wheeler-dealers who did me wrong. And that's precisely what I did. I mean the ticket part. Righting the wrong took some doing.

Part One

RETRIBUTIVE JUSTICE MOSCOW-STYLE

Chapter One.

"All the world's a stage," proclaims Shakespeare memorably in one of his early comedies. Then he zips through the parts we get to play on that stage during our lifetime. The child, the schoolboy, the lover, the soldier. Question: What about the in-between, the hybrid parts? Yesterday's student, now a soldier, can still conceivably be a lover until the trumpet calls to join his regiment before sunup . . . As to my transition from a film student to a programmer to an amateur sleuth to a lover in the time of a coup to a Boca Raton research assistant, it was by no means accidental or surprising. You could almost say I'd been setting myself up for it. But then, who would have thought the transformation possible at all given my consistently demonstrated lack of a pathfinder's sense of smell, let alone a killer's instinct? And even if I did possess said qualities, I wouldn't know how to deploy them if my life depended on it. A gunslinger's knack for shooting point-blank, however figurative, is an acquired skill that I never considered expedient to acquire. My old college professor Sam Goldstein, who, incidentally, once taught a course on Westerns, said it best, if not first, so the credit, in part, should go to him.

On a warm, drizzly evening in early September, the day before catching the red-eye to Moscow, I paid Sam a visit in Soho, where he was staying in a friend's loft. His friend, a documentary filmmaker of some renown or an experimental filmmaker with a sizable following, I don't remember which, was at the time in Rotterdam on the lecture circuit, unless he was attending his long-overdue retrospective in Berlin. When I told Sam over jasmine tea, which he brewed for us in a funky Buddha-shaped dark-green kettle, that I was going to Russia and explained why, he smacked his lips audibly, then cracked a smile. "Sorry, but I just don't smell a murderer on you, Mark. Chances are, neither did your so-called business associates." I remembered that smile. Back in school, it had made a brief cameo on his fleshy mug shortly before he gave me a B-minus for a thirty-minute structural video travelogue that took two semesters to complete and left me drained emotionally and financially. My opus, detailing an imaginary journey undertaken by Dr. Freud and his patient, a captivating social butterfly turned socialist revolutionary, one Glaphira Pertkin, the not so notorious woman-hedgehog case, through the expanse of the Arizona desert lacked, per Sam's critique, both depth and coherence. Plus, was there any compelling reason for shooting the entire thing in soft focus? Sam inquired pointedly in front of the small group of distracted grad students whose attitude issues stemmed, in part, from the excessive fixation on mid-career Godard. I was frayed for a week but didn't let hard feelings get in the way of our extracurricular friendship.

"C'mon, Sam, take a good whiff," I quickly raised my elbow over my head. Ever since I dropped out of San Francisco State U., where he taught film theory and video production, I could afford an occasional breach of propriety when around Sam.

"Nope, nothing," he said, shaking his head mock-ruefully.

"Could it possibly be because I never killed anyone or have any immediate plans to?" I offered. "You recall that movie about a dystopian society where manslaughter was not openly condemned, just frowned upon? You whack one too many, you get your knuckles rapped? You dispatch the entire community, you do community service in the neighboring community? So long that there's someone to appreciate the fruit of your forced labor? Until the hero winds up in a miniature replica of the Garden of Eden-type place? Talk about unjust deserts."

He remembered, albeit vaguely, for sci-fi was never really his thing. He thought the genre too didactic, too parabolic, too something.

"Sounds *Twilight Zone*-ish. Also, Greg Davis-y."

"Greg who-y?" The name was new to me.

"Greg Davis, the unsung pioneer of American cinema," elaborated Sam, ushering me to the door, "had a character blow his nose into the greatly shrunk universe. And you thought you were the only Mr. Irreverent on God's green Earth, didn't you?"

And before I had the time for a half-decent rejoinder, he bid me goodbye, asking to take good care of myself in the heart of the "Evil Empire" where I, jet-lagged and hungover from the above-average intake of Jack on the rocks onboard, landed the next afternoon and got settled in a nondescript two-room apartment (a so-called *dvushka*) in Moscow's bedroom district of Kuntsevo three days later.

Why Kuntsevo, a good ten miles from downtown Moscow rather than more centrally located neighborhoods only marginally pricier than my temporary abode featuring the faded gold-on-violet wallpaper in the living room, the black-and-white TV in the bedroom, and the sticky oilcloth-covered table by the kitchen window giving onto the poplar trees in the courtyard whose most prominent attributes included the row of Lego-size garages and the rusty '60s era swing set that made me feel like I had never left the country of my birth in the first place? I'll tell you why. Call me sentimental, call me a fool for love long gone to the dogs, but Kuntsevo was the neighborhood where my ex, Lilly K., grew up. Did I have a thing for my spry doppelgänger, or did I still have a thing for her? Why do I keep calling her "my doppelgänger" anyway? She looked nothing like me; was more of a hazel-eyed, well-shaped soulmate, or so it seemed at the time. It'd been three years since we broke up; we had lived together for six. By all calculations, I should have been over her by now. That is, if there's any truth in the saying that it takes half the time you are with someone before that someone is out of your system for good. Why, then, the imperative to breathe the same autumnal air she had breathed as a toddler taken on walks by her now long-deceased mom and her handsome dad, who has since remarried? Why was I dead set on seeing the same poplar trees, only taller, that she saw daily on her way home from school? Masochism thinly veiled as pining for lost love? Or are they more or less the same entity, like the conjoined twins bound by the forces of destiny, now more commonly referred to as genetically determined late and incomplete egg division, and as such better left untouched by the surgeon's scalpel? Funnily enough, we even bought two pairs of identical white bell-bottoms, she and I, when we started going out. Only hers fit her to a tee, while I had to lie down on the carpeted floor in my parent's bedroom and let the force of gravity do its thing, i.e., flatten my belly before I was able to pull my pair up and zip it up and button that sole tough-to-button button with attendant huffing and puffing.

Come to think, it was huffing and puffing—plenty of bickering too—that marked my six long years with Lilly as it was becoming plain to my Orpheus-like glance rearward augmented by the steady flow of Jacks aboard Boeing 747 on my way back to the former USSR. A looker when she put half a mind to it, effortlessly sexy around men of all ages, not an ageist in the slightest when it came to throwing her cute little ass around—towards the end of our cohabitation, she took to affecting laughter, school-girlish and intermittent, which irritated me no end given the end she used it to. She could also flare her nostrils when feigning indignation and twist her tongue 180 degrees clockwise and counterclockwise. No mean feat when performed purposefully and in tight quarters. A fashionista to a fault, she could do her prematurely thinning hair in five different ways, the top knot bun with curls cascading down her prominent forehead amongst her favorites. A dancer, too. Not professional by any stretch, but proficient enough at her syncopated marionette-like moves. Think for a second of the sinusoid pas interrupted by staccato feet stomping and head shaking accentuated by double finger snapping and rotations of wrists like she was skipping an invisible rope, starting with the simple jump and then proceeding to the more challenging crisscross and you'll get the picture, maybe. And let's not forget elbows akimbo, and pursed lips. Cumulative effect: mock-serious, gracefully clowning. She made dance-clowning look sexy, just like she claimed I made caricatures look serious. Not sure how far I'd go along with that take on the doodles I liked to occupy my spare time with back then. Who was it said, "We are all God's cartoons?" And if the notion is true only in part, then a human cartoon doodling away will give anyone enough food for thought, doodle-thought, or noodle-thought, but so what? Curiously, back in the day, doodling was my dancing, just like dancing was her doodling. I think we complemented each other that way. She called my graphic efforts a testosterone-propelled *letka-enka* dance on paper, and I called her dancing Jackson Pollock on the air. To this day, I still have only a vague idea of what I meant by that, but she didn't seem to mind and never asked for elaboration.

Lilly K. noodled her way into my life one fine weekend in April via a phone call. She was seeking trivial advice regarding her college entry art portfolio. One thing I don't like to talk about is that it was my childhood buddy Sashka Lerman who furnished her with my phone number en route to the US. The fact is that Sashka Lerman had a fling with Lilly K. in Rome while both of them were waiting for their visas to enter the

States. That long stay in Italy was their first exposure to the West, a first glimpse of the new customs and attitudes, just like it was for hundreds of thousands of ex-Soviets who opted for the US rather than Israel as their final destination. With plenty of time on their hands and boundless curiosity vis-à-vis the new mores and practices, they quickly—and briefly—became a couple, Lilly K. on her way to the States solo, Sashka traveling with his mother whose unshaken conviction about her son's smarts, looks, academic superiority, potential or actual, and success rate with the opposite sex knew no bounds. All you have to do is whistle, she'd tell him, and they'll come flocking in. She was right on the money, too. Flock they did. Sashka, not known for a lack of self-confidence anyway, was an instant hit with the young Russian- and Ukrainian Jewish ladies in transit who were duly smitten with his dark good looks, quick wit, and way with words. Lilly K. later claimed she just went with the flow, curious to see what the big deal was. Nothing special, she reported matter-of-factly when we started going steady in New York. Came in a matter of minutes. Like I cared. Or maybe I did. As for Sashka, he never took my new romance seriously (until it got to be nothing but); he would say to Lilly's face that chicks are never chosen over old friends, it's just not done. I felt awkward about his old-country machismo and the whole affair. Was I betraying him? Stealing his girl? But wasn't he unfaithful to his Tonechka who stayed behind, Tonechka the blonde sad-eyed daughter of a stern Soviet army colonel who wasn't exactly thrilled when his daughter started seeing a Jewboy to begin with. And look what happened; he is gone with the west wind though he said he'd come back and get her as soon as he got settled—yeah, right...

They were drawn to each other naturally, my ex Lilly K. and Sashka; they had the same taste in books and movies, loved art, and quite casually, went to bed a few times. She had her own ideas about chivalry, which happened to be diametrically opposite to his; he was reluctant to pay for her pizza and Coke, as a man, an employed man at that, she thought he ought to. Sashka, who knew some English, was hired by the resettlement agency while Lilly K. was getting by on her modest monthly émigré assistance check. Then she headed for New York, and Sashka chose Chicago. Before they parted ways, he gave her my phone number, just in case.

She called one Saturday afternoon in mid-April, and we agreed to go to the theatre the following weekend. I think it was something interminable by O'Neill in an off-Broadway theatre on Thirteenth Street, a play for which her friend was an understudy. I didn't mind the length of the play: long is how you want to sit in the dark next to an attractive twenty-one-year-old girl in the warm month of April. Or wait. Wasn't it *Annie Hall* that we went to see that night? Funny how things blur phonetically, not just chronologically, when you try to recapture the past: Doesn't O'Neill sort of sound like Annie Hall? Can you measure time by phonemes or reset it by unscrambling them? At half past five Jacks, maybe you can. Her English was nonexistent then, but she never let on that she didn't get much of what was going on in the wordy Woody Allen rom-com. She only asked for help when the snippets of Alvy's inner monologue were presented through subtitles, which at some point read, "I wonder what she looks like naked?" Lilly asked what "naked" meant. I translated. She nodded like it was a given. A week later, we kissed under a plane tree outside the three-story building in Astoria, where she shared an apartment with her relatives. Her lips were the softest. Most of my kissing had been done in the old country seven months prior. A change of pattern of the most welcome kind. My first American kiss.

A few months later, we agreed to have lunch: Lilly, me, and Sashka, who came to town on the Fourth of July. We met on the second floor of Burger King on West Third St. and Avenue of the Americas. It felt pretty weird; my childhood friend had just ended a relationship, call it en route, call it a Roman holiday affair, but now I was sleeping with his girl, not en route to anyplace—we were a real item, Lilly and I. Yet feeling weird was as far as it went the first six months: happy-go-lucky, no hard feelings, no retroactive jealousy pretty much described my state of mind back then. Not that we saw Sashka much since. I'm not sure what got into me along the way but half a year later, I recall roaming the deserted streets of Berkeley after lectures, talking to myself like a raving lunatic, halting in my tracks every half a block, burning with rancor, thinking how duped and cheated I felt by letting myself get involved with, and later marrying, the woman a friend of mine had fucked! It just hurt so! Even when she told me to stop this nonsense and asked why I didn't try feeling like the king of the hill who won his queen's love instead, it didn't help. Someone along the line made a choice, and it wasn't my choice. I followed; I didn't lead. I should have been that guy whom she got involved with in Rome or anywhere, damn it all to hell! I should have been with her then! They slept together; she called me out of the blue; we clicked. But the choice was made for me. So what if it had happened before she met me? It happened. It happened for real. He was inside of my love. Sometimes, to make matters worse, he'd say point-blank, like he did in New York after that lunch at Burger King, "Didn't you notice how she was ogling me from across the table?" I had to confess I didn't see anything out of the ordinary, or maybe I was just incapable of reading people like Sashka did. Later, though, I noticed that that was the look she reserved for almost any man of her acquaintance: sly, whimsical, effortlessly inviting.

Sashka Lerman's visit on that Independence Day, the first Fourth of July for both of us, culminated in our crossing

New York Harbor, he and I leaning against the railing, taking in the fireworks exploding behind the Statue of Liberty, the blazing many-colored bouquets swirling around in the dark-blue sky. Sashka and I were talking about the difference between the American Revolution, which we knew next to nothing about, and the Russian Revolution, which we knew a lot more about from Soviet textbooks that we reasonably suspected to be a very slanted riff on the actual events. We finally concluded that the American Revolution was infinitely more significant historically. "Isn't it why we are watching the fireworks on this side of the Atlantic?" I said. "True, but how do you measure the significance quantitatively?" Sashka, the eternal contrarian, queried. "Surely not by the number of victims left in its wake? Or maybe by its import for the country's bid to stay competitive on the global scene?"

The following day, my friend Sashka left for Chicago, where he was to start a new job at the World Bank right after the holiday weekend.

Chapter Two.

My granddad took a shine to Lilly K. the moment he laid his myopic eyes on her in The Three Sisters, a Sheepshead Bay eatery, a few weeks later. The '70s Russian invasion of South Brooklyn at its peak, the place was a-throb with multiple precision strikes spearheaded by Chicken Kiev hot-butter-fueled breadcrumbs covered missile-shaped cutlets, sour-cream-enhanced tomato and cuke salads "Nostalgié" discharging their vitamin-rich bursts on impact with willing casualties' quivering palates and the dressed-to-kill sequined-mini-skirt-clad chanteuses completing the gaudy theatre of operations. I watched my granddad watch Lilly closely, the disco lights' reflections churning recklessly in his rimless bifocals, as she danced the *freilachs* in controlled abandon encircled by the ample-bosomed heavily mascaraed relatives of Granddad's second wife on The Three Sisters slippery parquet floor. Lilly always seemed to know which dance to dance and when to dance it. Coming from a half-Jewish family, her other option would have conceivably been the traditional Russian squat dance favored by her Slavic forefathers. I also wondered if sirtaki wouldn't have been too tall an order had I come from a solid Greek stock and the festivities were taking place in one of Astoria's special events pantheons stuffed with cheap plastered copies of pagan deities staring each other down along the mirrored hallways. At some point, Granddad asked her to dance, too. She seemed hesitant for a moment, all modesty and reserve, then obliged, mustering all the poise she could after her third shot of Absolut. Round and round they went, slow-walking rather than dancing, the stooping section eight doyen, his gait wobbly, leaning on my sprightly wife-to-be who was leading unhurriedly but resolutely like she was a nurse administering the pre-swimming poolside recreational set of exercises to the sound of Sophia Rotaru's infectious covers. Was Granddad partial to Lilly because she was a foot-stomping, hip-swaying young cutie slender of limb and supple of torso, and let's not forget that mischievous sparkle in her hazel eyes? Or because she was a woman-in-the-making capable of perpetuating the Neider family bloodline given proper care and attention? Probably both.

Next time—which was the last time—we saw Granddad, I had a cassette tape recorder with me. He was pushing eighty-six, we were about to blow New York and embark on our one-way journey to California, and I thought his memories of things past could come in handy one day. Actually, I gave Lilly the portable recorder for her birthday, and we wanted to try it out. Two birds with one stone. I gave her a cassette with John Lennon's *Imagine* to go with it. She played the tape nonstop. Or hummed the songs on it. Or tried to sing along to it. Her older brother thought the songs were no more complex than lullabies and dismissed them outright. I believe he was a Stravinsky kinda guy. I'm cool with that, but does one hear Stravinsky hummed a lot? After a short Q&A session at Granddad's taped to our satisfaction, we headed to the Bronx Zoo a few blocks from Granddad's apartment in Pelham Parkway.

Imagine a breezy, sunny afternoon in late August, not a cloud in the sky. Imagine a Puerto Rican vendor in a white apron selling rainbow-colored shaved ice by the zoo entrance. Imagine crossing the street slowly, watching for traffic, the two of us with Granddad in the middle, pausing every ten feet. Just as Granddad used to take me to the zoo in our hometown, a much smaller zoo, which looked huge to the much smaller me, the zoo with the requisite tray-holding mid-size bear effigy on its hind legs inside the ticket office, so we took Granddad to the zoo in the new country, one of the biggest. Not much continuity between circuses here and there, no Russian TV or movies at the time. But animals are animals no matter where you pay to watch them do their animal stuff. And continuity does count for something when you are of a certain age and find yourself in a foreign land, like a bug-eyed fish out of damn water gasping for air. No cultural exchange back in those days either. An occasional Moscow poet reading at Queens College or Hunter. A sole Russian-language newspaper, briefly sharing the readership with another one targeting us, the new Americans of the so-called third wave of Russian emigration. And about twenty third-wave new American relations from Granddad's second wife's side who had come to the USA a year before us, all quick with business advice and a round or two of Smirnoff...

Grandpa liked the zoo so much that, in his excitement, he started mixing up place-names when we resumed taping the interview on the bench outside the monkey house. He kept calling New York Odesa and vice versa. "Here in Odesa," he'd say, or "When we moved to New York in 1923..." Then he'd pause, seemingly embarrassed every time I corrected him. Then I stopped correcting him altogether, just making a mental note every time he misspoke. Then I told myself, "To hell with mental notes, misspeak away, you're entitled to!"... Maybe the caged animals of the New World reminded him of their undernourished counterparts back in the socialist Zoolandia and triggered memories of the old country? Llamas will do it every time. For Lilly, it was the ride on the enormous African elephant, her red-rimmed blue pleated skirt complemented nicely by the ruby-red kilim mat she was perched upon during the ride. All of a sudden, she started giggling hysterically like she was a nine-year-old on a field trip, and there was no stopping her until the ride came to a halt, and the elephant, heeding the guide's orders, bent her forelimbs, flapped her ears a few times, and lowered her entire body while the guide courteously helped Lilly disembark.

A month later, Lilly and I were getting ready to hit Highway I-80. "Don't waste your time going to college," a visiting UC Berkeley law student friend was instructing me by way of a valediction. He had been staying with us for a couple of days. His wife had just graduated from Berkeley with a BA in psychology and was on her way to start a new job in Vienna. Her lawyer-to-be husband liked Lilly right away and tried to work his charm on her. I found his efforts amusing. Then there was a big faux pas involving the one-hundred-dollar bills he attempted to hang from a desiccated Christmas tree to impress his wife before we picked her up at JFK. We had kept the tree from the last New Year's in our one-bedroom apartment in Flushing. As he was hanging the bills from the prickly branches, he noted that there was a good chance we'd never see so much dough in one place, namely, our place—or such large denominations. So enjoy the show while you can. Right after he made that remark, he got visibly ashamed. Then, he tried to turn his crassness into a joke. Provided my Moscow-Boca mission bears the belated fruit, i.e., I finally get paid in full, wouldn't it be great to stick it to him, invite him over for a real New Year's, and trim the tree with fifty hundred-dollar bills for him to take in, maybe do a little dance around the tree, hopefully, with Tasha . . .

Anyhow, back in New York, the would-be lawyer said to me, "You have a fertile mind, Mark, unschooled yet quick. Don't let the curriculum clutter your head with things unnecessary and cumbersome. You know the story of the guy who made a fortune selling pet rocks?" I didn't. So he dutifully related the amazing story of the American success that capitalized on the fad that had swept the nation a few years back. Or started the fad, can't think of the proper chronology right now.

"For some," he ended his tale on a moralistic note, "school is a gigantic detour, a waste of time and money. You take a long way to California, you'll drive through ten states, maybe more. Don't waste your time; use it. And use your head. Do some research. See what people like. Try to single out and then fill that demand." Frankly, all I saw on our way westward was that folks liked cars a lot. Everything revolved around cars in my new home country: gas stations, highways, car dealerships, rest areas, car washes, car rentals, lines at DMV offices seemed the longest, two-garage houses abounded, there was even a new wave band called The Cars. How do you take advantage of that obsession? In a sense, and in a roundabout way, I did, if only partially: cars were what Vik Z-sky was in the market for, and in large quantities, too. And cars were what I helped him get. And have yet to collect for services rendered.

Reminiscing about my life and my wife aboard a Boeing 747 on my way to Moscow after bumming around in the West for fifteen years, I got so worked up in my aisle seat that I literally lost count ordering Jacks on the rocks from the ruddy-cheeked pursed-lipped flight attendant Evdokiya and thought it might be to everyone's advantage if I spent part of the flight in the restroom, thus unpremeditatedly channeling the USSR-bound character in a Beatles song written about a quarter-century before my journey. I mean the one about the passenger who keeps the paper bag on his knee and professes to have an interest in hearing the balalaika and seeing the snowy mountain peaks down south . . . Sashka Lerman, a bona fide Beatlemaniac, once told me it was Paul who played the drums on the track; Ringo was otherwise engaged, or plain pissed, during that particular session. Weird. But that's how bands break up. Marriages too. Wasn't Lilly all but missing from the picture the last few years of our cohabitation? Didn't she keep herself busy in those little pockets of activity I was denied full access to: tai chi, jazz dance, aerobics? But Ringo!

Sometimes, I had to take Sashka's word about pop trivia. Not that it mattered much; Ringo or not, it's still a great song and it opens a great album.

Feeling more at ease after driving the porcelain bus in the airplane lavatory for ten minutes and making a beeline back to my seat, I had a most vivid and protracted daydream, which seemed to last for the rest of the flight. Pretty much grounded in reality, it featured our honeymoon trip south of the border when my ex Lilly, and I witnessed a bizarre scene that revolved around an open-air circus act, namely, boxing. Until then, I'd been under the solid impression that kangaroos were the only mammals known to man who exhibited a verifiable interest in boxing. Was I wrong! At a crowded mid-May fair on a windy Saturday afternoon someplace Michoacan, Lilly and I watched a thirty-foot pole being hoisted up in the middle of the village square, a pair of boxing gloves hanging from the hook atop the pole, and shortly after, a midsize bear starting to make her way up said pole to reach the gloves that by all appearances were coveted both by the crowd of onlookers down below and her furry self. The bear was roaring with delight, and here's why: the wooden pole covered with lard to make the climb more challenging, stimulated her inadvertently by rubbing her inner thighs on the climb. By the time she reached the top of the pole and snatched the pair of prized gloves off the hook with her fangs, she was in seventh heaven. The cheering crowd didn't seem to mind the occasional droplets of the animal's vaginal juices bespattering the gawkers. Then the boxing match ensued as the final bets were placed either on the she-bear or her mustachioed hunchbacked ringmaster. All I can say is the obvious: I wish I'd had my camera. I'd left it back in the adobe hut where Lilly and I were staying. Some honeymoon. Your basic student variety, no frills but tons of thrills. I say I wish I'd had my camera because, in the third round, the hunchback won a convincing victory over the bear by knocking her down and then kicking her in the belly with his pointy boot as she was lying prostrate on the ground whining pathetically, though the last touch, or rather, the last kick seemed both cruel and unwarranted. For a brief moment, and given the attention lavished upon the ursine fighter, it seemed that Lilly and I were watching a circus number someplace Moscow or Odesa rather than witnessing an ill-kempt bear clearly trained to take a fall for an extra serving of the post-match honey in the Mexican village square. After the fight, the ringmaster passed around his sombrero and, I believe, made out like a bandit, which I think he was anyway.

"Remember Grandpa Krylov: 'The peasant had not breathed a sound before the bear had got him on the ground?'" Lilly quoted from the famous fable before she took a bite of the warm chicken tamale we bought from an elderly street vendor across the square. Then she added, "Looks like the tables have been turned here."

"Funny," I said. "Here we are watching a Mexican traveling show in a Michoacan village square in the late twentieth century, yet we can't stop quoting fables penned by an early nineteenth-century Russian poet!"

"Isn't that why you married a Russian girl?" grinned Lilly K., half-done with her tamale.

"And a hot little one at that," I chuckled stupidly and pinched her cute ass.

And there I was a decade and few emcees later, fastening my seat belt aboard the plane, preparing to land, thinking about my ex but also of ways to keep in check that pervasive and peculiar Russian habit of dropping quotations all over the place, and of looking at yourself, consciously or not, as part of a song you liked to get down to with your ex, and considering what it might take to lose that ill-fitting imaginary frock worn by a character in the book you read as a raw youth and modeled your early years on. There's got to be a safe and permanent means of egress from a mesh of references to fables, songs, movies, and books that forever make you feel trapped in someone else's puppet show written and directed way before you even made your first entrance. Can you have your say in the production? What if the strings are just too taut or the lighting too harsh? Or one more dress rehearsal is needed before the curtain goes up? What if you want your input vis-à-vis background music to be heeded? What if.

Chapter Three.

What I gathered after a week of hanging out in the hot spots of Moscow, where the dollar went pretty far, though often in the wrong direction, was that tracking down Vik Z-sky was easier planned than done. The same went for his daughter, Alena the ice queen, and Mr. Vodovozkind. None of them, for one reason or another, were showing their faces in any of the clubs or casinos on my list. (Yes, random as my search might appear, I did put together a list of places their kind was likely to patronize) For motives that hardly need elaborating, I preferred to frequent the night clubs in the company of two square-shouldered bodyguards, the Afghan campaign vet Decibel Petro and his silent civilian cousin Orlov whom I privately nicknamed Sharpshooter and Troubleshooter, the latter given to wearing a pair of extra-strength earplugs and Ray-Ban sunglasses even after dark. No great fan of the industrial music that was de rigueur in Moscow clubland that fall, I could relate to the plugs but was reluctant to ask Orlov what his take on the *Terminator* movies might be. The cousins were business contacts of Uncle Shura, who had been active in the nascent cooperative scene in Moscow before he decided to move his store to New York and try his luck there with unexceptional results so far. Uncle Shura recommended the cousins' protection services, and I had no reason to question his judgment. Not only was he an old family friend, but he also had a small stake in my trip's successful outcome—those business lunches at the Russian Tea Room and many a cab ride to JFK and back that he paid for were not cheap. If Uncle Shura was content with the duo's hands-on protection of the chain of consignment stores he once owned, I reasoned, all I had to worry about was my own security before collecting the dough from my so-called partners. I thought the actual meeting with Vik Z-sky and co, would be a cinch. And in a sense, it was, at least, for me. Because I never got to show up for it.

Meeting the cousins for a job interview in the spacious Rossiya Hotel, where I stayed for three days before finding the Kuntsevo apartment, was surreal. The cousins lived forty-five minutes from the city center in one of Moscow's bedroom neighborhoods, Chertanovo. Getting there by metro or taxi would have made for a two-hour round trip, maybe longer, since I didn't know my way around the city metro system then. Also, knowing the difference between a trustworthy cabbie and a rip-off artist was a skill I had yet to master. I was still groggy and jet-lagged after the boozy night aboard the plane, and for now, my main concern was that a face-to-face with a visibly distraught and disheveled American whacko who reeked of whiskey might bring about a hefty surcharge when it came to negotiating the cousins' fees. In a word, I got so freaked out before our meeting that you would think it was me looking to land a job and the cousins were the underworld HR team doing the screening.

At first blush, the hotel was a far cry from the Rossiya of my adolescence, its light façade quite a bit duller, its lobby shabbier. What I did once inside, even before getting in the long check-in line, was to buy a desk-calendar-size paperback of Joseph Brodsky's poems at the lobby newsstand. If for no other reason than for the incongruity of the purchase: I had plenty of the celebrated poet's volumes on my living room shelves in New York, but the post-Nobel prize Brodsky, once exiled, now published in his home country, was the first for me.

There was still a cafeteria on every other hotel floor where you could get a cup of coffee with a cheese Danish (*vatrushka*) or a salami and Holland cheese sandwich and hard-boiled eggs like you used to in the heyday of socialism. But a tangible sense of things falling apart hung heavily over the interior. The carpets that ran the length of the hallways were either badly stained or faded, the wall paint was peeling off in places, occasionally an elevator door was missing entirely or stood leaning against the wall, next to the dark shaft yawning at your feet. Then, the strangest thing happened. As I was looking for my room on the eleventh floor, I started rapping lightly on door after door, most of the doors left ajar, then peering into the rooms and tiptoeing inside a moment later. Just for the hell of it, I can't think of a rationale. Chalk it up to the Jack Daniels aboard the plane. Almost half of the rooms appeared vacant; the maid had already cleaned some, and others looked as if they were being cleaned and the maid had just stepped out. Behind the third door, I saw a short-haired woman in a gray wool dress with big glasses astride her pointy nose, her body peculiarly transparent in the sunlight coming aslant from the window. She also seemed to be glowing. The woman extended her arms, angling for a hug, greeting me in broken English and smiling pleasantly but in a peculiarly blurry fashion. She looked vaguely familiar too, said how nice it was to see me after all these years, then switched to Russian, which also sounded accented like she came from one of the Baltic republics. She then asked if she could take my coat (I didn't have one on; it was early September). I tried to blink away the apparition, which reminded me faintly of Uncle Shura's late wife, Aunt Nusia Tiraspolsky. Aunt Nusia was almost gone now, yet in a way, still there. I couldn't quite make out her features; her face shifted before me inexplicably, faster than faces do, even faces in motion; or maybe it was twitching. Then, all at once, it came back to me as if a living room window had been flung open, letting in the smells and sounds of a winter past.

Once, while on vacation in Moscow, my parents, myself, and Aunt Nusia were paid a visit by our American cousin's friends. They were his buddies from college in Belgium, where they studied medicine as foreign students; they figured they'd come over on a three-day tour of Moscow and Leningrad. Don, our distant cousin, couldn't join them for some reason. We, the Neiders, were days away from applying for exit visas to the US. Anyhow, Aunt Nusia, who was staying at the Rossiya Hotel on the floor above us, suddenly entered our room where the visiting Americans were sitting around, some of them on the floor cross-legged (which I thought was really cool, almost countercultural of them), as they were trying to address my parents' many pressing questions in my lame translation. ("What is it that we hear about the economic crisis in the USA?" "Ah, not to worry, it's not going to affect the banks, that's where we keep our money. Do we look worried to you?" "How exactly does a market economy work?" "Well, you see, it's all about supply and demand. Let's say, just as an example, that you manufacture fur hats . . .") So Aunt Nusia walks in and greets the Americans with her disarming smile, extending her hand, introducing herself, "Hi, my name's Vika!" As if by giving the Americans an assumed name, she was covering her bony ass. Nice try. All the rooms, of course, were bugged floor to ceiling back then. The guys in the control room were most likely trained well enough to tell a fake Vika from a real Nusia. I think at some point, she even volunteered to show one of the guests—a tall, silent man with a hooked nose and piercing eyes—a few *letka-enka* moves (kick to the left, kick to the right), holding him by the waist if for no reason than to prove to the American tourists that Russians know how to have fun, too. Anyhow, all these years later, I was standing in the middle of the room, which, as it turned out, was also our room back then, or maybe it was a similar room—you couldn't really tell the standard hotel rooms apart, the voices of the past ringing in my ears, seeing the specter of Aunt Nusia make its eerie appearance, which I tried to get out of my hair, literally, by taking a long shower, brushing my teeth, rinsing my mouth with Scope from a travel-size bottle, and then changing into a clean shirt and jeans, ready now to interview the cousins.

They arrived almost on time, seemed decent, well groomed, and reasonably intelligent. Particularly Decibel Petro, who had a bushy mustache that concealed a slight harelip, but otherwise was rather handsome. Both cousins appeared broad-shouldered by nature but also because of the cut of their double-breasted cashmere jackets. Petro sported mutton chops, Orlov was baldish and shy. They spoke of Uncle Shura with respect verging on reverence and were of the impression that he'd made it spectacularly huge in the United States. I tried to play along noncommittally without sounding too ridiculous, then concisely explained what it was that I'd be trying to accomplish during my stay in Moscow and went through the job description, pointing out that the nightclubs and casinos would be my primary target and the theatre was something I was thinking of going to on my days off, just to unwind a little, stock up on culture, you know. They agreed to everything and promised to furnish me with a more comprehensive list of clubs than I had at my disposal; the fee for their services sounded reasonable; the fifteen percent cut they requested didn't seem excessive either. However, upon hearing the word "theatre," they did a double take and exclaimed (quite theatrically, I should add) that that would cost me extra. And when they quoted precisely how much extra it would be, I said, "Forget theatre, *gospoda-tovarischi*. Let's concentrate on protection in casinos, nightclubs, and the rest of the capital's dens of iniquity. How much in harm's way does one want to put oneself taking in high culture anyway? Belinsky's famous adage, 'Go to the theatre, live there, and die there . . .' was nothing if not a figure of speech, am I right?"

(Another double take). "Of course, Lincoln's ill-fated theatre experience may be the exception that proves the rule," I said. (A pause punctuated by a double throat-clear). "Anyhow," I concluded, "I believe gangsters and greasepaint don't mix, do they?" Finally, Orlov, Decibel Petro, and I shook on it and sealed the deal by partaking of the Jack Daniels that I'd purchased in the Sheremetyevo duty-free shop and cracked open before you could ask, "On the rocks or straight up, dear gents-comrades?" Not that there was any ice in the room's mini-fridge anyway. And since only two glasses were sitting on the tray by the desk mirror, I filled them to the brim, clinked the bottle against them, then took a big swig from it, quite pleased with my new employees' look of appreciation that I glimpsed reflected in the mirror out of the corner of my eye. And that was my first wobbly day in Moscow, the white-walled capital on the seven hills, the place that used to endlessly fascinate me as a kid, the golden-domed majestic city that spelled art, culture, and theatre for me as far back as I could remember.

Chapter Four.

Come to think of it, the theatre has always loomed large for the Neider family. My dad was an inveterate theatregoer in the old country where theatre reigned supreme before the Soviets, under the Soviets, after the Soviets. Next time you're in Moscow, do yourself a favor and check out the Novodevichy cemetery. You'll know exactly what I'm talking about. Every third tomb in your path commemorates an actress, a stage director, or a playwright. Ballerinas and top government officials come a close second. The story my dad likes to share around the dinner table features him attending theatrical performances seventeen times while on a two-week college winter break in Moscow. This feat must have included occasional matinees if his account and my math are accurate. I know he is telling the truth, for the number of performances in his story never varies. "A good liar has to have a great memory" is one of Dad's favorite sayings. It helps to know what line you gave them if you plan to stick to it later. Dad's story has a true ring to it, regardless. I must have taken after him by default, I suppose. And I don't mean the honesty bit. I mean theatre. He and Mom attended premieres like clockwork in our hometown. Didn't make for a hectic leisure activity, though—there were just four theatre companies back in the fair city of Odesa: the Ukrainian Theatre, the Russian Theatre, the Operetta, and the Opera, a baroque marvel on a par with the Vienna Opera house. Of course, I didn't count the Theatre for a Young Audience and the Puppet Theatre, which I should have for accuracy's sake. Mom and Dad were also loathe to miss new productions when visiting Moscow. Babysitters were not an option back in the day, much less so when one was away from home. Leaving the kid to his own devices in a hotel room at night would be deemed uncouth even by my parents' bare-bones approach to child-rearing. So they'd take me along with them and even try to engage in after-show critiques on our way back to either the prewar Hotel Moscow or the then just completed spanking clean modernist Rossiya Hotel, depending on where we were staying. Once, because of some glitch in booking, we had to switch hotels mid-stay. Since the theatre was on our menu that night, like most of our nights in Moscow, I recall crossing Red Square on foot in January after the theatre to get from Moscow to Rossiya on the other side of the enormous deserted and spooky square. It was probably arranged that we pick up our luggage the morning after.

Light snow was falling on the square's wet cobblestones, the brightly lit red flag atop the domed roof behind the Kremlin wall was rippling in the wind, and you could see a minuscule pair of soldiers in the distance, rifle bayonets pressed to their sides, guarding the entrance to Lenin's granite tomb. It feels like a performance in retrospect, street theatre in its own right, perhaps a toy show starring the toy replica of the Neider family, especially if you factor in the size of the motionless guards and the granite box housing the embalmed leader of the world proletariat. My young parents in winter coats and fur hats, Dad's square brown one, Mom's light, spherical one, snowflakes landing on the furs of Mom's hat only to thaw into a myriad of glistening droplets seconds later, myself in tow, cheeks numb from the punishing wind, mittens attached to the coat sleeves by rubber strings, briskly crossing the square I had previously known only from picture books or military parades on black-and-white TV back home. Exciting and spooky! Two days later, the diminutive three of us wound up in a red-and-white plastic sphere with the thumb nail magnifying glass you had to peek into to see us pose against the dark tomb in the background. Dad looking proud of his attractively stylish young wife, his hand on his big-eyed boy's shoulder, the family on their first trip to the capital ready to gorge on the new sights and sounds and theatre, but also the restaurants, yes, let's not forget the restaurants, please, most of them named after the capitals of the Soviet bloc countries, some after the Soviet republics, except maybe Tsentralny and Slavyansky Bazaar, all of them offering cuisine to die for: shredded white radish and boiled tongue and fried onion salad, the specialty of Uzbekistan Restaurant, anyone? Or cream and mushroom hot juliennes baked to perfection and served in small piping hot metal pots just about everywhere? Ah, the quill of Gogol or Bulgakov, where are you when one needs you the most? "Say 'Cheese!'" not among the instructions favored by street photographers in the old country, no one is as much as pretending to smile in the picture. We wouldn't get the knack of baring our teeth for total strangers until after we had crossed the Atlantic. So far, we are just three very formal and solemn-looking thumb-nail-size exemplary Soviet citizens inside the plastic ball. Years later, I had the picture extracted from the ball. Enlarged and framed, its colors faded by now, it hangs on the wall above the desk in my midtown New York apartment.

What was the play that we saw on the night of our crossing the main square of the nation, the heart of the heart of our "great Soviet Motherland" with the cold corpse resting eternally in the middle of it, ready to extend his wordless welcome to the early morning visitors forming a line as endless, cold, and silent as eternity itself? Could it have been the Taganka Theatre production of *Hamlet* in Pasternak's spirited translation with his poems from *Doctor Zhivago* scattered throughout the play? Possible. The portentous curtain dominated the scenery, moving every which way as it swept the characters along like a bunch of listless marionettes lost in the implacable tides of history. Occasionally, the curtain resembled a spider web with actors clinging to it for dear life, going through convulsions as they tried to stay suspended midair. Porous and treacherous, it failed to save Polonius from Hamlet's sword or Ophelia from her descent into madness. Did the curtain ultimately stand for the "not to be" part of the play's central equation, that is, death herself? my parents pondered on the cold winter night, the white steam coming out of their mouths in waves commingling in the dark, for, in their excitement, they often interrupted each other.

What could I have possibly contributed to the animated post-theatre discussion in the falling snow? The only theatre I had seen prior was what seems in retrospect a semblance of a morality play mounted by the Operetta Theatre in my hometown: the stage design taken over by a red-and-black color scheme, a figure in tights and a cloak gesticulating wildly and mocking other characters who were either supposed to be dead or seemed dead because they were lit a certain way, or maybe because they didn't move about much. Unless it was the intrinsic nature of the spectacle, any spectacle, to resurrect the dead? The cloaked character did most of the talking. Then, a fight ensued between him and a fellow in a silver coat and elbow-length gloves who came from the fly system up above. At first, they were hurling insults at each other, then things got physical as each tried to pull a languid young lady clad in a white tunic towards himself. She was letting out faint whimpers, seemingly of two minds as to which way to go, then chose the silver-gloved chap and spat in his rival's face. The latter recoiled, then hobbled stage left, apparently hurt but full of resolve to take revenge the first chance he got. Granted, the entire experience was not too subtle as plays go, but impressive enough for a seven-year-old novice.

Of course, I liked the Taganka production of *Hamlet*; infinitely more nuanced and sophisticated it was than the vaudeville morality play seen in Odesa two years previously. But more than anything, I liked being a part of the Moscow theatregoing crowd, even for a brief winter recess period; the sense of belonging thrilled me to the bone. After all, it was one of the few things my parents lived for in the land of the commissars long ago and far away, and so did their circle of friends (the ones who could afford the infrequent trips to the capital, that is), ditto the Soviet intelligentsia at large: Moscow theatres, the fragile platform where things thought-provoking could be articulated however obliquely, the controversial status of Taganka, one of a handful of theatres all but inaccessible without the proper connections, Vysotsky, the legendary semi-legit singer as the guitar-playing melancholy prince engaging the audience by addressing it directly, Pasternak's soaring verses from the notorious novel by then still unpublished in his home country . . . How much more privileged could one feel culturally, politically, or aesthetically? Theatre, then, was your inalienable access to the locus of dissent, however muted or partial, your pass to a domain of transcendence and sanctified madness where rules were temporarily suspended or turned upside down, your transient yet much needed refuge from the mundane or the officious. Don't get me wrong: I'm not rhapsodizing about the country my family and I were happy to get the hell out of as soon as the opportunity knocked. Nor am I waxing lyrical about the ruthless founder of the state taking his eternal nap in the entrails of the tomb by the Kremlin wall—the monomaniacal, syphilitic fuck who masterminded the Red Terror that eventually cost the country the lives of untold millions. I'm just focusing on the cultural activity that made my childhood special and my early years endurable regardless of which puppet master behind said wall was running the show, then called "advanced socialism", at the inception of perestroika, to be hastily rechristened as "stagnation."

Is it any wonder that the first serious stab at culture in the Home of the Brave was my getting the discounted tickets to a Broadway show for the entire family rather than opting for the movies or, say, the Met on Fifth Avenue? Can't get a handle on the chaotic new world you were plunged into by the forces of fate (okay, make it the vicissitudes of high politics between the two superpowers)? Not a problem. Try a little dramatic order, a pinch of poetic justice, however artificially flavored and cookie-cutter it might seem. Hello, Broadway! We thought it was Broadway anyway. Vaguely aware of the theatre district situated roughly between Fortieth St. and Fifty-Third St. on the west side of town, we figured that getting off the Flushing train at Times Square would be playing it safe. We miscalculated. As it transpired, the theatre was located on Broadway all right, yet it was an off-Broadway production and the address was way up in the high Seventies. A mistake that made for a long and hurried walk on an early Sunday afternoon in May. T-shirt and hot dog vendors of all skin colors hawking their wares half-heartedly, blocks upon blocks mercifully barren of sex workers sleeping off the shift of the night before, the absence that prompted me to thank the gods of profligacy silently, loath as I was to let my mom get a glimpse of the seamy part of the city that never sleeps (or seldom does in the same bed twice as the case may be); the Camel man blowing out Hula Hoops of gray smoke into the air . . . Finally, half an hour after the curtain went up, out of breath and perspiring, we entered the Promenade Theatre, clambered up the stairs, and stumbled towards our balcony seats in the pitch dark. By then, we had been residents of New York for three confusing months, and my English was shaky, to say the least; the same went for my parents. Yet it didn't take us long to figure that according to Dick Shawn, the playwright and the star of the one-man show titled *The Second Greatest Entertainer in the Whole Wide World,* the greatest entertainer in the world was God Almighty

Himself, and Dick Shawn, or rather the homeless person he was portraying, was the second greatest. Not the Devil, mind you, supposedly no slouch in flamboyant showmanship in his own right, but the God's clown down on his luck.

Ah, how I wish this story were but a mere blow-by-blow of my theatregoing back in the old country, then in the US, then in the old country again, with brief reviews of memorable flicks thrown in for good measure, like nothing that happened in between ever mattered, if for no other reason than nothing much did, or whatever did happen in between had a lot to do with theatre or the movies. Because next up, chronologically, would be my account of the legendary Broadway production of *Oh! Calcutta!* with contributions from the likes of Samuel Beckett and John Lennon, the experience that made you feel like you were, indeed, smack at the center of the world you'd been drooling over back in the land of the commissars . . . But I have another story to tell here. And this story only in part concerns making sure that Vik Z-sky got his just deserts, though one thing necessarily led to another and then yet another, as it always does in our mesh of the ever-expanding universe. It is, to a great degree, the story of the life and the times of Mr. Greg Davis, an American film director, who, incidentally, cut his teeth in a Yiddish provincial theatre in Ukraine where he had been employed, first as an actor, then an assistant director up until the October Revolution forced his family to flee the Russian Empire for Europe and eventually settle in the United States . . . It is the story of Greg Davis, once a prominent figure in American cinema, now all but forgotten by audiences and critics alike, whose silent film *The Wild Ass's Skin* I had a chance to watch towards the end of my stay in Russia when Tasha T's Aunt Oksana Zhuravel, a thirty-nine-year-old film scholar from Leningrad came to Moscow, three weeks after the dust of the attempted October coup settled, to deliver a lecture on Mr. Davis's early work. So, when tasked with the

Boca Raton job, I already knew a bit about Greg Davis, the director. I feel funny calling the Boca Raton assignment a job, though. But then, everything is a job in this adopted country of mine. Nose job, snow job, put-up job, hand job, botch job, even goo-goo g'joob job, by Job, is a job! So . . . will you follow me, my reader?

Chapter Five.

The thing to keep in mind when you find yourself in your native land after a long stretch abroad is that you can't help feeling a little freaked out most of the time. Think Odysseus back in Ithaca, only no faithful Argos to wag his tail upon getting a whiff of this traveler returned. Think Dostoyevsky's Count Myshkin manifesting a certain degree of estrangement in St. Petersburg after his stay on a Swiss funny farm. All the more reason to hide your confused ass in the theatre, Orlov and Decibel's balking at covering the said ass while it did theatre notwithstanding. Drama or comedy, opera or ballet sure beat moshing the nights away in *Manhattan, 2x2, Bunker*, or the then recently opened *Pilot* for catharsis any day. Except maybe on weekends. For it was weekend clubbing, from the get-go, that was business as usual for me, the search for Vik Z-sky and co in Moscow hot clubs at the top of my agenda, casinos coming a close second. Hoping against hope for a blitzkrieg, I started with nightclubs that also housed casinos—two birds with one stone. Like the glitzy *Metelitsa* on New Arbat, a gambling house, I think I had heard Vik Z-sky mention casually to Alena the Primrose of the Underworld back in New York.

Reasoning that there was an off chance it might be their hangout du jour, I commenced my quest there, closely observing the clientele dressed to the nines Moscow style, but budget traveler that I was, never succumbing to the gambling bug myself, a tall order what with the blindingly decollated shapely ladies in sheer stockings gyrating next to me as I watched the intoxicated crowd swarm around croupiers' tables. Another observation post was my table for one partially obscured by a lavish ficus tree in the corner of the half-decent restaurant downstairs where I occasionally stayed for dinner, my bodyguards Orlov and Decibel planting their broad-shouldered selves at the next table. There, after downing the requisite hundred grams of vodka, quickly followed by pickled herring in sour cream sauce and a bite of beef stroganoff, I also did a bit of dancing with friendly casino ladies. It rarely went further than that; though on some occasions, I have to confess, it did. Listen, one is liable to feel lonely in a strange place, okay? Better the refined me (such was my thinking as I paid for the intimate services rendered) than some scuzzball businessman from Boondocks, USA, treated to the after-dinner entertainment by former Moscow mid-level Party bosses who now owned this town. I also regularly tipped Oleg, the pug-nosed headwaiter in a starched shirt and tiny black bowtie peeking out from under his clean-shaved double chin. Oleg indicated, though not in so many words, and upon my similarly roundabout query, that he knew Vik Z-sky, at least by sight, so when the moment came, Oleg would be sure to cue me accordingly. Or rather, he'd point out the man I was after to Orlov and Decibel, whom I introduced to Oleg as my college buddies in town for some archery competition training. Don't get me wrong, nothing outlandish was in the offing. No taking the law, or whatever passed for it in post-Soviet Russia, into my own hands. I wouldn't know what to do with a handgun if my life depended on it. No killer instinct, remember? All I was trying to accomplish was make sure that the IOUs that Vik Z-sky had handed to me over the two-vodka-gimlet lunch savored in New York's Russian Tea Room next to the transparent polar bear with the bellyful of drowsy goldfishes as witnessed by Uncle Shura, Alena the Oxfordian belle, and comrade Vodovozkind were honored in full, forget the interest but do factor in travel and accommodation expenses, however negligible they might be in the larger scheme of things. It made sense and seemed fair enough, though the moment of truth was sure slow in coming. So slow that upon hearing the truncated version of my tale of retributive justice in the making, my new Moscow friend, the street-smart punk princess Tasha Tschelicheva of the asymmetrical haircut and pierced everything, suggested then and there that I write off the money I was looking to recover as one gigantic and lamentable loss, pack up my bags, and head the hell back where I came from in a jiffy—much safer that way. Though she personally would miss me quite a bit because I was kinda cute and sorta fun. Quote unquote.

I bumped into Tasha T. in a Stalin-era House of Culture recently converted into The Shudder of Recognition, an exclusive nightclub with a killer sound system and clientele to match. While TSR's occasional live Brit electronica imports typically left the patrons gasping for air, the domestic and Europop fare overlaid with industrial music never failed to get them up and boogeying, often till the wee hours. For a large portion of the night in question, Tasha, a petite golden-haired young woman with a sizable shiner under her left eye, was busy pirouetting around the tables, guzzling drinks abandoned by revelers shaking their booties on the dance floor to Ace of Base's ubiquitous "All That She Wants." From time to time, the dancers waved exaggerated hellos to the non-dancers lurking in the dark recesses of the club, then shuffled over to them across the floor, swaying and twisting grotesquely, only to bring their friends into the spotlight, put their arms around them, and continue twirling and bopping. Joviality ruled; leather outfits held sway, cocktail waitresses were obliging and civilized to a fault. Next to the service industry elsewhere in town, the personnel carried on as if they'd graduated from top schools of hospitality in London or Paris before landing a job at The Shudder of Recognition.

All of a sudden, Tasha stopped mid-pas, waltzed right up to my table, and hit me with her trademark mix of studied nonchalance and understated disdain, "Kurt Vonnegut has just offed himself. Tragic, huh?" Of course, she actually meant Kurt Cobain, whom I knew next to nothing about at the time, which happened to be roughly the extent of Tasha's familiarity with Vonnegut's status or body of work. Still, the apparent disconnect mattered little: we hit it off swimmingly that night. She looked vaguely familiar, too. And I don't just mean her uncanny resemblance to the young Tatiana Doronina, a movie actress I had a crush on in the eighth grade. She also looked like someone I thought I had spotted at the Tarantula gig at the Bunker club a week earlier. Could she have been that girl jumping up and down at the back of the thinnish crowd every time the Sankt Petersburg neo-punk outfit's front man in tall lace-up boots got on his knees and tried to lick the purposefully spilled peach juice off the stage floor? Bunker was a much cooler venue than the places I usually patronized in search of my debtors. Of course, running into them in Bunker would have been like finding a bunch of albino elephants in the refrigerator; it's just that now and then, I felt the urge to chill someplace half appealing.

It was Tasha's idea to do some theatre soon—she indicated as much while slipping me a napkin with her phone number scribbled on it as we were leaving the club an hour later. So theatre we did aplenty, everything else falling into its proper place in no time, too. Not sure how she got on the subject of bears that night but she did. But first, I asked her if she thought drinking from strangers' glassware was sanitarily sound.

"Sanitarily, my ass!" Tasha hunched her shoulders. "Everyone smokes hash here anyway. The drinks are just for show, barely touched." How did she know? "Observation." Tasha gave me an emphatic wink. "Look, dude, they dance like bears, clumsy and graceless. That's hash bear moves for you. So Moscow *is* crawling with bears," she chuckled. "You foreigners are onto something after all. Only they are the club-crawling kind."

"Listen," I said. "I'm not a total foreigner, lady. I know my bears."

"Even better," said Tasha. "That's our bear connection right there, America."

Then she gave me this whole rambling spiel about her first toy ever. It featured, wouldn't you know it, a bear. Namely, something like a two-dimensional plastic contraption made up of a boxer and a bear, the latter on his hind legs, both with a pair of miniature boxing gloves on. The lever attached to the contraption allowed you to simulate the boxing match, though the opponents' gloves could barely touch. So, the advantage of one fighter over the other was arbitrary and solely in the eye of the prepubescent beholder Tasha. You could say the fighters were locked in a permanent draw, she added. The toy was the size of an adult's hand. The entire culture at your fingertips. Broken in two at some point to see if boxing was a sport you could do without a partner. "Nope. Takes two to get a fat lip. Or a black eye, whatever the case may be," Tasha concluded, touching her shiner gingerly. "A lesson learned early on."

"What happened?" I asked.

"Mother. Damn her and her booze. Things got out of hand the other day."

"Sorry to hear. It seems out of place on this pretty face." I pointed to her black eye.

"Face, place," Tasha twisted her mouth. "What, you a poet, America?"

"Nah, not me. A mid-level globe-trotter at best. Your story sounds like a prose poem, though. Very cute," I gushed. "'The Boxer and the Bear.' Just like the storyteller, cuter than cute." I put my hand on Tasha's beat-up leather jacket sleeve and gave it a light squeeze. It is worth noting at this juncture that my flirting technique, below par to begin with, gets a little bear-like when I'm inebriated. For a fuller picture, keep in mind the two pairs of watchful eyes of my bodyguards, Orlov and Decibel Petro, trained on us from across the room throughout the entire fun night at TSR. Ray-Ban and Rain Man. You try flirting under close surveillance—see how far you get.

"You married?" asked Tasha out of the blue as she slid her arm away from me.

"Divorced. No children. No regrets. Why?"

"Bull," said Tasha. "No such thing as no regrets. I don't care what Édith Piaf croons on the subject. What was she like?"

"Why? We just met, lady."

"C'mon, dish. What you hiding in that conjugal closet, America?"

"Nothing. Not a bone. One thing I will say. What she liked to purr before we'd get cozy was, 'Hey, bear. Let's roar and scare the hare.' I swear. Sort of a mating call with her."

Tasha threw her head back, let out a howl, clapped her hands loudly, grabbed my drink, and finished it in one noisy gulp. Then she moved a little closer. "I like that! 'Hey, bear . . .' Poetry, I don't care what you say!"

"But," I continued, staring into her enormous dark eyes. "Funny thing, I have a bear story for you, too. Just like yours, only real. Wanna hear it?"

"What do you mean 'only real?' Mine was totally real!"

"I mean, mine is not a toy story, okay?"

"Shoot," she said, moving a little closer and propping her chin on her hands like a good schoolgirl in her Ruslit class would, only with an impish exaggeration complete with brief pouting and blinking. Even the music subsided for a bit, so I didn't have to raise my voice much. I put my hand on her sleeve again. She didn't move it away this time.

"Are you married?"

"Widowed," she said casually.

"What?! Aren't you, ah, a little too young for that?"

"Accident on a job, whatcha gonna do? Contract job, to be exact. Welcome to Moscow, America. So what's your story, anyway?"

"Ah, okay . . . But let's order drinks first. What's your non-leftover poison?"

"Gin and tonic. And let's don't rub the leftover business in. I'm a budget club kid, you know. You have a problem with that?"

So I flagged down the rail-thin waitress in a leather mini, ordered two Tanqueray gin and tonics, cleared my throat, and launched into my honeymoon boxing match bear story almost unabridged. Though I did try to go light on details of ursine physiology and unnecessary human cruelty.

"And that is," I concluded in a mock-solemn tone of voice, "but one example of the universal appeal of bears as entertainers, the fodder for mythology, our four-legged friends in need, and even the occasional providers. And we haven't even touched upon the likable Misha the bear, the mascot of the Moscow 1980 Olympics who failed to impress half the globe into lifting its boycott on the event, despite his benevolent smile and Mickey Mouse ears."

"Friends in need and providers, my ass! What a waste of time: trying to win the love of half the globe that doesn't give a fuck about you anyway. Never did," Tasha frowned, then changed her tune. "But hey, that's quite a story. Kinda gives my 2D toy contraption a real-life dimension. Talk about weird honeymoons. Which brings us back to your ex. What happened? Come on, dish already," and by encouragement, she gave me a light punch in the stomach with her fist as we were blowing The Shudder of Recognition a quarter of an hour later. Light, but it hurt. That's how she turned out: flippant, temperamental, but ultimately reasonable and well-meaning.

"Why young winsome ladies are so curious about the exes of newly met men a generation older is a mystery wrapped in an enigma," I wondered out loud as we entered the metro station where I tried to feed the turnstile I remembered from childhood, only the feed I fumbled for in my pockets had gone up about six hundred times since.

"I'm twenty-five," said Tasha. "And you sure don't look anywhere near forty, America. So, who's a generation older? And who were the two fellas staring at us from across the room? You know, the ones you had a word with on your way to take a piss? Just curious."

"Some people I know. Why?" I answered, marveling at her power of observation, for I indeed had stopped by Orlov and Decibel's table and instructed them to make themselves scarce and allow for some privacy before we left the club.

"Not Koroviev and Azazello?" she queried, referring to the otherworldly characters from Mikhail Bulgakov's famous novel.

"What? Not a chance. What would that make me? Woland the Prince of Darkness?" I mused.

"Nah. Too cheerful and chatty for 'part of that force that always wills the evil and always does the good.' Unless the whole thing was cast against type this time around."

I must confess I had no idea what she was jabbering about. One thing was clear: there was another connection between us: *The Master and Margarita,* Bulgakov's masterwork that had acquired cult status over the decades since its belated publication in the '60s, the novel quoted from by every literate Russian, young and old. Even my first unremarkable dining experience in Moscow that fall took place in a tiny dimly lit pizza parlor, Chez Margarita, in Patriarch's Ponds, a park central to the book's opening scene.

"Too cheerful? Cast against what type?"

"Later, America," chortled Tasha. "This is me. Call me, okay? What do you think of the avant-garde theatre anyway? Yes, no, maybe, don't give a hoot? Ever heard of Pogrebnichko?"

And before I had the time to respond to her rapid-fire multiple-choice query, she gave me a big fat kiss on the lips and bolted out of the train at Smolenskaya station.

Chapter Six.

Over the next week, between theatregoing, club-hopping, and lovemaking in my Kuntsevo digs, I was slowly filling Tasha in on why I'd come to Moscow. Doing it in toto and right away didn't seem wise: the whole matter was too important, too sensitive, and not entirely legit. At first, though, I tried twisting the truth, coming up with all kinds of stories of varying plausibility: research for a video project ("Really? So where's your camera, dude?"), a series of articles for the *Village Voice* ("I don't see you take any notes, ever. Who do you take me for, America? A village idiot?"), a search for a companion because I just couldn't see myself with an American woman ("Plan to look much further, mister?"). Then, after we'd been together for a week, I figured my punk princess was a decent girl with a bit of a chip on her shoulder, and I could confide in her unreservedly. So, finally, without naming too many names, I gave her the entire story. Plus, I had to come up with some explanation regarding the 24/7 attention bestowed upon me by my trusty, if somewhat sluggish bodyguards Orlov and Decibel, the former also doubling as my personal driver, at least when his *Shesterka* beater wasn't hoisted up on the hydraulic lift in one of Chertanovo's body shops not too far from his five-storied apartment building.

Tasha's initial reaction was emphatically negative to the point of her calling me insane and plain stupid for trying to take on the Russian mafia on their own turf (for this is exactly who Vik Z-sky and co were in Tasha's view), but, by degrees, she warmed up to the idea of recovering the money by hook or by crook and finally gave in. She also sensed that by hanging out with me in public, she was putting herself in a precarious position as well, a fact that didn't necessarily faze her; it just made her more careful and selective with regard to the places we frequented together. Also, as she put it, the whole "crime and punishment" dimension of my quest added a pinch of spice to our budding relationship, thus making it more enticing for her. Whatever. Not to mention that she was something of a streetwise kid, a child of the roaring '90s who lived through the putsch of August '91, and then there was also that violent demise of her husband that she mentioned the night we met at TSR. Plus, coming from old—but more to the point, new—believer stock (devout Christian grandparents, hardcore Commie parents), she wouldn't be averse to seeing justice served on the bad guys by any means deemed necessary.

Her nomenklatura dad left the family (actually, abandoned the third grader Tasha in a public place one foggy December afternoon and vanished without a trace—what a piece of shit scumbag!), so she was raised by her abusive boozer mother and her second uncle Foma Alexandrovich who, it so happened, was a dead ringer for Leon Trotsky: the cap, the goatee, the pince-nez, the argumentative puissance. Not much to put on a resume, you would think. But as a mirror image of the fiery Red Army commissar, he did once sit for Diego Riviera's celebrated *The Fourth International* mural and, as such, got to hold the banner right next to Marx and Engels for hours on end, or rather next to the local bearded peasant passably impersonating the two founding fathers of Marxism alternately, and therefore getting paid double for the sessions: fair is fair. The real Trotsky, very much alive at the time, had to go into hiding that week: the rumors of his hired assassin at large were getting too real to be dismissed. The family lore remained reticent on what it was precisely that Foma Alexandrovich, a real-life

Red Army brigade commander who received a contusion on the southern front during the civil war, was doing in Mexico City in the late '30s. Be that as it may, Tasha and her bedridden and rarely sober mother Maria Vassilievna, never in a million years, no matter how pressed for cash, would consider selling the charcoal sketches from the prewar sessions that Diego Riviera brought as a present for his old pal Foma Alexandrovich on the artist's trip to Moscow in 1956 shortly before leaving this world for the greater and presumably more socially equal beyond. Whenever I'd stay the night at Tasha's in Starokoniushenny ("Come on over, America, and pump my ass like you mean it. It's been two long days. I may be a princess, but I sure ain't no nun"), she'd mix an extra dose of sleeping powder in the alcohol detox drink that her mother was supposed to take before going to sleep so that my honey and I could do whatever we pleased without the slightest regard for the attendant sounds of lovemaking punctuated by the headboard thumping against the wallpapered wall. My punk princess was noisily expansive in bed, and her customary biting of the pillow's corner for its muffling effect didn't always do the trick. That technique was also fraught with nasty side effects: she almost gagged on goose feathers once, or maybe pretended she did, audibly coughing them up and spitting them out onto the kitchen linoleum floor the morning after, startling her black Siberian cat, Behemoth. My little Doronina was a bit of an actress in her own right.

Chapter Seven.

I suppose it shouldn't be a great challenge to figure out what Tasha and I did in our downtime in the weeks that followed, that is, when I wasn't trying to track down Vik Z-sky and co in Moscow hot spots, and she had her nights off from the Arbat antique shop that employed her as a salesgirl. You can't avoid doing theatre while residing, even temporarily, in the theatre capital of the known universe. Theatre is what you do to reclaim your sanity, find your bearings, transcend or lose yourself, trace back your steps to the carefree days of your childhood, contract and contain the Artaudian contagion within the span of two and a half hours, or pass the time, especially when the everyday street theatre around you becomes too much to bear. Because street theatre is precisely what the new reality of your homeland looks like to you after you've spent almost half of your lifetime elsewhere. And so, as an antidote to heart-rending encounters with the frazzled tent dwellers camping under the starry skies between Red Square and the Rossiya Hotel, their grievances scribbled on pieces of cardboard pasted to their scraggly fur hats, or high school teachers in threadbare coats selling shivering puppies in Novy Arbat pedestrian underpasses, or every other small establishment from shoe repair places to flower shops converted to hard currency exchanges with the obligatory pair of semiautomatic-wielding special forces policemen guarding their entrances (a source of endless consternation to Moscow's senior citizens), you develop a strong interest in the Russian and Soviet classics in bold new interpretations, or better yet, in reverentially faithful traditional adaptations, if only to avert your eyes from the sights unfamiliar and unnerving. You sense the need to get to know the new, exciting stars of the stage or check out how the old ones are holding up. Catharsis galore, dramatic justice served unfailingly, the fallen hero dies a beautiful death in the breathtaking finale only to get back on his feet and take a bow moments later, hands pressed to his cranberry juice besmeared shirt. Theatre, theatre, theatre as an instrument for buoying your spirits or alleviating distress. Not always effective, truth be told. The aesthetics of a society in a state of flux can be vexing in its own right. Take the Moscow Theatre for a Young Audience's interpretation of Dostoyevsky's *Notes from the Underground* featuring the office clerk as narrator, his endless monologue accentuated by the consumption of large quantities of food intermittently regurgitated and spat out into his cupped hands, all the while addressing the fleshy taciturn harlot lying buck naked on the brass bed next to him. No one has yet called me a prude, but I must say that wall-to-wall nudity in *Oh! Calcutta!* seen on Broadway back in the day seemed a whole lot less disconcerting than this spiced up take on the venerable classic . . . The venues were sometimes confusing, too. Like the eight-hour staging of Aeschylus's gorefest *Oresteia* directed by Peter Stein. The German maverick's three-part play of vengeance and revenge took me aback right away: was the huge bas-relief red star up on the Moscow Soviet Army Theatre ceiling covered up by a white cloth for reasons of thespian expediency? Or, it being the early '90s, the gesture had something to do with domestic political changes in the air? Maybe both? It took the constitutional crisis I lived through in the early days of October to help wrap my mind around the simple and irrefutable fact: the red stars and what they stood for never really vanished from Moscow interiors, public or private, mental or physical, symbolic or real.

Chapter Eight.

A week before the aborted coup, Tasha grabbed me by the lapels, anxious to hear about my life in the United States. Made sense, too. I was the first foreigner or faux foreigner she'd ever met and gone to bed with. More specifically, she demanded to know what it was like setting foot in the States for the first time. Just like she tried to drill me about my ex Lilly ten minutes into our first encounter in The Shudder of Recognition. The same intensity of a curious mind, only this time fueled by the round or two of vodka shots chased with Heinekens.

"Truth, the whole truth, and nothing but," said my new friend mockingly, but there was an urgency in her voice, a vibe that I didn't feel like going along with, not just yet. We were hanging out in a recently opened sports bar on Kalininsky, one of the few places in town where you could enjoy MTV on a big screen, though neither of us was too keen on following Boy George's chameleon moves or Peter Gabriel's surreal claymation metamorphoses on the TV above the bar. Of course, I had stories for Tasha, stories of strife mostly, but it just didn't feel right to give our early exchanges too dramatic a spin. So, I opted for a facetious register, which felt more appropriate to my mood and the setting.

"Truth, the whole truth, and nothing but coming your way, Tasha," I said, my voice briefly acquiring a robotic ring. "So help me, mighty King Kong, the totem of the Empire State Bildungsroman. What is crucial to ascertain upon landing in a new country, my friend, is whether you'll still be able to get a bang out of things you enjoyed back home. Why hit the road if you don't think you can? With any luck, the new thrills will unfold before you eventually, but what do you fall back on while you wait for that glorious moment? Granted, the things that go by the same name may—and often will—turn out different. Apples are apples no matter how you slice them, you would think, right? But before long, you'll find the overseas variety as edible as pool table balls. And please don't get me started on tomatoes! You remember enjoying an after-school chess game in the well-aired chess club, silky curtains billowing in the afternoon breeze, the parquet floor waxed so shiny you could see your acne-blemished forehead in it? Forget all that. No Young Pioneer palaces in downtown New York City last I checked. Welcome to musty holes in the wall on Thompson St. crammed with pungent Popeye lookalikes swearing by the Sicilian defense and sporting crumpled shirts snatched from nearby public laundromats back in the Nixon administration. You do know Popeye? Funny, you should know Popeye, yet you say you've never heard of Doronina . . . Mismatches are too many, and they are a two-way street. Take branzino. Scrumptious when properly cooked and deboned in New York's fine eating establishments, it is only passably tender on the Amalfi Coast, as my ex Lilly and myself were quick to discover on our backpacking trip through Italy in the mid-'80s. Not even sure it was the same fish. Same family, at best. A distant relation, in all likelihood. A bony, myopic spinster aunt, maybe? A tourist trap, no doubt: they know we're bonkers about branzini in the States, let's see if we take the overpriced bait in the south of Italy. Hey, it's your vacation, live a little, fall into a tourist trap or two. Worse comes to worst, it'll make for a nice after-dinner story back home . . . But enough about me. Your turn, lady."

"My turn—what? You out of your mind, Mark? I haven't been anywhere outside Russia except for a weekend trip to Finland. I never heard of branzino," Tasha scoffed. "There's a

Bronzino in the Pushkin Museum, which I always had a soft spot for . . ."

"No, I mean your first steps in changing Russia? Also a new territory, right?"

"Oh that . . . Well. What's there to report? The beginning sure was heady," Tasha twisted her mouth like she always did when she'd get tense. "New freedoms, the whole glasnost thing. Some friends got rich; others got whacked. Overwhelmed by the new choices, most of them unaffordable anyway. The winds of change not always fair. Still, some hope left, though things did go south dramatically. South and sour. Poverty rules, pensions laughable, crime unprecedented. I guess I'm with this writer guy, can't think of the name, who said, 'You judge the fair by your own market.' The market around you might be booming, but if your personal profit is a few bucks and change . . . Listen, let's go someplace else. O'Grady?"

"So: How has your market been so far, Mark?" the tenacious Tasha inquired a few days later, picking up where she left off like she never did. "Other than that regretful branzino setback and the chess clubs that could use industrial-strength air fresheners? What were your first steps in the new land like? The giant steps for Mark the first man on the dark side of the moon? How dark was that side anyway?"

By then, we were already a bona fide item, so there was little need to BS her or play for time. Plus, I had already let her in on what it was that I was doing in Moscow. And she didn't really have to be Sofiya Kovalevskaya, the nineteenth-century Russian math genius, to figure that if I chose to get involved with the Russian businessmen of dubious ethics, then whatever promise the good old US of A held for me had been slow in materializing. In a word, a moment of truth, truth, and nothing but was upon us that night when we stayed home in my Kuntsevo apartment, drinking instant coffee by the gallon and consuming bologna and cheese sandwiches at the sticky oilcloth-covered kitchen table by the window overlooking the moonlit courtyard below.

"Okay, Tasha. Here goes nothing. Who was it said, 'Out of darkness, light?' The story gets underway on a blizzardy winter day in '77," I began. "Our first day in the country. Dad pointed to the row of snow-covered metal coffins on wheels parked bumper-to-bumper on a narrow street in the Bronx where we temporarily holed up with some friends. 'So, what do you think of American cars, sonny?' 'Big, they sure are big, Dad,' sonny shrugged. A month later, opening a bank account: 'And this is an American bank, sonny. What do you say?' Sonny: 'Check out the rugs. And the phones, two per desk, wow!' That was the beginning of the journey to parts unknown and often unpalatable. The first Christmas in an Indian restaurant on Bleecker St., one of the few places open that night. The holiday wasn't that familiar, plus the spicy cuisine was fraught with tongue and palate burns. 'Spare some change,' the undecipherable mantra chanted by prostatitis-defying panhandlers sitting on cold sidewalks of the new land (in stark contrast to their not-too-visible counterparts back in the USSR) . . . My iffy command of English made it hard to get a grip on precisely what it was I was asked to spare. Another issue that begged elucidation was why the exhibit of early Chagall paintings at the Pierre Matisse Gallery on Fifty-Seventh Street was listed in *People*'s entertainment section. Is Chagall an entertainment? Back home, he was the subject of the kitchen opposition's endless reflection. So what was considered high art in the New World then? Not *Jaws 2* by any fluke?

"But fundamentally, and perhaps, more seriously," I continued, "The thing about the New World is that, upon arrival, you don't know which part of it is new, old, or universal. You are first engaged with it on a purely visual level: billboards, advertising, and magazine covers in quantities you had never seen before. A tiny little dead-end lane someplace Elizabeth, NJ is ten times better lit at night than Gorky St., the main drag of Russia's capital during the holiday season. Billboards, billboards, billboards: so much to sell, so little time, which still is money, I don't care what they say in your time zone. And you are all itching to exercise that proverbial freedom of expression that made you embark on the journey to begin with. Because it's not the blenders or the new, improved potato peeler that you packed your bags and bid adieu to Pushkin and Chekhov for, is it... But where do you start exactly? Jimmy Page, your everlasting guitar God and guiding spirit, who sported the white silk scarf on the cover of *Creem* magazine when emulated by you in midtown Manhattan, cause your garment district Puerto Rican coworkers to sneer. 'You gay or somepin?' they inquire over a second round of Bacardis in a corner bar one Friday night after work, and they give you a good-natured slap on the back followed by a loud cackle. 'No,' you answer. 'Why?' 'What's that rag doing round your neck, then, buddy boy?' 'But isn't America...' And your head begins to spin, and your English as a second language gets slurred. You step outside for a breath of air. The dusk falls on Seventh Ave., and the office girls in midi-dresses all aglow in neon lights smile hazily as they glide past you in slo-mo. America, America, the land of... what? Not conformity by any chance? And that night, sloshed to the gills, you barely make it home to your one-bedroom apartment that you share with your parents. And you extract the crumpled wad from your jeans pockets, your week's pay. And you throw the bills up in the air and watch the swirling tens and twenties land on the cherry-colored wall-to-wall rug, and you feel powerless. You probably need to be making more and move the hell out. Or find a better job and stay and save and eventually move to California, but not before you negotiate your right to bring home lady friends. Only you don't have any lady friends to bring home.

"Once you bought a *Penthouse* from a tobacco store next door to a pizza place around the corner, a parlor where you had your first calzone experience. So bouts of self-gratification in the West, at least initially, became intertwined for you with the taste of calzone. Whenever you'd start touching yourself, you'd taste a warm calzone melt in your mouth. Weird, right? So you returned to your empty apartment, the magazine in a brown paper bag under your arm, your parents out grocery shopping, and you plopped down on the cherry-colored rug, and you put the magazine between your legs, and you opened it to the centerfold of a brunette beauty who also had her legs spread, only she had black seamed nylons and shiny high heels on, which in some pictures wound up in the air. And you pulled down your pants and trunks and started playing with yourself. And then the jangling of the key in the keyhole interrupted your solitary session; all you had the time for was to pull up your pants and jump up, leaving the magazine on the floor in plain view. And after dropping the shopping bags on the open kitchen floor, your father glanced at the beauty splayed out at his feet, then looked at you and shook his head wordlessly, if a little too emphatically. Were you being seduced by the permissive society at its most visceral and blatant, as in "you've been curious what cunts and erect nipples look like; here's a few examples for your viewing and tactile pleasure," in two dimensions so far, but hey, you've got to start somewhere? But wasn't any and all advertising a form of pornography—constructed, mediated, and addressed to the void within that contained your innermost desires, just like tits and asses were only under different guises? Were you ever to find a 3D flesh-and-bone companion? Certainly not if you kept jerking off in the apartment you shared with your parents.

"Hits and misses, but mostly misses. Every job you ever interviewed for, every job you ever got or didn't get, because you weren't sure how to dress for the interview or because your visible sweat-inducing discomfort during the interview made you feel like a character out of Dreiser, not that you ever liked Dreiser's ponderous style, his heavy-handed messages, his split infinitives or, for that matter, the jobs you were interviewed for. Like leaving your workstation at the major publishing house unbeknownst to your shipping department supervisor, a middle-aged gent from Barbados, mild-mannered, good-natured, yet in a subtle way condescending. To say that his English was flawed is to do a great disservice to ESL speakers the world over. So you excuse yourself to Fernando because you couldn't quit your workstation just like that, only you don't tell him where you're headed, and you steal to the elevator in the hallway with your college pencil and charcoal drawings rolled up under your arm. And you are five minutes early for your appointment with the head of the Art Department, who you thought might give you a few pointers on your future career. After all, you are an art major. And you wait for him in the reception room. And you wait. And he finally shows up in a very nice light-green summer suit, a matching tie, and a nice tan. I guess heads of departments at big corporations are supposed to have that look and walk that walk and talk that talk. So this is the talk he talked upon seeing my semester's worth of studio assignments. He said he had to be honest with me, perhaps even brutally honest, but he didn't see much promise in what he was looking at and suggested that I return to my place in the Shipping Department where my talents, in his view, would be utilized best. And that was that. And . . . as you know, I'm currently enjoying a career vastly different from that of a commercial artist for a publishing house, and I am in Moscow on a different mission altogether, and am preoccupied with other matters entirely. But . . . come to think, my artwork wasn't all that horrible, Tasha. And all I can say at this point is that I think his brutal honesty was uncalled for and misdirected, and a little milk of human kindness in a workplace (not the most ease-inspiring environment to begin with) goes a long way—it's not like I was asking the jerk for a job, or anything—so all I can say is if there's justice in this world or, more realistically, in the next one, I do hope he rots in hell along with his nice light-green summer suit and matching tie, and tan too, and his beige horn-rimmed glasses, and cigarette in a long cigarette holder, and his smug demeanor, and expensive haircut. Because the wounds inflicted upon you when you're nineteen don't heal that easily. Moron, a fucking moron—what a creep. Sorry, I got sidetracked a little here. What a fucking jerk. I mean, can you believe that asshole?"

Chapter Nine.

"I've boarded a boat, but the little boat, it was made out of yesterday's paper," the blonde beehived beauty crooned throatily to her own guitar accompaniment in the popular black-and-white movie of my adolescence. Tatiana Doronina! . . . The very same actress that now, twenty years later, I was literally falling all over myself running down Tverskoy Blvd. to see in the theatre she reigned over for years as its artistic director and star. It almost felt like a date. A platonic date with my past. Goes some ways to explaining why I didn't even bother asking Tasha if she cared to join, not that she would: she had to work her shift at the antique store that day.

Chasing the past, though, as it slowly dawned on me towards the end of my first month in Moscow, rates highly on the scale of futile human pursuits, perhaps a notch below efforts to bring back the dead. Unless you are vested with supernatural powers or have acquired the requisite professional skills. Exhuming a corpse, beautifying it expertly as you stare into the empty sockets of the half-decomposed face before dusting off its prominent cheekbones with a camel hair brush, then carefully applying makeup, hoping against hope for eye contact or a trace of a smile. What contact, what smile? To travel down that road, you must be seriously delusional and disillusioned by the present. Not this voyager. This voyager was reasonably happy with his IT job at a major New York City insurance company, inasmuch as it allowed him to keep a decent one-bedroom place midtown, a stone's throw from Central Park, enjoy a weekly meal or two out, and take an occasional vacation in Europe or South America with or without a lady friend. Who could ask for more? Apparently, I could. Because I did. And I don't believe I need to elaborate further why I chose to get involved with Vik Z-sky and co back in New York. Suffice it to say, I don't think anything is intrinsically wrong with trying to make an extra buck in a market economy. Or making sure you collect your pay in an unregulated economy that held sway over the land of perestroika and acceleration. Acceleration of what precisely, by the way? The number of empty shelves in department stores? The hordes of old ladies reselling salami and toilet paper off of Tverskaya St. sidewalks? Or the frequency of shootouts between rival gangs? Need I remind myself that I was in Moscow not to chase days long gone but to take care of unfinished business, preferably peaceably and conclusively, and that that was the long and the short of it?

Dry poplar leaves were dancing their weird sisters' dance along Tverskoy Blvd. on that chilly evening in early October. And the air seemed even colder on my scurrying back from the theatre. The difference two hours at Moscow's autumnal sunset make . . . As for the play, it also had all the makings of a reheated soufflé, cold and clumpy, possibly one of the more insufferable productions I had seen so far. Tatiana Doronina, the actress I used to have a crush on back when she was trying to sail that flimsy boat in the song from the movie, now twenty years older and many a pound heavier, was starring in Bulgakov's *Zoyka's Apartment*, a 1920s play that hadn't aged gracefully either. In my mind's eye, I could still see Doronina's more delicate and winsome incarnation as Dulcinea in *Man of La Mancha* a long time before and far away when the Mayakovsky Theatre came to my hometown the year I graduated high school. After the performance, for reasons I still find difficult to explain, I thought it an excellent idea to follow her and a group of actors, including the tall guy who took turns playing Don Quixote and Cervantes in Mitch Leigh's musical, the same tall, dark, and handsome actor who played opposite Doronina in the movie *One More Time about Love,* where she sang about the boat that never sailed, and at the very end died in a plane crash. And so, that balmy night in June, I walked behind the knight of the sad countenance and the sweet lady del Toboso, down Pasteur Street in the dark, past the medical clinic where my mom worked as a cardiologist, past the barbershop where Uncle Misha the barber would give me excellent cuts and praise the shape of my head to high heaven. I followed the actors as they traversed the Soviet Army Square to the hotel way past 10:00 p.m., crossing the street to the opposite side whenever the group paused at an intersection, waited for the lights to change. Then, surreptitiously crossing back to their side of the street... What was my aim exactly? No aim. Just silently shadowing my heroes to their hotel on Primorsky Blvd., slowly, in the soft summer night. Finally, they reached the hotel and were swallowed up by the massive revolving door, never to appear again...

What I had to deal with now, twenty years later, was trying to get Zoyka's stale aftertaste out of my system, and her apartment too, a very uninspired and insipid production, the entire affair highlighting the lameness of the situation I found myself in: on my own in a strange place, grasping at Tasha like she was my lifesaver, hunting my debtors with no leads to go by in a city of eight million plus countless out-of-towners. And as I was walking down the boulevard shuffling my feet through the autumnal leaves, just like when I liked to hear them rustle as a kid on my way to school, and still liking it now, on my way back from the play that I chose to walk out of during the intermission, I was thinking how most things you used to like back in the day more often than not didn't do much for you anymore. And, as I was walking down Tverskoy Blvd., chilled to the bone, I was thinking, if this was the turn things were taking, what would the fount of joy look like for me twenty years down the road? What would those pockets of positivity be: Would they be empty or half-full if the past clearly ain't where it's at? Would it be Hollywood's chewing gum for the eyes in one pocket and a paycheck from a not overly exciting job in the other pocket, and are we talking gold pieces or loose change and some lint, and would 180K, if recovered, ultimately make that much difference in the overall scheme of things, an old lady shuffles up to me, obviously a part of what they still referred to as "the old Russian intelligentsia," and the old lady asks me out of nowhere, "Did you hear the 'rat-ata-tatat' in the distance, young man? What was that? And the truck full of soldiers that drove by just now? Did you see that?" And I tell her, "Nope, didn't see the truck, but whatever that sound was, it wasn't shooting, not just yet, not to worry, lady." Like I had ever witnessed any military action in my entire life, like I knew what the gunfire in the big city's autumnal air at dusk might sound like. Because that was precisely what it was.

Chapter Ten.

Thinking back on that momentous night in the relative safety of my seclusion in Boca Raton, FL, I mean my life is not threatened in any way as far as I know, and upon completion of the project, a tidy stash of money will hopefully be put in my coffer, I say—thinking back on the first night of the failed coup—it seems bizarre how the gunshots in the distance sounded like an extension of the play I walked out of at the New Moscow Art Theatre. But then, did not traveling to distant places often carry with it the make-believe aura of histrionics? Didn't the sounds of a foreign language whispered at the next table in a Copenhagen coffee house for no apparent reason give a faint promise of mystery, magic, seduction even? Though the main thrust of the chitchat most likely didn't stray too far from any coffee shop conversation downtown Manhattan: boyfriend trouble, landlord disputes, office ennui? Granted, the sights and sounds of your home country quickly congeal into familiar words and easily interpretable signs, but the context, after a long absence, could always use a bit of fine-tuning. Were they habitually rude to me last week in the dairy section line at my local Kuntsevo gastronom? Or just unnecessarily snarky? Personal space still an ill-defined concept in post-Soviet Russia, it did hurt for real when a big-boned lady in her late '40s invaded it by stepping on my shoe and just kept pressing on it for fifteen excruciating seconds till the tears began welling in my eyes. And the absurdity of her forgoing an apology and cussing me out instead, thus turning the whole incident into a farce . . .

So where were those soldiers going? Were they perhaps just a bunch of extras, and if so, what tree was the Mosfilm helmer and his trusty AD hiding in? Then, as the days passed, unfamiliar pieces gradually began to make up the gruesome puzzle. Blood spilled and casualties untold started to feel all too real. Ditto the tanks shelling the Parliament building (aka the White House) in grave and weighty support of President Yeltsin's decree aimed at dissolving parliament, which quickly retaliated with a move to oust Yeltsin. Russians shooting at fellow Russians for the first time since when? The civil war of 1918-1920? Or Stalin's purges? Windows rattling in Tasha's Old Arbat apartment, scaring the bejesus out of her mother and Behemoth, a mere five blocks from the standoff scene. A sniper lodged behind the Aeroflot globe emblem atop the restaurant at the intersection of New Arbat and Smolenskaya. TV and telephone service dead for days. Parents going berserk back in New York, kicking themselves for going along with my cockamamy plan to visit my home country, however lucrative the visit's potential outcome might be. Tasha's erring on the dramatic side calling the state of emergency a revolution, but then, what do you call a situation wherein military units storm the government building on presidential orders while the vice-president, in a countermove, initiates the attack on the Ostankino TV tower, a curfew gets imposed until further notice, or groups of men in uniform flag down Orlov and Decibel's *Shesterka* to random check our papers, the muzzles of their guns sticking in our faces through the car windows? I favored the more level-headed definition I heard used on the BBC—incidentally, one of the two foreign channels that continued TV broadcasts throughout the turmoil, the other being CNN. The BBC called the confrontation a coup d'état, eventually toning it down to a constitutional crisis. Or maybe I was just more comfortable with the Western media after getting a taste of Moscow newspapers of the day: variegated, contradictory, often lewd or sensational, certainly a qualitative and quantitative leap from the informational paucity of *Pravda* and *Izvestia* of the Soviet era but, barring a few exceptions, confusing and speculative. Plus, the one or two Russian TV channels that did continue to work during those crazy days, for one reason or another, highlighted the ultranationalist party leader Vladimir Zhirinovsky, the notorious clown-politician who peppered his incendiary speeches with guarantees of all sorts, including the more liberal attitude towards such sexual practices as masturbation. ("Ura!!" shrieked Tasha and I in excited unison when we heard that promise of the new freedom and started jumping up and down on the sofa with the gaiety of five-year-olds, her face remaining somber, while I managed to put some mock-pep into my reaction).

Be that as it may, the armed conflict was a first for me, no matter what you called it. Every once in a while, I thought of it as the near-death convulsions of the last empire under the sun, though I never voiced that insight so as not to rub the concerned citizen Tasha up the wrong way. All in all, Tasha, who witnessed the bloodshed of the first coup in August 1991, was better equipped to handle the free-for-all of early October, yet once or twice, she betrayed signs of genuine distress as the crisis unfolded. For one, she, an on-again off-again smoker, now went through a pack a day, despite her mother screaming her head off in the next room admonishing Tasha to stop stinking up the apartment. Dunhills, Dunhill Lights, Dunhill menthols, Kents, Marlboro Lights, Virginia Slims, Sobranies, mostly knockoffs, all went for roughly a dollar a pack, so she would grab the first thing that stared at her between the jars of ersatz black caviar, bottles of diesel-cut Absolut vodka, and rubber male genitalia in commercial kiosks' windows that had mushroomed around the city over the past few years.

After a week, the coup was conclusively squashed by Yeltsin, and things slowly started going back to normal. I was finally able to brave an occasional trip to the Central Market, now entirely void of locals, a stray hard-currency-loaded foreigner trying his broken Russian on vendors who, for some reason, resembled college teachers more than ever. Wait. What's going on here? Are we back to street theatrics all over again? Why, then, is a young round-cheeked ethnic Russian tangerine seller, a lock of blond hair hanging down from under her headscarf, affecting a Georgian accent? Is she being funny in a self-deprecating manner, playing the part imposed on her by her vitamin C-enriched produce, citrus plants traditionally grown in the Republic of Georgia? Don't ask this confused Count Myshkin – he's just trying to get some veggies, farmer's cheese, and honey in honeycombs for his girl and her ailing mom awaiting him in their Arbat apartment.

Though I must say I did feel a palpable antipathy from Maria Vassilievna from the get-go, she didn't seem to mind my staying the night at their place throughout the crisis. An avid though rarely sober reader, now on a Latin American kick, she took to referring to my relationship with her daughter as *Love in the Time of Cholera*, which I thought was accurate and funny enough, though I'd never actually read the Márquez book, just knew it by the title. Yet I politely chuckled every time the foul-mouthed, ex-basketball coach, ex-Komsomol leader hooch hound pointed her crutch at us and howled hysterically from her bed: "Love in the time of cholera! Love in the time of fucking cholera!" Do check out the book when and if you get back to New York was a mental note I remember making as Tasha and I sat on the sofa in front of the TV in the living room, holding hands and watching the black smoke wafting up from the charred façade of the White House.

Around that time, my punk princess's queries regarding my breakup with Lilly grew more persistent. Deflecting them before the crisis was a no-brainer: I'd either laugh her questions right off or change the subject by launching into inconsequential tales from my life in the USA instead. Say, how crazy I was about branzino or how the early Scorsese changed my life in more ways than I cared to count. That seemed to do the trick when we were in the first throes of passion, sometimes not leaving the bedroom till noon on her days off from the Old Arbat antique store or when we were busy planning our theatregoing, or otherwise occupied by things mundane, such as grocery shopping and looking for meds for Tasha's mother. Now that the residual commotion in the streets had ground our activities to a screeching halt and we were mostly confined to her Old Arbat flat, there wasn't much wiggle room for me to keep dodging her questions. Plus, I figured that talking about my past at length might keep her mind off the nasty goings-on outside. Yet I kept stalling as much as I could, using all kinds of excuses, citing, by way of adverse example, my own lack of interest in her past (false: I was dying to get to the bottom of what happened to her husband), or my having to get busy mapping out the next move in my search for Vik Z-sky and co (very true).

Indeed, a few weeks after the failed coup, it was business as usual for me again. I was spending three nights a week in the capital's clubs and casinos looking for my debtors in the company of Orlov and Decibel Petro, who weren't exactly ready to call it quits—so long as I paid them in a timely fashion, which I did—yet were clearly of the opinion that the blitzkrieg I was hoping for wouldn't materialize. I also continued going to the theatre occasionally with my golden-haired punk princess. We went to check out Lermontov's *The Masquerade*, Bulgakov's *The Heart of the Dog*, Chekhov's *Ivanov*, and we loved them all. Something about the lived-through chaos of civil unrest and its effect on one's take on dramatic art. By mid-October, I was finally able to call my mom and, on a separate occasion, my dad and report to them that the crisis no longer affected most of my activities, be it searching for my debtors, getting whatever produce the irascible babushkas were peddling out of wooden crates next to the Kuntsevo metro station, or, for that matter, nurturing a relationship with the sweet if somewhat moody girl who lived with her mother and her cat on the other side of town. Yes, I brought my folks up to date on my relationship status, which was beginning to feel like the real thing to this traveler. At least, the few days and nights that we didn't see each other, Tasha was on my mind as obstinately as my ex once had been when we were starting our journey together, everything else except my hunt for the caddie scumbags taking the back seat vis-à-vis this new feeling.

By the way, not that it should be anyone's concern, but why not get it over with right here and now? The way we circumvented Tasha's multiple piercings fashion statement wasn't as complicated as that and fell roughly into the following pattern we rarely departed from. Before we went to bed, she would take out her lower-lip ring, keeping her nose ring in; tongue stud removal was optional, and the same went for her nipple rings and multiple earrings. As far as her intimate multicolor bead piercing, it was always taken out upon my request. My lady friend was more than obliging that way. And, of course, my helping her put the accessories back in reverse order the morning after added an extra measure of tenderness to our trysts. I miss everything about her as I write this within the confines of my Boca bungalow, as you can probably tell by now.

Chapter Eleven.

In the second week of November, Tasha and I decided to check out the screening of Greg Davis's early silent masterwork *The Wild Ass's Skin* that Tasha's Aunt Oksana Zhuravel was scheduled to present at the Kino Center in Krasnaya Presnya. We thought it best to get there by metro. I was into my third month in Moscow, my money was beginning to dwindle, and it made sense to use my bodyguards outside of any night club-related activity only when absolutely necessary. Before picking Tasha up at her Old Arbat apartment, I had a brief meeting with the cousins at the Novy Arbat sports bar to pay the duo for the semi-idle mode they had been sputtering in for a month because of the crisis and provide them with the nightclub schedule for the upcoming week.

Half an hour later, as Tasha and I were waiting for our train on the platform of the imposing Arbatskaya station with its chandeliers the size of minibuses hanging from its vaulted ceilings, I thought I'd try to buoy my friend's spirits by finally making good on my promise to tell her about my breakup. But first, I thought I'd go through a little warm-up routine. Then try to tease out the story about her perished ex. And only then . . .

The curfew lifted recently, the metro returned to its pre-coup schedule, but the semiautomatic-wielding OMON policemen in groups of three still patrolled the station, reminding passengers of the dire events of early October. Something I learned to deal with coolly during the conflict, something I was looking forward to getting the hell away from when my private mission was accomplished. I also hoped that Tasha would agree to visit me in New York at some point, though I hadn't broached the subject yet. Of the few ways of lifting people's spirits, the one I thought I was proficient in was banter. And banter I did while waiting for our train, rattling off some observational comedy; only in retrospect, it didn't seem all that amusing and was only tangentially observational. Lucky for the reader, I can't for the life of me think of what it was that I said to her that evening on the platform. One thing I'm sure of is that my routine did not involve the bears and only marginally touched on branzino. I recall that in response, Tasha managed to squeeze out half a smirk as I was holding forth.

"Dude, you sure get long-winded when in plain view of armed men in uniform!" she said, smiling. That's what I was shooting for: a smile, a glimmer in her eye, anything but the surly look I'd see on her face for almost a month. "So. It seems you did get your hands on branzino after all. Scorsese, too. Anything else? Jackson Pollock and Michael Jackson? Michael Jordan and Tom and Jerry? You had your Lilly of the valley, and you lost your Lilly of the valley. Or did she get lost on her own, petals and all? What the hell happened, dude? Should I get on my knees in plain view of armed men in uniform and beg you?" scoffed my punk princess and gave me a light but emphatic punch in the gut as we were boarding the train.

"You go first, lady," I said and shook my head. "And you go first this minute. What happened to your ex? I'm all ears."

"I don't feel like talking about it, Mark. How many times do I have to tell you that? He's gone," said Tasha. "What else is there to say?"

"Please," I said. "We've been together almost two months now, Tasha. Please?"

"Persistent, are we, America?" breathed out Tasha before giving me the following rapid-fire account without as much as looking me in the eye. "Ambushed in his car near Baumanskaya. A *vnedorozhnik* SUV pulled up next to his beamer, a masked gunman rolled down the window, stuck out his AK-47, and riddled Felix's car with bullets. The driver got hit, too, ambled out of the car, and tried to blend in with the crowd of protesters—no such luck. The poor chap didn't look like your typical Joe Blow activist, what with his tracksuit and gold chains. So he got stabbed to death in plain view, in cold blood. The motherfuckers were clean out of bullets. Wounds to his neck, chest, groin. Massive blood loss. Animals. The Solntsevskaya group, the roughest motherfuckers in town. Felix died of multiple wounds after he was rushed to the ER. A sweet, bookish kid, college dropout, carried my books from school, mom's a dissident, spoon-fed neuroleptics in Lefortovo, dad taught physics in college. Studied biochemistry in Polytech, Felix did, smart as a whip, went into business like everyone else. Knew his Tyutchev, was crazy for Tyutchev, actually. Even tried reciting Tyutchev on his deathbed. A nurse told me on our way to the morgue. I got there ten minutes late. Happy now?"

"You kidding? Happy? Not happy at all! But why, Tasha? Why?"

"Why what?"

"Why was he murdered? I'm in shock, and . . . ah, poor, poor girl!"

Shocked, dumbfounded, petrified, speechless was more or less how I felt. It all sounded so unreal, so horrific and inhumane. Godforsaken and ruthless land, which makes her people turn against each other like a bunch of wild animals. Only animals don't go after their own kind . . .

"Territorial disputes, what else? Competition taken to its logical extreme. He wouldn't budge, wouldn't negotiate. I mean, he was protected, sure. But it was time for that extra layer of 'cover' over his head . . ."

"What did he trade in?!"

"Oh, a little bit of everything. Consumer electronics, mostly. All legit stuff. Kickbacks to 'the special importer' boys, like everyone else. Owned three stores here in town and two warehouses in Mytischi. We had a nice flat, Mark. A nice lifestyle. Not your typical conspicuous consumers, though. The kid was twenty-four, for Pete's sake! A year older than me. Welcome to Moscow, m'friend, by way of Chicago, 1920s style."

"Speechless. Seems like a nice fellow who got sucked into some swamp and . . ."

"Not really, Mark. I, for one, never asked for much. He didn't have to become a part of gangland. He just didn't."

"But it doesn't seem like he did. I mean, from what you're saying? A victim of the unregulated market, maybe?"

"Unregulated is right. Got me unregulated, derailed, too. A widow at twenty-five, penniless; Felix's partner kept all the assets. Mom's a cripple. Abusive and unbearable, but still a mom. You say your friend Dostoyevsky was dark? Try real life for size. And I don't just mean a coup every other year . . . But enough about me and Felix the Cat. That's what I used to call him; he just loved that *multik*. What about your true love gone to shit? At least she's alive and kicking someplace Nebraska, Alaska? Your turn, America!"

There was no point in stalling any longer, not after hearing the horrid story she had just divulged in such vivid detail. Still, I nodded a few times in momentary deliberation, then cleared my throat, and as I leaned against the metro car door that said "NO LEANING," or, actually, some jokey variation thereof, attained by a prankster's hand that scraped off several letters from the sign that now spelled "NO LENIN" (I'm giving you an English approximation), I told Tasha about my breakup with Lilly K. on our way to Krasnaya Presnya Film Center.

"My story is so . . . blah compared to yours, Tash. Definitely not a high drama with a Prohibition-era finale. A comedy of manners? Maybe. Only not too funny as comedies go. After we made it to Northern California and got settled in a place we could call our own, it didn't escape my notice that out of us two, Lilly'd be the one more readily engaged in conversation by friends and strangers alike. Could it have been her clothes? Her dancing? Or her infectious laughter? Not that she danced nonstop or laughed 24/7 like a teenage moron.

"What, then? Her silver backpack? Her pointy shoes? Why silver? Why pointy? She always aimed to stand out in a crowd. And stand out she did. Nothing wrong with that, sure. Except I was also the one she started keeping her distance from, at least in public. I recall us leaving for Europe on what was to become our only trip overseas and her friend Ashley throwing a bon voyage party for us. It turned out Ashley was the only one in on the fact that it was both of us going away! For one reason or another, the rest of the happy revelers thought Lilly was traveling solo. I must say that rubbed me up the wrong way big time. I can practice Buddhist self-effacement till the cows come home, but when perfect strangers start giving my lawful wife pointers on how a single woman should carry herself in small Sicilian towns, I draw the line... This is us, Krasnoresnenskaya? After you.

"Getting high was what we liked to do for recreation once in a blue moon. Only grass would make me chattier and her gloomier. Once, we passed the joint around after dinner with some friends. Dancing to *Speaking in Tongues* in their living room, I got so psyched by the album's B-side, which I heard maybe for the twentieth time, and us getting down to it with such abandon; plus, Talking Heads were indeed gods incarnate to us at the time, that I blurted out something to the extent that no matter what I did later in life it would never match that level of perfection. Lilly took issue with that. Why did I say that?! How could I make such self-defeating statements? Aren't I an artist, too?! She got incensed out of all proportion. Why was she getting increasingly mad at me with every passing day? Yelling at me in public for a moment's hesitation whether to ask for seconds at someone's barbeque party! Why are you so afraid to help yourself to more coleslaw, for fuck's sake?! Because it was a test, a litmus test. If you raise your voice at me over some stupid coleslaw, then fuck you, fuck you, fuck you. And fuck your dead mamma from Kuntsevo, too. I don't want to deal with any of this bullshit anymore, you hear me?! Let's cross here.

"Ugh, why do I get so worked up over a ghost of a marriage, feelings no longer there, Tasha? Memories would do it, I guess. Speaking of ghosts, you've seen *Ghost* the movie, right? So, you know who Whoopi Goldberg is? Believe it or not, she was there in the flesh almost the day we decided to call it a day. Shortly before this trip, in shoebox number twenty-four in my closet in New York, I found pictures of myself and my slim-limbed ex engaged in the act of sexual congress or, alternately, taking a breather in between. Frankly, you can't see much. Wielding a bulky Nikon in front of the mirror and reaching a crescendo from behind was a tall order even back in my more acrobatically daring years. What you do see is my waist being roughly the width of my you-know-what: extra pounds were never an issue back in college; rather, three square meals a day were. Anyhow, a few years later, we took the pictures to a local photo place, just for the hell of it. And who do you think is standing behind us in line? Whoopi Goldberg herself. She was a Berkeley stand-up comedian at the time, performing locally, maybe down in LA too, but certainly not nationally. No movie gigs yet, either. And she didn't like our bickering at all (for that was precisely what we were engaged in), automatically taking the woman's side. So when I snapped back at her, 'We do what we damn please, lady, and certainly are not in the market for marriage counseling from strangers in photo labs, being a couple and whatnot,' Whoopi cackled, 'Not for long, pal!' Period. Which I thought was rude and presumptuous. But my ex Lilly said, 'You got that right, miss.' Well, I, too, knew Whoopi got that right because this was the question we debated almost daily in those days. Anyhow, our marriage was on its last legs, and it was sensed by strangers and friends alike. And then it just drew its last breath, rolled over, and conked out. And that's that. The amazing story of the events leading up to the breakup with my ex. We parted for good three days later."

"Man, oh man," Tasha whispered under her breath after a bit of silence as we approached the Kino Center building, whose colored neon lights were already on. It was getting dark and foggy outside. Did I overdo my rambling confession? Spruce it up with too many unnecessary details? But hadn't she been pelting me with questions about my divorce since the night we met? She asked for it, and she got it.

Moments later, we sat at a high table in Arlequino, a fancy little restaurant in the same building as the Kino Center. We arrived fifteen minutes before the screening and had just enough time for coffee and a slice of Prague cake, so we decided to split it two ways. Then Tasha spoke.

"That certainly was over and above, I'll tell you," she said. "My thoughts? Your ex sure managed to crawl under your skin, and then some. Or rather, you let her do the crawling. Just curious: Is she done munching on your liver pâté and pancreas mousse, do you think? I mean the richness of detail, the subtlety of the narrative. The high-calorie memories. Master-storytelling, dude. Even your facial expression briefly changed when you were doing her lines. And it's been, what, four years?"

"Three."

"Three! And you chose Kuntsevo, of all places, to stay in Moscow! Any chance she might crawl out your backside any time soon? Or scoot over? Ain't enough room for the two of us inside one big-hearted Mark pining for that entrails-gobbling ex-spouse. I mean, by comparison, the stories of your hunt for the scumbags who gypped you out of a small fortune sure got short shrift."

"Hey, scumbags I don't know from Adam. Lilly and I lived together for six long years!"

"Sounded twice as long from your tale of woe. What's she up to now anyway?"

"How would I know?" I said. "I last saw her in San Francisco, the height of the AIDS crisis. We're not in touch. I hope she's okay. Anyway, thanks for lending your ear. I guess I did chew it a bit there. Water under the bridge."

"If you say so." Tasha twisted her mouth.

"We should probably go. It's five to. One last thing, Tash. Just so you know. What's happening between you and me now is more important. More important than the dancing shadows on the wall of an old decrepit house long slated for demolition. And, by the way, I chose to settle in Kuntsevo before I met you. So there."

"You could move someplace else, you know. Or stay with us when Aunt Oksana leaves. She has to go back soon; can't leave her Valerka for over a week."

"Your mother may have other ideas."

"My mother's never sober enough to have any ideas!"

"She seems to hate my Jewish American guts with a passion, drunk or sober."

"It's all in your head, Mark."

"And my eyes. Can't unsee the look she gives me sometimes."

"You shoulda seen how she looked at Felix! He stood for everything she detested. The only dry eyes at his funeral were Mom's."

"Poor Tasha. A mom from hell, if I may be so bold."

"Hey, hell or limbo, she's still my mom. Let me ask you this, though. Say your mission's accomplished. This month or next, you find who you've been looking for. What next? I mean, for us?"

"Simple. I go back. I send you an invitation. They give you a visa. Your mother stays here, so they have no reason to deny it. No risk of you jumping ship. You come to visit for a month, maybe two. See how you like it. Maybe you'll like it enough to stay."

"And Mom?"

"You go back and get her. For good. Maybe there's a cure for her in the States."

"No, I mean while I'm visiting? She's paralyzed from the waist down, remember? Who'll be taking care of her while I'm away?"

"A nurse. A relative. With the dough I stand to recover, things will work out fine. We're late. And let's deal with problems as they arise, ok?"

"Optimism is Americanism. Tocqueville was right on the money."

"That what he said?"

"How the fuck would I know?" smiled my lover and gave me a peck on the cheek which I promptly returned.

Chapter Twelve.

On our ride back to Arbatskaya station, I made a mistake, which I had to pay for in spades, at least for a few days. This is not to say that our after-screening exchange with Tasha didn't start on an amiable note. During our walk from the Kino Center to Krasnopresnenskaya, she and I agreed that the film just seen was enjoyable and Oksana's lecture very informative. I spoke appreciatively of her aunt's erudite opening notes and of the movie that was striking both on its own and in comparison to the silents of the era I was familiar with from my film studies. The twenty-five-year-old Greg Davis's groundbreaking approach included his use of floating intertitles and even bits of animation, like that famous squiggle of an epigraph that precedes Balzac's novel, which, I should mention, I've read both in Russian and in English translations. All of a sudden, the squiggle that appears ten minutes into the movie morphs into a text in Arabic that the down-at-the-heels Raphael makes out in the back of the magic skin in the old curiosity shop, and then the letters disappear like smoke, or actually, they reappear as real smoke coming from the pipe his friend Eugene is puffing on in the next scene. Or the row of hats that the casino cloakroom attendant keeps on the counter, something like ten of them, the camera slowly dollying alongside fedoras, top hats, straw hats, and cabbie hats until it finally reveals the figure of the withered attendant watching over them unblinking, a pack of cards folding and unfolding, as if pulsating where his heart ought to be. Boldly entertaining is what the silent film proved to be, and it also pointed to Greg Davis's acclaimed future sound film productions, which, according to Oksana's intro, regretfully and inexplicably came to a halt by the late '40s.

It was also evident that the film, incidentally transplanted from early nineteenth-century Paris to Prohibition-era New York, occupied a niche at the crossroads between the illusionist flights of fancy of Georges Méliès and the hard-edged realism of early narrative cinema giants such as G. W. Griffith. Oksana, an attractive if slightly overweight blonde woman in her late '30s, was clearly fascinated with her subject and, though a tad disorganized initially, picked up steam halfway through the talk and ultimately came across as an expert in Greg Davis's early work, American silent cinema in general, and the social and historical context of the period. She also argued that the self-perpetuating nature of Davis's version of *The Magic Skin* formed a narrative loop as the shagreen at the center of the movie turned into a perpetuum mobile of sorts, allowing for sequels (never filmed) since Raphael's last wish involved the skin itself. He asked the piece of shagreen, now shrunk to a thumbnail because of the wishes it granted him, that it restore itself to its former size and take back all the worldly possessions and advantages it had bestowed upon its owner. And that would set him back penniless yet equipped with his newly acquired wisdom. So the film's ending, every bit as moralistic as the novel's, was also a lot happier, as it behooved an American production. At least Raphael lived in Davis's version of the story. And that knack for having his cake and eating it too, per Oksana Zhuravel's insight, was one of the qualities that distinguished Davis's future body of work.

Tasha seemed so pleased with my show of regard for Oksana's presentation that she squeezed my hand on our way to the station and kept holding it as we boarded the train and took our seats. Aglow in the refracted light of my praise for her brainy aunt, my punk princess added a few details that had escaped my notice. For instance, some intertitles stayed on the screen longer than was common in silents; also, the sheer number of them was greater than was the custom back then. Thus, the film targeted a more literate and sophisticated viewer than your average two-reeler audience that patronized the Nickelodeons of the day. The last bit Tasha heard privately from Oksana, who never referred to it in her lecture. And yes, her scholarly aunt was working on her dissertation on Russian- and Ukrainian-born American directors' contributions to Hollywood and even spent some time in the US with her husband, a philandering cad if ever there was one, whom she broke up with while finishing her post-doctorate research at the Art Institute of Chicago. The wily bastard also had a hand in putting Oksana's name on the INS list of undesirables should she choose to reenter the country in the future. His way of getting back at her for leaving him while expecting Valerka. Yet she did have to go back to the States at some point to conduct additional fieldwork on Greg Davis, do the interviews, use film archives, etc.

"Amazing," I said, putting my arm around Tasha's waist and drawing her close. "Also funny how a director who is nearly forgotten in the States is studied in today's Russia, a place in transition, not to say upheaval, that could probably do a better job taking care of her own seasoned filmmakers. But then, gloria mundi being the fickle little bitch that she is . . ." And then, for no good reason, blathering fool that I am, I started telling Tasha about my visit to the Kino Center a few days before meeting her at The Shudder of Recognition. I took a metro ride from Kuntsevo to the Center to attend the premiere of a comedy inanely titled *It's Always Sunny Weather on Deribasovskaya, It's Raining Non-Stop in Brighton Beach*, by Leonid Gaidai, a director who made scores of funny movies that I had kept seeing over and over back in the day and knew almost frame by frame. But the subject matter of his new film was poorly chosen and under-researched, and the outcome, humorless and tedious, was unworthy of the Gaidai I knew from his golden period. Stuff happens, no argument there. "But what added insult to injury," I continued holding forth though Tasha, by then disengaged from my hug and sitting a good foot away, was beginning to look like she'd rather be sitting across the aisle from me or better yet, in the next car, "was that at the end of the screening Gaidai, who happened to be in the audience, stood up, took an awkward bow in response to some applause, then blurted out, 'I'm not going on stage for a little speech as they asked me to. Not going to happen. And for a simple reason. When I demanded a modest fee for it, a hundred dollars, to be exact, they wouldn't hear about it. In America,' he added bitterly, 'directors of my stature get paid thousands of dollars for a crummy five-minute appearance.' Indignant, he then sat down. It was downright embarrassing. That someone of his renown should make such a big deal of a measly fee and make that reference to America, the country his new film was trying to satirize and whatnot."

To that, Tasha, who, as I finally noticed, was pulling on her lip ring and hyperventilating, said testily, "Geez. Listen, Mark. People are poor here, okay? Directors, actors, pensioners, and even underpaid bodyguards. Poor. I barely make ends meet, too, you know. And you, you still have no clue as to what's going on here, do you? Too much clubbing and theatre gone to your curly head, huh? Just trying to collect your pay from a bunch of lowlifes and then it's 'farewell, unwashed Russia'? A little empathy goes a long way. Hello, America!? And by the way, ever thought of one little snag in your great master plan? What if I am not too keen on going anywhere with or without you? Don't want to leave the country of my birth? What if I want to stay here and see how things shake out in the land my people died fighting for? Ever thought of that little glitch?"

I didn't really see it coming, nor had I ever seen her get so worked up in the two months that we'd been together. So this is what I said to her as I touched her shoulder (she abruptly pulled away from me): "Hey, all I'm trying to say is it was embarrassing all around, okay? The Kino Center refusing to pay Gaidai, and Gaidai voicing his chagrin in public. Period. As to your coming over for a visit, it's not like you'd be making any life-changing decisions, you know. See how it sits with you."

And it was then that Tasha, having let my last words roll off of her, started drilling me with all sorts of questions that I was not ready for. "So what *do* you know about the first coup anyway, Mark the bounty hunter? It didn't exactly make headlines in New York, New York, did it?" To repeat, the question caught me unawares, and I remember going silent for fifteen seconds, feeling a little piqued as our discussions rarely turned to politics save the recent crisis. And as I was collecting my thoughts and looking around for help (what help?), I noticed a fellow sitting at the far end of the train. He wore an aviator helmet, and his face, with its prominent aquiline nose and dark piercing eyes, seemed vaguely familiar. His right leg was in a cast up to his knee, he was leaning on a crutch, a guitar case to his left, and a young strawberry blonde female companion to his right, and they were engaged in a quiet conversation. Her coat was partially open, and I glimpsed the tight dark-green skirt she had on, too short for the season, and the tall boots, the height of Moscow fashion that fall. Was it the afflicted fellow who, for all I knew, could have been wounded in recent skirmishes that triggered my punk princess's harsh and loaded questions? Hard to say. Proceed with caution, I thought to myself before answering.

"Matter of fact, I do remember August '91 well, Natalya. I was staying with my folks at the time, something you do in the States, too, sometimes. Like when you are right out of college or between jobs. And I remember this endless commute on the Long Island Expressway and morning radio hosts riffing off the 'ya' sound in putschists' last names, i.e., Yanayev, Yazov, etc. Not a word about the losses or the motives. None."

Tasha was hanging on every word I was saying. I don't believe I'd ever seen her this focused before. Moments later, she spoke. "The word about the two boys squashed by the tanks and the third one who got shot got around later. The obligatory *Swan Lake* on TV made the grandmas wonder how bad the Kremlin shuffle really was this time around. You know how they play that Tchaikovsky schmaltz every time someone gets the fucking boot at the highest echelon? Later, we learned that the hardcore faction of the Soviet government was battling for power with the Russian Federation's government. The result? The USSR was no more. Bye-bye, Gorby! Yeltsin's the man at the helm. Fast-forward to the last month. The black dents still mar the façade of the White House while you and I enjoy the unprecedented flourishing of dramatic arts in Russia's capital." Tasha finished her diatribe and twisted her mouth. She was visibly unsettled.

"Tasha, I get it. Don't rub it in, okay? What's with you? It's a bumpy time for the country." I was trying to steer clear of platitudes or pandering notes. "But . . . things'll get better. Looks like the worst is over. The last thing the country needs is a civil war. And it is not going to happen."

"Oh really? And how exactly do you know what is or is not going to happen? Are you some kind of visionary? A political scientist? Not even a terribly concerned bystander, far as I can tell. How would you know how long it'll take to go back to normal? Just curious?"

"I don't. I just hope it was all for the better."

By then, we were off the train, out of the marble echo chamber of Arbatskaya station with its enormous chandeliers, and were briskly walking past the late-night book vendors in the dark pedestrian underpass next to the Khudozhestvenny movie theatre. The lurid covers of books made recently available by the tides of glasnost looked ludicrous in the dim fluorescent light: Lolita's skinny knees in anachronistically frivolous torn fishnet stockings, Lara and Dr. Zhivago French kissing against multicolored onion domes in the snowy distance, two cutout figures engaged in what seemed like intercourse on the cover of Limonov's bestselling *It's Me, Eddie.*

"Argh. You really get my goat when you talk this way, Mark!"

"Which way is that?"

"A groundlessly benign and oh so disarmingly positive way. The friendly American way."

"Beats the unreasonably cantankerous bitchy Russian way any day, if you ask me."

"Not bitchy. Just not overly impressed with your show of sincerity and compassion."

"My show of what?! Are you insane? I'm not out to impress anyone, Tasha!" I was beginning to lose it. "Least of all, the ingrate little grouch who doesn't know what's good for her!"

"Wasting time on a pushover from the land of Land Rovers is not good for anyone in her right mind, pal!"

"Not sure what that means."

"Use your head for a change, Mr. World Trotter. You might like the feel of it. Those little wheels humming away inside of your thick skull!"

"What is this barrage of abuse, Tasha? Now I'm curious. I thought we . . . I don't know, knew better than that."

"Apparently, not."

"So long as we don't regret it later."

"Regret what, excuse me? You in my life?! Take the money and scram. Take a hike, this ain't no Klondike."

"What the hell are you blabbering about?"

"Your superior attitude. And don't bother seeing me off! I can take it from here!"

"Tasha, cut it out before I say things I don't mean!"

"Not before you suck my dick, Mr. Business Opportunity Knocks. And yes, before I forget: screw you and screw your get rich quick mentality!"

"Look who's talking!" I believe it was then that my voice reached the point of screaming. So glad Old Arbat was deserted. Or almost deserted. "A girl from the city crawling with gangsters! A widow of a get rich quick man who got whacked in a hurry . . ."

"Leave Felix out of it, okay? You piece of nothing who has no feelings for this land or any sympathy for me . . ."

Boy, was she on a tear! Truth be told, she looked kind of ugly to me in the middle of that tongue-lashing, a reverse transformation of a princess into a punk frog if I ever saw one, her pierced face contorted and pasty in the green neon light of the Prague restaurant sign on the corner of Old Arbat. Beauty is in the eye of the beholder, sure. Only this beholder felt like splitting then and there so as to take a break from beholding what was left of the beauty (not much).

"The piece of nothing is rich. Stooping pretty low now, aren't we? I actually want to make a suggestion." I was trying to sound calm and mature under the circumstances. "Let's stop seeing each other for a while. The distance may do us some good."

"I thought you'd never ask," Tasha said impassively. "Let's."

"Glad we're on the same page. Take five. We've been through a lot. And then . . ."

"Then what?"

"See who wins this staring contest in reverse."

"Meaning?"

"Whoever misses the other more, calls her. Or him."

"Her, Mark. Her. Don't kid yourself for once, please."

"Whatever. And then maybe we'll go see a play?" I said.

"What? What play?!"

"Any play. A make-up play. Would be nice, catharsis-wise."

"Catharsis huyarsis," said Tasha. "Just don't let Orlov and Decibel out of sight for long. Healthier for your thick skin." With that, she flipped me off with both hands, two birds with one stone, as it were, then took a sarcastic low bow, did an abrupt about-face, and walked away into the foggy night.

Chapter Thirteen.

As I watched her diminutive figure recede into nothingness on Old Arbat and debated within myself whether I should head straight home to Kuntsevo or stop by for a quick drink at Rosie O'Grady's, a funny thing happened. Granted, the ensuing encounter was perplexing in its own right, and the exchange between my midnight interlocutor and myself was nothing short of bizarre—but so were the circumstances that led to the man from the train appearing in front of me, practically out of nowhere. Towering a good head over me, he was leaning on a crutch and swaying faintly in the chilly wind all by himself (sans the strawberry blonde companion, sans the guitar case), squinting his piercing eyes as he addressed me in English in his low pleasant voice, "Passport, Mark Efimovich Neider? Your passport. Glad I've caught up with you. I'm a fast walker, all right, used to run marathons even. Way back in the day. But not with this damn hairline fracture . . ."

Obviously, the stranger had already peeked inside my passport, which I apparently dropped on the train in the heat of my argument with Tasha. The fact of the matter is, I made a habit of never leaving my apartment without it even before the coup, to say nothing of taking it with me during the peak of recent events. So I thanked the poor man, shook his icy hand, and said it was awfully nice of him to get off the train and follow me to hand back the document, which would have taken forever to reinstate at the US embassy. "Think nothing of it," he responded magnanimously, then laughed a strange velvety laugh. "Surely you don't believe I got off because of your papers? Arbatskaya happens to be my stop, too. So, it all worked out nicely. As it always does, all things being equal. Listen," the stranger looked around, then shifted his weight slightly, "I hope I'm not imposing, but . . . what do you say we grab a quick drink? Rosie O'Grady's isn't too far, and it's one hell of a bleak night. Just tell me if I'm imposing. Please."

"Hey, I'm game," I sighed. "Sure could use one right now," and I patted my coat pockets for cigarettes.

"Tell me about it, *tovarich*," the stranger gave me an exaggerated wink, though his angular face remained surprisingly stern. "Isn't she a bit of a hothead, your friend Tasha? Don't mean to pry, but sometimes the best strategy . . ."

"Wait. How do you know her name?" I frowned as he clutched my elbow. God, I don't appreciate when people do that, even the fair sex. I mean the clutching part. But the guy was obviously trying to keep his balance while tottering by my side. His lone crutch just wouldn't cut it. I couldn't help wondering how he managed to catch up with me. I also hoped I was doing an okay job as his human crutch.

"You kidding? You were practically screaming it on the train. People in the next car could hear you, I'm sure!" He laughed his peculiar laugh again, then gave me a sidelong glance.

"Hey, you were there too, weren't you?" There was exhilaration in his faintly accented voice, an exotic amalgamation of rolling "r"s and hisses as if he were part French, part Portuguese, though, it turned out, he was neither. "You saw *The Skin*! My friend and I were sitting practically three rows behind you!"

"Small world, isn't it?" All of a sudden, I felt a little too fatigued for a keener show of surprise, though the coincidence was indeed striking.

"Make it the universe while you're at it!" My interlocutor was apparently prone to quirky generalizations. "No, but what did you think?" he asked. "Let's use the underpass there. So many good limbs to go around if you catch my drift."

I did, almost.

"I thought it was good," I shrugged. "At times, brilliant." Still steaming after my squabble with Tasha, I tried to sound civilized as best I could. "Great introduction by the lady scholar, too."

"I know, right? Minor work, yes, sure. But. Hey. We're not nitpicking here. Still packs a punch. Right? Sure, his great ones came later, in the '40s, and '50s. An art circuit darling where I come from—pride of place in my private pantheon. I even met the gent briefly, though the big shot probably has no recollection of it," the gregarious stranger declared with a mixture of modesty and conviction. "But yeah, considered a prodigious talent in my neck of the woods."

"Where's that?" I was intrigued by the man's enthusiasm. "I mean, where are you from?"

"Saint Pete by way of Sweden. A dash of Bavaria in my veins, too. A US citizen, naturalized, naturally. A blend in a band, here on tour, aujourd'hui and toujours!" he announced with a quick flourish of his crutch and good-natured chuckle. "Played Bunker for a week. A residence gig. Killed it, too. If I am to believe the local press. Not that I pay much heed, local or global. Healthier that way."

"Hold on just a sec!" I exclaimed, watching him let go of my elbow, thrust the tip of his crutch up in the air, strum its handle comically, and emit a few loud discordant sounds like he was playing electric guitar through reverb.

"That's how I know you!" I cackled at his silly antics in the dark. "I saw your set at Bunker—wowee zowee! Just don't break your other leg on me! You guys were . . . a-w-e-s-o-m-e!" Excited, I just had to spell out the last word of my compliment.

My companion smiled vaguely, though his expression remained unchanged, as he slipped his arm through the crook of mine before we resumed our walk. In a short while, we found ourselves in front of Rosie O'Grady's, whereupon the fellow quickly pulled out an unadorned silver cigarette case from his pocket, inquired in a mock baritone what type of cancer sticks I preferred, and gave out his intermittent laugh before I had a chance to respond. "Ain't it crazy?" he continued.

"What is?"

"Everyone and his little niece quoting from *The Master and Margarita* here! Like I did just now. I saw that look of complicity, can't fool me, comrade! The book's okay, no ifs or buts . . . Though I've obviously read better. But the status! The reverence! Ah, the land of cults and posthumous devotional rites! A little tour inside the Garden Ring will make you feel part of a sprawling installation: the repressed and the executed staring at you from every other building façade. Nothing wrong with memorial plaques, nothing wrong with belated regard. Just don't put your writers in front of the firing squad with such dismaying regularity before canonizing them. You do that with impunity, and you feel you can get away with invading a sovereign country a century later. Parliament, okay?"

He stared at me as I extracted a cigarette from his case. Then he flicked the wheel of the Zippo lighter that, like a variety show magician would, he took out from the side of his helmet, which looked scaly in the dark. Then he turned his left cheek to me, revealing the secret little pocket where he kept the lighter. The flame's dancing shadows distorted his profile momentarily as its hue changed to orange, then pink, only to be subsumed by the reflected crimson light of the establishment's neon sign.

"What sovereign country?" I tried to give him back his smokes, but he refused with a silent shake of his head. "You don't mean the Prague Spring? Because that happened hardly a century later."

"Nice try," the man returned. "But you are cold. Cold as stone, *khlopchis'ko.* The old war machine gobbling up her own progeny, then turning her hideous maw on her neighbor's. Wish I was wrong, but you just wait till the chickens come rumbling home to roost."

"I guess it's all about control," I said, letting his non sequiturs slide, same goes for his getting a little too familiar and choosing to call me "a kid" in Ukrainian. "You know, the Artist vs. the State dynamic. Poets here are more than poets, as this poet once said. Back in the States, they're prone to go to bed hungry. If they don't teach, that is. The dreadful custom here was to put them away without correspondence privileges. That's a euphemism for capital punishment for you. Things seem to have changed."

"Blessed are the believers, to quote the author, I normally try not to," he said gravely. "Shall we go in? You can finish your ciggie inside. This ain't no home of the brave health nuts."

"Man, I still can't believe it's you. I mean the Tarantula! You guys were something else," I gushed as we clambered onto barstools beside each other, though he took a bit longer. "Even the peach juice licking bit seemed . . . I don't know, somehow apropos. Just a tiny bit excessive, maybe. But hey, we all need our schticks, I suppose. The whole image thing. No biz like showbiz."

He chuckled again, apparently pleased with my reaction, then slapped his hands together like he was mosquito-hunting, though, in fact, he was trying to get the bartender's attention. The bartender, a gaunt and sinewy guy in white shirtsleeves, seemed to know him from before. "Not merely a schtick," the stranger explained, half-turning to me. "I make like I lick the juice off the floor when we break into the beefed-up version of 'If You Don't Want My Peaches.'"

"Oh, that's what it was!" I smiled. "And I thought I knew the song. The one and only Irving Berlin. Loved your post-punk take on it! And the new lyrics to 'Sympathy for the Devil?' What was that all about?"

"What new lyrics?" the fellow seemed puzzled. "We don't do 'Sympathy.' You sure it was us you saw at Bunker, hehe?"

"Well, yeah," I shrugged. "I could swear . . ."

"Let you in on a little secret, buddy. All it takes is a ticker, speeded-up rim section, plus the vocals weaving in and out exponentially. Fatten up the chords through reverb. Let the solo stand out, let it hover above the white noise. Staying this side of chaos, seeing order behind it, warp and weft—yeah, man! The whole Nietzsche's butterfly thing. Pick up the pieces just before they get shattered, hitting the ground. Shattered! Goes beyond music, man. Look back on random things, you see a pattern. Make the universe shrink incrementally by doing your bit. What's your poison anyway? I'll get the first round."

"Maker's Mark, straight up, thanks."

"Make it two Makers', Seerozha. Rocks for me." My new friend showed the peace sign to the bartender. In return, the latter tried to give him a clumsy high five before reaching for two glasses under the counter.

It was right about then that I started to lose my chatty interlocutor: his train of thought was beginning to rattle a little, to take occasional unexpected turns. His speech acquired an improbable Jamaican ring, only to lose it moments later. So, I figured I'd switch to things commonsensical after we clinked our glasses. What better way to keep tabs on the situation? And that's what I did.

"Anyway, what happened to your lady friend?" I asked. "Last time I looked, she was sitting next to you."

"Rita? Got off at Kievskaya. A test tomorrow. The second to last time *I* looked, she was expecting. Also, a little, you know, hot to trot. The brittle Rita, the queen of Germanic studies . . . Women. Can't live with them, can't break them on Catherine's wheel, right?"

"Say what?"

"Just busting your chops, buddy!" The man opened his cavernous mouth as if getting ready to laugh again only no sound issued from it, just a lone golden tooth shone dully from within its depth. I hadn't noticed that dental embellishment in my companion's oral cavity before but then it was the first time that I saw his bony clean-shaven face with the aquiline nose up close, well lit and animated.

"I don't mean to pry," he said after a pause. "But I believe you should be the one to give your friend a call. Listen, man was created first, at least, according to that universally beloved fairy tale, the telephone came a bit later, and only then . . . Anyhoo, it's all about communication. And miscommunication. Did you see *Uncle Vanya* at Maly yet, by the bye?"

"Much obliged," I interrupted and raised my hand as if trying to halt the oncoming traffic. "I'm sure we'll straighten things out on our own just fine. Same goes for our theatre options."

"Oops. I think I just did. I mean, pry. An issue, I know. So does my shrink. Fuck, man, what's the matter with me and my big kisser? Keep your nose out of other people's affairs—argh," he concluded, obviously discomposed. "Seerozha, let's do another one," he called out to the bartender and jiggled the ice around in his empty glass.

"You have a shrink here?"

"Stockholm. I divide my time between Stockholm, New York, and Saint Pete. Though can you really do that? I mean, divide time?"

"What's your name anyway, Mr. Globe Trotter?" I inquired, ignoring his stab at cleverness. "Time we got mutually acquainted."

"I go by a few. Bandmates call me Arhi. With the 'h,'" he said.

"The 'h' where?"

"Where it belongs, where do you think? Right after the 'r'!" Arhi bent his knee the best he could and tapped the cast with his long forefinger. The cast was smudgy and covered with scribblings, some more legible than the others, some written over the barely visible old ones, forming the soiled palimpsest: "You can't stand the heat, stay out of the kitchen, Arhi, man!" "Poor devil up to your old tricks?" "Let 'em have it like it was the real White House!!" "Don't get meth, Arhi! Get Evian!" Some made more sense than others; some seemed to morph into others, not unlike the intertitles of the movie we both had just seen. The last part was the weirdest, and I promised myself then and there that the next Maker's Mark would be my last. It had been a long day. But it was far from over.

"You have a lot of friends, Arhi, man," I observed stiffly, for a brief moment stung by jealousy. "My cast would look pretty blank under similar circumstances."

"Man, I make friends wherever I roam. Sure, is a bit of an effort. I mean, when not touring, I tend to keep to myself," he confessed. "But . . . let me assure you, comrade, you'd never find yourself in circumstances like mine."

"Why do you say that, Arhi? My bones are as fragile as the next fellow's."

"Yeah, but. I mean the circumstances that led to the fracture. Can't have your cake and eat it, too. Remember, got to serve somebody? What a guy, that Zimmerman, forever stuck in limbo, but so what. Sure, there are exceptions. Double agents. Come double payday, they are happy troopers. But, say, you get your ass nabbed? Boy, you stand to take a pounding from both sides! Like when you happen to work for Yeltsin *and* his opposition? Don't try it at home, bud. Know what I'm sayin'?"

"What *are* you saying? You were employed by Yeltsin? In what capacity, Arhi?"

"And Gorby before him! Strategic info brokering, Neider." Arhi gave me a wink. "Hooked up his team with a bunch of economist whiz kids from Harvard . . . Boris Nikolayevich prevailed. Good for him and his kith and kin. Let's see how the country fares now."

"So. Let me get this straight. You did some government-level consulting for Russia's first president? As well as the last Soviet leader? Must've been a rough ride. A bit of a departure for a musician, too?"

"Comes with the territory. Just try not to patronize me if you can."

"How am I patronizing you?"

"You just are. Nothing rough about double brokering. Not too legal. But if you're in my shoes and keep an eye on the big picture, legal takes the back seat."

"What big picture is that?"

"Boy, you ask a lot of questions. Let's have another one. Let you pay this time. The big pic? Looking past the petty thugs snapping at each other's heels would be a good place to start. I try and see right past them. Though they shit their pants every time they see me play. Like I was their boss-*nachalnik*. That I very well may be, it's just that they're not supposed to be in on it."

Arhi showed Seerozha his empty glass; Seerozha nodded vigorously, blew him a kiss, bared his teeth (he appeared to be missing an incisor), and flailed his hairy arms like he was doing an imitation of "The Dying Swan" dance.

In the meantime, the scene inside Rosie O'Grady's was getting progressively unsettling. A pair of chubby young ladies were giggling impetuously as they bumped into each other on their way out of the establishment; for a brief moment, they halted in the doorway, hiked up their coats, and showed us the seats of their baby-blue underpants. Seerozha frowned, pitched a sizable ice cube at them, missed the target by two feet, then let out a frustrated yelp.

"What brings you to Moscow anyway, friend?" asked Arhi, ignoring Seerozha's antics and the pickled ladies' midnight lack of restraint.

"Research," I said distractedly, trying to mull over what I just heard. A strategic advisor to Yeltsin, how odd, I thought. And a possible mafia clandestine bigwig? All that on top of being a punk rocker? Is Arhi missing a screw? Is he a victim of a contusion he failed to mention just yet? What's with the scaly aviator helmet and goggles anyway? And maybe it is time I headed home for some rest?

"To your success in the land of the commissars, then! Bottoms up! Just like the merry barflies just now! Martha, my dear, and friend whose name escapes me as well it should. They're always here." Arhi raised his glass over his head and then took a small sip. "'People die for metal, hahaha?'" he sang in a pleasant operatic baritone. "Did Gounod have in mind the crime-infested Russia of today, or was he just dishing out platitudes like any artist worth his salt sometimes has to? Don't want to lose the audience. How you say it? To risk is noble? You don't need me to tell you that!"

"Tell you what? I mean, tell me what?"

"How tight the money thing gets when you're out of school, and she plays you for a god's fool!"

Arhi rounded his dark eyes in anticipation of my surprise. I didn't give him the satisfaction.

"What school did *you* go to anyway? You sound like a college man," I inquired instead.

"Other than the school of hard knocks? San Francisco State, why?"

"Get the fuck out!" I almost fell off my barstool. "My alma mater?!"

"You shitting me," he whispered, widening his eyes again. "When were you there?"

"'88 to '91."

"Class of '87," he patted himself on the chest and smacked his lips jocularly. "Missed you by one year. The faculty bozos still need to see the final cut. So, technically, I haven't graduated. Technically. Been too long."

"No fucking way! You a film major?"

"Sure am. Small universe, anyway you pork it. Getting smaller by the second. Every coincidence—quote, unquote—shrinks it some. I don't care what science has to say on the subject. Way overrated in my book, science is. Something about us, expats," he lowered his voice as he leaned towards me, "breakdancing on the same wavelength without half trying. A weird place your home country is, bro. Inside out and back. A weird time to be visiting. 'Blessed is he who visits this life at its fateful moments of strife.' Easy for Tyutchev to rhapsodize. See how you like nipping away with a hairline fracture. Friendly fire, my ass. What's so friendly about it if I'm constitutionally unfit to take sides? A broken bone broker with ties to Brocken. There's a rap number in it somewhere, no?"

He was blathering away a mile a minute now, fluctuating between not too coherent and utterly impenetrable and, as he abruptly took off his scaly aviator helmet with goggles, I finally got a full view of his peculiar haircut, but not until I walked around him on my way to the men's room a short while later: his partially shaved occiput, a two-inch tattoo comprised of a spread-out compass with the square and the eye inside, and the semicircular inscription "Lux e tenebris" around it, pencil-thin sideburns, and a small scar on the back of his long neck. What a character.

"Look here. Let's simplify things for argument's sake. If the universe is expanding like they say it is, how can you be sure the things said or written today mean precisely what they meant yesterday? You just can't. Incrementally so, negligibly so, but the meaning changes. Because everything flows, remember Heraclitus? What a chap. I'd do him in a heartbeat. Just shitting you, what?" Arhi was talking fast now as if in a trance, yet his rant sounded like he had given the subject some prior thought. "What I mean is every word signifies what it does plus something extra. The meaning is rarely bolted down. It vibrates along with the context. It buzzes like the fluorescent lights that buzz in the underpasses of the capital of your motherland at night. Don't give me that puzzled look, motherchugger. Don't tell me it stopped being your motherland just because you up and left with your hapless folks for greener pastures one fine day many a moon ago, who are you kidding, *khlopchis'ko*? My field is gray, by contrast. Yet I sure try to make sure the equilibrium is maintained. Your kind leaves, there's got to be something coming in, for harmony's sake. But what is it? And can you put out what hasn't been yet put in? Though you sure wish you could. Instrumentally speaking, the bridge is never too far. So what if you can't see it for the trees."

"Are you talking about . . . your music?" I asked, letting his crudeness and the motherland jab slide. Not sure how he figured out where I was from. My accent? Wait. My passport! The place of birth paragraph in my passport, of course. Odessa, USSR. Is that why he kept calling me *khlopchis'ko*?

Still, I must say I had a hard time following him. Truth be told, I was falling way behind. For a whiskey-soaked minute, which felt like a miniature replica of eternity, before me appeared a vision of Arhi standing on the top of a hill in the distance as I was lying flat on my back in a yellow valley below amidst the swaying daisies and dandelions shedding their fuzzy petals on my brow and heaving chest. His voice could barely reach me, yet every word he uttered came through loud and clear. There was also a newly manifested bond between us, tangible though immaterial, the difference in altitudes notwithstanding. Was he trying to drag me to the gray realm he had just referred to? But the realm above his pinhead-sized head looked blue to my eye . . .

Both of us were standing at the edge of the tar-covered roof of the tenement building now, below us the flea market abustle with a multitude of buyers and sellers, Arhi's arm resting on my shoulder fraternally, the other arm clutching a three-liter bottle of pickled tomatoes in muddy brine. "Wanna jump?" he queried softly, giving me a mischievous wink. "Just four stories high, not counting the basement. Should be a synch." "You jump," I returned. "You can do it in your sleep, can't you?"

Then, as if someone was treating me to a slideshow projected on my cranium, a jeans-clad image of Arhi appeared sitting cross-legged on the Rossiya Hotel room floor, dragging on a Marlboro Light, blowing out perfect rings of smoke that wafted up in the beam of light coming from the window as he exchanged pleasantries with the transparent Aunt Nusia Tiraspolsky who was standing right next to him and playing absently with his curly hair. "Vika, not Nusia," she intoned, sticking out the tip of her tongue. Suddenly, he jumped to his feet, took an exaggerated bow, and extended his hand toward her as she asked him for a round of *letka-enka*. Then Aunt Nusia laughed a short, flirty laugh and said, "Friends are leaving for warmer climes like so many rooks. Sad part is I'll never get to see them castle again. Why are you doing this to us?"

Then Arhi turned invisible, though I could swear it was him squatting at my feet and tickling Alena the primadonna between her thighs under the table at Dock's. A double dirty Martini, he announced in an undertone as he encouraged me to take a whiff of his long, moist fingers. Little wonder it was me who got slapped hard on the cheek by the peeved young woman. Tokens of immodest attention couldn't have come from Vodovozkind, Vjollca, or Victor Z-sky, who shared our table by the window overlooking Third Ave. Funny, but in my Maker's Mark-induced trance, I enjoyed the smell of her pungent cunt juice as well as the sharp and sudden blow. Unless both were brought on by Arhi post factum. Still not unpleasant. Who the hell was he? I remember beginning to ponder right about then. The brief slideshow was over, though I wished it had gone on longer.

"Equilibrium between two forces, dude," he said emphatically. "Keeping things from collapsing. The losing side gets demonized every time the shit hits the fan. Can't let it happen for longer than expedient. How long is that? There are formulas, we ain't no amateurs. Vkraina will prevail, nukes or no nukes. Just get ready to tighten your belt while picking up the tab." His explanations had a way of muddying up the preceding statement. Out of the corner of my eye, I noticed that Arhi didn't look too comfortable either. Wetting his thin lips with his uncommonly long tongue, he asked Seerozha for a spare napkin and some salty peanuts. Seerozha obliged momentarily, whereupon Arhi daubed his high forehead with the folded napkin, took a nip of Maker's Mark, and uttered impassively, "Questions, comments, all-consuming concerns?"

"So, how do you make sure things don't collapse?" I asked, looking around furtively. The bar was deserted now, and the overhead lights dimmed. All at once, I realized how desperately I needed to go home, get in bed, maybe catch an old Soviet-era movie on TV. Yet an uncanny force had me glued to my seat. Call it chemistry, call it metaphysics, but it had me hanging on every word, however bizarre, that issued from Arhi's thin lips.

"That little extra meaning is my domain," he said readily yet ruefully. "Time and space unity is an Aristotelian conceit, useful in a spectacle but otherwise quite worthless. Take this exchange of ours. It is a spectacle only if viewed or heard from a vantage point. And I don't mean the good man Seerozha here, who is congenitally deaf, by the way. I mean time and space that make up the stage of the universe, with energy and matter as its dramatis personae."

His voice was beginning to have a droning lull. I can't say it was soothing, but it had a way of putting me at ease. Was I being hypnotized? Seduced? To what end? What did he want with me?

"Are you a hundred percent sure we are having this chat in Rosie O'Grady's on Znamenka, downtown Moscow, past midnight?" he continued. "Or in Rosie O'Grady's on Seventh Ave. and Fifty-Second midtown Manhattan during happy hour two years back? The interiors are similar, the franchise rule and whatnot. The frolicking beauties fending off the untoward advances of a bunch of foreigners a mere fifteen minutes ago while going through the contents of their breast pockets in that corner over there could have been a couple of mail order brides just off the plane in the Big Apple ready to wet their whistles before stopping by at Samovar to meet their long-distance betrotheds from the Midwest... And more to the point: Who gives a fuck? The words exchanged are what counts, the consequences are what's at stake. You can be in two separate places at once, or successively, you don't even have to leave your birdhouse. Saves tons on airfare, no skin off your beak. Like that performance space in Alphabet City. King Tut's Wah Wah Hut, was it? The place I bumped into your missus one summer night while you were playing footsie with that lanky film student chick in black tights during the *Berlin Alexanderplatz* screening at the Red Vic? You know how to pick 'em, *khlopchis'ko*!"

"Wait, who'd I pick? Who do I know how to pick?" I almost spit out the ice cube that I was sucking on distractedly. Then it hit me like a ton of bricks: the guy, sadly, was a loon.

I had never played footsie with anyone at the Red Vic, an art movie house on Haight in San Francisco, though maybe I wish I had. And even if I had, how would he know it? He bumped into Lilly, he said? The guy was certainly a nutcase, not threatening or sociopathic as far as I could tell, just not too pleasant to be around longer than necessary. Try not to contradict him, I remember thinking. You don't want him to fly off the handle on you and start pounding you on the head with that crutch.

"Our objects of desire, or their trans-world doubles, it matters little," he said, proceeding with his lecture from hell. "If A equals B, then all A's tchotchkes are equal to B's tchotchkes. They can swap 'em, and no one will know the difference. Call it a lateral flashback. If there's the ultimate evil, there's got to be the ultimate good. You would think, right? But can you tell them apart in the short run? Who are you to pass judgment? Is the ultimate good the same as the ultimate truth? If so, wouldn't it follow that lies are evil? Then everyone's evil, only for a different reason and to a different degree. Can we liken good and evil to the two ladies in torn fishnets and see-through prosthetic bellies with canine embryos knocking around inside them, you know, the performers from King Tut's Wah Wah Hut?"

"What performers?! You keep saying performers, but I don't know who the hell you're talking about!?" I screamed, then quickly checked myself and started considering a few exit scenarios. One: ask him for a Parliament, then step outside and run like hell to Arbatskaya station. Two: forget the cigarette, just bolt for it.

"Saxon, and what's her face? Iobst? Hi-la-ti-ous ! Ah, the ur-feminist crypto-fascist pseudo catfights they used to have! Hair-raising! Avenue A? Not unlike the forces that shelled the White House last month and the guys on the inside. The parallel is not far-fetched. Battling it out for the good of Russia? Or a banal power struggle? Surely not a pre-rehearsed made for television spectacle? Revolutions always contain the seeds of counterrevolutions. What I did was advise Boris Nikolayevich to draft and ratify that oh so fateful decree. You didn't have to be a logician to anticipate that the parliament would put up a fight. They did. Though not for long. So, was I right or was I right to be there and see it come to pass? Peacekeeping troops? Bah! Try war-keeping truths. Try riding that war machine before it gets appropriated by the state. Do you suppose Deleuze was delusional?"

"So what is the truth? I mean, in this instance? Was it on Yeltsin's side?" I asked with all the urgency I could muster while conversing with a raving lunatic, who was making offhand references to French theorists after three Maker's Marks past midnight.

"Truth is," Arhi responded, though I could swear his lips were not entirely in sync with his words now (a filmmaker, lapsed or not, I had an eye for such things), "Truth is everyone has his own. There's no overreaching truth, valid and immutable for eternity. What is your personal truth, then, Mark? Like your mission here . . ."

"What about it?"

"À la recherche de l'argent perdu, *khlopchis'ko*?"

"What do you know about my mission? And please, stop calling me *khlopchis'ko.*"

"Only what I overheard on the train, dude."

"And? What does it have to do with anything?"

"Not much, I'm afraid. Whatever you came for, you go check out the Tarantula and yours truly at Bunker, then *It rains on Brighton,* and you do theatre like it's going out of fashion. Is this your way of prioritizing things?"

"How do you know about theatre?"

"Read my lips if you can," said Arhi. "You miss your land bad, dude. Everything else is a goddamn pretext, smoke and mirrors. Take it from this lame fortune teller wannabe who's had one too many. And chew it over, for fuck's sake!"

Insane or not, his observation had all the makings of a direct hit, though I'd be the last person on the planet to either refute it or admit it, so instead of getting mired in the swampy terrain he was trying to suck me into, call it a gray area, call it a provocation, I thought I'd switch the subject to matters familiar and obvious. Again. My tried-and-true tactic that never backfires.

"Enough about me, Arhi, please. What was your unfinished project, anyway? Just curious."

"Oh, water under the bridge, my brother."

"Pray tell."

"Here we go again. The old switcheroo, huh? You really want me to get into all that?"

"Sure do. I told you lots. And what I didn't, you seem to have picked up on the train . . ."

"What the hell. You know who Kleist is?"

"The German romantic?"

Arhi nodded enthusiastically. "If you must know, what I basically did in voiceover," he continued, "I went over the highlights of Kleist's essay on marionette theatre. You know, the one where he talks about the movement of the puppet master's body and the advantages of the puppet over living dancers? And how puppets are infinitely more graceful than dancers. Then I concluded with the story Kleist also concludes his piece with, i.e., detailing the narrator's trip to Russia and the bizarre fencing match that occurred between him and the bear, which was no match at all, really: all the narrator's thrusts and feints were parried by the beast without effort! That latter part I did in animation as if it were the stage performance watched by the family from their orchestra seats. Though the main character, a twelve-year-old kid, was almost forced to stay home as punishment for his outrageous behavior. So, while the highlights of Kleist's piece were done in voiceover from the kid's POV, the live-action visuals focused on the kid in his early teens and his mom and dad in their early '40. They're getting ready to see a play by the Royal Dramatic Theatre of Stockholm directed by the great Ingmar Bergman. You could hear Mom in the next room, gushing to a friend on the phone, how hard it was to get tickets for the Stravinsky opera, what dress she'd wear for tonight's outing, etc. Dad just home from work, shaving in the bathroom. The kid dressed up, feeling bored and prankish. Maybe also possessed by his puppet master; who can tell? How else to explain this episode of temporary insanity: his carefully spacing three pairs of spectacles out on the linoleum-covered hallway floor in front of the bathroom and hiding in the kitchen, panting and sweating in anticipation, waiting for Dad to come out? Dad, his turquoise bathrobe wrapped tightly around him, emerging from the bathroom, skipping the first pair placed too close to the bathroom threshold, and as he notices the second pair and the third one, his stride not wide enough to avoid both, he misses the second pair. Still, he steps right on the third one, crushing both the lenses and the frame, nearly losing his balance and falling on the floor. Almost. Indignant, he gives the kid hell, slaps him some for good measure, and threatens to ground the little rascal for the entire month of June, no theatre or movies, no bicycle, or trip to Denmark the family had been planning since winter, then cooling off and reconsidering. Pre-theatre mad theatrics, right? Almost done with postproduction. On hiatus because of touring. Next stop Kyiv, an open-air gig. What do you think?"

"I have to read Kleist's essay first. Sounds promising, though maybe a bit convoluted. So you think the kid was temporarily possessed by an evil spirit or something?"

"Maybe. Maybe not. Think suspension of disbelief. Think open endings. Think Bergman incidentally monikered the demon director. Also, *The Rake's Progress* had a bit of a reputation in its own right. That's the opera they went to see that night. Kleist's essay was just an intertextual liberty I took. Hey, it's my project, right?"

"Nice. I may actually have a bear story for you, too. For your next project, maybe? Though it's getting pretty late," I said matter-of-factly as I slid off my barstool. "But first, let me take a long-overdue leak."

"Take your time, comrade," Arhi said magnanimously. "They don't close until two. Right, Seerozha?" He showed Seerozha the victory sign again. The latter nodded.

Very curiously, the outlandish night also had an open-ended finale if I ever did see one. When I returned from the men's room three minutes later, my gregarious interlocutor was gone. I peeked out of Rosie's and scoped the empty street, just in case. Nothing.

"The guy who was sitting next to me?" I addressed Seerozha in the sign language of my invention. "What happened?" Seerozha, who was seemingly having trouble understanding me, spread his wet hands wide. "The fellow in helmet and goggles, you damn well know who I'm talking about?" I persisted, raising my voice a notch. At last, he explained, also gesturally, that while he was washing and rinsing glasses with his back to the room, Arhi vanished without a trace, apparently stiffing him on a tip. Something Seerozha self-consciously asked me to make up for in easily interpretable signs. Reluctantly, I obliged and bid him good night.

Chapter Fourteen.

I started missing Tasha forty-eight hours into our trial separation. No surprise there: over the past seven weeks, we'd seen each other almost daily, and the old "out of sight, out of mind" maxim goes only so far until the body comes into play and starts aching for another body. Decibel and Orlov were busy showing the capital to an out-of-town relative, so with my clubbing activities on a temporary hold, at night, I stayed home and tried to finish this sci-fi book by the newbie Viktor Pelevin that I picked up in Dom Knigi on Tverskaya or watched TV, which had a surprisingly soothing effect on me. During the daytime, I just sat by the kitchen window staring at the bare poplar trees swaying in the wind and bingeing on instant coffee and the cheese *zapekanka* that Tasha had made for us the week before.

On the third night of my self-imposed house arrest, my mother called. It was about 3:00 p.m. in New York, and she had some bad news to deliver. My former IT colleague from Prudential called. Larry had no idea I was in Moscow. All Larry knew was that I quit my job, and since my answering machine in New York was full, he made it his business to look up my mother and convey to her the news about our colleague Vjollca Lleshi's death—she was killed instantly in a car accident early that morning. The memorial service was scheduled for next weekend. "Isn't that your Albanian lady friend?" asked my mother. "So sorry to hear, Mark. I know you were close."
"I'm sorry too, Mom."

I was trying to collect my thoughts, but for some reason, all I could think about were Vjollca Lleshi's shoes and maroon pedicured toenails that she encouraged me to cover with smooches occasionally. I swear I could still taste the scent of the cucumber lotion and, more faintly, patchouli favored by Vjollca as I spoke to Mom. Vjollca Lleshi had a thing for crazy shoes, and I remembered clearly one pair in particular that featured thick transparent heels filled with water where tiny polliwogs swam about, some of them barely alive, others quite animated given their constrained habitat, while another pair looked just like two ponies complete with miniature gear: straps, reins, girth. Sometimes, she wore that pair to bed, and when she did, she'd assume "the horsewoman astride a steed" position and even did a bit of neighing while in the throes of passion because I just wouldn't. "When you coming home, Marik?" Mom sounded peeved, impatient. "Haven't you had enough excitement in the land of the Bolsheviks?" "Soon, Mom," I said. "Almost done here, I promise. Be home for New Year's." "New Year's? New Year's is more than a month away?"

Ah, poor Vjollca, with whom we used to sneak a cigarette outside our office building on Third Ave. after open season on smokers was declared! The art-loving fashionista Vjollca, who looked fifteen years younger than her age and was apt to come to work with a bare midriff and in cutoffs on casual Fridays, was no longer among the living. She was more friendly to me from the get-go than anyone in the entire department, perhaps excepting Larry Friggs, a seriously overweight consultant who was in a way responsible for Vjollca's befriending me and then some. Because of his bulk, Larry was forced to use the stall in the men's room, generally reserved for the handicapped. I believe Larry even had a custom-designed chair ordered for him that barely fit inside his cubicle, that's how oversized the guy was. For someone who weighed 275 lbs in his blemished socks, Larry's well-coiffed wife on the photo pinned to the wall by his terminal looked rather cute, despite or maybe because of her slightly cleft chin. Good for him, I thought, though I couldn't quite fathom certain technical aspects of their marital life, not that it was any of my business.

Larry and I would share lunches in the cafeteria on the seventh floor and occasionally walk to Grand Central together, trading bad jokes and office gossip. Funny, Larry proved a brisk walker for someone of his poundage while I'd get all out of breath trying to keep up with him tearing half a block ahead of me. "What's your hurry?" I'd grumble, panting. "Slow down, dude. You move too fast." We both knew our Simon and Garfunkel. "Wait till you get hitched, you'll know what the hurry is," he'd say, slowing down for a bit. He owned a house not far from Stamford, Connecticut, and though he wasn't thrilled with his job and often spoke dismissively of it, there was Selma Friggs, the mother of his three-year-old daughter and another one in the oven. And, as Larry himself once observed dryly, if you don't put up a framed family picture next to your terminal, you won't have much going by way of a daily reminder of why you do what you do nine-to-five, year in year out till the day you croak or retire, whichever comes first. Not the most upbeat outlook, if you ask me, but not entirely inaccurate either. Anyhow, a few days after I heard that bit of wisdom, I pinned a photo of the medium-sized cut-up fish, exposed glistening guts and all, drying in the sun that I had snapped in Barbados a year before. Just for the hell of it. Or maybe as a sad reminder that I really had nobody at the time to bring home the bacon or fish fillet to. Larry, who stepped into my cubicle before lunch that same day, ventured a guess: "Your nephew? Must be a real cut-up . . . Nice family you gut. Gut, get it?" I cracked a smile and nodded while Larry doubled up laughing, not an easy proposition given his bulk and limited agility.

Enter Vjollca Lleshi, who had been on the periphery of my carnal vision since the last Christmas office party when she got sloshed senseless on Burgundy, then scotch, then more

Burgundy, and for a chaser tried to entice Santa from the Rent-a-Miracle agency to join her in the supplies room for a quick heart-to-heart. After the bearded fellow demurred, mumbling that it was, sadly, against the job regulations, she and I did a bit of dancing to the mixtape featuring several versions of Alanis Morrisette's "Too Hot," a fast song that Vjollca chose to slow dance to, swaying her opulent hips while pressing her bosom against my chest. A breathy invitation to spend the night at her house in Fair Lawn, NJ, followed. Why I took a rain check that night, I'm still not too sure. Though I did help her flag down a cab outside the building, then took a long walk home in the falling snow, had a smoke in bed, and jerked myself off to sleep. The way Vjollca carried herself in the office the next week, I could swear the episode was completely wiped from her memory. Not so fast.

The third week of the new year, Vjollca blew into my cubicle, took in the photo of the eviscerated fish on my wall, and sniggered: "What the hell? You scare me, Mark! You a closet fisherman or what?"

I said, "Hey, Vjol, some conventions are there to be broken. Consider this my lame stab at irreverence. It's like Larry said . . ."

"Forget that lard-ass," she interrupted. "You excuse me for a sec, I may have something for you by way of irreverence." In less than a minute, she blew back in and handed me two Polaroid snapshots of her posing on what looked like a sun-lit well-manicured lawn in front of a split-level house, smiling innocently in one picture, pouting mischievously in the other, her breasts completely exposed in both of them. "How do you like them melons?" she chortled and arched her brow.

"I like them fine," I conceded, finding it hard to keep my eyes off my colleague's big brown nipples staring right back at me from the photographs. Not only did her bosom look just as ample as it had felt during our slow dance, but her topless self, so inappropriate in the workplace, made the whole thing piquantly transgressive to the point of giving me an instant boner. Now, if that wasn't a come-on, I don't know what is. I think we even skipped the obligatory coffee or lunch that day, not even a cigarette outside that she and I liked to have sometimes. We rushed to Port Authority and hopped on the next bus to Fair Lawn, where she lived alone. Once enveloped by the dark of the Lincoln Tunnel, she started probing the inside of my ear with her moist tongue. I reciprocated by feeling her up under her skirt, both of us getting a kick out of carrying on like two teenagers in heat. Then we got off the bus, got into her purple Nissan, reached her split-level Dutch colonial, had a couple of swigs of brandy straight out of the bottle, helped each other out of our clothes, and repaired to her bedroom. She turned out to be loud, smelly, sweaty, and got dripping wet the moment I resumed fingering her down there. Minutes after we got under the sheets, she made herself comfy, perching on my face, her smooth cheeks pressing down on my cheeks that had a five o'clock shadow by then. Breathing at some point became a challenge, but I still managed to stick my tongue inside her and flick it up and down, up and down, like a good boy, inhaling through my nostrils all the while. I'll stop right here; why get excited over the tragically expired ex-lover, but let me add just one thing: our first night was nothing if not memorable. I think she was the first partner I ever had who insisted on swallowing my cum which she did three times that night, and every time she did, her eyes glazed over, and she let out a barely audible squeal. Also, her pubic hair was like nothing I'd seen before, not even in *Oui* magazine that Lilly got me subscribed to for my birthday when we were breaking up, whether out of malice or levity, I can't say for sure. I remember well, though, that the big hair was all the rage back when she and I were splitting up, and in all quarters, too. Same with Vjollca, who sported a regular retro afro (albo?) down there, and we were already well into the '90s. Intimate haircuts had apparently yet to make inroads in Albania, where she had come from four years prior. I'm not sure why she got divorced or maybe just separated. She seldom mentioned her husband, but it sounded like he had a dependency issue, plus he was something of a gambler and a malcontent. Not a healthy mix. Anyhow, I enjoyed the six months we stayed together, actually five and a half, not counting the two weeks she took off from our steamy romance when her twin sons came home on a college break.

Another thing about my exotic paramour: she possessed kick-ass energy and superior intelligence and was nuts about art. Soho gallery-hopping is what we did every week, heading to galleries and art spaces on Thursdays and Fridays after work, making sure we didn't miss out on openings, lectures, or artist talks. We heard Peter Wollen speak at the Kitchen on the dynamic nature of the cult of Salome in turn of the century European iconography, and Gary Indiana deliver the opening notes for the Alexander Kluge retrospective at MoMA, or Slavoj Zizek at the old Deitch project, clips from Hitchcock's *Vertigo* liberally interspersed through the jittery Slovenian's talk, as was his wont, to illustrate this or that post-Freudian point. Then Vjollca, not a single self-conscious bone in her shapely body, walked up to the celeb thinker and chatted with him about some people they supposedly knew back in Ljubljana.

She seemed to know everyone who was anyone in downtown New York: art dealers, collectors, artists, and fellow art lovers. Once, during an opening at Postmasters, we bumped into my dad and his gorgeous bell-bottomed curator girlfriend Tatiana from Bryansk, who were also doing the gallery rounds that night. We had a queasy chit-chat with them, all the while sipping pinot noir out of plastic cups and talking contemporary art of the Marxist bent that my dad wouldn't be caught dead anywhere near had it not been for the artistic and intellectual predilections of his leggy flame in a pantsuit. That was shortly before he invested a tidy sum in a little storefront gallery space on Suffolk that she lorded over with an iron hand as director-slash-curator. It just seemed a bit queer dating Vjol, who was almost Dad's age, while he was sleeping with a woman slightly younger than me who happened to have a penchant for vintage clothes that went back to Dad's bell-bottomed adolescence in Odesa. I'm sure Zizek would have gotten some mileage out of this misalliance underlying the libidinal nostalgia localized at the interstice between the Symbolic and the Real.

Vjollca would bring the extra set of clothes to work every time the opening was on our menu and change into her leather pants and S&M-themed heel shoes with or without the polliwogs or boots with golden inlays on the back of the heels and suede miniskirt with sexy zippers coming out of yin-yang. Then after checking out the galleries on Greene or Wooster, soaking up the shows that featured cutting-edge multichannel videos, high-tech installations, or neo-geo pieces, and getting buzzed up on free wine, we'd grab a bite at Lucky Strike or Raoul and hail a cab to my midtown place where we'd spend the entire next Saturday indoors fucking like rabbits. More accurately, I fucked like a rabbit, while she was more of a python, and I don't mean it in a pejorative sense, nor do I merely imply our body-type differences (the sinuous Vjollca vs. a few extra pounds me) but a temperamental contrast as well. I'd get twitchy and quivering as I came on her firm stomach while she was all stillness and poise, even when buck naked, taking her time savoring my semen, her eyes half-closed and her cunt breathing softly and steadily under my cupped hand. She was into role-playing, too. So if her Soho outfit on any given night were a variation on the theme of "discipline and punish," she'd get plenty rough with me in the boudoir: biting, sucking me dry while digging her nails into my buttocks, scratching my chest till it hurt, even strangling me lightly with her pantyhose which smelled of cucumber lotion and patchouli. I'd try to give as good as I got, slapping her around, spanking her till her ass was the color of her lipstick (a pale shade of candy apple red). Once, I tried to whip her playfully with my Diesel pants' leather belt, but evidently, it hurts more when you do it sans the simultaneous penetration. So she shrieked, in pain and disgust, "Don't just beat the shit out of me; fuck me too, fucking asshole!" She made her point all right, and I made sure I never repeated that mistake.

She was an art collector, too. The money she made as a senior developer and her savings allowed her to invest in small pieces now and again, like abstract photography or works on paper that she bought from Pierogi Gallery, which just opened in Williamsburg across the East River, or from the new crop of then tiny Chelsea galleries. One Saturday morning, after a night of boozy sex at her place in Fair Lawn, she asked me to join her on an art-hunting expedition across the two rivers. I agreed, and once we reached Pierogi, I remember us putting on white gloves upon the gallery owner's request before he let us go through the content of the so-called flat files. The gloves made us look like two Bugs Bunnies, only one of us silly wabbits was a big-bosomed Bugs in a leather miniskirt and silver tights, while the other sported a newly grown patchy beard, had a pair of Diesel pants on, and improbably, a Versace shirt that he got from his dad for his thirtieth birthday. She blew $480 on three watercolors and a Mondrian-flavored piece, which was actually just a glorified contact sheet of 8 mm film negative strips glued to an ochre background. Then we took a train and a bus back to her place. I offered a hand hanging the pieces on the living room walls, and while I was up on the highest step of the short ladder, she wasted no time unzipping my Diesels and, as a reward for help in domestic matters, gave me a sloppy blow job that changed the way I looked at Mondrian or his epigones for some time to come. More biting and scratching ensued in the bedroom upstairs, then she put on her apron and got busy fixing dinner for us as I lazed about watching CNN on her plasma TV. I mean, Vjollca had energy to burn, and though I was seventeen years her junior, it was I who would periodically need to charge my batteries off of her generator when we hung together, not the other way around. You can take this metaphor or leave it.

It was during that Italian dinner, complete with an arugula salad that she asked me to help her toss, the mouthwatering homemade lasagna and the runny but delicious tiramisu plus a nice bottle of Barolo that my lover inquired bluntly if my plans for the foreseeable future might include settling down and having a family. I mumbled something to the extent that at some point and with the right person, they probably would, but I had just turned thirty and was still trying to catch my breath after a rocky marriage. "Just thirty!" exclaimed my expansive lover, giving me a start with her howling laughter so loud and sudden that I nearly spilled the wine on my pants. "You know how old I was when I got married?" "Do tell," I said. "Nineteen!" she thundered. "Nineteen years of age!" "You don't have to yell, dear. I can hear you fine from where I sit," I said calmly. "And for all I know, that may be a common occurrence in your part of the world. Or maybe you were good and ready to tie the knot. None of it applies to this particular case, I'm sorry to say. People get married late in the US. And I, for one, am certainly not there yet. Plus, can you, in all honesty, claim that your choice was all you ever hoped it would be?"

"Suit yourself," Vjollca shook her head in resignation. "Just keep one thing in mind. Statistically speaking, singles' funerals tend to be under-attended. More tiramisu?"

"Very funny," I said. "But then, does it really matter how many people show up for your funeral, statistically? The departed isn't exactly expected to engage in much mingling at the event anyway . . ."

The dinner continued as if nothing had happened: more wine flowed, job-related gossip was exchanged, soft music kept on wafting from her stereo by the sofa, we went to bed early, and the rabbit/python dynamic deployed that night was enjoyable like make-up sex often tends to be, though we didn't exactly fight so technically it was just enjoyable, period. But from then on, a rift in our relationship was beginning to make itself felt: the taunts, the unkind observations vis-à-vis my appearance or physique, and uncalled-for touches of sarcasm became an oft-repeated occurrence. Never in a hurry to attribute possible inter-relational ethnic blunders or inanities to antisemitism, once or twice I swear I was close to calling her out precisely on that. Like when I made an exaggeratedly grotesque gesture during dinner in a newly opened Greek place in the East Village one hot night in June, just trying to be facetious, illustrating a point, someone else's point at that, and my hand movement illustrating the point was no more than a gestural quote, so to speak, so what Vjollca did in response, she mimicked the gesture, apparently taking it at face value, then added, "Well, this is precisely why no one is particularly crazy about your kind." "My kind?!" And my fork fell on the tiled floor with a ringing sound that resonated in more than one sense. How is a single gesture supposed to summarize the four-thousand-year history of my kind? I thought I misheard or misunderstood her, then reckoned it was in my best interest to let it slide. Why such nastiness? Was she expecting me to take her not too subtle hint and propose to a single forty-nine-year-old mother of two college boys right there upon finishing my runny tiramisu?

Soon after, another taboo was broken. During our lunch in the company cafeteria, Vjollca observed that she was pulling in almost twice as much as I was and asked how it made me feel. Funny, but my pointing out that I started the job just a year ago while she was employed as a programmer in Albania forever, plus she had four years of experience in major New York corporations had no truck with her. I told her I was pretty happy with my midtown apartment, which she seemed to enjoy sometimes too, and that I made enough to go Dutch with her when we ate out or sometimes even take care of the entire check. She responded that as a European woman, she expected to be treated all the time, pampered even, not when one felt like one could afford it. Well, welcome to America, Vjol, I couldn't resist saying to her dour face by way of ending the discussion.

I've seen a few solid relationships go south, then straight to the dogs, and the process usually started with petty bickering. But then, nothing ever starts with that; bickering is already a sign of something profound percolating underneath the surface, and it better be diagnosed and addressed early on. Take Tasha and me, who came from vastly different backgrounds, yet at the core, there was a bond between us, starting with those silly bear tales of our childhood and ending with her being my equal in many ways. Like our sharing an appreciation of Pushkin, no surprise there (though she confessed to just liking his fairy tales, oh well), and Tarkovsky (his entire oeuvre, whew!), and, of course, Bulgakov, her undisputed literary guiding light. So what if her bedroom walls were hung with posters of Tsoy, a handsome rocker that I had no idea about, and Queen whose music I had little tolerance for, and so what if she could care less about Talking Heads and Monty Python? You can't win them all, can you? She was by far the coolest and the youngest girlfriend I had ever had, with lots to learn and energy and curiosity to do it, so there was no doubt in my mind that things would work out between us should we give it half a try. Living through a crisis as we did could break up families, not to mention shatter nascent relationships to pieces, I was reasoning sitting at the kitchen table and chain-smoking Dunhill menthols past midnight, yet we chose to hold onto each other through it all and just had our first tiff ever, and over Gaidai, a comedy director, of all people, big fucking deal! I could, should, be more sensitive to her fellow citizens' plight, but let's face it, I was a stranger in my own land. Just like she could, should cut me some slack precisely because of that. Something I couldn't do with Vjollca when she started to show her nasty side. Sex was good with her, no argument there, but was sex enough? Maybe it was too good; is such a thing even possible? Maybe all that biting and scratching and swallowing (and did I mention her kicking me on occasion where it hurt with those shoes full of freaked out pollywogs?) pointed to something dark and disconcerting in her character? What do I, your basic missionary position kind of guy, know about sex as the flip side of one's personality anyway? But when by the end of our romance, or actually, when the romance was already over, she invited me to have lunch at Dock's on Third Ave. kitty-corner from our office building and introduced me to her ex-husband's former associate named Vik Z-sky, whose nasal hair, I believe, made his speech phonetically nasal too, as well as his stony-faced daughter Alena who touched her dad's earlobe with her stubby fingers as she whispered into his ear the Russian translations of menu choices while Vjollca whispered into mine, "This is your chance to make an extra buck so you look good vis-à-vis your next flame. Don't let it slip through your fingers,"—how could I say "no" to 200K for a three-day job? And even if it didn't work out as expected, I'd have never come to the land of commissars, looking for Vik Z-sky and co, and I wouldn't have met my punk princess Tasha Tschelicheva. So it was all good, all good.

Thinking about my blustery love affair with Vjollca made me sort of accept the fact that she was killed in the car crash.

I mean, sure, I felt sorry for her kids, whom I had never had a chance to meet, and I did hope her death was instant and painless. But more than anything, I felt numb about the entire thing and also wised-up to the fact that there was no love interest or emotional attachment other than my parents awaiting me in New York now, whether I go back as a relatively wealthy man or your basic one-check-away-from-poverty kind of guy.

Then, for whatever reason, my thoughts turned to Kristen and how I didn't know her at first in that coffee place on Bleecker and McDougal where she waitressed tables, looking like someone else, someone younger because she let her hair grow out and dyed it raven black during the three months that it took me to tidy things up in San Francisco and get ready for my big move back East. How Kris and I once had gotten hella stoned and then argued at the Grateful Dead gig on Ventura Beach whether the concert had already started or if it was just a protracted tuning up that the band treated us to after our five-hour drive down Highway 1 to see Jerry and the guys live. How she and I used to amuse our friends doing a precarious sixty-nine position vertically (her feet up in the air, my nose planted snugly in her crotch) while dancing in I-Beam on Haight to some monotonous synth-pop tracks neither of us cared for much. Or how we'd walk out of the Castro theatre forty minutes into a movie to show our non-bohemian friends sitting next to us that we were way above the bourgeois fare of the mid-career Woody Allen, or was it a rural epic by the Taviani brothers? And then she just up and skedaddled to New York, leaving me in the lurch.

In her New York incarnation, Kristen was bouncy and fun to hang with, as usual. Her shapely foot in the door of independent film, she had yet to stop couch surfing and find a place of her own. Meanwhile, she was staying in a friend's loft with a few on-again, off-again roommates, which made spending the night with her a crapshoot, never knowing for sure if the night in question would indeed be the night. She landed a script girl position on a no budget movie that was being shot on location in Alphabet City, in somebody's bombed-out squat and around it. The place actually belonged to one of the gaffers, an emaciated guy everyone called Bunga who was high as a kite half of the time on and off the set. The deferred payment was what everyone agreed to work for, including Mark, the smitten PA from SF, soon to start his first serious IT job at Prudential. In the meantime, I had to wince every time Frank, the longhaired cameraman, called Kristen the tits-and-ass of the project to her face, facetiously, no doubt, because Kristen was of a delicate build and somewhat underendowed in either department. But you don't really get mad or possessive or publicly drop hints that you are in a relationship during the shoot, so I just had to take the seasoned indie cameraman Frank aside on a lunch break one afternoon and ask him outright to dial down the adolescent joviality because Kristen and I were getting engaged next month, you see, and our new status could use a little respect from the crew. Frank grumbled under his breath but acquiesced. I probably should've proposed to Kristen for real around that time, too, if for no reason than to see her jaw drop an inch and her eyes roll shortly after.

Sometimes we'd break the set around 3:00 a.m., and the big-hearted Bunga would let Kristen and myself crash at his place, where we'd make our makeshift bed on the stained mattress on the kitchen floor and hump away quietly with all due consideration for the host snoring thinly in the adjacent room. In the morning, I'd quickly get dressed, kiss my sleeping beauty on her sweet lips, and grab some coffee with toasted everything and cream cheese from a Delancey deli for the three of us so that by 9:00 a.m., we'd be good and ready for the next fifteen-hour shoot. Too bad there was no phone in the apartment: I wonder if things might have panned out differently had we used the deli's takeout service. Bunga, a hook-nosed geek with beady eyes, never took off his imitation leather jacket, which was so old and weather-beaten that it was actually a moldy green instead of black and smelled of mold, too. Not that it bothered Kristen any. Why did I ever let her go work on that project in Toronto? With geeky Bunga, of all people? But then, can you really stop anyone from doing what they think is right for them, career-wise or Bunga-wise? She was so beautiful in a way that transcended the pervasive new wave look of the time, so benign, so talented. I still have the drawing she mailed to me from Toronto: a damsel in no apparent distress, rather all aflutter in her long see-through gown, a fire-breathing dragon with its spiky tail against the elaborately rendered mountains by the lake, all done with the blue ballpoint pen on folded toilet paper—not the toilet roll but the oval-shaped one that you put on the seat in a public bathroom. Creative? I'll say. A possible hidden message? Art and negativity walk hand in hand, cheek to cheek even? Nothing to create beauty out of other than shit. I loved her cheek, her cheeks, too; her pussy was the tightest, most fragrant I've ever smelled, an absolute joy to lick before penetrating, the loveliest tiny tits, an ass I adored to squeeze and pinch.

Thinking of Kristen made me want to conduct a simple test I don't believe I had attempted since the ninth grade when I used it to ascertain firsthand, as it were, which of the girls in my class I had the most hots for. What I did back then was I'd put my hand on my cock and start stroking it slowly, thinking of my classmates one after another to see who got me hard the fastest. And this is what I did during my self-imposed house arrest now. I started thinking of Kristen, then Vjollca, Lilly, too. When it was Lilly's turn, I thought of the time Lilly and I were breaking up. She was staying with a friend, crashing in a sleeping bag on the floor. I'd come to visit her not entirely sober, or actually pretty stoned, and whisper in her ear that I didn't care a fig whether she was running around with every

Tom, Dick, and Harry in town, and that I was still mad for her, and no one else but her and that was the God's honest truth, and then she'd let me do it to her right there on the floor. I knew I was taking my chances using no protection, occasionally coming on the bag that Lilly borrowed from her friend Ashley, thus inadvertently using Ashley's sleeping bag as a canvas for my postcoital bodily doodles. I had to recall that instance of tenderness, too, for the purity of the experiment's sake. Then, last but, of course, not least, I thought of my punk princess Tasha to see if her image got me hard the fastest and the longest, yet trying to keep her apart from the rest of the emcees in my mind's eye was not a simple proposition: images tend to blur and morph into one another with time. Granted, it was a totally embarrassing pastime for a thirty-one-year-old professional, but what with the limited social interaction that I had to endure for the past couple of days and the news of Vjollca's death hitting me hard, perhaps a forgivable bit of singularity. Long story short, it was Tasha who got me up the fastest, Lilly coming a close second, and Kristen vying for third place with some delays. Little surprise there: Kristen was out of the picture banging Bunga in Toronto, Vjollca was dead as a doornail, Lilly not entirely out of my system, and Tasha . . . And I promised myself then and there to call Tasha first thing in the morning, no matter what. To hell with pride or conventions—was the last thing I remember thinking as I fell fast asleep.

Chapter Fifteen.

The next morning, renovations started in the apartment next door. The racket the construction workers were making was so thunderous that it could have easily been produced by a team twice as big. My hunch was they were gutting the place, not sure how else to explain the buzz of drills, the clang of hammers, and the squeal of saws going nonstop and all at once. Surely they weren't quartering a medium-sized domestic animal, readying it for some kind of perestroika-themed ritual to be performed by the swing set in the courtyard below? Be that as it may, I thought it best to stay in bed till noon with the pillow pressed over my head and wait till they broke for lunch so I could call Tasha at work. Just as well: her antique shop bosses weren't too keen on her spending more than two minutes discussing non-Faberge-related matters over the phone.

"Was it good for you too?" I bleated nervously, lighting my first Dunhill of the day. Turning the whole thing into a joke seemed one way to deal with my bombing the separation test. Not that I was too self-conscious about it.

"What you mean, America?" Tasha tried to hit her trademark note halfway between ridicule and nonchalance.

"Abstinence, my dear."

"Who was abstinent again?" she said.

"Funny. No, I'm serious. You won, okay? Just don't gloat."

"Not my bag, gloating. So. Who chooses the make-up play?"

"Does it matter?"

"Let's grab a bite first. Make a night of it. Someplace they don't shoot you point-blank," she seemed chattier than usual.

"The House of Actors in your hood? Casual and nice?"

"Perfection. Don't forget to call your duo, though. Play it safe."

"Deal. So what are we seeing, Tash? You want to do *Uncle Vanya*?"

"Let's. A little postmod and excessive, but hey, why not? Okay, got to go make a few bucks for the store. Later, alligator."

"See you at six?" Boy, was I happy to be talking to my Moscow girl again!

Uncle Vanya it was, then. Directed by Solovyov, said the theatre guide that I kept on my nightstand. Solovyov, a film director whose work I wasn't necessarily smitten by—you had to be there was how Tasha explained my not getting Solovyov's body of work—a hypothesis I had nothing to counter with. One thing I knew for certain: so psyched was I by the prospect of hanging with Tasha again, doing theatre, whatever, I didn't care how postmod, mod, or premod, and going to the restaurant before the theatre, anyhow, I got so excited, that I thought to myself then and there, "Stupid fool, are you in love again, Marik?" And then my inner Marik said to my big sentimental Mark, "Anything wrong with that, pal?"

Then I shaved, got dressed in a hurry, dialed Orlov and Decibel Petro, asked them to meet me at ten to six at the Old Arbat House of Actors restaurant, and left my apartment, as chance would have it, never to cross its threshold again.

On my way from Smolenskaya station to the new House of Actors across from the Vakhtangov Theatre, I eyed the street vendors peddling matryoshkas, hot *khachapuris* (a Georgian bread and cheese concoction), as well as hideous miniature acrylic landscapes à la Russe lamely executed on rectangular pieces of plywood that featured the unavoidable dystrophic birch tree, the pale-blue squiggle of a river, and the shit blob of a melancholy hut with grey smoke rising from its smokestack. Donkey rides and photo ops with cardboard cutouts of

Yeltsin's grinning semblance were offered aplenty, something vaguely Christian about the former, tawdry and pagan about the latter. The ubiquitous live covers of Lennon-McCartney compositions, a staple of downtown Moscow street corners and underpasses, filled the chilly autumnal air on my way to meet my lover and friend.

Inside the House of Actors restaurant on the sixth floor, Tasha, dressed in an uncharacteristically festive indigo-and-white polka dot blouse and skirt, was waiting for me at a table set for two. Stiff starched napkins rolled into tubes sticking out of the two crystal wine glasses placed on the snow-white tablecloth, Orlov and Decibel Petro were planted at a table close to the stage where a flutist and a violinist dressed in black coats over pink shirts were playing—what else?—an early Beatles medley. Tasha suggested we sit next to each other in case we felt like holding hands, which we did in no time. Before we did, though, she extended her right hand toward me and silently motioned that I do the same. We interlocked our pinkies in the pinky swear Russian style as she chanted something out of the deep recesses of my childhood, "V mireh, v mireh navsegda, v ssoreh, v ssorreh nikogda" (let there be peace forever, let there never be any quarreling). She had already placed an order, so our waiter started bringing out assorted salads, the trademark Ossetian pie, herring à la Borodino, and Chicken Kiev, which we asked him to halve for us. The chemistry between us palpable, the flutist readily jumped off the stage, shortly followed by the pudgier violinist, and the two positioned themselves a mere ten feet from our table. I raised my hand to quell my bodyguards' momentarily heightened state of alert before the musicians broke into a decent rendition of "Here, There, and Everywhere." Truth be told, I wished the dinner would have never ended: the food was scrumptious, the clientele a far cry from the garish women and racketeer types I knew from the places I had patronized on my own until then. By contrast, seated around us were actors or theatre people speaking in a polite undertone; our waiter was old-school courteous, and even the cascading white curtains that spelled the officious '50s didn't look tacky or jarring.

I don't remember how Tasha and I got onto the subject of elections, but we did. Maybe it was our way of offsetting the excess of mushiness between us. I thought I'd tell her how I voted in the US for the first time and took my new civic responsibility so damn seriously that I even put on my only jacket and a tie that nearly choked me to death. The polling station was set up in someone's garage across from my apartment building; a nonagenarian lady supervising the entire constitutionally guaranteed process was gracious yet forbidding. Later that afternoon, my college buddies at San Francisco State were wondering what was with the getup and if I had been looking for a job. I guess the popular assumption in my adopted country, I added, was that the only occasion non-casual attire was called for was when you tried to do something related to making a living. Choosing the Commander-in-Chief for the next four years didn't even come close. Tasha replied that voting for Russia's first president two years back was a big deal; the polls were packed, it was Yeltsin or bust for many people, and folks standing next to parked cars listening to the radio was a common sight. Idealism was in the air, hope for a free Russia on people's minds. And if that also meant bidding farewell to a sausage for two rubles twenty kopecks per kilo, then fuck the sausage for two rubles twenty kopecks per kilo. She also said that maybe, just maybe two hundred years of democratic elections down the line, future generations of Russians would be voting for the man in Kremlin in their nighties and slippers, too. We laughed and kissed, and then I took care of the check, included a very decent tip for the Beatles Forever duo, and we left the restaurant, Orlov and Decibel flanking us on our way to the car parked on Starokoniushenniy. We made it to Maly ten minutes before the curtain call, Orlov and Decibel on call, the pay phone (should I need to make a call) a few meters away from Alexander Ostrovsky, the Shakespeare of Russian theatre, slouching broodingly in his armchair in front of the theatre façade oblivious to the gaggle of ladies of the night surrounding the Marx monument a stone's throw from the celebrated dramatist. Then destiny called.

Chapter Sixteen.

After the first act of the German-sponsored *Uncle Vanya* production, postmod as postmod can be and complete with two disoriented borzois ambling around the proscenium for a good five minutes before the human actors made their appearance, Tasha and I were accosted by a gangly cloakroom attendant with salt-and-pepper hair and a stammer, who upon closer scrutiny turned out to be none other than my debtor's associate Samuil Yakovlevich Vodovozkind, for that was his full name. And Samuil Yakovlevich Vodovozkind beckoned us with his crooked forefinger to follow him to a little nook between the cafeteria entrance and the fire extinguisher box, where he brought it home to us emphatically yet in a surprisingly unhurried fashion, that skipping the fair town of Moscow before you can say knife might be my only viable alternative to an involuntarily assisted flight out the kitchen window of the seventh floor of my Kuntsevo digs where, by the way, the fake renovation next door hasn't started just by coincidence. And that I had about forty-eight hours to pack. Or not to pack, for time was of the essence, and Tasha would always be on hand (if I played my cards right, the bugger added) to forward my personal effects to NYC. What's more, it seemed that I had every reason to take his words at face value, for not only did he know my exact Kuntsevo whereabouts, including the building and the apartment number, but also the approximate date of my arrival in Moscow last September. In essence, that was the cloakroom attendant's measured response to Tasha's petulant, "Who the fuck do you think you are, and why the fuck should we trust you?" Then, after a moment's hesitation, S. Y. Vodovozkind elaborated that he had recently had a big dustup with Viktor Z-sky, and since, as the old saying goes, an enemy of my enemy is my friend, technically, all he was trying to do was just that: help. Help who? I raised my voice. Your friends, or ex-friends, owe me big time, and you know it. I turn tail now, then what exactly have I been doing in Moscow for the past two and a half months? I mean, other than culture and a little recreational gambling? "Listen," the cloakroom attendant returned curtly. "Let me be b-blunt with you, young man. The going rate for a contract job in this town is roughly $5000. From what I g-gathered they owe you forty times that. How's your math anyway?" What was Samuil Yakovlevich doing exchanging coats for tickets and vice versa? Love for the stage. He always loved the boards. Was even an amateur actor back in school theatre. Played Khlestakov in Gogol's *The Government Inspector* to some acclaim, too. Plus, a man has to have something to fall back on when the racket loses appeal or starts to sputter. Doing something legit had its advantages, too: Who in his right mind would think of tracking him down in Maly?

Need I add that *Uncle Vanya* was the last Moscow production I saw that season, thus inadvertently turning Stanislavsky's famous dictum "The theatre begins with the cloakroom" on its head? For me, that's precisely where it ended. However, we actually stayed for the second act instead of heading back home right away. Back to Tasha's place, obviously. My Kuntsevo digs didn't feel too safe all of a sudden. And as we watched Uncle Vanya and Sonya crunch the numbers in the play's textbook finale from our maroon orchestra seats and take vows to work hard for others so that they could finally rest when their hour came and the life they would see would be beautiful and tender like a caress, I was doing just that in my head sans the vows: tallying up my Moscow expenses, wondering what would happen should I fail to collect the money (a very likely scenario), and would I have enough left for my airfare back home and a little extra for Tasha and her mother's medical expenses. We stayed for the second act—unable to leave the magically beautiful house, so what if I had just forty-eight hours to pack (or not to pack)—and as Uncle Vanya and Sonya talked about the time when they'd hear the angels sing and see the sky festooned with stars as bright as diamonds, I remember thinking, "Not so fast, Sonya, no diamonds for this itinerant soul just yet. Let's see how my own private drama plays out first."

Chapter Seventeen.

My Kuntsevo digs ostensibly compromised beyond repair, we thought it best to have our powwow with Orlov and Decibel in Tasha's Old Arbat apartment for security reasons and proximity to Maly. As it turned out, we would have been better off had we gone elsewhere. But where? Another noisy nightclub? A restaurant? I had reasons to believe my bodyguards had had enough of them. So had I. Plus, can you really think straight at 11:00 p.m. after it's been made abundantly clear to you that you're on somebody's hit list and don't have much time on your hands?

The duo picked us up from a spot right in front of the brooding Ostrovsky, and twenty minutes later, we were already drinking piping hot tea from tea glasses in prewar silver tea holders adorned with hammers and sickles, border patrol guards with dogs by their side on the lookout for miscreant trespassers, young pioneer heroes ready to turn in their class enemy parents at the drop of a hat for the sake of a brighter future, and a couple of planes peeking out from the billowing clouds up above where the handle met the cylindrical body of the tea holder. Our motley crew was sitting under the lampshade: Tasha's mother, Maria Vassilievna, a disheveled, big-bosomed middle-aged woman whom I had never seen in a seated position before, a pair of crutches next to her, Tasha's film scholar aunt Oksana who was staying with them, and Tasha who already had a cigarette going, as well as my trusty bodyguards who felt a little out of place in a domestic setting.

Maria Vassilievna seemed annoyed with Tasha for bringing late company over, and strangers to boot, plus she and

Oksana were in the middle of a spat. Oksana, who looked even more attractive up close than she seemed in the Kino Center, also appeared unusually tall, broad-shouldered, and pretty high-strung. She had been trying to convince Maria Vassilievna that her best bet was privatizing her apartment like many Moscovites recently had. Maria Vassilievna countered snappily that she saw no sense in doing that because when Tashenka, God willing, moved out, she'd be in a position to take in tenants, including foreigners and expats, the so-called *firmachi* who were coming to Moscow in droves trying to do business and thus she'd be able to supplement her income and disability paycheck. Tasha was listening distractedly, holding her hand to her cheek, then said, "Sorry to interrupt. But the hour is getting late, and we have a bit of an emergency here, don't we, fellas?"

"What now?" said Tasha's mother. "And will you put out that stinking cigarette?"

"Long story short," returned Tasha, taking the last drag on her cigarette before squashing it in the crystal ashtray. "My good friend Mark here didn't come to our city just to pay his respects to the Tsar Cannon, the Tsar Bell, and that Tsar of the Russian letters, Fedor Mikhailovich Dostoevsky, though all three were pretty much covered during his stay. Especially, the top hat of the latter encased in a glass box in his museum was fun, right, Marco? Mark came here to collect the money owed him by his New York associates and our fellow citizens who shall remain anonymous, and he has been actively looking for them so far to no avail. Or almost no avail. As luck would have it, earlier this evening we had a bit of a breakthrough in Maly, of all places. A theatre cloakroom attendant we bumped into, a gent formerly associated with Mark's business partner, informed Mark that his partner was aware of Mark's being in town and that Mark was looking for them. Moreover, he didn't take kindly to it to the point of putting Mark on his hit list. Simple math: getting rid of Mark would cost just a fraction of what he stands to part with by honoring his commitment. Big words, to be sure, "honoring" and "commitment" given the circumstances or his business ethics. And that Mark has forty-eight, actually (Tasha looked at her Casio digital watch), forty-six hours between now and boarding the plane to New York, all things being equal and Mark being in one piece at boarding time. Questions?"

"Question. I don't mean to be blunt but what's all this got to do with you?" a surly Oksana asked. "Like we don't have enough problems of our own here, you hang out with someone on someone's hit list and you turn your mother's place into a mob apartment? What if they followed you here? What if they come here looking for you tomorrow?"

"What if you stop worrying and bugging everyone, Aunt Oksana? In two days, you'll be back in the cradle of the revolution, the city of Leningrad, with your lovely little *karapuzik* Valerka, teaching Eisenstein at the Institute for Theatre, Music, and Cinema. Unless you maybe want to go back home sooner? What's all this to you?" Tasha shot back.

"Voicing concern for my aunt, for one. And for my reckless niece. They obviously spotted you and your American friend hanging together. You speak any Russian?" Oksana turned abruptly to me.

"Oksana, he *is* Russian!" Tasha anticipated my answer.

"Ah, an emigrant!" cried Oksana, rubbing her hands with feigned enthusiasm. "Isn't that peachy! I just love your sort. How's life in Brighton Beach anyway?"

"Raining cats and dogs," I said dryly.

Oksana let the reference slide. "I lived in Chicago for three years. The only time I had to deal with the local Russians outside my marriage was when I went grocery shopping."

"A crying shame," I sighed. "How did you find the produce anyway? Beats the Bush's chicken legs sold out of crates in underpasses here in town, huh?"

"Break!" exclaimed Tasha like she was a referee, and we were two boxing bears locked in a clinch. Then she added: "Shall we focus on the issue at hand, maybe? Option one: Mark leaves town in forty-six hours."

"No!" Maria Vassilievna interjected. "Option one: your Maly attendant is full of crap. And your friend Mark is in no danger whatsoever!"

"Then why the hell did he have to bullshit us, come up with the whole 'run, Mark, run' story?" demanded Tasha and lit another Dunhill.

"Question. Did you ever see that attendant before, in the States or elsewhere?" asked Oksana.

"Sure did," I said. "Three months ago, in New York, to be exact. He was a part of my partner's retinue. An active part. But 'run, Mark, run' is not enough, I'm afraid, Tasha. I still want to collect my goddamn dough. And that's where my colleagues enter the picture." And I pointed towards Orlov and Petro, who had been quietly drinking their tea until then.

"Listen. It's your decision. But . . . a second opinion, a voice of reason, whatever. What if you buy a ticket tomorrow and leave the day after, like nothing ever happened?" said Tasha.

"No can do, sorry. I'm 10K in the hole, Tash. That's a lot of money for this faux *firmach*. Money that I am contractually owed."

"Contractually! Owed!" scoffed Maria Vassielvna, spilling tea on her cardigan and leaning sideways to pick up her crutch, which hit the parquet floor with a thud that put a full stop to her bout of hilarity. "You are not in Chicago, my dear. Remember Marshak's poem? Forget that word along with a few others while in Moscow."

"Frankly, I almost had the moment I landed in Sheremetyevo, Maria Vassilievna," I said with a poise and dignity worthy of the Maly stage. "That is why I'm employing the services of citizens Orlov and Decibel Petro here, the latter nicknamed so, incidentally, because his hearing is not what it used to be. A result of exposure to one too many artillery raids while in Afghanistan, you see. Belated thanks are due to late comrade Brezhnev for that lame campaign, by the way. Decibel is a unit of sound pressure, am I right, Petro?"

"Thank your shit for brains Reagan, the clown in chief, why don't you!" countered Tasha's mother angrily and looked at Orlov and Petro, not sure which of the two I just referred to.

Decibel didn't catch half of what was being said but smiled pleasantly anyway, kindhearted fellow that he was, too good for a sharpshooter or a bodyguard, I thought, and suggested we stayed out of politics. Mariya Vassilievna and Oksana looked at me as if I had just broken wind and failed to apologize.

"I suggest," said Decibel Petro after a pregnant pause punctuated by his slurping tea out of his saucer after blowing on it as old ladies did in the plays I'd seen aplenty recently, "I suggest my cousin and myself go back and check out the play tomorrow night. Though, I don't have to remind Mark of my take on dramatic arts. Chekhov the singer of melancholia in particular, ugh! But then remind Mark I might while I'm at it. Back in the day, boss, they kept the Soviet plebs entertained and edified by the theatre while depriving them of any political engagement whatsoever. Why bother: a few hints dropped oh so daringly here, a little melodrama that will make you laugh or cry there—and drab reality doesn't seem so drab anymore. These days, you have to be, with all due respect, an even greater moron to waste your time enjoying the fruits of the new uncensored theatre while everyone is getting crazy rich using old connections in the upper echelons of power and the opportunities of Yeltsin's newly corrupt Russia! Grab all the dough you can get your hands on first, get all the culture you need later. There, I've said my piece." And he flashed everyone the improbable Nixon-style double victory sign and even stood up and took a dignified bow.

My jaw dropped slightly, and that's not just a figure of speech. I hadn't had the foggiest idea that Decibel had it in him. I mean the vocabulary and the argumentative verve that ran opposite everything I held dear then and still hold dear now. Do make a habit of talking to your bodyguards more often, I recall making a mental note as Decibel helped himself to a few teaspoons of apricot jam and held forth.

"The amount, which shall remain undisclosed, will be retrieved and the debtee reimbursed. We intend to collect money by fair means or foul. Such were the terms of our accepting Mark's employment. We did all we could looking for Mark's debtor, leaving no stone unturned. Now that we have a solid lead, it would be laughable and counterintuitive to turn tail, heed threats, and board that plane to New York; motherfuckers have to learn their lesson, pardon my French, and Mark will be reimbursed for his efforts and his trouble. Take it from someone who had a year of law school before his draft put the kibosh on his pursuit of knowledge. Granted, taking the law into your hands is morally wrong and plain barbaric. However, when the law of the land is lawlessness, it's the fastest one on the draw who catches the early worm. No, wait. I think I got it ass-backwards here."

"You sure did, man," Oksana chimed in. "What's your name again? Decibel, you got your metaphors mixed. Your signals, too. It's not some 1920s Warner Brothers movie where everyone gets knocked off because a truckload of illicit booze wasn't delivered on time. It's the land of Pushkin and Dostoyevsky, and, yes, Chekhov and Pasternak, we are talking about here! But you, you walk into Maly toting your heaters, and then what? Bump off the cloakroom attendant if you don't get what you want? Is that your plan? An attempted or successfully carried out assassination in the theatre founded in the mid-eighteenth century, a theatre whose stage was once graced by the performances of Schepkin and Yermolova!? I move that you have your high noon moment elsewhere. How does Liubertsi sound? Biriulyovo, maybe?"

Orlov, who had been keeping quiet, finally spoke, his voice low and a tad menacing. "Listen, lady, I don't know your Schepkin from Adam, okay? But your niece here says you know shitloads about old movies. I happen to like 'em, too. *Traktoristy, Volga-Volga* . . . I have a suggestion for you. You stick to your old movies and let us finish our job, okay?"

"And what job might that be?" Oksana raised her voice. "Shooting people at close range?"

"Righting the wrong, for fuck's sake, Aunt Oksana," Tasha intervened.

"Oh really?" Oksana scoffed. "You sure know a lot about righting the wrong, young lady, don't you? Ratting out Felix to the narc squad like you did?"

"What? What was that?" I looked at Tasha in disbelief.

"Do me a favor, don't listen to her, Mark. Her ripe imagination is getting the best of her. Must have OD'd on movies at some point," Tasha said in an undertone.

I kept quiet, trying to process the ratting out part, while Tasha leaned close to me and whispered in my ear as if there was no one else in the living room but us.

"Listen. Aunt Oksana's mom was helping my mom raise me when Dad pulled the disappearance act, which fucked us up royally. Grandma Olya would take the Red Arrow train here once a month like clockwork. Of course, Oksana could use help back in Leningrad. And so there were tensions—that's how families are, right? But there has never been any ratting out. Except maybe Oksana's ex ratted her out to INS and is now trying to rescind it. And pay for the damages. Talk about unstable. And unfaithful."

"I know you are stressed out, Aunt Oksana." Tasha continued out loud. "Maybe that's why you say the things you don't mean. Please don't. 'Cos it's getting late, and we have a long day tomorrow. We are staying here. Full house, but hey, I'll crash on the sofa, Mark will use the armchair. It is indeedy not Chicago, my dear. I'll get your tickets for *Uncle Vanya* during my lunch break, gents. It's not bad really, once you get past the borzois. Then you do what you have to do. Which I assume is to ask the dude a few questions. Like where his former boss resides. Remember, a thin guy with salt-and-pepper hair and a stutter. Don't think I'm telling you your job, but a stutter is best identified when you get someone to talk . . ."

"Really?" said Decibel Petro. "Either you have a very dry sense of humor, lady, or you take us for a couple of complete nincompoops!"

"Humor, humor, no worries, Petro," Tasha cackled nervously.

"Wait." Maria Vassilievna raised her hand like she was at a local chapter of the communist party meeting. "And for the last time Natalya: put that cigarette out! There are still a few things that bug the crap outa me. Mark's in town to get paid by some criminals, am I right? These two are going to make sure he does. He gets on the plane, cash in his carry-on. A lot of cash by our lights, I'm guessing. By our lights, any cash is a lot of cash. So what if a few days pass and the criminals go after my daughter because she was associated with Mark? And then what happens to us, the two helpless women in the gangland that is Moscow today? Given it any thought, young man?"

Decibel Petro spoke first.

"Piece of cake, lady. This is how it'll play out. When we have our little chat with Mark's debtor, he'll have no choice but to acknowledge his debt. No way he'll want to make any counterclaims or file any retroactive appeals to the powers that be. Gangland powers that be, for that would be our so-called arbitration court. You see, the world we are a part of, lady, has its laws and regulations. Immutable and stringent. Violating them comes at a price. Often the ultimate price. And who is insane enough to be willing to pay that?"

"Also," I said, "if you feel that some protection might be helpful, my pals Orlov and Petro will always be on hand. Just give me a transatlantic holler, and I will let them know. Or you contact them directly."

"You seem to have all the answers, Mark Efimovich," blurted Maria Vassilievna, and started drumming her thick fingers on her left temple as if she were conducting a neurological test of some sort. "My daughter is not a whore, though. Just a friendly reminder: not everyone in these parts is. Not a whore and will never be! My Natalya here is not a fucking whore!"

"Whoa, wait just a minute!" I exclaimed, turning red. "Where did that notion come from?"

Tasha's mother was fuming now, her forehead perspiring. Oksana seemed weirded out even more than Tasha while my bodyguards did a double take.

"What did I ever say that made you suppose?"

She didn't let me finish.

"Well, you were hiding out your ass in here throughout the entire coup, Mark. Sure, it's dangerous out there, I know. You'd mix some foul potion into my tea every night, which I poured right out under my bed the moment I smelled it. I can't walk, but the rest of my faculties are intact, young man! Then you went at each other like two crazed monkeys in heat, and in the morning, I was supposed to be all smiles and make my double hobble omelet special for you: four eggs, two slices of tomato, some dry Moskovskaya sausage, two crutches by my side. And now, it's goodbye to Russia, just like it was goodbye to Russia in the '70s when you and your ilk fucked over the country that gave you free fucking education and left for

America in a hurry where you got yourself good jobs using that education! And now—now you are trying to fuck us over once again with some tidy sum in your pocket. Plus, it's goodbye to the young, smart, and beautiful woman who kept you company for the past two months! Not a whore—not my daughter! And will never be!"

"Mom, will you stop already!" Tasha screamed at her mother, who was obviously having a huge midnight meltdown. "No one is screwing over anyone here, okay? I can speak for myself, too, you know. If you let me. For a change. Maybe I'll go to New York to check out what it's like. Maybe I'll like it—nothing like a little change. You should know that. A Komsomol poster girl in your basketball team, a hero of labor in your factory, wife of a nomenklatura jerk who fucked you over, then a seamless transition to a God-fearing adept of the new economic reforms. And the moment the communists you voted for in '91 lost momentum, you jumped ship, crutches and all. Right, Ma?"

"Fuck you, you little bitch. And fuck your Jew fuck, too! Get the fuck out of my apartment! This instant! And pray to God I don't make a phone call first thing in the morning! Just one crummy little phone call, and your lover Jewboy here gets detained. Either before his musclemen try to shake down whoever or when he tries to take the loot through the security gates! Just pray to God, Natalya. Don't make me do it!"

Mariya Vassilievna's voice was cracking and her face turned beet red. Tears were swelling in her eyes, and her lips were quivering—insanity on the Old Arbat, pure and simple.

"Aunt Masha, please," said Oksana. "Don't you think this has gone far enough? From what I've gathered, Mark would like to see your daughter in New York at some point. He is offering you protection should you need it here. I don't believe aggravating matters further is in anyone's interest!"

A teatime scandal, like something straight out of Dostoyevsky himself; it was the first serious confrontation ever witnessed by my trusty duo during their stint working for me. I even noticed Orlov take the handgun out of his pants pocket and stealthily put it between his inner thighs under the table, but I made such a horrible face at him that he put it right back. Shooting your girlfriend's mother, however casually petulant or chronically inebriated, while drinking tea in her living room is the stuff of unfunny mother-in-law jokes. So I just had to whisper into Orlov's ear, "Are you out of your fucking mind, buddy?" Then, after finishing the last of my tea, I stood up, all poise and determination. "Thank you for your hospitality and valediction—can't think of a better word for what I just heard. Time for this Jewboy and his shiksa friend to hit the sack. Too crowded in here, even if it didn't feel like I outstayed my welcome. I'm sure we'll find a suitable hotel room even at this late hour. Goodbye, goodbye. And Oksana, I never had a chance to thank you for your lecture at the Kino Center. A great experience, a great director, and thorough research. Gregory Davis has a significant following in Sweden too, they tell me. Can't wait to learn more about him and am glad to finally express my appreciation in person, though the circumstances could have been a little more appropriate for a little film chat."

And then I just grabbed my coat, let Tasha and our retinue through the door first, and left the Old Arbat apartment.

Chapter Eighteen.

The Rossiya hotel was our obvious first choice. Still relatively inexpensive, it reeked of nostalgia for me, and since I was beginning to get a strong feeling that my days, if not hours, in Moscow were numbered, regardless of the outcome of Orlov and Petro's encounter with Vodovozkind, staying in Rossiya, to me, "rhymed" with the very early days of my Moscow visit. Plus, the mood was right to grab a gin and tonic at the Manhattan Club downstairs and watch the coltish *putanas* in miniskirts prance in circles, drinks in hand, while me, Tasha, and the indomitable duo tried to chill before finally calling it a night.

"Well, that was some tea party," Petro cackled after we ordered the first round. "Freaking cra-azy!"

"You think?" said Orlov.

"You don't?" snapped his cousin.

"What, you didn't like Mom's apricot jam?" asked Tasha. "That's from the summer before. Our dacha was rented out this summer."

"I mean the high drama," said Petro. "What jam?"

"Guys, guys," I said, "Something I've been meaning to share. Talk about drama."

"What?" said Petro.

"A few days back, I had the weirdest encounter with the most peculiar individual who plays in the band and—this takes the cake—apparently served as an advisor to Yeltsin during recent events. Strategic info broker, no less. What do you think?"

"Apparently? Since when you hang with strangers when you're by yourself?" Orlov hissed through his teeth. "You want us to hike our fee on you, or what? Either that or break the contract altogether? Your choice, man."

"Listen, guys," I pleaded, "It was an exception. I can explain."

"A Russian rock 'n' roller who is also in politics? That would be the first," Tasha said.

"He is a Swede."

"What band?"

"The Tarantula. I saw them at Bunker."

"Never heard of 'em. When was that?" Tasha seemed intrigued.

"Before we even met."

"Hmm. Does he have a name?"

"Arhi."

"I know Arhi," said my girlfriend matter-of-factly. "Horny bastard. Was hot for my bod, like, for months. Never mentioned the band, though."

"A different Arhi?" I offered.

"How many Arhi's are there in Moscow, you think?" she scoffed. "He asked me out like two years ago."

"And?"

"And nothing. Not my type. Plus, um, I was in mourning back then."

"What did he look like?" asked Petro. "I used to know an Arhi."

"Blond receding hair, short, shifty eyes, a judo nut. Great ass," she rattled off.

"Wrong Arhi," I said. "Can't vouch for his ass, but my Arhi was tall and lanky. Walked with a crutch."

"Not the guy from the train?" ventured Tasha.

"The guy from the train. You noticed him?"

"The jerk was eyeing me, like, the entire ride, looking past the girl he was with. I hate it when they do that. Sure, I noticed him. What did you two talk about? And when?"

"Right after... after you bid me a heartfelt goodbye in front of Prague."

"Oh. So you just poured your heart out to a total stranger in the middle of Arbat?"

"Rosie O'Grady's. He did most of the pouring, actually."

"What about? Not the bears?"

"That too. Funny you should mention it. But also the doubles, the war machine, lateral swaps, whatever the hell that means. Most of it went right over my head. He was a little insane, I think. Kept calling me *khlopchis'ko*. At some point, I thought I'd get the hell out. Only he was one step ahead of me. Came back from the man's room, and he was gone."

"What's *khlopchis'ko*?" asked Tasha.

"A kid," volunteered Petro.

"Thank you. Mark's not a kid, though."

"The guy I knew was Harry, not Arhi—it just came to me," said Petro. "No slouch with, whatchamacallit, transubstantiation."

"How do you mean?"

"Tried to shoot him point-blank. At the outset of perestroika. Hit the soda machine in the back of him instead. Vanished into thin air. Demon is who he was, I think. Don't want to mess with their kind."

"What demon? My guy was no demon."

"Oh, and how do you know that?" said Petro. "He hand you his card that said 'I'm no demon' in bold print?"

"No horns, no hooves."

"Old school," said Tasha. "Though he did have a limp, right?"

"Wounded in action."

"Yep, like a zillion years back, maybe? A long free fall from grace?"

"During the coup, Tasha. Give me a break. Funny part: he went to my school in San Francisco!"

"Creepy," concluded Tasha.

"And to top it all off, he said he bumped into my ex in New York!"

"A liar or missing something upstairs. Forget him."

"Trying to."

"Moscow's full of weirdos," said Tasha. "Remember the Hitler lookalike guy we spotted at the Vakhtangov Theatre before the Brecht play? Your guy . . . could have been impersonating somebody, too. Glad he—I don't know—didn't steal your soul or whatever they do."

"Old school, Tasha."

"I mean whatever passes for it today."

"Like what?"

"Self-regenerating genes. An extra-large memory chip."

"You don't seriously believe in that sci-fi claptrap, do you?"

"I believe it's almost one thirty, and your buddies are zonking out here, and we could use some sleep too, Mark."

And that's what we did: finished our drinks, I paid the tab, asked the cousins to leave a message for me tomorrow right after they had their evening chat with Mr. Vodovozkind at Maly, bid them goodnight, and took the elevator up to our room.

The only intimate activity directly associated with the Rossiya back in the day was my nightly masturbatory sessions at age fifteen featuring the mental image of my father's colleague's bespectacled teenage daughter Regina, with whom I had seen a few theatre productions on winter break. It was Regina's family's last visit to Moscow; they were emigrating to Israel in a few months. She was definitely not my type, but no one really had to be back then to tickle my pubescent fancy. Anyhow, that had been then, this was now. And it would have been a gross understatement were I to take Tasha's mother's colorful cue at face value and describe our roughhousing behind closed doors as two crazed monkeys in heat having a go at each other. Twelve monkeys on speed would have done more justice to our protracted bonking with wall-to-wall fireworks and sound effects. Up until now, reader, I have been shying away from what might come across as too graphic a depiction of Tasha's and her truly's carnal pursuits, so let me go out on a limb here and briefly describe what took place in our room until the early hours of the morning, which turned out to be my last morning in the city of Moscow.

Since the six female monkeys of the afore-described equation happened to be having their period and the six male monkeys were of Jewish extraction and thus opposed to and even put out by the Slavic monkeys' appeals and entreaties to undertake penetration without any regard for the attendant blood emissions (the mere thought of violating the ancient prohibition law sending shivers down the six male primates' Judaic spines), the monkey business Tasha and I got down to started with a slow shower taken jointly in the smallish tiled bathroom before retiring to bed. Washing each other down with the tiny hotel soap bar was just a part of the ritual we were making up as we went along. The rest relied on time-tested patterns. With the warm shower going nonstop, she squatted in front of me and commenced to suck and lick my cock and balls with her studded tongue as I reached over and circled my forefinger around her asshole, applying no slight pressure to it—a technique she enjoyed but only to a degree. On the other hand, I appreciated her tongue stud doing its subtle work on my skin more than ever. Once in bed, on fresh bedsheets which had a faint scent of hotel detergent, she played footsie with my erect member, her smooth and delicate feet assuming the otherworldly grandeur of a large extraterrestrial vagina ready to engulf me whole: dick first, then the pelvis, then the rest of the rapturous me (did I have two or three gin and tonics downstairs?). Be that as it may, I enjoyed the foreplay immensely. Playing with my punk princess' tits, her smallish, deliciously supple nipples . . . I mean, I could write a chapter-length blank verse poem about her pierced titties alone, but sucking on them is what I miss about Tasha the most now as I pen these lines in my Boca seclusion. I even tried anilingus with her briefly, though I can't say it was my thing. But with all the other ports of call on temporary lockdown, I felt adventurous and mischievous. Then she sucked my cock for close to half an hour while I sniffed her feet and nibbled on her lovely pungent toes one by one. I think it was our best night ever. Monkey see, monkey do. Only my beautiful monkey is now far away from her despondent and lovelorn hunky. At least till Christmas, anyway.

Around four a.m., she was lying next to me, smoking in the dark, casting occasional glances in the direction of the black-and-white TV across the room, whispering loudly: "Butusov, yeah! Patricia Kaas, you go, girl!" as someone she knew (and I didn't) flickered across the screen and crooned into the mic. Then she said, "Mark, I'm sorry for my mother's shitfit, man. It's not you, trust me. She's been feeling lousy for a week now, plus Oksana's overstaying her welcome, and then us barging in like we did in the middle of the night . . ."

"No big deal," I replied. "It's not like your mom is the first Jew-hater I had to deal with on either side of the Atlantic. And, in all likelihood, not the last one. Like I said, No worries."

"But she's not an antisemite, I promise! It's like she gets possessed whenever she gets on that track. She almost never does, though, I swear. My bad, bringing up her glorious Komsomol past. Last time I did, I wound up with a shiner, remember? There was no call for that yesterday."

"Whatever. Let bygones be bygones. The question is whether she has it in her to make that phone call. That could make my going through security one hell of a challenge, with or without dough."

"No way, Mark. You kidding me? She'll get plenty pissed, she'll say things she doesn't mean. She even hit the late Felix with her crutch once, his spine hurt for days. Over some Gorbachev speech. But she'll never squeal. She knows what honor is. My uncle Foma was in the civil war, grandpa died in WWII. The Tschelichevs are no squealers or Stalinist scum. Just like Oksàna's rant on me supposedly ratting out Felix. Also, to freak Mom out. Never happened. We both could be nicer to her, my aunt and I."

"Yeah, I didn't get the part about Felix... Also, your mother saying you weren't a whore? What was that about? Another flight of temper?"

"Like I'm saying, when she gets derailed, she says crazy things. Feels sorry about it later. And... something I'm not proud to admit, though. But hey, pillow talk has its unwritten rules. Here comes the truth or dare part. Ready?"

"As I'll ever be."

"Once upon a time, and a very lean time it was— crazy inflation, ruble in free fall, no money for food or Mom's meds, Felix gone and buried. So... I never told this to anyone, and I wish I never told Mom. But then, how do I explain going from no food and no meds to food and meds in two nights? Simple: you turn two tricks per night, your tax-free take home is five hundred bucks, a small fortune two years ago. Still is."

"Wow... Well... Please, don't get me wrong. I'm not being judgmental or anything," I said. "Maybe just a bit freaked out. Jealous, too. But that takes some doing. Good for your mother. To have such a daughter, I mean. She probably shouldn't bandy that word about so much. She thought I was just another client, then, a long-term client, who's taking advantage of her Natashenka? Because I'm not. And you know it. And she is wrong. We, the Neiders, are also all about honor. Decency, too."

"'Course, America. I know you'd be hush-hush about it. Don't want my little foray into putanadom to make the front page of *The New York Times* when you return to the land of the free . . . bees?"

"Free . . . bees? Yeah, right. You are funny. Mum's the word, you little *putana*. My dirty little slut, come home to daddy this instant," I whispered.

And with this I started sniffing and probing and then licking her mild Roquefort-flavored armpits covered with prickly undergrowth, just like two baby hedgehogs, simultaneously playing with her soft pubic hair, pulling on her clit-piercing ever so gingerly with the forefinger and the thumb of one hand and squeezing her angelic buttocks with the other, getting an instant hard-on. And she, my Moscow odalisque slash punk princess intoning, "Kinky, kinky, Mark, one more time with feeling, though we should be up with the lark," dove under the blanket with her trademark agility that I loved so and sucked me to sleep slowly and diligently like my mother used to breastfeed me to sleep, like your mother, I'm guessing, just tell me how wide off the mark I am, used to sing you to sleep, so Tasha sucked me to sleep, and I hope you see the parallel here: sucking, feeding, singing? Sure you do: they all revolve around oral activity and unconditional affection.

Chapter Nineteen.

The next morning, we fooled around some more till about ten thirty, before showering, before breakfast, before the cleaning lady rapped on the door only to hear our "Thanks, maybe a little later?" when suddenly the phone rang, reminding us of the day's schedule and import. Orlov and Decibel Petro were calling from the lobby. They wanted to let us in on their plans change and were on their way up. "Meet you in fifteen minutes in the northwest corner café on our floor," I said into the receiver. That gave us enough time to shower and get dressed.

Orlov and Petro were sporting dark-blue tracksuits and oversized leather jackets. Noting their attire bulging in places, I figured they were packing. Much to our surprise, they also brought Mr. Vodovozkind with them. Dragged him more like. The gangly genleman was visibly distraught, wouldn't look me straight in the eye, and kept pressing a crumpled napkin to his prominent nose. We ordered coffee and *vatrushkas* from the lethargic vendor behind the glass counter. Samuil Yakovlevich insisted faintly that he couldn't start his day without a hard-boiled egg and kefir for his blood pressure, ulcers, and something else. I'd never seen anyone take such great care cracking the egg with the teaspoon, extracting the hard yolk from it, and chewing it with utmost deliberation while taking tiny sips of kefir from the glass. It played like the last meal taken by an inmate on death row.

The Red Square and Kremlin seen in the distance through the morning fog outside the wall-to-wall café window lent gravity to our conference, as if we were planning yet another coup instead of figuring out how to extract a modest amount of cash from a small-time mafioso. The change of plans, partially implemented, went like this. Rather than wait till the evening performance at Maly, take their chances in a crowded place, and waste everybody's time, which, indeed, was of the essence (less than thirty-six hours till my purported departure), Orlov and Decibel Petro thought it best to head directly to Maly at the open of business, talk to the theatre HR people as politely as possible (what with Schepkin-Pepkin, and the rest of the sacred cows, Orlov added), get Samuil Yakovlevich's home address from them, pay him an early visit, and take it from there. And that's precisely what they did; they didn't even have to brandish their Makarovs in his face much, said Petro smugly as he patted the side of his jacket.

"We have to act and act f-fast," urged Samuel Yakovlevich, looking up dourly at me and spraying kefir on his jacket as he tried to control his speech impediment. I was wondering what happened to him. Hopefully, nothing too ugly—all things considered, he seemed a decent fellow. How did he get mixed up with Vik Z-sky and co to begin with? But then, how did I? "We gotta be there ins-inside of an hour."

"Where's there?" I said.

"Two blocks from Tretyakovka is where Vik Z-sky makes his home," Orlov answered.

"Great," I exclaimed. "So. Our next move would be . . ?"

"Next move," said Decibel Petro as Tasha started her first cigarette. "Now that we know Vik Z-sky's whereabouts, we head there with Samuil Yakovlevich (man, get some ice for your nozzle, willya?), he shows his face to the CCS camera, lets us through, and we make a forced entry. It's not like his henchmen guard Vik 24/7, mid-level racketeer that he is, who, by the way, recently tied the knot with someone half his age, legs rumored to start around the Baltics and stretch down to the Black Sea—in a word, a very leggy girl he got himself for a wifie. I mean, the voodoo man here says this hot little number is one leggy broad. Legato, lo!"

"I think I got that," I said. "His new wife has a pair of remarkable legs."

"Name's Alena, you've met the b-bitch," announced Samuil Yakovlevich, his face contorted. "And mine, by the way, is Vodovozkind."

"What? They do that here now?" I shouted. "I mean, I thought it was a universal no-no!"

"No-no, my ass," replied Vodovozkind calmly. "She's not his daughter. Passed her off as one so they could check in hotels under Alena's boyfriend's radar. The guy eats small fry like Z-sky for lunch!"

As I was trying to process that last minor plot twist, Petro reiterated dreamily, "Remarkable. Long and beautiful pins. So," he continued. "Z-sky is a distracted newlywed, not prepared for our visit. Didn't even pick up when you called your boss or ex-boss. She did, right?"

"Sure did," said Samuil Yakovlevich, scooping up the last of his kefir with a spoon and smacking his lips behind his napkin. "Then she put him on. Like I said, they ex-expect me within an hour. Oh, yeah, and shall we talk the finder's fee? How does fifteen percent sound?"

"Five," I said without thinking.

"Ten," Vodovozkind shot back.

"Deal," I said. "But how do you know he'll have cash at his place? How do you know he won't put up a fight?"

"Simple," said Decibel Petro. "Technically, we are your bodyguards. But we're also your protection in a larger scheme of things."

"What scheme?"

"He fucked you over, Mark. We are in a position to get the money from him. In other words, if he chooses to get *his* protection involved and we escalate the dispute one level higher, then a certain penalty for damages incurred shall be imposed should he lose. And it may be as steep as the amount owed. Half a mil for Vik Z-sky is a hefty chunk of money. He won't want to go there. Beauty part is he knows who we are. What he doesn't know is that the man we have on our side is Samuil Yakovlevich here. So if he doesn't want to play by the rules again, open the safe like a good *malchik* and put the money in the Adidas bag, there's coercion or arbitration. Samuil Yakovlevich, by the way, told him he wanted to meet him because of the new info he had on you. Questions?"

"Do we go with you?"

"You don't have to. If things get messier than expected, you'd need it like a hole in the head. Maybe literally."

"What are you saying, Petro? We just finish our little breakfast here, then stay in our room, watch some TV? Or do some sightseeing? Maybe the Tretyakov gallery, close to the place of reckoning?"

"Don't be ridiculous, Mark," snarled Petro. "You go get your plane ticket. Make sure it's the open kind for a couple hundred extra bucks. You don't leave tonight, say, things don't get resolved, there's arbitration one level higher, you leave three days from now. But be ready to fly tonight. We get the money, bets are off, no reason to rush nowhere. Stay another month, do more Chekhov, whatever. But for now, you don't need us to run your errands. Just like we don't need you around when we talk sense to your acquaintance."

"So. Okay. If that's how you want to play it. But . . . and don't get me wrong, fellas. How do I know you guys won't take the money and go someplace nice? Like Majorca, on a long vacay? Or transfer it to your off-shore account in Cyprus?"

Tasha nodded a vigorous "Yes" when I said this. Orlov gave her a nasty glance and grunted. But I loved my streetwise baby more than ever for her silent show of support when she did that. God, how I wished her period was over and there was an entire afternoon free of worldly concerns before us. It was not in the stars for us, though.

"Listen," Orlov said, "we have a reputation to maintain, man—an international reputation. Uncle Shura is like a real uncle to us, what with the time he did with my mom in the mid-'60s, bribery charges, you know the story (I didn't). Plus, we already had our chance to fuck you over multiple times. Like asking for fifty percent of our fee upfront, then calling in sick, very sick. Or call OVIR and suggest they keep an eye on you. Many ways to shake down the innocent abroad. Can we stop this discussion? We got a job to do."

"I'll go with you," said Tasha, slamming her palm on the table.

"Like hell you will, lady," Orlov and Decibel Petro exclaimed in unison while Samuil Yakovlevich shook his balding head and wiped his lower lip and then his upper lip, which, as I could see now, was a little on the swollen side.

"I'll go with you," repeated my punk princess. "We do trust you, gentlemen. No ifs or buts. But as Mark's former president once said to Mikhail Sergeyevich, 'Doveriai, no proveryai.'"

"When did he say that?" asked Orlov while Decibel Petro looked on glumly. "Very unnecessary and undesirable . . . Yet, since we work for Mark, and not for you, we'll take you along only on his say-so. Under protest, mind you."

"Mark, say 'so' already," pleaded Tasha. "And here's why. I'm telling you like it is in front of your protection and our esteemed lead. By the way, for a racketeer, an attendant in a venerable theatre institution strikes me as a very odd employment choice. I don't get it. You must really live for theatre, man. And what was the nature of your spat with Vik Z-sky anyway?"

"Young lady," returned Samuil Yakovlevich, cocking his head in a dignified yet slightly jocular way. "Do you mind if I answer your questions in the order in which they were received but at a later point? We don't have the whole day!"

"Not a prob, old man, just curious," snickered Tasha. "Anyhow. Things go wrong, things get complicated, armed guards crawl out from under the floorboards, Alena, the leggy newlywed, sings . . . There's got to be someone who has Mark's trust, which I humbly assume I do. Someone in a position to deliver the goodies should things go awry."

"Say no more," said Decibel Petro after a brief pause.

"You made your point," added Samuil Yakovlevich.

"Do you know how to handle a weapon?" inquired Orlov. "I think we have an extra bulletproof vest in the trunk."

"You think you do or you do?" I asked.

"I do," said Orlov. "I do."

"You show me how," answered Tasha. "I remember civil defense from high school. The foe across the ocean kept us on our toes. Right, Mark?"

"You sure you want to, Tash?" I said, still not entirely sold on the idea. "I can go too, you know. With you, or better yet, instead of you?"

"Mark, listen. You are a foreigner in a foreign land," she said. "Cops get involved, then what? They don't treat foreign nationals kindly in prison. The same goes for court."

"What about you?" I asked. "You get pinched, who's going to take care of your mother?"

"Mark, can we stop entertaining every fucking angle here? It's not like we are robbing a bank. We are hitting the guy who owes you money. And, like Petro said, he knows it. We'll get your dough for you." With that, she flashed me a cute smile. "Happy to be of help. Come on, everything will be okay," she added throatily, and it seemed for a second that she was imitating Doronina from the old movie *One More Time about Love,* which I could swear she'd told me she had never seen.

"Okay, if you say so," I said, squeezing her hand.

"Can you wait for us at Pushka between 3:00 and 5:00 p.m.?" said Decibel Petro. "The plane out to New York is not before eight something?"

"No problem. Where's Pushka?" I said.

"A spot in front of the Pushkin monument? You know the one on Tverskaya, right?" Tasha shook her head in disbelief.

"Yeah, I know the monument. I just didn't know they call it Pushka."

"Even between 3:00 and 4:00 should work," said Orlov. "What's there to discuss with Vik Z-sky for more than ten minutes if he is a man of reason? Or for more than three minutes if he is a stupid moron who doesn't know what's good for him?"

"Well," said Tasha. "If we have an hour to kill before hitting the Leningrad highway to the airport, we grab a bite in Aragvi before we do. Even if we show up at 3:30, it'll give us plenty of time."

"Listen," I said. "It's 11:30. Say, I get tickets around 12:30. Either here in the tourist office or at Savoy. A smaller hotel, the lines are shorter. So. I should be standing in front of Pushkin freezing my butt off around 2:00, maybe 2:30 p.m."

"No need to freeze your cute butt off," chimed in Tasha. "McDonald's is right across the street."

"No way," I said. "Not for my last meal in town. Better freeze than to feast on frozen meat."

"Suit yourself, snob," said Tasha, frowning. "Okay then. To recap: we don't show up by three with the money, we show up with info re arbitration by, say, four or four thirty. We don't show up by five, I wouldn't expect either the money or the good news. Just flag the first cab you see and hit the Leningrad highway."

"Wait just a minute," said Orlov. "Since when you get to give the instructions here, young lady? Not security-related instructions, anyway. Uh-huh, not your department."

"Okay, what'd your take on Mark's actions be, Spinoza?" asked Tasha.

"What did you just call me?" Orlov said. "You're asking for it, young lady. Watch your tongue, okay?"

"If we don't leave n-now," interjected Samuil Yakovlevich, "I might as well g-go home and take a nap. I work for a living, you know. Late hours, too. Culture is work. Hard work, sometimes."

"Please, gents," I said. "Let's get a move on."

"Vovka, hold on, man," said Decibel Petro. (I'd be damned if I knew that Vovka was Orlov's first name) "Tasha has a point here. No show at Pushka with the dough by 3:00 p.m., no show with the third-party arbitration plan by 4:30 p.m., then it's grab a cab, hit the Leningrad highway to Sheremetyevo. Must mean nothing came out of our little encounter."

"Ladies, gents! Let's not reinvent the wheel, please," I said. "What we are dealing with here is a simple if/then/else statement. To recap: if 3:00 p.m., with money, then a plane as scheduled. Else: 4:30 p.m. with no money, then a plane as scheduled."

"Isn't it what I just said?" asked Decibel Petro.

"You did. I just codified it a little. Once a programmer . . ."

"We got to go," said Orlov. "Now."

"Good luck, you guys," I said, getting up from my chair. "And promise you'll be careful, please." Then I hugged and kissed Tasha on her lips, but, actually, I was addressing the entire group as they stood up from the table and headed for the only working elevator on the floor.

Chapter Twenty.

2:45 p.m. Pushka is a peculiar place. Even on a chilly afternoon in mid-November with snowflakes landing on the bronze curly head of the "Sun of the Russian poetry" gazing down from his pedestal upon us, the mortals scurrying about below like so many particles in Brownian motion or navigating the slippery stairs of Tverskaya underpass tentatively, or waiting for tardy rosy-cheeked sweethearts in *varenka* coats and fur-fringed ankle boots, Pushka is still a very crowded place. So crowded that there seems no safer spot in the entire city for a rendezvous, however illicit, extramarital, or pregnant with dire consequences for state security. No kidnapping a business partner's fetching daughter, shooting a conniving competitor point-blank, or shadowing a suspect before apprehending her is easily perpetrated in Pushka. Don't even think about it. Plenty of other locations in town better suited for acts of malice and revenge.

3:00 p.m. Dressed in a Vietnamese down jacket purchased in the underpass kiosk half an hour prior, the Turkish-manufactured fake leather quilt bag across my shoulder (also brand new), the Aeroflot ticket in my pocket, all errands completed in under two hours, I was freezing my butt off as accurately foretold by Tasha earlier that morning. But the line to McDonald's seen from across Tverskaya was so off-putting, so reminiscent of the long lines to Lenin's tomb of the olden days, that the entire prospect of patronizing the capital's first American fast-food establishment, even to keep pneumonia at bay, seemed very unappealing.

3:25 p.m. Questions that race through your mind in no particular succession as you're getting progressively edgier waiting for your lover's return from one heck of a mission may include: Why did you let her join the people, gunmen, really, only two of whom you can trust? Vodovozkind, I didn't know from Adam; his initial intentions murky at best. He wanted to help? Why? The last-minute pecuniary considerations apart, what were his ulterior motives for approaching Tasha and me in Maly's foyer? And what if, in the worst-case scenario, Tasha gets her ass nabbed? Before the dough is retrieved or after? What if the whole thing is ultimately pinned on her? Do I fly back from the States to bear witness at her trial? Wait till she's done serving her term doing what exactly in the meantime? Things wouldn't go that far, that I knew. I hoped they wouldn't anyway. Am I dealing with amateurs here, or what? Isn't Vik Z-sky aware that he owes me, and when reminded of it, won't he fucking cough it up?

3:45 p.m. Funny, when Tasha and I just started dating, she kept bugging me about my childhood recollections of Moscow. I think I told her how striking to me were the invisible fans located somewhere between the double doors that blew hot air at you the moment you stepped inside big department stores or metro stations back in the '60s. It felt like civilization was right at your feet, waiting to envelop you in her warm embrace as soon as you crossed the threshold between the wintry outside and the man-made inside. No such primeval separation between the cold and warmth back in my hometown: no metro, no harsh winters, no big department stores. Small-town lifestyle, small-time mentality. Is that why Dad up and packed our things one fine day in the early '60s and moved Mom and myself to Moscow when I was just six months old? To pursue his ambitions for a better life in the capital where his hometown buddies had already been sitting pretty raking it in in various fields of human endeavor, not all of them entirely legit? Heck, *none* of them legit, let's call a spade a spade. So technically, there were a few things I could have seen or felt before my exposure to Moscow's fans blowing warm air at age eight. The only glitch was that I couldn't remember any of them. I was six months old, for Pete's sake! What I did know from my Mom's stories was that my parents rented a place in Maly Gnezdikovsky, a stone's throw from where I presently was doing a poor imitation of Fred Astaire's hoofing, what with the mercury hovering around five degrees Celsius and the early Moscow dusk falling upon me rapidly, I'd say, what I knew from Mom's stories was that the Pushkin monument was the place she took me to in a stroller for daily fresh air. So was it any wonder that Pushka felt familiar beyond the textbook familiarity with the monument itself, or Pushkin's poems, or his ubiquitous portraits and larger-than-life persona, his unshakeable status, his legend that kept on living, his presence that kept on giving, streets named after him in every Soviet city, anecdotes about him abounding, monuments to him gracing city squares, metro stations named after him, as well as theatres, concert halls, and museums, his poems set to music, movies and operas based on his plays, a ship or three christened after him etc., etc. What was one supposed to write or do to acquire such staying power so that he effortlessly entered your field of vision everywhere you went one hundred and sixty years after his death? From whence this capacity to vie for centrality in the national psyche matched only by the bald bogeyman laid to rest in the Red Square mausoleum, or perhaps eclipsing it, just as Pushkin himself envisioned in his poem *The Monument,* a stanza from it engraved on the pedestal ten feet away from me still sending a shudder of excitement down the spine of any true blue Russian or this blue-in-the-face faux Russian on the verge of pneumonia, and—one hopes not—a nervous breakdown: too much theatre, too much drinking, too much frolicking indoors, too long a stretch away from New York, my Vietnamese down jacket too thin, a shoddy pair of autumn shoes making me feel like a poor clerk in a Gogol story, my feet ice-cold, nose running, nerves ragged . . .

Dad's round of Moscow false starts and dead ends culminated in a business meeting with a friend who was doing quite well in Moscow's underground economy, an encounter during which the old friend, instead of making a hoped-for job offer, said amiably as he pointed to the porcelain bowl of large tangerines sitting in the middle of his office desk, "Fima, old man, do me a favor, try one of these, they're real killers. Juicy like I don't know what." Mom and Dad packed their things and returned to Odesa two weeks later. I'm curious if they did much theatre during Dad's three-month dry spell in Moscow. Probably not.

4:34 p.m. So it got past "the action" time and "the mission accomplished" time, and it was starting to get close to "the arbitration at a higher level" time. Still okay, if one sticks to his guns, figuratively speaking, so long as there are no real gunshots exchanged, I could deal with figurative. Half an hour to go before you start suspecting the worst. Say, your bodyguards realigning their priorities on the dime and maybe thinking it a good idea to fuck you over after all. Or maybe Tasha was in cahoots with them, too, now? Split the dough three ways after taking care of Vodovozkind's finder's fee. But why go to such lengths to shake me down? Surely, there were less elaborate ways to get rid of me, if that's what they were after . . .

4:42 p.m. Sue me, but every time I start thinking a person is a piece of shit, I find it useful to think nice things about that same person first and give him a fair shake. Can't live your life suspecting everyone is out to get you, can you? Call it a last-ditch effort to play it fair, but I began recollecting what few bits and pieces Tasha revealed to me over the past two months. Funny how the young woman with dark purple nails that had seen better days, multiply pierced ears, and, on occasion, eyebrows would get misty-eyed recounting the times her father took her to the Patriarch's Ponds and how she loved it more than anything in the world. "Patriki" was where she played with the other kids, even in the light drizzle and the falling snow, always looking forward to taking the metro to get there and crying her little heart out when it was time to leave. Or sobbing quietly as she was sharing with me fifteen years later how her father had left her there on the bench by the pond, all alone and shivering, with her little kitty Beggie in her lap when Tasha was nine. Some man in a woolen beige coat and a cap volunteered to give her a ride home in a chauffeur-driven black Volga parked at the park's edge that night in December. She remembered looking back to see if her father might still be somewhere there among the trees, but all she saw was the frozen pond and the soldier's footprints (he looked like a soldier to her) in the fresh snow that covered the paths of the deserted park. And how her mother was despondent for a whole year, looking for her missing husband who vanished without a trace: quit his government job, no forwarding address, police was quite useless too. Then Maria Vassilievna was forced to take a second job cleaning people's apartments so she could fend for her daughter and herself; then, by degrees, she let herself go; then paralysis struck; and finally, she took to the bottle. Tasha was growing up a cheerful kid despite it all, a decent student too, though the scars of that December night at the Patriarch's Ponds never did heal entirely. A few years later, she won a trip to a Crimean summer camp and during that stay, she told me, she befriended a big-mouthed redhead Lenochka, a girl six months her senior, whose father was a higher-up in a Moscow regional party organization. Lenochka, at thirteen, was big into things British and American, like rock 'n' roll and movies, and flares and oversized colorful pin buttons, and she was, actually, the one who started calling Natasha "Tasha" because she knew Natasha was the most popular Russian female name in the States, and also the real name of Natalie Wood who supposedly came to the States from Russia as a child soon to become a big movie star in Hollywood. And then, Lenochka, who, of course, insisted on being reciprocally called Helen, taught Tasha a neat trick: how to wear a token on a thread around her waist and let the contraption hang down low inside of her panties so that it came in direct contact with Tasha's little clit and rubbed against Tasha's clit while Tasha was out and about; and that clandestine pendulum, when set in motion, made Tasha's strolls appreciably more exciting. When I asked my friend if she didn't think that thirteen years of age perhaps was a little too early for such carnal experiments, she looked at me as if my intergalactic spaceship just crash-landed in the middle of her Old Arbat kitchen, then elaborated that some girls from school were no longer virgins by age thirteen . . . Talk about acceleration, I muttered in response to that bit of statistics. Lenochka, now a bona fide Helen, most of her anglophone dreams having come true, married a British national and was raising two lovely kids in Notting Hill, London. Then my thoughts turned to what Tasha had to go through to help pay for her mother's meds and family's living expenses. I'm hardly a prude, but then there was something uncool about that entire love-for-sale episode. And what about that violent death of her husband, Felix the Cat, and her being just a little too matter-of-fact and stenographic when recounting it? Ten shells at the scene of the crime . . . Who exactly counted them anyway? She didn't even mention the police. Was the crime ever solved, perpetrators apprehended? The driver's multiple knife wounds . . . Cartoonish and grotesque, that's what it seemed in retrospect. Tyutchev on his deathbed, give me a fucking break! But then, wasn't Moscow, as I got to know it, violent beyond belief? And didn't everyone and his uncle recite poetry at the drop of a hat, serial killers being no exception? More or less. Shootouts and explosions an everyday occurrence. Then poetry slams. Tasha and I once even checked out a reading held at Moscow State University, which featured a group of poets who called themselves The Order of Courteous Mannerists, an experience wherein for five dollars apiece, we got to sit on the stage within earshot of the mannerists, have a glass of tepid champagne and an orange each while listening to an overweight curly haired young poet with heavy eyelids recite his verses, though they seemed neither memorable nor distinct. Also, what didn't quite add up was how come Tasha, the street-smart cookie that she was, let her husband's scumbag of a partner get away with conning her out of her share? I wished I could take care of her when she made it to New York, I thought, but then my programmer's pay was nothing to write home about . . . We'll see. First, I'd like to hear her explain why she didn't keep her end of the deal. What happened? Should I stay in town and blow my Kuntsevo digs for someplace safer if the renovation, just like Vodovozkind said, was part of an elaborate plan to off yours truly? Thing is, I didn't want to take any chances. Let's say the threat was real, let's say the money wasn't at Vik Z-sky's apartment, or things got messy; let's say not everyone survived the holdup. I'd find out soon enough after I make it to the States; there's international phone connection, mail, faxes too . . .

5:00 p.m. To recap before I hail a cab: having stayed in Moscow for two months, my resources completely depleted, instead of finding the fuckers who fucked me over big time in New York, I fell in love with the girl who volunteered to join my bodyguards in what I think is called a hit. Why? She didn't want me to get in trouble should things go wrong. Things seemed to have gone wrong. How else do I explain the no-show, whether she stood me up or not, but our date was crucial, I was thinking to myself.

At 5:05 p.m., as I finally stepped down from the sidewalk and onto the slushy road ready to flag down the cab or a moonlighting *bombila* driver in a half-decent car, all of a sudden, a familiar *Shesterka* slowed down and came to a halt in front of me. The driver's door opened, and who emerged from the vehicle in the dusk but Samuil Yakovlevich Vodovozkind himself and motioned me to get in. I followed his directions, no doubt in my mind that he was still on our side, though ten minutes prior, the question of everyone's loyalty, including that of the cloakroom dude, had been up in the air. I guess I was really happy to see anyone from our team finally show up. He was pressing a napkin to his nose again. It was covered with dark smudges.

"What the hell happened?" I yelled, panting as I got inside the car. "What's going on?!" I always tend to pant when I get extra nervous.

"A nose-b-bleed," he screeched.

"Fuck your nosebleed, man! How come you're late?" I kept yelling. "I have a plane to catch, remember? Where's Tasha? Where the fuck is everyone?!"

"Things went a b-bit haywire, Mark." Vodovozkind shook his head in resignation. Then he quoted—who else—Pushkin. "As Saadi sang in earlier ages, some are f-far distant, some are dead. Please keep your voice down."

"Will you give me a fucking break with your quotes, moron!?" I screamed as he released the break, put car into first, and pressed the pedal, going into second, then third gear. "Who's dead?!"

"Your b-bodyguards, I'm very sorry to say, joined the majority, young man. T-Tasha's in the hospital. Thank God for that vest. A scratch, nothing to worry about, really. But still, you know. Best attended to in a sterile environment. The Sklif clinic seemed a good choice. I know the department head. A t-tetanus shot and whatnot. You would like to stop by and say a quick hello, wouldn't you? P-pick up the loot, too?"

"Course I would! If she'll see me. What's with the shoot-out? Who started it? How come the cousins are dead? What a horror story!"

"Were they related? I-I didn't know that."

"Yeah, they were related. What does it matter now? Who else got hit? Why the high noon in the high-rise?!"

"Long horror story short? We get inside the b-building. I show my face to the intercom. V-vik Z-sky buzzes us in. The rest of us squatting. I ring the doorbell on the ninth floor. Vik opens his reinforced door a crack. We exchange hellos, he gives me a b-bear hug—after all, I've worked for the b-badass for years. Until he thought he could get away paying me b-bubkes while raking in a king's ransom. 'So you wanna make peace?' he says. 'Why do you think I'm here?' I say. Then, the bodyguards force their way in, pull out their heaters, and take aim. 'Does the name Mark Neider mean anything to you, fuck-head?' the smart one says. 'The fellow who helped you purchase upwards of seventeen mils' worth of Cadillacs, and his stipulated fee was two hundred thousand dollars?! Only there was a breach of contract on your lousy part?' I am not giving you an accurate ren-rendition, Mark, but certainly something to that effect," Vodovozkind said ruefully.

"Fuck the rendition!" I screamed at the top of my voice again. "Where was Tasha hit? Is she even conscious?"

"I won't stand for this type of t-talk," said the old man calmly as he gave me a stern look at the intersection. "I can d-drop you off right here, you know, and you'll have to cab it to the airport. How does that sit with you, *loch*? I'm almost twice your age! Just fucking think about it for a moment. Have some respect and civility, you pathetic fuck!"

"Sorry, man," I muttered, taking it a notch down. "I'm just unbelievably, insanely upset, and you know why . . ."

"Course I do," he said, changing his tune too. "And so am I, believe me. Plus, it's been a long day for me too, maybe? She's hit in the shoulder, the bullet grazed her skin, minor bleeding. Like I said, thank God for that vest. It could have been worse. A lot worse. The Sklif people don't know what really happened, of course. Nor do they know Tasha's real name. She was admitted as Lilly K."

"Lilly who?"

"K. Some name she made up. She'll be out in a d-day or two. Worse comes to worst, we'll hide our asses at my dacha an hour from here. Though I doubt we'll need to. What with the shit happening around town, who are you kidding? I mean, no one will start a proper investigation. Not to mention that Vik Z-sky had something less than a stellar rep."

"But what the fuck happened? You're not telling me what happened?!"

"M-maybe if you shut up for a minute? And let me do the talking? Anyhow, this Petro guy explains to my ex-boss at g-gunpoint that you don't run out on your commitments. He says it's a bit more than 200K owed now, what with s-surcharge and penalty, shipping and manhandling, whatever. And Petro suggests the matter gets settled then and there. Without taking it to a higher *krysha* arbitration, which might be f-fraught with f-further f-fines. Vik Z-sky is surprisingly cooperative. The marriage mellowed him out some, no doubt. Who wants to play with fire, you keep all the games for the boudoir. That hottie. Shoulda never introduced her to Vik. Had a fling with her too, right before she got hitched to that Odesa *zhlob* when she turned nineteen.

"Anyhow, Vik Z-sky shuffles over to the safe next to his enormous Sony HD TV, Sonechka the schmuck calls it, f-fusses with the knob, unlocks it, and starts counting out the money. Money's in pretty thick bricks from where I am standing. Then, he asks Petro to name the sum he's supposed to fork over with extra thrown in for breaching the contract so that the matter is settled once and for all. And as Petro responds, 'Make it an even 400K, that will make us square,' this piece of work wife of his, this newlywed purebred Alena who'd given you a boner without half trying, am I right? This bitch with just a see-through silk nighty on emerges from the bedroom, her hair all tousled up, screaming like a hyena in heat, all twitching and shaking like she's ready to pee herself. And she takes in Vik Z-sky stooping over the open safe, a guy next to him pointing his gun at her fucker, and she fires two shots, a Saturday Night special. I hated her with a passion, Mark, ever since she, ah, never mind. One bullet hits Petro in the head, the other one grazes the shoulder of your lady friend who was standing next to him.

"What happened next took place within five seconds, maybe less. Your other bodyguard f-fires his gun at the bitch till she's dead. Vik obviously doesn't like what he sees, so he grabs a gun he had stashed away in the safe and plugs the other guy on the spot. While I snatch the second guard's heater in the n-nick of time and hit Vik between the eyes before he can hit me or further hurt Tasha. What kind of name is that, anyway? She's not a fake American like you by any chance, is she?"

"She's not. And neither am I."

"Anyhow. Here we are, the emergency d-department. Impressive, huh? Could house a museum. I tell you, the tears shall yet be shed for the Union of Soviet Socialist Republics and the care the country took of her p-people's well-being and health. So, we grabbed w-whatever was in the safe, looked like close to half a mil, give or take, locked the safe, and made a run for it. Finding the keys to the guys' *Shesterka* was the tricky part. I didn't want to leave prints on their tracksuits.

But leaving the four bodies in the mob apartment, I personally am not going to lose much sleep over."

"What if they trace the whole thing to you? Or Tasha?"

"Like I said. I have a dacha outside of Moscow. Sit it out if need be. Totally winterized. But I don't think anyone will bother much with the dead run-of-the-mill m-mafiosi. The bodies are going to be chalked up to yet another territorial *razborka* between rival gangs. And come to think, was it anything but? Tasha wants to wait things out in Shchelkovo? Be my guest. That shouldn't be your concern right now. It's her aunt who is ready to tear you limb from limb that you might want to think about. She's up there with Tasha, and she didn't like the shape she found her niece in at all. You don't believe me, look at my fresh nosebleed. What, you didn't think it was my old nosebleed?"

Chapter Twenty-One.

There were three beds, four including Tasha's, in the Sklif clinic ward. An old man, his chest bandaged up tightly, was lying flat on his back in one of them; next to him an old emaciated woman with a pointy chin, nothing visibly wrong with her except her drainage bag was in need of emptying, and a creature of indeterminate gender, long-haired and shivering who was peering at the ceiling and spouting obscenities intermittently, like he was slowly counting sheep while trying to fall asleep, only saying, "twenty fucking three, twenty up yours doggie-style four," etc., all in all, not a pleasant sight to look at. From a distance, I thought that the potty-mouthed patient was Tasha, and then I saw Tasha's bed in the corner by the window. She was waving her unbandaged right arm at me weakly.

The first thing I uttered when I approached her bed was the obvious, "How bad? How bad were you hit? Are you in pain, dear?"

"A little," responded my impaired princess dismissively. "Much voodoo about nothing, really." I looked closely at her left upper arm and shoulder, which was bandaged along her clavicle.

"I shouldn't have let you," I whispered. "What a stupid pathetic son of a bitch I am! What a moron—how I hate myself, Tasha . . ."

She put her finger to her lips. Then I noticed her aunt Oksana lumbering towards the foot of her bed. She wasn't looking at me or Samuil Yakovlevich standing three feet from us and hunching his shoulders. Oksana was seething. Oksana was clenching her fists and hyperventilating. Oksana was ready to pounce.

"Can I ask you to step outside for a sec, young man? I've got something to tell you in private," she hissed, leading the way out of the ward. She was a good head and shoulders taller than me in her cloggers, which were clearly wrong for the season.

Tasha gave me an imploring look and shook her head; so did Vodovozkind, but I followed Oksana anyway. She's not going to kill me, I remember thinking. She didn't, of course. However, once in the hallway, Oksana barked at me, "I could just about break your goddam head in two right now! What were you trying to do? Get my niece killed? Was that the idea?" Then she socked me one in the eye, quickly followed with a one-two punch in the gut, really hard, then a third one, even harder, as I shrieked in pain, doubling over, then squatting and whimpering quietly like a hurt puppy.

"What's with you, lady? You lose your fucking marbles?" I finally squealed, breathing with considerable difficulty.

"Something I picked up in the Windy City." Oksana gave me a crooked smile as she leaned over me so close I could smell her stale breath. "No time to go Aikido on your sorry ass, moron. One call, though, and you'll be spending the rest of your pathetic life in the Surgut region, where it gets dark so early, no one will notice the second asshole your new friends will tear next to your old one. Just don't want to implicate my bonehead niece, so I'm letting you off easy, creep. Love is mean; it'll make you fall for a cretin. You remember our proverbs so rich in imagery?"

I thought it best to remain silent as I slowly got back up on my feet and took a step back.

"Why did you have to put her in harm's way, numbskull?"

"I'm sorry," I mumbled. "I really am. But listen, she went on her own accord."

"But it's your stupid business and your stupid concerns, not hers! She has got enough to worry about, meathead!"

"I said I was sorry, lady . . ."

"Sorry, my ass. Get the fuck out of here before I call the cops. And don't forget to pick up your loot. And read the letter my niece enclosed. Make yourself useful for a change, see how it sits with you!"

She turned around clumsily, flung a heavy backpack over her shoulder (my hunch was she was leaving for St. Pete that night), and slowly walked towards the elevator, no goodbyes, no looking back. Correction: she flipped me off before the elevator doors opened. Just like Tasha did instead of goodbye a few days ago. Must run in the family. A couple of disheveled orderlies came out of the elevator, laughing their heads off and high-fiving.

I tiptoed back to the ward where Samuil Yakovlevich was busy explaining to a nurse that I was Lilly K.'s ex-husband from Tallinn ("Funny accent, huh?") and that she phoned me right away and told me all about her accident at work (a gun went off during a circus rehearsal where she was assisting an animal trainer of some renown) and wondering if Lilly would be in a position to be discharged tomorrow. "Make it the day after," the nurse said. "Not much of a wound, but seeing how the tetanus vaccine takes, plus changing the bandages, might take up the whole extra day. Play it safe. And, truth be told, our food here is not half bad."

Then, I asked my newly converted accomplice to leave the ward and hang out in the hallway so that Tasha and I could have a private moment. The kind soul Vodovozkind obliged, all courtesy, tact, and the residual nose bleeding.

"Tasha," I said, cringing and pressing one hand to my stomach, "Oksana and I have said our goodbyes. No bandages needed, maybe a quick X-ray and some ice . . .".

"Don't be silly, Mark. And don't hold it against her," Tasha begged. "She's sooo pissed. Like I've never seen her pissed before. And I've seen her plenty pissed. She was so against the whole thing from the get-go. Let me see your shiner . . ."

"Never mind. She has the brawn of Wonder Woman to go with that brain of hers, that's for sure."

"Her dad was an academic," Tasha responded faintly. "It's all about good genes . . . I'm sorry."

"You should be sorry? I feel like such a jerk," I sighed. "I feel . . ."

"Don't. It was my idea, okay?"

"How bad does it hurt?"

"A little."

"What kind of pain?"

"Sharp. But also dull. Listen, I'll be okay. Could've been worse. Thank God for that vest. You need to go, though. You have a plane to catch, remember?"

"I can't leave you like this! What are you talking about?"

"You can. And you will. It's a scratch, I tell you. You shoulda seen that ballerina's pirouette and her overfed swan's taking his final bow courtesy of our cloakroom friend. For comparison."

"I can't leave my wounded girlfriend in the hospital, Tasha! Who may be on the wanted list for all I know! What do you think I am?" I whispered, looking around to see if the weird trio was listening to our exchange.

"Mark, no need to get dramatic. I'll be out in no time. What list? You're not in Chicago, my dear. Or maybe you are." Tasha said. "Down there," she pointed under the bed, "is what you came to the land of the bears for. The rest is incidental music."

"Stop it, please!" I said. "You and I were not incidental. My feelings are not incidental. Just get well as soon as you can and come to New York. So we can be together."

"There you go again, making our global plans." Tasha smiled. "Meanwhile, I'm thinking of hanging out at Vodovozkind's dacha for a bit. With his kind permission. You will be all right, too, by the way. Eventually."

"In what sense?" I asked, thinking once again that I detected the low throaty notes of Doronina's voice from that movie I liked as a kid.

"Close to half a mil in the bag under the bed," Tasha said faintly. "If my hasty count was accurate. A hefty penalty for pain and suffering. And a few stiffs. My pain. Your suffering. Stiffs all around. The bitch started firing first, no tears for her bony ass. It's your pals I feel awful for."

"I do, too. Believe me . . ."

"Mark, you'd better get going. I'm totally bushed, and you don't want to miss your flight. And don't forget the bag!"

So I pulled the bag from under her bed, took out about half of its paper-wrapped stacks, shoved them in my quilted Turkish bag, and then zipped it up. "No time to do a proper count," I said.

"What the hell are you doing?" she asked quietly.

"Partners in crime splitting the loot two ways. Only right, no?" I said quietly. "Vodovozkind gets his fee out of my half."

"Take the rest this instance," Tasha said gravely. "You want to leave me something, so leave five stacks, ten stacks. More than enough for Mom's meds and shit. No haggling over the dough in the hospital, not in front of everybody, please! Don't be ridiculous. You have a cab to hail. Not a great idea for Vodovozkind to take you to Sheremetyevo in the getaway car."

"You're right," I said. "When you're right, you're right. And you're right, Tasha."

However, instead of doing what she asked me to, I knelt by the side of her bed, blocked her view with my back, acted like I was taking the stacks from her bag and counting them when, in fact, I was leaving the content of her Adidas bag untouched. Done with my silly pantomime, I stood up, leaned over, and kissed my Moscow punk princess on her lips, slowly and tenderly; and the sigh that issued from my lips was heavy with sorrow and longing.

"Oh yeah," I said. "What about the letter your iron-fisted aunt mentioned?"

"Here," Tasha reached under the pillow and pulled out an envelope. "Read it on your way to the airport. It's important. Self-explanatory, too."

"See you soon? Before the New Year?"

"It's a plan, man."

I stuck the letter inside my Turkish bag and headed for the exit. Out of the corner of my eye, I glimpsed that two out of three of Tasha's ward mates were fast asleep. The third one kept counting fucking sheep under his breath. Once in the hall, I shook Samuil Yakovlevich's hand, extracted five stacks from my bag, and handed his fee to him. "Much appreciated, young man," he intoned, and as he opened his arms, angling for a hug, I noticed tears swelling in the theatre-loving gangster's eyes. Ah, Russia cannot be fathomed by the mind alone; Tyutchev was so right when he penned it way back. On the one hand, I wanted to stay with Tasha and see her recover entirely, and I felt she could use knowing that I cared for her while she was recovering. Also, let's be honest here, I wanted to fuck the brains out of my afflicted angel more than anything on God's green Earth. Yet I was also happy I was getting the hell out of Russia, money at long last in my possession, thinking of beating the traffic on my way to Sheremetyevo, imagining what it would be like to finally see my parents after two month's stay in my former home country that had managed to turn into a dangerous gangland while I was busy making a life for myself in my new country. My former country felt former beyond repair—a place where I'd survived an attempted coup, avoided a hit by a mafiosi whose blacklist I'd wound up on, and lost my bodyguards. Also, you may chalk it up to Western ethics making inroads into my consciousness, but the two things I was feeling okay about as I was trying to flag down the car in front of the Sklif's pillared façade were managing to fulfill my financial obligation vis-à-vis my Kuntsevo landlord, rent paid up in full, as well as squaring money matters with the cousins for their services rendered through the end of November. Though there was no chance in hell they'd now be able to take advantage of my due diligence.

Chapter Twenty-Two.

I flagged down the first car I laid my eyes on in the Sklif parking lot; everyone seemed gung-ho to make a quick thirty smackeroonies in the former land of the red commissars: hospital visitors, orderlies, not sure about moonlighting doctors or the just discharged patients but my driver happened to be a male nurse, who had a five o'clock shadow and smoked like a chimney. It didn't take him long to figure I was no local. Locals don't insist they'd rather sit in the back like we are used to in the States. So when asked where I was from, I had to say Tallinn and add that I just loved Moscow theatre, cuisine, and even the post-coup politics, but that it was time to fly back home to my wife and twin daughters. He was just about to start drilling me for my opinions on Yeltsin and the coup's consequences for the economy and my take on Ukraine's giving up her nukes now that it was an independent state, but I apologized, saying that I had a letter to read and could use a bit of privacy. Not sure he knew the meaning of the word, but he shot me a nasty look in the rearview mirror, shut his mouth, and didn't open it until we got to the airport an hour later. I tried to make the most of the silence as I read Tasha's letter. At first, it felt like I'd been had big time, whether by Tasha or her aunt Oksana the middleweight, or even Vodovozkind, I couldn't tell just yet. My next thought was: if you choose to use someone else to pull chestnuts out of the fire for you, this is precisely what you get. And lastly, as I got the gist of Tasha's missive, I thought I was lucky to know my girl, to whom I felt forever in debt, even more than before if such a thing was even conceivable.

"Mark, my friend," the letter said,

"So much to tell you, so little time. Plus, writing is not something I am capable of doing for long. I'll be brief and hope itemizing things will help keep the letter short.

1. There was half a mil in the bag, give or take. The money is yours, no ifs or buts, *tovarisch* capitalist.
2. The slight snag is they don't let people flying international take more than $10,000 out of the country. For half a mil, you'd get your ass nabbed, Mark, whether it's declared or not. Confiscation till further notice wouldn't be out of the question. In our particular case, tracing the money to this afternoon's events would muddle matters further. Much as she has an axe to grind with you, Oksana brought it to my attention as they were putting bandages on my arm.
3. So, not to waste more time than you will have before your flight or expend more strength than I have left (gotta nurse that scratch, still oozing a little), what we did, we asked Samuil Yakovlevich, a pro in such matters, to run home and bring back the props. We took the liberty of creating a so-called *kukla,* the fake stacks. In other words, only the top hundred-dollar bill and the bottom hundred in each stack are real money. The rest is paper to give it bulk and the shape, so that it looked like the real thing to you (sorry). And it is best discarded on your way to the airport or, at the very latest, in the men's room. Definitely before you clear the customs. Thus, the actual content of the bag you have next to you, as you hopefully read this, is no greater than ten grand, which is exactly what you're legally allowed to take on board. The rest, roughly $490,000, will be kept with me and my aunt Oksana as collateral.
4. Now, the tricky part. The balance you will collect in the USA over some time, and the length of the period will depend on how fast you work. Here's how:

5. Once you make it back, you will be approached by Oksana's ex-husband Mike, a Chicago real estate big shot. Per Oksana's request, he will meet you at JFK.
6. Oksana and Mike, not to engage in untimely gossip yet to give you a bare-bones back story, parted ways on less than amicable terms. In brief: as a result of their messy divorce-in-progress, Oksana, while still in Chicago, developed a nervous condition that led to her dropping out of the PhD program at the Chicago Art Institute, cutting short her stay in the US and aborting her plans on writing a book-length study of the Hollywood directors born in the Russian Empire, including our old buddy Greg Davis. Mike owes her, and he knows he does—he still has some scruples left in that real estate *golova* of his. Plus, she has a child from that marriage, she came back to St. Pete pregnant, and she tries to take care of her kid. So Mike is willing to pay, settle out of court, and repay for damages incurred. In a sense, and with your indirect help, a windfall, really, Oksana has already been paid handsomely. It could have been fourteen dollars and change, or 200K in that safe, but it turned out more than twice as much. Now, it's up to you to make sure you get paid by Mike.
7. With his help, you will get in touch with Greg Davis's sister, who lives someplace in Florida, as Oksana found out. And you will have to convince her to divulge any info pertaining to her director brother. Conduct interviews, what have you. Write them down. You will get further instructions from Oksana through Mike. Challenging, huh? Fun, too! Good thing, the pay's not bad by any standards, maybe up to 3K per page, maybe more. Oksana expects around 150 pages of raw data. It's a deal you can't refuse, Mark. You need the money, which is yours, after all. Oksana needs Greg's story to finish her dissertation and write her book, which is her life's work. She'd love

to do research herself; the glitch is, thanks to Mike, she can't enter the country. The things we do in the heat of the fucking moment. He sure did. Can't get into it now. Anyway, you'll be her long-distance research assistant: you studied film, Greg Davis was also born in Ukraine, so it's all perfect. All that's required is making sure his sister talks. They say she still has glamour and poise to spare and is no recluse, though her vision is impaired.

8. Goodbye, my transatlantic lover. It's been real. Your wounded bear gives you a big, one-armed bear hug and a kiss and hopes to see you one happy day. Lots of luck to you. They say the first mil is the hardest. Well, the first half a mil should be a piece of cake.

Love, Tasha

PS. Oh, yeah. Apropos nothing. Or rather, that boat that never sailed, though you can say ours did, to be honest. I must have seen *One More Time about Love* five times, easy. Sorry for misleading you. Sometimes I do that, don't ask why. Mislead, that is. And I do know I'm a dead ringer for the young cuddly Doronina. Why do you think I went the whole nine yards on the road to punkdom at the tender age of 17? Couldn't handle living my life as a goody-two-shoes little blonde teddy bear is all . . . Have yourself a safe flight, okay, America?"

Chapter Twenty-Three.

Of course, I knew better than to spend the rest of the ride wallowing in useless reflections on how stupid and naive I was not to check beforehand the limit imposed on the dollar amount allowed to take out of the country, what with the Russian international banking in its infancy wrapped in swaddling clothes of fraud and embezzlement. Instead, I did something more practical and timely: I started skimming a hundred off the top and a hundred off the bottom of each of twenty-five stacks of cut paper, double-checking as I went along that nothing of monetary value was left in the bag. Had the rest of the padding been real, each stack would have had $10K in it, and the total value of my bag's content would have been roughly $250K, also a rough equivalent of what I thought I left under Tasha's bed though it was actually only around $5K. But then, my math was off since I left five fake stacks with Vodovozkind, totaling a thousand, though I thought I was paying him $50K. Anyhow, 490K for my research efforts that Oksana's ex was supposed to pay me gradually as I conducted my interviews was subject to fine-tuning. But I must say I felt like a rich man, though obviously prematurely so.

After dumping my bag's newsprint content in the men's room, five stacks per stall, I declared five thousand dollars, five thousand short of what I was permitted to take out of the country, cleared the customs under the unblinking gaze of the flat-faced customs officer Anna D. Snegina, and boarded the Boeing 747. Once on board, I made myself reasonably comfy in my window seat, resolving to abstain from my ritual midair intake of Jacks, all the while thinking about my poor girlfriend in that hospital bed next to the afflicted trio, then about Orlov and Petro left at the scene of the crime, wondering if I should ask Tasha to send their families some dough anonymously (and let Oksana's ex withhold an equal amount) as some very poor compensation for their demise in the line of duty. I thought I should. And I would.

Mike, a short, fidgety man sporting a Barneys beige camel coat, a paper banner in hand that said, "Hi, Mark! I'm Mike," was waving at me with the banner, a superfluous bouquet of roses in a cellophane cone pressed to his chest. I thought, briefly, that he was trying to play good cop to Oksana's foul-mouthed Aikido-practicing cop. "What's with the flowers?" I couldn't help commenting. "I'd prefer cash, you know." He took care of that, too: twenty-five thousand in a manila envelope handed over to me in his white chauffeur-driven limo on our way to the island of Manhattan was a well-timed and promising touch. "Not a bunch of *kuklas*?" I asked, just in case. "Cause I've grown accustomed to them. The entire *kuklas* clan left soaking in the Sheremetyevo latrine." I don't believe he registered my stab at humor as he returned, "The real deal, Mark. No worries." I figured the retainer (retainer number two, really) was about five percent of what I stood to collect upon my completion of the Boca Raton Assignment, and it was also about ten percent of what I hauled my ass to Russia for in the first place. Of course, I counted the money twice as we entered the Midtown tunnel that I emerged from with the rough equivalent of more than six months of programming take-home in my bulging breast pocket.

Before dropping me off at my walk-up midtown, Mike suggested we stop at Gemini's diner on Second Ave., right across from the tunnel. The place was almost empty because of the early hour, which was okay with us, given the nature of our discussion. We slid into a booth equidistant from the cashier and the kitchen. I quickly picked eggs over easy, home fries, bacon, semolina toast, and coffee, the morning fare I had desperately missed while bounty hunting in Moscow. Mike, in town for reasons more substantial than our little half-a-mil deal, said that his favorite place for breakfast or brunch was Café Carlyle on Mad Ave., but they opened much later. He also said that he would take me there for dinner when my end of the agreement was fulfilled. "I don't know if the cabaret is your bag," he added pleasantly, "but the ambiance is something else." He seemed quite a man about town—any town. "Deal," I said. "Though when all's said and done, and I get paid in full, I'll be in a position to invite you to, say, Chanterelle." It was Mike's turn to say, "Deal" and slap me on the wrist coyly. You can always engage in a bit of the restaurant name-dropping tug-of-war with a wealthy guy if you leaf through *Time Out* with any regularity. Then he started pouring his heart out to me over his spinach salad with boiled egg whites and croutons. A little too early in the day for a confession after a long flight, but he was technically my employer, so I couldn't really snarl at him, "Cut to the chase, buddy." Also, not sure if his oversharing was coming out rambling on his end or I was processing it through the haze of jetlag, but Mike's cri de coeur seemed all over the place, so much so that I wished my eggs came with the unscramble box and a pair of earplugs on the side.

"Listen. I know I wasn't much of a husband, Mark," said my new acquaintance. "But believe me, I tried to make her happy in my own way. I did. I loved her dearly, probably always will. Even when she flipped out on me and we stopped sleeping together, and it was getting to be a challenge to keep up with her mood swings. At some point, all she wanted was a child; she thought it'd help her claw her way out of depression, so I gave her the child. Not right away, though. We kept trying and trying. It just wouldn't happen. After we'd do it, she'd spend half an hour with her feet up in the air. Just picture that giraffe with her tootsies pointing skyward. Ridiculous. And sweet. But so is life. And is money not ridiculous? Yet, is it not sweet? People live for it, and people die for it. You got burnt by some crooks, you went to Moscow, you fell in love, your girl got burnt by the same crooks, literally, though, thank God, not lethally. I got burnt by love too, Mark. Who knew that depression works in insidious ways? At least, I made my fortune (and I do mean fortune; I get to New York in my private bizjet) by taking advantage of what this country has to offer. As opposed to risking my life in the Russian jungle where law and human rights, human life really, have no meaning. Never did. That wretched land of eternal serfs and murderous snitches! Stay away from it is my motto. Not shaming you, Mark. Just making an observation. We got married here, I'm a third-waver, just like you, the late '70s exodus. I was taking night drawing classes at her school in Chicago. I'm not all business all the time, you know. I fell in love with Oksana, she was in my class. Love happens. Fell for her smarts, looks, drive, her derriere.

"Loved everything about her. I like them tall, so Oksie was my type, all right. She'd bust my chops for going muff-diving on her standing up. Whatever. Things were fun, but then they stopped being fun. What else is new? And it's not just the thing I have for guys which she couldn't abide . . . I had to be in the office 24/7, build a business from scratch, worry about seed money, investors, partners, advertising. She was buried in her dissertation but also needed attention, was desperate for it, really. She needed it come midnight every goddamn night. I just couldn't keep up, I had business on my mind. She wanted it from behind five-speed bicycle style, look ma, no hands. Then she'd lick her honey off of my little dipper. Then she'd ask me to smack her some with it. Or spatula. Or both. She wanted domination, humiliation even. Could talk about the Marshall Plan for hours. Like Marshall was her personal enemy. I swear we did it three times a week, mostly on weekends. Weekdays felt empty to her. She's no nymphomaniac sex fiend, don't get me wrong. Just wanted to get her fill, she said. Like she was some rocker on tour, and I was her male groupie . . . So she started having mood swings, insisted I stop seeing men, insisted we have a child. I took her to St. Thomas, I took her to St. Lucia. I took her everywhere. Fucked her through the early months of pregnancy. She was funny about it, too. In a sick kinda way, come to think. Junior's no bigger than a can of coke, she'd say. Just be careful, don't tamper with that ring. Then, out of the blue, she'd start accusing me of God knows what. Like I wrote an anonymous letter to INS, and they put her on their blacklist. What blacklist? Or that I was interfering with her Greg Davis research, kidnapped him even to sabotage her project. That's where I had to draw the line. I didn't kidnap the man, that's fucking crazy, he vanished on his own, it was all over the goddam papers."

"Who vanished on whose own?" I said, picking up a crusty strip of bacon and dipping it in the runny yolk.

"Greg Davis left his suite at the Algonquin hotel here in town and never came back. You are to interview his sister, Rosalyn, a Boca Raton, Florida resident. They were close, but not that close, different politics, she was more of a radical, at least for a while. That's what I remember from Oksana's research. She's legally blind, too, Rosalyn is. So you have to gain her confidence . . ."

"Wait. I thought Greg Davis was dead or something?"

"Nope. A missing person don't mean a dead person."

"True. But . . . how do I do that? I mean, gain his sister's confidence?"

"Up to you. I'd start with using your head, your charm. Oksana's niece says you're not lacking in either department. I spoke to Oksana this morning. She apologizes for going mental—and physical—on your ass. Man, she was incensed about you dragging Tasha into this . . ."

"How's she now? I mean, Tasha?"

"Better. Oksana said she's home."

"Thank God! Thank God. But listen. Let's get one thing straight. I didn't drag her into anything. It was Tasha's decision. A very unfortunate one at that, and I shouldn't've let her. But she's an adult, Mike. And I'm very, very sorry she got hit. It was a light one, though. Thank God for that bullet-proof vest!"

"You can say that again. But hey, she got hurt, and judging by your shiner there, Oksana tried to teach you a lesson!?"

"You might want to examine my abdomen for a fuller picture."

"That won't be necessary. Some other time, maybe?" Mike heehawed like a moron spilling coffee on the Formica tabletop, then continued. "Anyhow. Every other day myself, and Oksana, whose sole executor's duties I take upon myself in this agreement, will expect you to fax over the single-spaced pages of a transcribed interview with Rosalyn Teal of Boca Raton, Florida. 3K per page; 15K will be wired to your account for every five-page batch. You want to get paid every week, you fax us what you get every Friday. Whatever difference between the earned amount and the real sum I owe Oksana (and now you) will be calculated in due time. It's all in the agreement." He slid a folder across the table towards me. "The thing is, Oksana can't enter the country to conduct the interview; no US visa in the cards for her. Not after she filed for divorce and . . . never mind. And even if she could, the money she would have gotten from me, which she actually already did, would have been taxed heavily on both ends. So it all worked out for her moneywise just splendissimo. Let's worry about your end of the deal. If you need to pay Rosalyn Teal a little, by all means, do. Though it's in your best interest to make sure it is not much. After all, it will have to come out of your pocket."

"Geez, Mike, aren't you all business! I don't care what you say. And I find it admirable, seriously. Business, business, business. Where did you say you got your MBA from? INS?"

"Hilarious, Mark. I thought you'd never ask," Mike, not fazed in the least, flashed his biggest smile yet and asked for a check. "University of Chicago. Top of my class, one of the top business schools in the nation."

"I just knew it." I was trying to control a tide of resentment suddenly surging inside me. "So how come you didn't find it in you to use your business acumen and interfere on Tasha's behalf when she lost everything after her husband's death?"

"Come again?" Mike straightened up in his seat, looking puzzled for the first time during our power breakfast.

"You heard me. Tasha's businessman husband Felix fell to the assassins' hit in broad daylight a few years back. And his stores, assets, and warehouses wound up in his partner's hands. While Tasha and her sick mother were left penniless. What does international law or simple human decency have to say on the subject? Plus, you were family at the time, too?"

"Not much, I'm afraid," said Mike, looking me straight in the eye. He went on weighing his every word. "And for a very simple reason: as far as I know, and I do know it beyond a reasonable doubt, for I indeed was a part of the family and technically still am because Oksana and I are not officially divorced yet. Anyhow, as far as I know, Tasha was never married. And her husband never fell victim to any gangland activity. There was never a husband, ditto shoot-outs, warehouses, and merchandise. There was always a street-smart club kid Tasha, who never showed much interest in a steady job, though taking care of her mom wasn't cheap (and that's where I came in chipping in and still am, if you must know), a smartass and a cutie but undereducated and somewhat ill-mannered. You know her better than I do. Not trying to give your sweetheart a bum rap here. One thing I do know for sure: she was never married. Not much interest in boyfriends either, for that matter. At least not since that lowlife drug dealing pal of hers OD'd on his own supply a few years back. Oksana believes she ratted him out, but I seriously doubt that. Would've been long dispatched by now. His pals had little patience with such breaches of loyalty."

Dumbfounded as I was by that last bit of news, I tried to compose myself the best I could and just asked:

"But why? I mean, why make up this elaborate noir story instead of telling me like it was?"

"I would take it up with Tasha," said Mike, getting up from our table. "Gotta bounce, buddy. Hate to be late for my next appointment. You could probably use some rest, too. What can I say? Maybe she wanted to appear more interesting? Maybe she's a pathological liar? Talk to her. Me, I've had enough of that family. Just want to keep up my end of the deal here. Valerka is almost two and daycare is expensive in St. Pete. In six months, I'll come for a visit and finalize the divorce. Meanwhile, best of luck to you. My fax's in the contract; sign it and fax it back to me, and don't forget to include your bank account. I hope this Rosalyn lady helps the research and maybe sheds some light on her brother's whereabouts. Maybe a missing person does mean a dead person."

"So my plan is," I said to Mike in the back seat of his white limo, crawling through morning traffic on our way to my place midtown. "Nurse my cheek for a day or two before I show my face to my parents. Then, get the economy ticket to Boca and find the lady. And then, if the lady talks . . ."

"She will," interrupted Mike. "People of a certain age, and Ms. Teal is ninety-two, don't have too many friends to talk to. None, give or take. She'll talk, Mark. One correction, though. Call it a suggestion: you may want to go to Boca sooner than that. Like tonight, after packing your summer things for the road. Also, let as few people in on it as possible. Your interviewee is ninety-two, and Oksana insists the project is time-sensitive for other reasons. She has a book to finish. So, I think you should see your folks after you're done with the project. Tell them you're taking a well-deserved long break. All things being equal, you will be enjoying it anyway in a month."

Part Two

THE BOCA RATON RECLUSE TALKS

Chapter Twenty-Four.

Mike was right. Mrs. Teal was willing to talk and then some. And I liked to hear what the old lady was saying. Even if I had been bored stiff with the job, even if I couldn't have cared less about the company of an immaculately coiffed old lady dressed in a timelessly elegant fashion favoring turquoise and lavender colors, I don't believe I would have been sending Oksana more than thirty-five pages a week. I wanted the job to last. Still, by the middle of December, I generated a backlog of over eighty pages of typed transcripts, money promptly wired to my account every week.

It also helped to know that Tasha would be coming to Boca on a fiancée visa for Christmas, and that shortly after, both of us would fly to New York to celebrate the completion of the BRA project and New Year, meet my parents, and just hang, check out Soho restaurants and boutiques, maybe do some theatre, maybe not. She got way psyched when I told her on the phone the night I arrived at Boca Raton airport that my immediate plans included taking care of her visa and airfare. Just like I was relieved to hear she was finally home and almost recovered. I did ask her, though, what the hell she was thinking stuffing the bag with stacks of cut paper in the hospital and writing that long letter instead of nursing her wound and why she made me haul the shitload of newsprint to the Moscow airport only to dump it in the latrine. Explaining the situation in ten words or less in the ward would have done the trick just fine. No one was in the mood to throw a tantrum over some stupid customs regulations because no one could really do anything to bend them. Tasha made light of the whole thing, cracked some jokes about all theatre all the time and props making the world go round or something like that, and said that it was actually the cloakroom Vodovozkind who wrote the letter from her dictation. Plus, spelling was not her forte anyway. On my part, I had enough tact to steer clear of any questions regarding Felix the Cat, whoever he might be to her, or why in the world she chose to check in the hospital under my ex's name. Let bygones be bygones already.

Mrs. Teal thought the idea of writing a book that would include a chapter on her missing brother timely and seemed thrilled that it would be done by a Russian scholar, whom she vaguely recollected receiving a phone call from three years ago. However, the long-distance discussion wasn't too conclusive. She also appreciated that the scholar—"Zhuravel? isn't it some kind of a winged creature in Russian?"—would publish her book-length dissertation on the Russian and Ukrainian-born American directors in the former Soviet Union, where there's supposedly more of a sense of history and tradition than in this country, she said. I thought I detected a tinge of bitterness in her voice, but didn't think contesting her observation would serve any practical purpose. She also warned me at the outset that her account might be long on biographical facts and short on Mr. Davis's moviemaking career per se because he was notoriously reluctant to talk shop with the family. "Believe me, whatever you remember, Mrs. Teal," I enthused, "would be godsent to me and my Sankt Peterburg employer."

"Well then," began Rosalyn Teal, turning her prepossessing face in stylish '60s shades towards the living room western window, "let's begin at the beginning. My brother was four years my senior, tall, handsome, well read, and lavishly gifted. And I'm not just saying this because I'm his little sister whom he was a mentor to when we were growing up. The only man I knew who seemed to have had no enemy in the world, on both sides of the Atlantic. None. Got along with everyone, or at least made an effort to. Producers, actors, agents, fans, and even Father. A trait not too common in a director. You have to know when to crack your whip, and do it often, too. Don't get me wrong, he had a backbone, to be sure, but he was always willing to hear out the other side. One thing that separated him from the lot in his profession—he was a good listener. I guess it's called fairness.

"Absolutely crazy about theatre, an actor with the Yiddish company back in the old country, then production manager. Father was against it vehemently. Greg would stay up nights, burning the midnight oil and copying out the parts for the entire troupe, which was an all-male troupe. Father would find the pages the morning after while Greg tried to catch what little sleep he could, and the old man would tear them up. Talk about unnecessary cruelty! Why not hide them for a time, give him a talking to, then give them back? Hours of hard work destroyed just to make a point! And what point was it? Wise up, theatre is not serious business. A point lost on Greg entirely.

"The next night, my brother would start from scratch, now hiding the pages under his pillow. They staged *Di Tsvey Kuni-Lemels, Uriel Da Costa,* and so on, all of which were in Yiddish. Even did the Yiddish *King Lear* and scenes from *The Thousand and One Nights*! He had a few fans, mostly lady fans and gymnasium students who could only afford gallery seats. They'd wait outside the theatre building, sometimes in cold weather, to get his autograph. A young man of twenty, a local celebrity, no less! I don't know if it ever went to his head; maybe it did a little. Sure, I looked up to him, but he made fun of me in his sly way and looked down on me and my boyfriends. Not that I had many, but the ones that I did dare bring home he considered a bunch of pathetic losers beneath my station, definitely not my equals in the smarts department.

I know it is supposed to be mostly about him, but you know how it is. We were very close, he and I. Very close.

"Greg had his quirks. Some I knew about from hearsay, others I was an accidental witness to. I thought it odd when I spotted him once in a dressing room, taking forever to put on makeup, a wig, and a dress. Like he was really enjoying it. Sure, you have to if you want to get under your character's skin, you have to know her, you have to love her. Only how far do you go? And was it Cordelia that he loved or himself as Cordelia? The old subject-object quandary: you're a college man, you know what I'm talking about.

"Once, I made the mistake of entering his dressing room without knocking. He wore a long dress, and a young gentleman, who played a page, was kneeling before him. You get the picture. He got embarrassed, then mad, quickly fixed his dress and raised his voice, 'How about knocking next time, young lady? We're rehearsing here!' Sure, Greg. Only I couldn't recall any scenes involving kneeling in the play. He just got off, as you young people might put it, on dressing in ladies' outfits, I suppose. Some do. Only, um, I don't know how far it went with him. Maybe it aroused him to the point of wanting to do it with people of his sex. Maybe it did not. He was married a few times, you know. Had two kids; one died of leukemia, Victor did. But does having kids really make a difference?

"Sometimes, he went out wearing a coat borrowed from Mother unbeknownst to her, her hat with the veil, too. Ladies' shoes he ordered from the catalog and had them delivered. Mother's shoes wouldn't fit him. I didn't know firsthand, thought it undignified to spy, let alone snitch on him. But I did find them stashed away behind the pile of boxes in his wardrobe. I believe Mother asked me to look for something or other in his room. That's how I found the shoes—three pairs of fancy shoes, suede, leather with tiny mother-of-pearl buttons and satin bows. People would recognize him in the street, veil or no veil. That didn't seem to faze him, quite the opposite. That's what made him tick, I suppose—that thin line, teetering on being exposed. In the States, he got in trouble because of his queer tendencies. I mean, he wasn't queer or anything, but you know what I mean. No charges were ever pressed, though. Especially when he got a bit of a taste of fame: mores in movies were more relaxed than elsewhere. The Hayes Code applied just to the on-screen, off-screen goings-on was a whole different ball game. Plus, he made a name for himself performing in drag on stage. The tricky part was ridding his act of any suggestion of homosexuality, making it acceptable to the audience who fell in love with the tall, leggy beauty strutting her stuff on stage and singing silly ditties packed with double-entendres. [*A chuckle.*]

"Our parents either looked the other way or never gave much credence to what the good people of our hometown whispered about. We did come from a proper family, you know. Possibly one of the best in town, not the most affluent, but distinct in many ways. Mother studied law, though she never got to practice; Father owned three bakeries, twelve employees worked for him at one point, so there was no need for extra income. But we stood apart from the rest. Plus, how many people do you know directly descended from dragonflies? Not that many, I bet. Am I right?"

"Beg your pardon?"

"Have you come across many people who descended from dragonflies? Either stateside or Europe?"

"I'm afraid I don't understand, Mrs. Teal..."

"Which part? A simple 'yes' or 'no' question, young man. Do you know the dragonfly people? Or you don't?"

At this point, I thought I'd much rather the subject of my interview was a decade or two younger, dementia being a nasty thing capable of corrupting the very act of communication. But for now, I just responded, "No, Mrs. Teal. To the best of my knowledge, none of my friends, relatives, acquaintances, or people known to me from hearsay descended directly or indirectly from dragonflies."

"I knew it! I just knew it! How could they, right? Well, our family did. Or at least that's the story Greg told me when I turned six. How did the dragonfly business come about? I knew you'd be curious. You're recording all this, right? Good. I believe it all started when I was in the first grade and before any losses in the family. Grandpas and grandmas on both sides were still alive and well and enjoying picnics in May and beaches in August. Uncle Moisey, a civil engineer, was still with us, too. So, my concern was purely theoretical. But I do recall the pangs of fear creeping into me stealthily during waking hours and keeping me up at night. I think it was the first thoughts of mortality stirring in my little chest. A certain heaviness, a premonition inside me, made itself felt for the first time. Ah, how dreadfully scary its emergence was, how disquieting, how vexing! The former serenity no longer there, the lightness of being forever gone. So I began pestering Greg (back then, he answered to Girshl, obviously) with all sorts of questions about what's going to happen when I die. 'Not much, sis,' Girshl shrugged. 'Stop fussing about it already, and stop bugging me. Do you really think much of the time before you were born? That must have been a very long stretch. A whole eternity, give or take. So there's an eternity ahead of you, too. Same thing. Don't you worry your little head over nothing.' I said, 'Well, okay, yeah, sure. But listen, now that I've been alive and actually started to get the hang of it, wouldn't it be an awful thing to stop being alive at some point, however distant, stop breathing and seeing, and moving?' Of course, I was only six then, so it didn't come out quite as articulate. But the gist of it is accurate. And then, seeing how worked up I was getting, and feeling how sweaty my little palms were (he was holding me by the hand the way he always did when he took me out for walks in Alexander's Park), and how miserable I must have looked, he up and blurted out, 'We the Kozinskys have nothing to worry about anyway, kiddo. Our family comes from dragonflies. Just think about our last name for a second (*strekozi* in Russian means *dragonflies*, does it not?). We are not like the rest of humans who come from monkeys. And if you don't know it by now, you will surely learn about it in your gymnasium in due time. Dragonflies are immortal.'

"Dragonflies are immortal! Imagine that. How did he think of such a thing? Right there on the spot, too! Talk about imagination. Talk about spontaneity. I believed him; I believed everything Greg ever said. I still do, or should I say, almost everything because he never gave me a heads-up before vanishing into the night like he did. Back then, his little lie seemed the most natural thing. Of course: Kozinsky-strekozinsky-*strekozi*-immortality. What was I thinking? Just look at them hovering around peonies and lilies, suspended in midair in the month of July, their angel-like iridescent wings emitting a barely audible hissing sound... The thin-tailed, bug-eyed messengers of immortality right outside of our dacha terrace!

"And if that wasn't proof enough, there were our parents, a couple of jittery dragonflies in their own right, hyperkinetic, irascible, busy making sure I had no care in the world, fussing about my health and my clothes, and my grades; but the world was quickly changing before our eyes. Before you could say 'land to the peasants, bread to the hungry,' it went topsy-turvy on us like a backdrop that wasn't bolted down properly to the stage floor. Only who do you ask for your money back if the real-life show flops because of poor stage management? We had to flee our sun-kissed town by the Black Sea where I was born and was attending a gymnasium for girls, the best in town or the only one in town, I can't recall, and it matters little.

"As a young girl, to digress, I used butterfly nets to a variety of ends. Mainly to catch dragonflies, naturally. I called them 'dragonplanes,' the military planes I knew about from the letters that Father's younger brother Moisey sent back home from the front. But I also pictured dragonflies as my parents, though it'd been years since I stopped believing Greg's ridiculous story. But you don't really need a story to keep the fantasy alive, do you? Images are enough. So I imagined that the dragonflies I was hunting for were, in fact, my bug-eyed, spontaneous, and benevolent Father (a kind man, despite his going medieval on Greg's theatre-loving backside) and Mother, a social butterfly—but then why not a social dragonfly?—forever worrying about my getting the flu or the mumps.

"Another fantasy my parents were trying to keep going for me for months and months had to do with Uncle Moisey still being alive while in fact he was killed in the battle north of Vilno six months after he was conscripted into the Imperial army to fight in the Great War. Actually, I think he volunteered like so many young men in town, gentiles and Jews alike. That got me really, really sad, even before the news of his death reached home. Not only did the word 'war' have a nasty ring for my ten-year-old self, but it also meant I wouldn't be getting all sorts of holiday presents from Moisey.

"Come Passover or the New Year, he'd go pagan on his little niece, bringing me beautiful animal masks made out of papier-mâché that smelled of glue and all sorts of hand puppets, even the prized porcelain wonders made by the Szrajer & Fingerhut factory he used for the puppet shows that he staged for me, his sole audience while hiding behind the two chairs standing them side by side in the living room. I was crazy about Uncle Moisey. He was twenty-five at the time, ten years my Father's junior, very handsome, sweet, and funny. And then he just went off to the war.

"At first, we'd get his letters from the Southwestern Front filled with stories that were hard to believe. At least some of them were. Like the one that I remember to this day where he barely survived the friendly fire by squatting down accidentally a split second before the cannonball behind him was fired by a Russian artillerist at the advancing German infantry. He didn't elaborate on why he had to squat. A felicitous call of nature? Or the one about trying to get drunk on cheap moonshine his buddies got from the Polish villagers during the lull in action and how they downed the glasses filled to the brim with muddy liquid, which was potent and smelled okay (they were told it was made from a mix of potato and bulrush) only to realize upon the customary after-drink belch that the substance used for brewing the potion was excrement, human or animal they couldn't tell nor did they feel like finding out for certain. Then, after a few more letters filled with funny stories that also tested our credulity, the correspondence petered out and finally stopped.

"For months and months after Armistice Day, they'd tell me that Moisey was on his way home, or detained in the hospital being treated for gangrene, or getting married someplace outside of Warsaw, etc., etc. When finally, as I was about to turn twelve, they told me that my favorite uncle had died in the battle of Vilno. I remember crying my eyes out for weeks on end, nonstop. I thought my little heart would break—nothing would console me. I couldn't bring myself to go to school or eat. I turned into a walking skeleton. Uncle Moisey's death hit me very hard. Then it dawned on me that it's not your own death that is the most terrible thing that can happen to you, but the death of your loved one—no easy way of handling it for the survivor. Greg was crushed, too, of course, but being almost seventeen then, I think he was better equipped to carry that burden.

"Anyway, school friends kept calling me the dragonfly girl way past when I came to my senses and dropped the entire *strekozi* business. Just like Father once said: 'Stop it, Rosie, you don't want to become a laughingstock of the entire school.' So I did . . . I wasn't the most capable of students, merely a good one, better than average, which was good enough for Mother and Father. Too many distractions, not necessarily boys—we were too young for boys. Boys came later, though not much later and not for long. We were getting ready to leave, you see. Packing for a long journey to a new land and coming of age ran neck and neck. Necking with schoolboys on half-packed chests. How do you pack for a one-way trip? First, I packed my precious collection: three albums filled with dried-out dragonflies, some crumbling, most with neatly handwritten labels in blue ink underneath the exhibits, the Latin name, date and year captured, etc. Some kids were into stamp collecting; the pursuit was supposed to expand one's knowledge of geography and history. My stamps were dragonflies. Don't laugh. Hunting them didn't necessarily expand anything. I wouldn't know how to begin studying my humming stamps with long, quivering tails and iridescent wings. Marveling at them is what I did. Stamps traveling from flower to flower, no envelopes or letters needed. Stamps that actually were letters with return addresses ever-changing and, therefore, unnecessary.

"My first watercolors had dragonflies and flowers, too, so entwined that it was hard to tell them apart. I liked the smell of watercolors, liked diluting and mixing them, then applying paint to paper ever so delicately with fine brush tips, stroke by glistening stroke. Even the way the paint spread out inside the jar filled with water, I liked to watch those ever-changing clouds of color, too. Cloudy green with a chance of occasional blue showers with daubs of yellow thunderstorms. Matter of fact, I still do. I picked up painting again; retirement is not without its privileges; widowhood, pardon my bluntness, can be a blessing in disguise, too. Of course, I had to stop when my eyesight deteriorated. Though I must say the stuff I did see in galleries in the '60s and the '70s, boy, someone had to be blind to get away with it. The critics, or viewers, maybe the artists too. It's been eight years since my husband passed on, forever since Greg disappeared; children visit twice a year, not nearly enough. I'll show you my artwork later if you want."

"Fascinating, Mrs. Teal. It truly is. I mean your childhood memories, your hobbies, the whole *strekozi* business . . . And it sounds like Mr. Davis had imagination to spare even in the early years. Speaking of, I wonder what Mr. Davis's friends and lovers were like back then? I mean, before your family fled the Russian Empire. He must've had a few," I ventured, though it was my philosophy to interrupt my interviewee as rarely as possible.

"In due time, young man. All in due time. I'm just warming up here. Patience is a virtue, as the ancients used to say," chuckled Mrs. Teal. Then she took a long sip of the can of Diet Sprite that was sitting on the small coffee table next to her armchair and continued.

Chapter Twenty-Five.

"I can still see before me the faces of my teachers like it was the day before yesterday. Memory has a knack for paring down life's events, turning them into sketches, reducing the people you used to know to caricatures. A gesture, a quirk, pants too short, a loose collar revealing a bobbing Adam's apple . . . What's stayed with me through the years are some grotesqueries; life's complexities are better suited for Rembrandts proficient in oil or Titians well versed in chiaroscuro. A tobacco-chewing algebra teacher who'd spit out light-brown gobs of tobacco with such precision they'd hit a spittoon ten feet away without fail. We called him The Spitter. More of a garbage pail than a spittoon. He would have never hit a spittoon from that distance, come to think. Or a Russian literature teacher, freckled, pale-skinned, and red-haired, who'd get visibly irate upon the slightest provocation, but in a very peculiar fashion. You'd see him turn red from the neck up, gradually, chameleon-like, only the hues of the environment had nothing to do with the transformation. Rather, the loud yelps of pranksters among us did. One of my girlfriends had a huge crush on him. She married an albino civil engineer eventually. Must have been a fixation with her. Gave birth to an albino baby, too. The boy grew up to denounce his parents, was decorated with a medal of some sort, and then disappeared into the labor camps himself. Such stories of savageries from the workers' paradise sure took a bit of wind out of the Upper West Side Trotskyites' sails floating around me aplenty back in the '30s, though not enough wind and not right away. Funny how slices of life, your life, wind up forming a palimpsest so layered that it's a challenge to keep those early memories apart, especially my life in the prewar decade in the US when I got married to an art dealer and eventually started practicing law and hung out with all the intellectual types in the Village. Was it that sensitive, curly haired Greek sculptor I had a brief fling with? Or the algebra spitter? Or his spitting image that I defended in that big fraud case that established my reputation as one of New York's top ten defense attorneys? Can't be the same person—a double, maybe?

"Greg did have a few friends back in those days, as well as fans. I don't recall having that many. As I said, our parents were well-off, and that put up an invisible wall between me and the rest of the class. Class was an issue back then. It always has been and always will be. And I don't just mean the 'blooming bracket,' as Greg's pal George Cukor would put it. I mean the lifestyle, values, and habits. You know as much as I do about it. I never did live in the victorious workers' and peasants' paradise like you did. I mean, the effort to build a classless society, the price you pay for it: repressions, bloodshed, more injustice. That's how revolutions start. Someone gets unhappy over time, the agitators seize the moment, the agitators start agitating, and the words 'I'm a professional revolutionary' are bandied about indiscriminately. Isn't it a lot like confessing to being a career criminal with a license to kill? Enough is enough, we'll show them who inherits the world and on whose terms. Before you know it, your estate is burning and you are heading for the hills. Does 'classless' always mean annihilating all classes except one, which becomes the ruling class? As a one-time reluctant New York Trotskyite, no more than a fellow traveler really, I had enough wits about me to say goodbye to such malarkey early on. Flirting with trendy ideas was something Greg could never relate to. I know this should be more about him, but we were very close before he went off to Hollywood, close in a mentor-pupil kind of way, so when I talk about myself, I'm really talking about him, in a sense. He always looked down on my hanging out with the Upper West Side sympathizer types. He even stopped talking to me for a year! But then, walking contradiction that he was, he dated my best friend Rita, a bona fide Marxist and anarchist to boot. Like many New York bohemians of the day, she claimed to be one without even bothering to read Marx or Bakunin. Poor Rita: got kicked out of the country for her views and her deeds, eventually . . .

"My closest two girlfriends in the old country got upset when they heard I was getting ready to leave. They got mad at me, truth be told. We'd spend an awful lot of time together and knew each other's secrets and secret crushes. We'd draw the curtains and light the candles in my parents' living room. And we'd whisper, though we didn't have to, my parents away in Saint Petersburg or maybe Yalta, my poor deaf nanny Nadezhda Petrovna fast asleep in her little room.

"It was kind of a game we played. Whispering, of course, implies secrecy, though nothing we did or said was shameful or illicit. I mean, sometimes we tried to evoke the spirits of the dead—not a federal offense, as far as I know. Think Orpheus. Think Aeneas and his golden bough. Think Greg or the entire moviemaking business, for that matter: live images of long-gone actors and actresses flickering on the screen, moving us, the living, to tears or laughter. Heaven on earth for the emotionally needy. Nothing much came out of our early efforts, though. The dead chose to play dumb.

"One of the first ones that we tried to commune with was Pushkin, who had had an affair with my friend Zinaida's great-great-great grand aunt, also named Zinaida, during the poet's year-long exile in Odessa. My friend's great-great-great grand aunt was the daughter of a Belgian-born city prosecutor and archeologist, the first to study the northern shore of the Black Sea in earnest, the gentleman who was also credited with founding the city's historical museum. And so, his descendant Zinochka Blaramberg would surreptitiously bring Pushkin's letters addressed to her great-great-great grand aunt to our séances and even read parts from them to entice the poet to leave the valley of the shadows and honor us with his incorporeal visit; but it helped little. All I remember is the not-too-subtle rhyme Zina/Mnemosyna, for parts of the letters were penned in verse. But then they were private love letters, so even if I did remember more, it wouldn't be too kosher to quote from them extensively, would it? Perhaps it is for the same reason that I'm not going to dwell too much on Greg's personal life, young man. Sorry to disappoint you or your esteemed researcher boss from Petersburg. Greg was a private man, never too keen on the whole glossies culture or mindset, so he would not have approved. Anyhow, we made sure that the letters, which we knew were priceless, were handled with utmost care. But Pushkin's ghost was most likely otherwise engaged at the time. Or maybe we were too young to stir the interest of the great poet's shadow or lacked the requisite mesmeric skills to invoke his spirit. My first American boyfriend rekindled my interest in spiritism. But, of course, that happened later. Do remind me to tell you about it. Greg never got involved in our New York séances, though. He was probably too busy honing his vaudevillian/stand-up comedian skills. There's more than one way to make fools part with their money." [*A hearty laugh.*]

Chapter Twenty-Six.

"It goes without saying that we lost everything in the revolution. Actually, we lost all our possessions before the revolution came to our hometown: the house, Father's bakeries, bank accounts. Took us all of two weeks to pack up and get the hell out. Because when you stand to lose everything, there's a good chance that next on the scales will be your life and your children's lives. And then you do all it takes to protect them, and you do it without delay.

"Though I had a few Jewish friends, most were non-Jewish. Not sure why, but I felt more comfortable around them. They seemed more easy-going, direct. Straight shooters? Not sure how to explain it. I remember strolling down the boulevard with Zinochka Blaramberg, the beautiful willowy blonde of Flemish extraction, and Nadia Sveshnik at the beginning of winter recess, my last winter in my hometown. Light snow was falling from the starless skies, forming haloes around gaslights glimmering in the mist. The Pushkin monument not twenty feet away, his dark face light with snow like a death mask. Like he'd only just been killed in that duel. We liked Pushkin, deified him even though he never seemed too removed from our time. His poetry, his persona, his circle of friends, and his influence were all too tangible.

"Our bonnets were white, too. So were our mittens and the collars of our coats. Yellow-white because of the street lamps. It felt like we were three sisters in a fairy tale and something magical was about to happen at any moment. Skating rink in the park next to the Opera house. Streets deserted. A lonely Belgian streetcar ringing its bell in the distance. Light snow falling on the ground. So much fun tossing wet snowballs at one another. They already knew I was leaving, so it was fun tinged with melancholy, fun to keep the sadness at bay. We tried to spend as much time together as we could. So we went back to my parents' place, drew the curtains, and lit the candles in the living room. And we whispered, trying to commune with the spirit of Pushkin: 'Oh, the father of Russian poetry, give us a sign, any sign!' [*A nervous chuckle.*] All of a sudden, a knock on the door. 'Come in,' said Zina, her voice trembling with anticipation. 'Reveal yourself, immortal genius of Russian poetry . . .' A silhouette in a top hat, a walking stick pressed to his chest, appeared in the doorway. The collar of his coat concealed the lower part of his face as he moved closer to our table and started to recite a poem, Pushkin's poem, though with a bit of a Yiddish accent, rolling his 'r's etc. 'The wondas moment of ouhr meeting . . . Still, I gemembah you appeah . . .' 'Girshl, you bastard!' I shrieked with delight, literally falling off the chair, laughing my head off, and rolling on the carpet like I was having a seizure. I knew it was my brother as soon as I saw his frame in the doorway. More precisely, I knew it was not Pushkin, who, as is well known, was rather diminutive, while Girshl stood six foot two without shoes or heels. We all burst into laughter like raving lunatics and woke up our parents; it was spooky and ridiculous, such theatrics on a cold night in January. Girshl, always a gentleman, saw Zina and Nadia home a little later."

And then Rosalyn doubled up laughing and slapped her knee with her large hand, knocking the Diet Sprite off the table but catching it midair in the nick of time, which was a little unsettling to observe. At least, I never saw her get this animated before. It seemed that whatever made her laugh so hysterically was a recollection she failed to verbalize, but it tickled her funny bone beyond measure. And I knew better than to ask her point-blank, "What's so funny, dear Rosalyn?"

Did it have anything to do with her brother dressed as Pushkin and her two girlfriends flanking him during the midnight walk in the falling snow down Pushkinksaya Street, where the real poet resided almost a century before the faux séance? And then, after a hearty laugh, unless it was uncontrollable sobbing, for I saw tears appear from under her shades, which she wiped with tissue paper quickly extracted from a box next to her, Rosalyn surprised me a bit more when she asked to reiterate what it was that I was doing in her living room and why I had a Russian accent, and why she was sharing her life story with me, and why I was taping it. "I may be blind, you know, but I'm not stupid, Nicholas," she added firmly.

"The name's Mark," I replied ever so tactfully. "I came to the USA from the USSR in the late '70s, Mrs. Teal. Hence the accent, though I do hope the grammar's not too shabby. I'm a research assistant for a Russian-based film scholar who is finishing her dissertation, later to be reworked into a book, which will include a long chapter on your brother Gregory. With your kind permission, and as stipulated in the agreement signed by you in the presence of your attorney, I'm taping and transcribing your story—and, inevitably, the story of Mr. Davis. We have also agreed on a fixed weekly amount for you to be reimbursed for your time and effort, Mrs. Teal. And something I would like to get to at some point is the reason or reasons why Mr. Gregory Davis stopped making movies in the late '40s, why he did it so abruptly and at the peak of his career, by then nothing if not illustrious."

She took it all in with utmost attention, nodded a few times, then inquired sternly, "Ever heard of McCarthyism, young man?"

"Sure have, Mrs. Teal. And if you recall, at the beginning of our sessions, I asked you if Mr. Davis was ever blacklisted or called to testify, and you answered in the negative."

"I do. And the answer is still no, he was not."

"So what's the connection, then? The last Davis production, *A Noose Too Loose* was released in 1948, two years before the second Red Scare started in 1950 . . . What gives?"

"Will you please let me go on with my story like I know it and like it happened, and stop interrupting me every five minutes, Mark? Something to be said about chronology, you know . . . Or good manners, for that matter. Plus, you got your Greg Davis filmography all wrong!"

At this point, I thought it best to apologize and promise to hold my tongue and let her tell her story, making a mental note to be as accommodating as possible, even in the face of occasional incongruities, whereupon she continued.

Chapter Twenty-Seven.

"The dark-eyed gentleman in uniform who shared our compartment, I believe we were on the train to Romania unless it was already after we crossed the Belgian border, was running a mild fever, and Greg, who tried to befriend him, offered him a cigarette. Greg preferred to roll his own, and they stepped out for a smoke, though Mother being Mother said, 'Maybe you shouldn't, young man, you seem under the weather.' But the soldier said it mattered little to him. In fact, tobacco was known for its medicinal power, at least in some instances, and you didn't have to be a Cherokee to subscribe to that theory. And if that doesn't work, he said, he had a much stronger medicine in his bag, a panacea, if you will. I didn't know what 'panacea' meant. I thought it was some kind of alcoholic beverage. There was a ring on his little finger, too. 'The guy's a mason,' Greg whispered into my ear. 'Get a load of his signet ring.' I nodded, pretending I knew what that was. A mason? I think there was a compass engraved on his ring, maybe a sphinx's head, maybe not, some writing in Latin, too. Things that stay with you.

"At first, the lieutenant was not too talkative. Was he being shy, or did the slight yet pronounced lisp impede his speech to the point of making him reticent? I don't know, and I don't remember much from that encounter other than how it ended. Dramatic doesn't begin to describe it. Our first encounter outside the Russian Empire—too outrageous for words. When Mother whispered, 'Rosie, offer the man some knishes and a piece of apple strudel,' I did just that, and he opened up a bit. Actually, he began by asking questions himself, mostly addressing Grandpa, who had a knack for instilling confidence in strangers and friends alike. Was it his white beard of a sage, his whooping cough that almost got him in trouble on Ellis Island, or his frequent and seemingly random quotes from the Torah, but he certainly commanded respect without even trying. Never one to talk to strangers himself, often coming across as reserved and not entirely friendly, Grandpa was not the chatty type. The nickname he went by in our family was Chatterbox Ben, though his real name was Ben-Zion.

"I recall the bedtime stories he liked to tell Girshl and me when we were little, and no matter how they ended, his tales always involved a train or a train station. [*A short laugh.*] Do you want to know why? The village he came from had recently added a new feature: a train station where trains were scheduled to stop twice a week. That new development certainly put Khristinovka on the map and gave its inhabitants a sense of purpose and brought work. Sort of like the invention of the movies provided jobs for thousands and a pastime for millions. Only Chatterbox Ben was a storytelling engine all by himself.

"Anyhow, the train (and the station) became the kernel of the stories Chatterbox Ben improvised so readily and inventively. I wonder if it might also account for trains being a prominent feature in several of Greg's pictures, almost to the exclusion of other locations in two of them. I'm referring to, firstly, *A Train to Reno* and *Voyagers in the Night*. Be that as it may, making up stories for our fellow passenger as he went along was a cinch for Grandpa. Like telling the lieutenant tall tales about our final destination being Brazil. Etc. 'You kidding me, right? Why Brazil, what's in Brazil? You have people in Brazil?' asked, er, . . . I can't think of his name right now, but it didn't seem that the lieutenant bought the Grandpa's Brazil story. 'Yes, distant relatives. Plus, the climate, business prospects, and a sizable Jewish community. One has to rely on his own kind, at least initially. What about you?' 'I'm being extradited,' the lieutenant said matter-of-factly. 'So my journey is very much one-way, too.' 'What happened?' Grandpa said. 'I hope I'm not meddling in someone else's affairs?' 'I feel peculiar talking about it,' the man said, shrugging. 'But since we don't stand a chance of ever seeing each other again, why the hell not? Strangers on a train often do. I mean, share stories. The main reason is I was part of the group that assassinated the tsar and his family.'

"A pregnant silence fell upon the entire compartment. Greg and I did a double take. It even felt for a moment like the train came to a stop. But it did not. Something inside of me did. 'Not directly, never pulled the trigger,' he continued. 'But I was a part of Nicholas II's escort. Tasked with making sure he and his kin got to Yekaterinburg safely. His retinue, too. So after everything was over, and the royal blood spilled in the Ipatyev house basement, I was given two choices: leave the country tout de suite or be executed on the spot. A tall order that. Nobody wanted any witnesses around, though.'

"Then the lieutenant started insisting, in a loud whisper, that Lenin was actually a German spy—the lieutenant personally had never had any doubts about that. So the lieutenant was, in fact, an indirect victim of greater circumstances. 'Aren't we all?' chimed in Father, who was rolling his eyes behind the stranger's back and making circles around his temple with his forefinger, indicating to Mother that he thought the soldier had a few screws loose. 'Oh yes, though some to a much greater degree than the rest,' the lieutenant rattled on. 'But now that the toppling of the Provisional Government by the Germans was a fait accompli because losing the war was a tough pill to swallow, and that coup was nothing if not Germany's way of getting back at Russia (and Europe), doesn't it change your way of thinking? Knowing it normally takes two to tango or scream 'bloody murder,' whichever the case may be. I mean, one does the screaming, the Menshevik gets his throat slit. Not to mention that reparations are a pittance when your newly expanded territory encompasses a huge empire rich in resources that spans half of Europe and two-thirds of Asia. Now that the Hapsburgs and the Ottomans are not on the map anymore. The crescent for the full moon! You call it fair? And I saw what happened to the Romanoffs with my own eyes!' Anyhow, as he was trying to put across, though not without difficulty, he was not a part of the firing squad. He was guarding the tsar and his family, that's all he did. Also, assisting Botkin who was the royal family doctor. He was never put on trial or attempted to be gotten rid of, Lenin's orders or no Lenin's orders. The victims . . . the bloody deed. In the basement. Blood streaming. Bullets bouncing off the princesses who had diamonds sewn in their clothing . . . He saw the whole thing, damn his eyes! So whether he was exaggerating the role of Germany in the revolution or not, he continued, Germany was affected by the diminished stature of Russia because of the war, and the revolution and the turmoil of the civil war . . . He sounded feverish and was barely coherent, sweating bullets and breathing heavily.

"Oh yes. I think I failed to mention, though it is important, if not critical, that I recall noticing a beautiful young lady who saw the lieutenant off at the station, her long dress with frills, her manservant in a silly hat with short flaps that belonged to the nineteenth century, certainly not to Europe ravaged by the Great War. Such refined features, such delicate manners, and poise she had! She also carried a patent leather *sac de voyage* in her gloved hands, which she passed over to her lieutenant friend almost as an afterthought but with the utmost care. As if she wasn't convinced that she wanted to part with it until the train started making loud hissing noises, ready to leave the station. Then they kissed goodbye, the lieutenant and his lady friend, perhaps longer than was common in public then. The time was November 1918, the station Lemberg.

"It transpired later—don't ask me when—that our fellow passenger had spent time in Switzerland before the Bolsheviks seized power and that he was directly involved in the publication and distribution of a socialist-revolutionary newspaper. Maybe even ran a press—you know how radicalized Zurich was at the turn of the century. Then, a complete turnaround in his worldview followed after months and months of perusing 'revolutionary literature' in the university library. So he actually was a Menshevik of some prominence who, at some point, became a Bolshevik, a change that his former associates still bore a grudge against him for. Therefore, he was facing double jeopardy: on the run from the two opposing factions. So much so that his lady friend from Lemberg, who, according to him, was none other than a great-great-grand niece of Balzac's wife Evelina Hanska by her first marriage (as I found out later), was vehemently opposed to his meddling in politics, and once or twice put it to him bluntly (he told us): 'Either you want to spend the rest of your life with me or in jail—a simple choice. But you just can't have it both ways. I'm not taking a vow to wait for you should you wind up in the stir. A Decembrist's wife, I'm not. Because whomsoever prevails, whomsoever seizes power and holds onto it, your flipping sides will be used against you as sure as night follows day. You want to be swallowed and digested by the revolution, be my guest.' So he was leaving Russia in the hope of uniting with her at some opportune moment in Belgium, where he was extradited.

"It was at this point that Greg, mild-mannered man that he was, up and crossed the t's and dotted the i's. 'Though we are headed in the same direction, at least for now, and you seem a reasonably intelligent fellow, not to mention you're under the weather, and it looks like you have a bad knee'—he did—'and probably should be left alone it is fair to suppose that you were among those directly or indirectly involved in bringing about the changes that made our life in the land of our birth not only difficult but actually impossible. Thank you so much for that! Running away from the tides of persecution and destruction is what my people historically thrive on, as is well known! Thank you for perpetuating that cycle, dunderhead!' And with that, he spits in the gent's eyes, thickly and forcefully, whereupon this Yuriy, his name just came to me, he introduced himself to us at the beginning of our journey as Yuriy Borisovich, this Yuriy slaps Greg in the face, hard. I got so scared, I almost peed myself, seeing the two men have a go at each other, one being my tender-hearted and fragile brother, the other a soldier who could have been armed for all I knew and who was big enough to strangle Greg with his bare hands. This Yuriy could have.

"The fight that ensued was quickly quenched by Father and Chatterbox Ben. So the two men figured they'd take it outside. Actually, my Greg dragged out the limping lieutenant bodily. A quarter an hour later, Greg returned with a black eye and fat lip. Yuriy didn't return at all. Greg told us that Yuriy went looking for another compartment, but what Greg actually did was push him off the speeding train in the middle of the night! Can you believe it? Is this how you start your journey to a new land? You bump someone off? I was scared senseless. Nothing left of our fellow traveler but his coat, cap, and patent leather *sac du voyage*. Greg said he'd come to pick up his things, but, naturally, he never did. Much to everyone's surprise, it wasn't a murder. Yuriy, a survivor to end all survivors, lived. Some people!"

Chapter Twenty-Eight.

"Like I said, Greg was never overly impressed with my so-called boyfriends back home. I say 'so-called' because none of them were anything other than platonic infatuations, even those from good families he considered not worth my while. Things got worse in New York when I started going out a bit. Neither Greg nor I ever went to a synagogue (that's where young men met young ladies back in the day), except early on, for high holidays, when I was in my mid-teens. Never really bought into the whole institutionalized religion charade, much to Chatterbox Ben's dismay. No dances either, since I thought dances were silly; too much fancy footwork, literally, to get to the point. There had to be a better way, a shortcut. Plus, who had the time for dances when I had to make a living, working ten to twelve hours a day?

"I must have gone through five jobs in New York in the first few years. Not that I couldn't keep a job or was too picky. I was a seamstress in a clothing factory where they made children's dresses and coats. It wasn't too bad, except our foreman was a brute and a total idiot, so I lasted no more than three months. As a post office clerk during the onset of the Red Scare, the first one, what with the packages blowing up all over town, I was breaking into a cold sweat every time I had to deliver them. That was right after the big explosion on Wall Street. Everyone was scared out of their wits, anticipating a new terrorist attack any day.

"Once, I was supposed to deliver a small package someplace across town. It was a part of my job—a foot messenger and a post office clerk rolled into one. Though I believe they were supposed to have two employees fill these separate positions. I don't think labor unions were really doing their job at the time. So whether it was the post office or any old office, they'd try to cut corners, and as a result, you'd get a lousy performance. Anyhow, I got on a streetcar, and I had to get off Bleecker, and I thought I'd quickly go through the contents of the package while I was in the car. I knew it was against the rules; I'd had to sign above the dotted line when I got hired. I just didn't want to blow up the entire car and the two horses who dragged it down Bleecker. Then I thought: What if the bomb goes off while I look for it? So I chucked the entire package out the streetcar window and onto a deserted block, got out of the car, and instead dropped in on my friend Rita, who modeled at an art school nearby, then reported to work an hour later. [*Giggles girlishly.*] Sure enough, the addressee lodged a complaint. So did the sender. I had a bit of explaining to do in my supervisor's office. Didn't help any. I got fired. Well, at least I stopped having nightmares about getting blown to smithereens.

"There must have been a few other jobs, but the one I recall most vividly was modeling. Art schools were among the few places young people could congregate and socialize. Like I said, my friend Rita modeled at one in the Village. She was a socialist and a tough cookie with a slight overbite. Very cute. A libertine, too. Lost her cousin in the Triangle factory disaster. That's all she ever talked about—greedy bastards, subhuman conditions, my poor, poor Sofochka. That and the big Armory Art Show she went to as a kid. The one trashed by Teddy Roosevelt. Before your time. Before my time, too. Politics tried to handle art with a velvet glove. Got a bit less velvety during WWII when Greg was offered a few battleships for free in exchange for the Pentagon reading and approving the script for an antiwar picture he was in preproduction for. He made the movie all right, though he had to make do with boat scale models. A matter of integrity for him. Don't mess with the artistic process. Rita, by then long out of Greg's life and out of the country, had come to New York before WWI from Kishinev. Sometimes, she'd let me sit in on the classes and do sketches. Sometimes, I'd substitute for her when she was sick or otherwise indisposed. Can't think of an easier way to pick up a few extra bucks. Just strip and don't stir, and try not to freeze your patooties in a draughty studio in wintertime.

"At first, I felt awkward posing in the buff, but then I got used to it. I just tried to imagine what it would be like to have a steady boyfriend like Rita did. Matt, her Italian American bartender beau who saved up and eventually opened his own bar, wasn't in on how she made a living. They looked alike, Matt and Rita: lean and raven-haired, both liked to have a few beers after work when it was still allowed. Greg, whom she left Matt for, knew about her modeling. She told him because she knew it'd be okay with him, the bohemian at heart that he was. She took a fancy to Greg right off the bat: handsome, talented, ambitious, and no stranger to dubious activities. I believe he got involved with some bootleggers for a while, too; there was no other way to raise the money for a small production he was trying to mount at the Progressive Yiddish theatre on Second Avenue. When Rita found out the play would have a socialist bent to it, I think it was loosely based on *Macbeth*, Lady Macbeth symbolizing US postwar imperialist ambitions (can you believe this crap? I can't), she begged me to introduce her to Greg, then begged him to let her be in the play. She said she'd be happy with the smallest part, a tree in the Birnam wood, anything, and she promised to help raise the funds. I think it was she who put my brother in touch with bootleggers. Cost him his freedom, almost: he was let go on bail, but at the end of the day, he had the money for the play, got himself a hot daredevil girlfriend, and got radicalized more than he ever had been, though not for long. And last but not least, he got a few favorable reviews in the Yiddish press. I think that was the last time when he actually paid attention to reviews.

"While Rita was helping Greg with the production, I took over her modeling job entirely. Though initially shy about getting undressed in front of people, I found a way to overcome that hurdle: I'd imagine every art student in front of me and back of me buck naked, just like me. So, in my mind, we were all on equal footing. Because stripping makes you feel inferior to the fully dressed person next to you, right? And, of course, I couldn't resist signing up for a few studio classes, though I couldn't afford the drawing paper, even the cheapest kind. So I drew on the wrapping paper that Father used for his pushcart goods. Or wait. I think he opened his first dry goods store by then. The pushcart was just the first year or two: too small for my entrepreneurial dad, who liked to think big. You can't hold the good man down. However, holding down is what my good old man did to Mother. Did I tell you she was among the first women to study law in our hometown? Or I think she was. My memory is not what it used to be. Anyhow, that was a big deal for a woman back then. Though she never practiced law either there or in the US. Father wouldn't let her. [*Sighs.*] What is it about the men in our family looking down on our choices, professional or personal? Too late to ask anyone: Father died before WWII and Greg has been missing for God knows how long. Mother died in the Depression; taking to the bottle at the height of Prohibition was both illegal and costly and not too healthy for a woman over fifty. Not too Hebraic either. I don't think she was ready for the New World, or the New World didn't prove to be too hospitable to her. A double-edged sword this thing is and has always been. Anyhow, *omnia mea mecum* portables, that's what Chatterbox Ben called Father's little store on wheels. Worked his ass off, sometimes fifteen hours a day, poor bastard. Not sure why I talk about Father so flippantly.

Maybe because he was against Greg pursuing his artistic ambitions? Or me pursuing boys? I had to twist his arm when the time came to apply to law school, too.

"Back to modeling. Rita, who came from Kansas, I mean Kishinev, as a nine-year-old, posed semi-nude, sometimes entirely in the buff. She intimated once that her biggest concern was not breaking wind in front of the art students but showing her Kotex pad. You know, 'If it's good for our soldiers, it is good for us' good old days of feminine hygiene? I mean, the surplus pads shipped to our boys in the trenches were used by female consumers back home after Armistice Day. Came in handy. My modeling career was short-lived, though. Not sure exactly how, but Chatterbox Ben got wind of what I did in art school when I wasn't drawing. Maybe through Greg, who learned it from Rita? Such a gossip that girl was! Grandpa said that if I didn't stop right then and there, he'd tell my parents, which would be the end of my art and possibly the end of me, too.

"I don't know why Greg broke up with Rita, who adored and worshipped him initially, but then started noticing tiny or not-so-tiny fault lines in his personality. Then they both realized they mixed about as well as oil and water. She was just too radical in her politics, too experimental in her artistic preferences and lifestyle, too knowing and embittered for her age. He was too tame by her lights, too mainstream, and she found his ambitions to succeed risible and later detestable. Though at first, that's what drew Rita to Greg, opposites attract, there's much truth in that. When he realized she was doing drugs, which were, in effect, responsible for her mood swings, it was too late. He was head over heels in love with her; he was beginning to enjoy a modicum of renown from directing his plays (he did three by the mid-'20s) and was already working on a motion picture as assistant director. Things were looking up for him, yet Rita and her antics seemed to be dragging him down. I'm no Miss Prim either, call me a stepchild of the Roaring Twenties: I came to know excess firsthand when I got a little older too, but I have to thank Greg's lucky stars that he could stay the straight and narrow. Bootlegger nonsense was just a fluke (many people I knew did just that, but none of them exactly fit the description of a gangster), and it was minor compared to the rift between Rita getting heavy with drugs and Greg keeping his nose clean. Not easy being with someone who drinks and snorts and comes up with all sorts of cockamamy ideas, like kidnapping an actor with the Stanislavsky troupe on tour in the US. Please remind me to tell you about it. That story alone requires a separate session. I'm so glad we are doing it daily now. Though I'm not even halfway through. But then, if you wanted shorthand, you'd pick up Greg's biography or his filmography. For context, there's nothing like eyewitnesses. Even the one that is blind as a bat is worth her weight in gold."

Chapter Twenty-Nine.

"My first serious boyfriend was a Chinese American art instructor who was in the war, that's the Great War, of course. An invalid with a missing arm, a dry sense of humor, and some uncanny, if sputtering, powers of hypnosis. Not sure why—and neither was he—they worked selectively and intermittently. Ah, the mysteries of the Orient! [*Guffaws.*] Sure managed to hypnotize this fetching young thing into falling head over heels for him . . .

"You could see many people beset with deformities in the streets of New York back in those days: some missing an arm, others on crutches. He was one of the very few people of his ethnicity to fight in the war on the American side. Made sense proportionately. Not too many Asians were admitted into the country when his parents made it here after the Boxer Uprising. I believe his parents were Christian. But no matter what your religion, the quotas based on pseudoscientific or plain rigged studies that proved the inferiority of Southern Europeans and Asians were strict. Just tell me if racism is not an inherently embedded part of our national psyche. The melting pot, as the newspapers eventually called it, was always boiling erratically and unevenly. John didn't technically fight in the war; he was drafted as a photographer. But then, mustard gas or airstrikes didn't care if you were there to document the battle or take part in it directly. The shrapnel hit his left arm, and his bone splintered into pieces. Spent two months convalescing in a Belgian hospital before they shipped him back home. He showed me the photographs he had taken there. Not for the faint of heart. People with missing noses, poorly matched prosthetic ears, and foreheads badly mangled. Not just the hospital photographs. He was wounded three weeks into his duty. So, there had been plenty of maiming and death around him even before he got hit. Goddamn war. I hate it with a passion as anyone in his right mind ought to. As Greg did, too, making his anti-Nazi movies before and during the Second War. Maybe it was his way of getting back at militarism for Uncle Moisey's death in the Great War. Maybe he was inspired to say his say out of patriotic feelings for his new country. Who can fathom the depths creativity springs from?

"He did three war pictures back-to-back. Selznik was particularly happy with Greg's *Keep 'Em Running*, an antiwar comedy that made both a bundle. Of course, you don't show the horrors of war when you make a product for a mass audience; you want to gloss things over and make it palatable. Something John wasn't concerned with documenting the wounded and the dead in WWI. I'm not sure what publication or government agency sent him to the front. Certainly have no clue why he thought it expedient to show me the pictures. Was he subjecting me to a test of sorts? See if I could be a convincing Jewish Desdemona to his Chinese American Othello? 'She loved me for the dangers I had passed, / And I loved her that she did pity them' bit?

"I remember John and me sitting on the bench next to Cleopatra's needle in Central Park on a sunny afternoon in May when he made me look at the pictures he kept in the leather-bound album. I can still see them in my mind's eye. What Cubism? A bullet can transform a hapless model's face more drastically than all the Picassos and Braques rolled into one. I was twelve years his junior, naive in most aspects of life; why put me to such a test? Cruelty takes so many forms. To see if I could empathize with what he'd been through? Even missing an arm, he was able to teach art and practice his craft as a photographer with uncommon dexterity, though developing pictures required two hands, and that's where I came in. An odd choice for a first boyfriend, you might think; also, an odd pursuit for a cripple. Of course, you don't bandy that word around much these days. I may be old school, but I'm not an old fogey. You say 'asymmetrically endowed' or some such nonsense. As a former lawyer, I'm well versed in ways to present the truth, make it easier to swallow, play with perspective and foreshadowing. So did John Wong, a first-generation American, whom I kept a secret from my family for months. Until he just showed up at our place on Rivington for Pesach, and nobody said anything. Because nobody noticed anything. Not that he was Oriental. That alone would have caused a few heart failures at the table during the Kiddush. Not that he was much older and missing an arm. They thought he was a Jewish kid from the Lower East Side. That's what I told my family ahead of time upon John's request: a friend from the neighborhood is coming to dinner, and that's how John introduced himself. 'Velvel,' he said, smiling. 'Chag Pesach sameach.' And no one noticed anything. Was it the light makeup he applied to his face or his prowess in tampering with people's perceptions? Probably both. I'll explain.

"Believe it or not, John was also proficient in the so-called spirit photography that came hand in hand with table-rapping séances, which were all the rage after the war—communing with the lost in action, summoning the spirits of deceased family members who stayed in the old country or perished in transit. So he had no lack of engagements from spiritually curious wealthy New Yorkers. He was also not above messing with facts. So if the spirits of the dead were slow in manifesting their presence, he'd augment the process to the point where they, or something, sometimes a mere shadow, a quasi-silhouette, was visible. That was the time of glass negatives. So, a few scratches here, a smudge in the upper-right corner.

And lo! Your dead uncle's presence in the picture was all but incontrovertible.

"Though the whole thing was always part real deal, part scam, he never ran the serious risk of being put away for a simple reason. You had to believe in ghosts and spirits to be willing to use the services of a medium, to begin with. Of course, some schemers were occasionally exposed and thrown in jail, but that never fazed John, a mere reporter documenting the event in which his clients had a prior conviction. As far as the state penal code went, it was a gray area. Essentially, John was asked to provide evidence of something intangible at best. And that he did, one way or another. Come to think, is it not like writing or moviemaking? You create something out of nothing. Of course, you do it in a social context, and if it's done well or strikes a chord, it has a way of influencing people, for better or for worse—sort of what Greg was practicing around the same time.

"While I was busy getting paranoid delivering packages all over town, or baring myself in front of twenty disheveled art geniuses, or assisting my lover in cheating the prim Fifth Ave. set out of their pocket change, Greg was honing his skills as a Lower East Side stand-up comedian, despite his heavy accent, iffy English, and jokes targeted mainly at an ethnic audience, a tough job for someone newly arrived who was trying to compete with silent movies and Yiddish theatre, or vaudeville. His act sometimes preceded the feature show or was presented during the intermission. So, get a load of this: every time Greg would get paid, though not too often initially, he'd try to split before he counted the money. His thinking was: better make a run for it before they get wise to his delivering counterfeit goods . . . All art is cheating; good art is skillful cheating. Perspective, trompe l'oeil, it's all about illusion and sleight of hand.

"Anyway, Greg got his big break at the Orpheum Theatre downtown. Booze, loose ladies, gambling was a big part of it, too. Though the booze patrons and proprietors had to kiss goodbye around 1920 . . . Rowdy patrons, maybe not firing their six-shooters at the feet of an actor doing Hamlet's soliloquy like they do in *My Darling Clementine*, but not particularly refined types either. So there was another goodbye for you: a goodbye to the highbrow theatre of the kind Greg was used to doing back home: high art wasn't where the money was when it came to the huddled masses. It was give 'em what they want for my dear brother, at least initially, his lofty aspirations put on the back burner until further notice. Just watch that flame while they simmer. [*Sigh.*]

"But back to John and his fooling the entire family into thinking he was a Jewish fella on the first night of Pesach. The prayers, the yarmulke, the partaking of the matzoh and *beitzah*, my Velvel-John pulled it off with flying colors. Chatterbox Ben and the rest of the Davises (by then, the Kozinskys had already made the transition to the Davises; when in Rome, you know the rest of it), they didn't even notice John was missing an arm. Or I think what he did was fix a plank to his elbow and bandage it up with gauze, claiming he broke his arm playing baseball with the kids from the neighborhood. Quite a feat! Even during the after-dinner chat with Granddad on Judaism, John, a moderate Confucian, tried to keep his views in check. 'Yes, but,' he objected timidly to Chatterbox Ben, who was holding forth on the virtues of monotheism. 'Confucianism is all about One, too. Another thing they have in common is that neither Confucianism nor Judaism subscribes to the notion of reincarnation. Destiny, yes, but—' 'True,' interrupted the old man, picking out a chunk of matzah from his beard. 'However, the premise shared by both religions is never do to others what you would not like them to do to you. That is the silver rule, or the golden rule, or the platinum rule. One thing it is not: it's not the platitudinous rule it is often passed as.' 'But neither is Manicheism,' said John. 'What good would good be if there was no evil?' 'I know,' acquiesced Chatterbox Ben quickly. 'Mani, that great apostle of light was sure one smart cookie. Have some strudel, kid.'

"For the life of me, I can't remember what language they conversed in. Why did John do it? I guess, a thrill-seeker that he was, he was trying out his hypnotic acumen. To him, if the scheme succeeded, it would be a benchmark accomplishment. If he could fool people in close quarters, the smoke and mirrors of his ghost-catching photo sessions would be a cinch. Boy, was he wrong! Also, years later, Chatterbox Ben confessed that he was onto the ethnicity of our Passover guest from the moment my beau crossed the threshold of our tiny place on Rivington. Granddad just didn't want to blow Velvel-John's cover, or mine, the bond between us as clear as day to him. Though my choice struck Chatterbox Ben as unorthodox, not to say a little bizarre.

"Initially, John never served as a medium per se, though he was employed by a few mediums of various competence and credibility, including some out-and-out con artists the industry was crawling with. [*Nervous chuckle.*] Of course, at first, he was not too picky regarding his employers' reputation. But as he gained experience and confidence, he was in more of a position to pick and choose. He also thought there was a certain parallel between his wartime photographs of people with missing body parts and pictures of the spirits of the dead who weren't maimed but were there only in part.

"His bulky camera and tripod at the ready, as well as his hefty magnesium lamps to better capture the apparitions in dimly lit quarters (that's where yours truly came in), I guess, the agreement between the medium and John the trick photographer stipulated that a visible trace of a spirit summoned should be discerned in a picture taken. It was around the time when John made a full transition to mediumship (ever quick with a quip he called his move 'cutting out the medium man') that my friend Rita came up with the insane idea of kidnapping an actor from Stanislavsky's Moscow Art Theatre then on tour in the US. Her thinking was that the ransom money paid by the Soviet theatre organization or the government could be used to finance Greg's film projects and then some. Funny part was that Greg, the sober and reasonable person that he was, went along with it, though initially he had his reservations. As for John, he argued that the whole scheme was foolproof and could work, but first, the Soviet actors should be asked if they wanted to stay in the country voluntarily. If they agreed, we would help with paperwork, temporary accommodation, and job search in exchange for some service fee. My beloved John, always the trickster, who, by the way, blew his whole Jewish Orthodox cover vis-à-vis Greg by then, sure had a way of blowing smoke in people's eyes. So had Rita, who was looking for a way to support her habit, which, sadly, was getting the best of her. Plus, John could use extra cash too—his séances took a downward turn around that time. I'm skipping around a bit, but once, actually, the third or the fourth time he assumed the role of the medium, with some clever devices up his sleeve, literally just one sleeve, while I was tasked with photographing the entire session, his bluff was called and he got bodily thrown out by the paying customer.

"In brief, this businessman wanted to summon the spirit of his wife's aunt, a gold digger, who had panned for gold alongside her husband, an Aussie, and one of the original 49ers. When her husband struck gold and died shortly after under mysterious circumstances, she continued panning, met with some success, and eventually became prosperous. Some of the Jezebel's fortune was stashed away, either buried or maybe invested—no one knew for sure. Since she left no progeny when she died right before the Great War, it was her second niece's wish, very much shared by her furrier husband, to evoke the spirit of Jezebel and see if she could shed some light on her fortune, posthumously. Long story short, while John was quite adept at creating all sorts of visual distractions and effects, it was Jezebel's voice that he had recorded using a gramophone, which was hidden under his chair and that he wound up on the sly during the session. The problem was that the record got cracked en route to the furrier's house in Harlem. As a result, Jezebel, while speaking (I was the one who did her voice, which I tried to make sound both old and eerie), started to stutter and repeat the same phrase over and over again: 'Search for gold in the back of St. Joseph's Portuguese Church in Oakland, California, fifteen feet from the back wall's southwest corner, the back of St. Joseph's Portuguese, the back, the back of St. Joseph's Portuguese Church . . .' ad nauseam. That's when the furrier and his wife saw right through John's little game, yanked the gramophone from under his chair, started screaming and shoving him around, kicked the gramophone, and even socked him a few. Poor Johnny! I think that was the end of his career as a medium or mine as his assistant . . . Greg was so amused by the story of our narrow escape that he eventually made a picture loosely based on it, and called the caper *Jenny Lee's Gold*."

Chapter Thirty.

"Anyhow, I think it was Stanislavsky's second tour of the United States, the Moscow Art Theatre doing eight performances a week, all in Russian, all to sold-out audiences of Russian émigrés and American theatregoers alike, the tide of fascination with all things Russian at its peak. However, I must say that not all the critics were uniformly taken by Chekhov's plays' melancholy or the productions' overbearing stage designs. Greg happened to be employed by an American impresario as an interpreter/liaison between the Russian troupe and a number of New York, Brooklyn, and New Jersey theatres that hosted the MAT performances, as well as some Yiddish theatres that Greg was directly involved with. So, it was towards the end of the tour that Rita, ever the opportunist, said to us: 'Listen, there's bound to be a few dissatisfied actors in Stanislavsky's ensemble who would consider staying on. Soviet Russia is not for everyone. Of course, the maestro himself is the theatre king in the land of the Bolsheviks and wouldn't even think of upping sticks. But for the rest . . . Not everyone's an idealist filled with lofty artistic aspirations. A bit part player's fee in a Hollywood picture would likely exceed *The Cherry Sisters* (*sic*!) lead's annual paycheck. Let me do a little survey backstage. Better yet, take the actors to a downtown speakeasy or two. Show them around, show them a good time. Help will be offered to anyone who wants to jump ship. Like John said, paperwork, legal help, initial lodging. Don't be stingy with promises. This is America. Create the need, then make a buck satisfying it. And if all fails, kidnap a lead, for fuck's sake'—so said the foul-mouthed Rita. 'Let them try and finish the tour without him. Or her. Trust me: they'll cough up the ransom money before the next night's curtain call.'

"Greg just scratched his head; that's all he did. I don't think he knew his wild girl had it in her. Same goes for my reaction. Puzzled. Talk about callous, talk about the anarchist turning on a dime into the entrepreneur trying to make a buck. But I suppose people change drastically and think up desperate plans to indulge their habits. Drinking got to be expensive, and it could get you in trouble during Prohibition. Plus, you can't really hide your bottle from outsiders or family. With opium, you can be a lot more discreet.

"Guess what. There were no takers for Rita's 'jump the boat' offers. Some actors were planning to defect anyway, you could just tell: their luggage was twice as bulky. Like a husband-and-wife couple, their name will come to me, who stayed in the country and enjoyed a long and productive career in American theatre and film. Starts with a 'D.' But quite a few of Stanislavsky's actors were wary of Rita's being a government employee; they thought she was a Soviet agent provocateur who might be out to implicate them in treasonous activities while abroad.

"So there was no choice left for the conniving friend of mine other than to go ahead with plan B, namely, kidnap one of the actors. A bungled effort, if there ever was one. [*Deep sigh.*] Greg and John were waiting for the show to end outside the theatre's back door in midtown Manhattan, Forty-Third Street, I think. Rita was behind the wheel of the borrowed Model T getaway car, her cap obscuring the upper half of her pale face, a Chesterfield dangling from her thin lips. Who did we borrow the automobile from? I can't remember for the life of me. Greg had a bouquet to be handed to Smyshkin, I believe that was the young actor's name that the co-conspirators thought was perfect for their plan (in good health, no danger of a heart attack during the kidnapping; somewhat prominent, almost indispensable to the ensemble).

"The play performed that night, if memory serves, was Gorky's *The Lower Depth*... What can I tell you? Man supposes, but God disposes... Smyshkin, whom we planned to abduct, was laid up with a minor flu that night and replaced by an understudy who looked like Smyshkin but was a much more robust version of Smyshkin, even taller than Greg, and whose physique couldn't begin to compare with John's, a wiry and tenacious man all right but certainly no Hercules. Plus, don't forget that missing arm.

"So, imagine a rainy, slushy New York night in the theatre district in late January, automobile lights' reflections floating along the glistening streets, two figures approaching a towering Soviet actor, surprising him with a bouquet of primroses and violas, one of them sticking a gun in his ribs, John's WWI trophy, which the actor proceeds to promptly wrestle from him while screaming at the top of his baritone, 'Polizia!!' The two mounted cops who happened to be riding by, get off their horses and handcuff Greg and John in a jiffy, while Rosie, I mean Rita revs up her borrowed Ford, runs a few traffic lights... Wait, I don't even remember if they used traffic lights back then. Were they invented later? Anyway, she is gone with the wind or, rather the windshield broken into smithereens upon impact with the brownstone railing. A fair-weather friend was what she turned out to be; she thought it expedient just to vanish on us.

"Well, lucky for all involved, as I watched the entire scene from across the street, shivering from head to toe in my thin overcoat, John thought he'd use his hypnotic powers right then and there. And guess what, this time, they worked like a charm! [*A short contented laugh.*] I saw the cops all of a sudden take the cuffs off Greg, then John, and apologize profusely. Then they yell to the actor, 'Scram, Bolshevik agitator, or we'll book you!' and shake their fists at poor Smyshkin's understudy. Then they hop back in their saddles and slowly take off, clippity-clopping down a slushy Forty-Third Street. Greg was staring at John, and John was staring back at Greg, but only one of them knew what happened.

"So much for Rita's get-rich-quick scheme. I'm just curious what would have happened had the real Smyshkin been in the play that night. Would we all have wound up in the slammer? Get deported like Rita did? She was certainly left-leaning and an anarchist at heart, though she rarely acted it out and never did anything criminal or subversive. I guess the pitch of the Red Scare hysteria was such that people would run afoul of the law for much milder offenses. Or maybe she did get thick with a bunch of bootleggers after all. And since she was a repeat offender, instead of being put on trial in a court of law, she got deported with the rest of the undesirables. We didn't see much of each other after the aborted kidnapping, so I don't really know what happened. Was she embarrassed about the whole Stanislavsky mess, or was it me who felt resentful about her crazy idea, which put us all in danger? Hard to say after so many years. But one night, I bumped into her former boyfriend Matt on Delancey, and he told me that two weeks after the botched kidnapping, they came after her, gave her half an hour to pack her things, and took her to the nearest precinct, I think it was on Orchard. The next day, she was put on a ship to England and then Russia. Never heard from her since. My first close friend in this country, the wild and beautiful Rita from Kishinev, Greg's first American lover . . . [*Sniffle*]

"For whatever reason, Greg's movie career took off right after his girlfriend, or by then his ex-girlfriend, was sent away. He got lucky, I guess, getting hired to direct his first big one, *The Wild Ass's Skin*. But luck had only so much to do with it. The skin did the rest. His lucky skin, I should say, his hide that protected him from all sorts of trouble later on. I mean the film's subject matter that touched the audiences so profoundly in the happy-go-lucky '20s, truly tapping into the zeitgeist of the nation hungry for quality entertainment. His first breakthrough success was his next picture, though. Also, the silent *Diary of a Scoundrel* was a huge hit, a blockbuster, as they would call it today."

"Wow, that is really breathtaking! I mean the events you and your brother were a part of," I exclaimed incredulously after a brief pause. "But perhaps we should stop for now and continue tomorrow, Mrs. Teal? It's been a long session, and we both could use a little rest, wouldn't you say?"

"I couldn't and I wouldn't," replied Mrs. Teal defiantly. "I'm not tired in the least. I could go on and on. Memories seem to work their rejuvenating magic on me, Mark!"

"Well, truth be told, I feel a little tired all of a sudden. Normally, I don't, but I do now. I hope you will excuse me. I can come back first thing tomorrow morning, Mrs. Teal."

"Whatever." She seemed a little disappointed. "Can you do me a big favor, though, and do some light grocery shopping for me before our session tomorrow, Mark? I hope I'm not imposing."

"Not at all. What would you like me to get?"

"I've run out of a few basics, OJ and milk, make sure it's organic, please. Seltzer, too. My home attendant came down with a stomach flu . . . Oh yes, Entenmann's cake, the one with the pecans and frosting. You know the kind. Henrietta does light baking, too. I'm so used to having dessert in the kitchen. We can have it tomorrow with coffee."

"Not a problem, Mrs. Teal. OJ, milk, seltzer, cake, anything else?"

"Some food for Honoré D. would be nice. Don't want to starve Mommy's big helper."

"Sure thing," I said. "Any particular kind?"

"A couple of bags of Taste of the Wild, his favorite. Again, please forgive me if I'm imposing. And I'll pay you right back. Unless you want the money now."

"Don't be silly! Your credit is good with me, Mrs. Teal."

"Fine then. You're a nice young man."

"And you are a super-intelligent lady with a memory that'll give anyone a run for their money, myself included. Speaking of which," I said, clearly pushing my luck, but the need to push it was pressing suddenly. "While we are making lists, can you give me a few titles of Mr. Davis's movies? Whatever comes to mind, and in no particular order. So that I can structure our next sessions a little better?"

"Of course I can, Mark. Though some I'll never recall. But a few stayed with me forever. A couple of musicals he did for MGM in the '30s and '40s. *Stepping out with Fate. Chock-Full o'Diamonds,* though I think that one was for Universal. And, of course, his later successes *Bad Boy Rob* and *Kiss Me, Sonny.*"

"Thank you so much, Mrs. Teal. This is very useful. Big thanks from me and, in advance, from Ms. Zhuravel, the Gregory Davis scholar."

Then I got up from my chair, said goodbye, patted Honoré D. on his big brown head, as was my custom, and stepped out into the Boca starry night feeling a little lost in time—a state of mind a good storytelling would put me in on occasion.

Chapter Thirty-One.

There is something refreshingly liberating about switching from first-person to third-person narration. An unspoken element of doubt, a certain textual distance can be introduced subtly into events recounted and recorded. Especially since it was right around this juncture that I was beginning to harbor serious suspicions regarding the partial or even general authenticity of Mrs. Teal's account. And I don't just mean the abundance of storybook adventures that befell her and her brother (she hadn't even covered half of them, she said); things do happen when you live long enough to witness or partake in them firsthand. I mean her dwelling on her growing up in the Russian Empire and coming of age in the US, steering clear of details of her brother's time in Hollywood and her somewhat confused memories of motion pictures that Mr. Gregory Davis directed in the '30s and '40s. The latter two points I attributed to the fact that Mrs. Teal's and her brother's paths diverged for twenty-odd years, starting at the end of the Great Depression. Occasionally, she would come out West to spend time with Greg when he was between productions or marriages. Nothing like little sister's advice or words of consolation when the love boat runs aground, as Greg's would do, sometimes with devastating results. Alternatively, he would visit what was left of the family in New York for high holidays, both Chatterbox Ben and her mother sadly gone by the late '30s.

Mrs. Teal's sketchy account of what happened to Mr. Davis in Hollywood included his friendship with the likes of George Cukor and Billy Wilder, both considerably better established than he was at the time; a succession of breakups: Mr. Davis wasn't known for maintaining lasting relationships; his rubbing shoulders with the high and the mighty, such as Carl Laemmle, the man himself, and Carl Laemmle Jr. on both coasts and in various capacities: director, friend, confidante. Also, when visiting New York, Mr. Davis would stay in the Laemmles' apartment on West End Ave., as witnessed by Mrs. Teal, by then a married woman taking care of two adorable toddlers and thus unable to accommodate her brother in her modest two-bedroom apartment on Riverside Drive. She was also invited to a few soirées at the Laemmles' and recounted in vivid detail one such party in the early '40s. The guests seemed to include a who's who of Tinseltown and Broadway. Humphry and Lauren, the moody Irving Thalberg, the young and perky Veronica Lake and her art director husband, Ben Hecht, who, as Mrs. Teal recalled, was treated with great respect rarely accorded screenwriters of the day, most likely because a number of movies based on his plays were big hits, but also for his activism, much admired by many and disparaged by some. The Hellbent Hecht, as he was known to both his friends and adversaries, was trying to galvanize Hollywood movers and shakers into anti-Nazi action, what with antisemitism rearing its ugly head in Germany, windows of Jewish-run stores being smashed, people either fleeing the country or getting deported en masse.

There followed a description of Humphry and Lauren, both chain-smoking, squinting, and blowing out smoke that created an effect that Mrs. Teal cleverly likened to that of the nylon stocking pulled over the lens in old pictures when the director was going for a beautified close-up of a female star. Only in this particular case, she added, it was the unisex effect that glamorized the Hollywood couple but also made it hard for nonsmokers in the room to breathe.

At some point, Moss Hart assumed center stage with a bottle of Veuve Clicquot sticking out of his enormous tweed coat's pocket (maybe it was a New Year's Eve party?) and launched into a story that Greg claimed to have heard from the Broadway's darling a few times before. In it, the eight-year-old Bobbie (Moss's real name) takes a train to Times Square, his first trip outside the Bronx, his first time in the isle of Manhattan on an errand to buy some sheet music for the store he worked in. The sights and sounds of the big city scared the boychik, naturally. The throngs scampering about everywhere were overwhelming. Twice, he stumbled and fell on the ground, swept along by the frenzied crowd flashing past him. Everybody waved American flags and pennants, small and large, chanting and cheering and laughing. "So this is what Manhattan looks like on a typical weekday?" thought little Bobbie. "How can people even walk here? It's nuts!" It turned out that it was the day Woodrow Wilson won the presidency over William Taft by a landslide. It was no ordinary day, not by a long shot, and certainly not the day to run errands. Everyone at the Laemmles' laughed. Only Bogey kept a stern face. At last, he blew smoke out through his nostrils and said gravely, "The guy who did a hell of a job helping the Allies beat the Krauts. We sure could use a guy like this in the highest office right now."

Two or three Greg Davis's war pictures later, the Germans defeated by the Allied forces, Mrs. Teal was visiting her brother, by then a newly married man who found conjugal happiness with one Felicite Bauhman, an aspiring actress from Kew Gardens rechristened Patricia Oliver by the studio heads. Pool parties, fun times, boozing it up into the small hours, German expat directors getting free rein to impose their Expressionist sensibilities on American-made pictures, the striking look of the sets exceeding what was called for by the paucity of plot-lines; Mrs. Teal's short-lived fling with a married MGM executive and a subsequent abortion she had with due discretion, and so on, and so on. Then some talk about the snitches that Hollywood was crawling with; Senator McCarthy's lackeys who were tapping filmmakers' phone lines; L. B. Meyer getting behind "the effort to ferret out the leftist roaches and send them scuttling back to Moscow where they belonged." Greg, seemingly unscathed by hearings yet concerned with people losing jobs all around him, forged ahead with *To Each His Own* and *About Last Winter*, which were made in 1951 and 1954, respectively. An anecdotal but telling story related to Mrs. Teal by her brother over the after-dinner port in her drawing room followed.

It featured Greg's friend Dimitri Tiomkin, a well-regarded expat composer from St. Petersburg who scored over 120 films during his long career in Hollywood, which boasted a music department specializing in knockoffs of Viennese operettas, a department that did military marches, romantic duets, and so on. Tiomkin could do just about everything. Selznik, a legendary producer, commissioned Tiomkin to write eleven main themes for the motion picture *Duel in the Sun*: the Spanish theme, the rancho theme, the love theme, and the orgasmic theme . . . "Orgasmic theme?" Tiomkin's eyebrow went up. "How do you score an orgasm?" "Just give it your best shot," Selznik replied. "I need a good *shtump* here." Tiomkin disappeared for a few weeks, then assembled an orchestra that included forty-one drummers and a chorus of one hundred male and female vocalists. Then he brought to Selznik the score for eleven themes. Selznik asked Tiomkin to whistle the love theme for him. Tiomkin whistled the love theme. "Great," said Selznik, rubbing his hands in excitement. "Now, how about the orgasmic theme?" Tiomkin obliged. Selznik shook his head. "No, no. No. This is not an orgasm," the producer said. Tiomkin went back home to do some rewrites. He added the sighs of cellos and the brass tremors of trombones that sounded, per his description, in the rhythm of a handsaw working away in a forest thicket. Again, he was invited to come to Selznik's studio, this time with a full orchestra. The theme was to be performed during the love scene between Gregory Peck and Jennifer Jones.

Everything was going well until the time had come to play the orgasmic theme. Selznik asked to play it again. And then again. "You probably are going to hate me right now," he finally said to the versatile composer. "But it is not beautiful." "But Mr. Selznik," returned Dimitri Tiomkin. "What exactly are you objecting to here? What is it that you don't like?" "I like everything," said the legendary Selznik. "But this is not the music of orgasm. This is not the *shtump*, Mr. Tiomkin. I don't screw like that." "Mr. Selznik, but you screw your way and I screw mine!" cried Dimitri Tiomkin in exasperation. "To my ear, this is precisely the music of orgasm!" And this time, the legendary David Selznik had nothing to counter the argument. Tiomkin told Mr. Davis the story when the composer was working on the score for Mr. Davis's picture *What Price Glory,* his only Western, shot on a relatively tight budget someplace Utah in 1957 with no-name actors, but a solid if a bit formulaic plot and excellent camera work by the ace lenser Peter Hall.

"Cut," I mentally said to myself and felt the strong urge to have a word with my old film professor, Sam Goldstein, right then and there. I had meant to do this for some time but had to put it off until the following day. For now, I thanked Mrs. Teal for her amazing behind-the-scenes story and bid her good night.

Chapter Thirty-Two.

The following day, bright and early, I called Sam, who seemed excited to hear my voice, just like I was happy to hear his. After all, it'd been close to four months since our last exchange, and except for my occasional phone chats with Tasha, Mrs. Teal's voice was almost the only voice I heard for the past few weeks.

"Sam, how's everything?"

"Fine. Toasted everything with lox and cream cheese would even be better right now. Bet you're missing that in the twilight zone?"

"I'm missing it in Boca Raton, Florida, Sam. I'm back. Have been for two weeks."

"No kidding? Still the twilight zone in my book. You know Florida is where Jules Verne sent his characters to the Moon from?"

"I had no idea."

"What's in Boca anyway? Happily retired, enjoying your new wealth?"

"Not quite there, Sam."

"What, then?"

"Long story short, I'm interviewing Greg Davis's sister. A paying gig."

"Oh? And I thought you swore off film for eternity."

"An offer I couldn't refuse. Got hired by a St. Petersburg scholar."

"They study Greg Davis in Russia? He is all but forgotten here!"

"I know."

"Disappeared into the night in the early '80s."

"Is that why we never studied him in school?"

"His last film was made in the late '40s. That's why."

"Well, Orson Welles's final decade was checkered too. Yet he is studied to pieces."

"Come on, Mark. Greg Davis is no Orson Welles."

"Still a productive career while it lasted, wouldn't you say?"

"What's your point?"

"Point is, and that's where your expertise comes in . . ."

"Cut to the chase, Neider."

"What I gathered from reference books I could get my hands on here, the last film Davis made was *A Noose Too Loose* in 1948. And that was that. No work for television, no movies since. Zilch. What he did for the thirty years before he pulled a Houdini is anybody's guess."

"Early retirement, Mark. McCarthyism?"

"Sam, McCarthyism didn't kick in until the early '50s."

"Maybe he was between projects? A long hiatus? And then got pinched by the House Un-American Activities Committee. Ever thought of that?"

"Sam, he had been making a movie a year until then. He was in great demand and in good shape, no breaks, no side projects. But that's also beside the point. Or rather, it needs further research. What really bugs the crap out of me is that Greg Davis's younger sister, Mrs. Teal, a person of sound mind and good memory, insists that her brother kept making movies well into the mid-'70s. Not only that. She actually remembers the movie titles, sometimes even names the actors who starred in them. Talk about the twilight zone!"

"Ever heard of senility? Mild or advanced?"

"But isn't it when people forget things? Repeat things unnecessarily? Here not only does she insist her brother never stopped working, she actually goes through the list of the movies he supposedly made. Like I said, no mention of them in the encyclopedia. None."

"So?"

"So the favor I'd like to ask you is: please check if the following titles were ever made at all? More specifically, were they ever made by Greg Davis?"

"Mark, I have a few deadlines here. Papers to grade, auteur geniuses to crack my whip at."

"I remember the whip, professor. But please, can you do me a favor, Sam? Can you?"

"Shoot, mother-father," said Sam. "What's the list?"

So I rattled off the list of the movies that Mrs. Teal mentioned throughout our sessions, in no particular order: *A Flat, Diary of a Scoundrel, The Wizard of Waltz, His Bride's Dowry, Nobody's Child, What Martha Knew, A Train to Reno, Up in Daisy's Attic, Voyagers in the Night, Keep 'Em Running, Jenny Lee's Gold, Stepping out with Fate, Chock-Full o'Diamonds, Bad Boy Rob, Kiss Me, Sonny, To Each His Own, About Last Winter,* and a few more culled from my notes plus, just to be safe, though I saw the movie with my own eyes a mere three weeks ago, *The Wild Ass's Skin.* Then I thanked my old professor friend and said I owed him one. A big fat one. Something valuable, rare, film-related, and offbeat, yet not entirely twilight zone-ish. Maybe Eisenstein's notes for his never-filmed *Das Kapital* adaptation? Ask Tasha next time I talk to her if her film scholar aunt knows how to get a hold of them.

Chapter Thirty-Three.

"You know well by now what I do, dear Mrs. Teal, and you know what I don't do. I'm a research assistant. Someone else will be writing the book based on my findings. What you kindly choose to share gets duly recorded and then committed to paper the same night. Not too challenging as jobs go. But it is a job. Accuracy, due diligence, and courtesy are all it takes, really. Some of it is stipulated in the contract we both signed. You reminisce, I record. I get paid, you get paid. Sometimes, we have a cup of coffee with chocolate chip macadamia cookies or Entenmann's cake; we chat a bit. Other times, I go straight back to my hotel. Memory is funny, as you said a few sessions back. The older we get, the sharper scenes from decades past come into focus. While the events of the last week, last year, or last decade may not be so easily summoned. Not to wax Shakespearean or get plain banal about it, but it is true, and people in the medical profession will second that observation.

"What I couldn't help noticing over the last few sessions, though, is the mounting number of inconsistencies and incongruities popping up in what you've been kindly relating here. At first, when mistakes were not too glaring, I'd just let it go. A battle here, a botched kidnapping of a phantom actor there, I'm neither a twentieth-century history buff nor a theatre scholar. A film school dropout and a programmer who also dabbled in import-export pretty much describes who I am professionally. Things will eventually get cross-referenced and checked by my scholar employer. Footnotes and a glossary will be furnished, too. Yet certain things couldn't escape my notice, even at this early stage of the project. The family history you shared with me so generously, a precious thing that it is to you and a real treasure trove for my employer, and, I should add, a fascinating narrative for myself to record and mull over, I accept unconditionally and with gratitude. Yet things don't seem to add up whenever you reminisce about the movies made by your lavishly gifted and celebrated brother. Once again, some of the movies you refer to are strangely missing from the film encyclopedia I have recently checked out. More specifically, the movies released, per your account, after the late '40s are not included in reference books at all. Moreover, when I consulted a film scholar friend, a person with some reputation in the field, one Sam Goldstein, he supported my hunch. The Technicolor productions of the late '50s, such as *The King of Flatbush, The Asphalt Cyclops, My Witness, My Neighbor, My Wife,* plus the '60s star vehicles such as the musical comedy/road movie *Bad Boy Rob* starring Bob Hope, *Kiss Me, Sonny,* and *The Big Scramble* with the teenage Al Pacino, were never made by Greg Davis or, for that matter, anyone else. How does one account for that? I am frankly at a loss here. How do I present this erroneous and misleading information to Ms. Oksana Zhuravel, the film scholar from St. Petersburg, Russia? If your memory plays tricks on you, what should we make of the fantasies generated with such great verve and so little effort? What are these flights of fancy? I need your help here, dear Mrs. Teal! I seriously do."

"I don't know what the dickens you're blabbing about, young man. And do me a favor, there's no need to dear me. You asked me to talk about my brother and his movies. I'm telling you about my brother and his movies. As I remember it, not ever checking with movie guides or what have you. If I missed a movie or two or even three, I obviously didn't do it deliberately. He made about forty pictures before he disappeared, how am I supposed to remember them all? Some were great, some were okay, others were obscure even for film scholars. Last I checked, Gregory Davis was dropped from college film courses entirely. Not sure when or why, but he was."

"Yes, but Mrs. Teal. Not to split hairs or challenge you unnecessarily, the last film he made was *A Noose Too Loose,* released in 1948, whether Mr. Davis is studied in today's academia or not. Not a single movie done since!"

"So? Mark, I told you before, and I'm telling you now. Chalk it up to McCarthyism. He didn't want to testify before the committee, didn't have it in him to pull a Kazan on his friends and colleagues. Some were sympathizers or left-leaning, certainly more so than he ever was, but he didn't want to rat on them. And that's why he was silenced, Mark. Couldn't get a single movie made for years. Some squealed and were spared. Too many to name named names. And it was then that Greg found himself on his own. A tough stretch for him, a trauma for the entire family, myself, my late husband, and the children. He was divorced at the time. Isolation is a beastly thing, Mark."

"I know, dear Mrs. Teal. I mean, scratch 'dear.' Sorry," I said softly as I watched her lift her dark glasses and wipe the tear with a tissue she pulled from a box beside her with remarkable dexterity. "But not to belabor the point, once again, didn't McCarthyism effectively start in 1950? And the blacklist campaign went full tilt a year or so later?"

"Yes, but testifying meant naming names, Mark. And he didn't want to do that. I can't see, but sometimes it feels like I'm talking to a deaf person."

"Point well taken, Mrs. Teal. Though he couldn't have been conceivably asked to testify as early as 1948 . . ."

"Of course not! Geez. He was asked to testify in 1952 or '53. I don't remember exactly, young man. Give me a break, will you? I'm turning ninety-two in a week. That is, if I survive this assault by a rabid researcher from hell!"

"I do apologize, Mrs. Teal. Just trying to see if maybe *Bad Boy Rob* and *Kiss Me, Sonny* were released under different titles?"

"They were made. Period. Made a bundle, too. Put yours truly right back in the saddle after the mid-'40s lull!"

"Put who back in the saddle, Mrs. Teal?" I said, leaning forward, thinking for a second that I might have misheard her.

"Mark, it's been a long session. Different from the rest because you did most of the talking. The uncalled-for talking!"

"I'm sorry if I've overstepped any boundaries, Mrs. Teal."

"I need a breather here. Is it me or is it awfully hot in here? Can you turn up the air conditioner for me? No one has committed any vile crimes in my family, as far as I know. Why such scrutiny instead of a casual interview? Who gave you the right to carry on like this, for Pete's sake? I'm a former attorney, you know. I can make life difficult for you. Break the agreement and you'll be left with a very unfinished project on your hands. As of today, for instance."

"Of course, it's your right, Mrs. Teal. And from now on, I'm perfectly willing just to listen, record and transcribe."

"You do that. Really, young man!"

"No problem. I do understand, Mrs. Teal. But . . . one last thing. Something I'd been meaning to ask when we started our sessions. Are there, by any chance, any pictures of you and Mr. Davis in your possession? Any family pictures? Any mementos would be truly invaluable for our project?"

"Didn't I tell you everything was destroyed in a fire a few years back?"

"Not that I remember."

"It was, Mark. Life records gone up in smoke. Furniture. But who cares about furniture? The entire house torched. Good thing I had a decent coverage."

"Malice?"

"Nah. Who would need to harm an old man's measly belongings? Left a kettle on the stove before seeing the eye doctor. Not an Alzheimer's case yet. But stuff does happen. Of course, I use the word 'see' advisedly. Optical nerves shot years ago . . ."

"And the word 'man'? How do you use that, Mrs. Teal? Man as in . . . human?"

"What are you talking about, Mark?"

"You just said 'an old man's measly belongings!'"

"Mark, you are beginning to annoy me. Do you realize that? I said 'an old hen's belongings.' Not 'an old man's belongings.'"

"Whatever, Mrs. Teal. It's getting late. And the whole thing is getting just a little bit strange. Tomorrow, the usual time?"

"Make it the day after, Mark. I need to take a day off. Your questions have a way of wearing me out. I could use a break. Check my archives. Test a hypothesis I need to think about. Maybe it'll give this thing a whole new spin, a zing to take home. A double loop free of poop."

"Huh? A double loop? You sure know how to keep the turkey suspended, Mrs. Teal."

"You're no turkey, Mark. Just a sweet kid trying to do his job. And maybe biting a little more than he can chew along the way. We've all been there. Some have managed to find their way back. Don't bother locking the door. I want to check my mail."

Chapter Thirty-Four.

There was no phone in my hotel room and, improbably, no pay phone in the tiny lobby either; so after I was done transcribing the previous day's tart exchange between me and Mrs. Teal, I had to drive to the nearest public phone, which happened to be inside a nondescript mall a few miles away. Nondescript is a misnomer: it looked like an oversized pizza with five toppings, only the toppings were on the inside, so they were actually more like stuffing rather than toppings: a jewelry store, Gap, a perfume store, a tourist tchotchkes store, and a pizza parlor proper. What I had on my mind as I was dialing Sam Goldstein's office on the San Francisco State U. campus across from the Modernist student union structure we called Battleship Potemkin was that my playing yesterday's tape back and forth revealed that Mrs. Teal indeed said "an old man's measly belongings" not "an old hen's measly belongings" and a few other blunders that she tried to explain away so lamely.

Why was I calling Sam? To hear from the horse's mouth once again that the films in question were never made. Though that was precisely what he had said before, this time, I needed to run a few more titles by him before calling Mike in Chicago to bring him up to date on the unexpected turn the research was taking and see if Oksana might have further instructions for me. I was past the midpoint in my sessions; a tidy sum had already accumulated in my savings account, and Tasha would be coming over in two weeks. Yet the responsible mensch that I was, I wanted to get my bearings in rapidly changing circumstances and do it without delay.

Sam's answering service greeted me with a few clicks, then ten tinny bars from "Somewhere over the Rainbow," followed by Sam's intoning in his best imitation of Dorothy's lilting voice, "You have ten seconds to leave your message in toto, too." Hilarious. He called back within five minutes.

"What's up, Mark?" he said.

"Not sure where to start . . . The sister is either losing her marbles in a hurry right before my eyes or never had a full set to begin with. Slips of the tongue compound, if that's what they are. I wish there were a way for you to check what's on my new list as we speak. Time is of the essence, Sam."

"You came to the right place, buddy. Databases at my fingertips. You want to run the titles by me and reverse the phone charges?"

"Not a problem."

So, I gave Sam the titles from my updated list, including the star vehicles, musicals, court dramas, you name it. No dice. None of them were ever made. There might have been some similar titles, but the last Greg Davis production ever released remained *A Noose Too Loose*.

"What was it about anyway, Sam? I mean, the *Noose* flick? You remember it offhand?"

"More or less. A Nazi fugitive from justice makes his home in New York. Runs a dog kennel. Business is booming. Everyone owns a pooch on the Upper West Side. After work, he plays Nazi anthems behind closed doors. Has a girlfriend fifteen years his junior. Her fiancé died in the war. The Nazi was involved in his death, big time. She has no clue, of course. Someone, a local baker, a Polish Jewish fellow, brings in a dog who needs to be put to sleep. Too old, can barely walk. The baker recognizes the Nazi with the help of his sick dog. So he changes his mind. Lets the eyewitness dog live. But the Nazi is in on the whole thing. So he kills the dog to save his skin. But not for long. Something like that."

"So why the title?"

"The baker hangs the Nazi in his kennel. He is a strong man, a former prizefighter or something. His first try fails. The noose is literally too loose. He gives it another go, much better results. The Nazi begs on his knees before he dangles: 'You can't do this. You bungle it the first time, you let the guy live. Laws of humanity, justice.' The baker laughs in his face: 'First, I tried to avenge my wife who died in the camps. This time is for your girl's fiancé.' Something along those lines."

"Not bad. Powerful stuff, come to think, right?"

"Right. Well executed too. So where does it leave us, Mark? My office hours start in five minutes."

"I plan to confront this Teal woman, Sam. I do. I'm going to get to the bottom of this. I already did speak up. Who does she take me for?"

"Hmm. Or vice versa?"

"What?"

"This should make your day, Mark. Or break it. Hold onto your hat and Bermudas. I'm scrolling the microfiche newspaper clips here, around the time of Greg Davis's vanishing in Manhattan ten years back. No sister is mentioned in obits or write-ups. Survived by children and grandchildren, ex-wives, list of movies made, honors garnered. But no surviving sister. How do you like dem apples, Marko?"

"I guess I'll talk to you later, Sam."

I hung up, suddenly feeling tired, dispirited, thirsty. I got myself a large diet Coke with plenty of crushed ice from the Rocket to the Moon pizza parlor across from the booth, then walked back, placed the cup on the shiny steel shelf next to the phone, and dialed Mike in Chicago. His secretary put me on a brief hold before the big shot answered.

"Hey, Mike. Listen. Something I've got to tell you."

"*You* have something to tell me? I left like five messages with your hotel reception this morning."

"Things are getting pretty hairy here, Mike."

"Mark, listen to me. Things got way out of hand on my end!"

"What happened?"

"Not sure how to break it."

"Try me."

"It's about Tasha."

"What about Tasha?"

"Mark, she passed away early this morning, Moscow time."

"She what?!"

"Sepsis. They took her to the hospital again a few days back. Looks like something went wrong there."

"What? What *is* sepsis?"

"Blood poisoning. They thought she was getting proper care at the Sklif, recuperating at home. Apparently she was not."

"Dear God . . . This is so fucked up. I . . . was it sudden? God, Mike!?"

At this point, I was sniffling audibly. Then I accidentally tilted my cup, spilling Coke all over my t-shirt. Then I tried to sit on the booth floor but could only squat down as low as the metal phone cord allowed me to. Then I thought of pounding the booth glass with the receiver, but quickly reconsidered.

"Oksana says she'd been getting worse over the past few days. And then she just drew her last breath. They tried antibiotics, I think. Nothing worked."

I went on sobbing and couldn't talk. Silently sobbing, opening my mouth wide, inhaling through it, and sobbing, sobbing like a wounded animal.

"What do I do now, Mike?" I finally said. "Get a gun and blow my brains out? It's all my fault, isn't it?"

"It is not *all* your fault, Mark. But . . . she did get mixed up in your affairs. Oksana's take on things. I'd go to Moscow in time for the funeral, pay your last respects, least you could do. But I'd watch your step. You don't want to wind up under the sod next to her. Oksana hates you with a passion. And frankly, I don't blame her much . . ."

"My God. Tasha . . ."

There was silence on the other end of the line. Then he spoke.

"So I guess that wraps up our project, Mark."

"Fuck our project, man! I just have to see this Teal woman one more time, who may actually be not a Teal woman for all I know! And then fly to Moscow."

"What do you mean Teal woman is not a Teal woman? Who is she then?"

"I don't know. An impostor?"

"You're not being delusional, Mark? 'Cause stress'll do it. I'll be there too. Moscow. I'm family, you know. I have no words. A tragedy, a twenty-five-year-old kid. Cut down in her prime."

"Mike, one more stupid cliché out of you and I'm hanging up, seriously."

"I just don't know what to say, Mark. Don't get righteous on my ass, please! I feel like crying myself."

"You do that. Have a good cry. And . . . so will I. Then we'll speak. I need time to process this . . . this thing."

Then, slowly, as if in a daze, I got into my Nissan Presea, fired up the engine, pushed the AC button, and ten minutes later reached my hotel. I needed to pack my bags and check my notes before my final session with my interviewee. I also felt severe pangs of hunger and needed some sleep. Was it a somatic response to the double punch in the solar plexus: bizarre news from San Francisco and god-awful news from Moscow by way of Chicago?

But before fixing myself an avocado, mozzarella, and alfalfa sprouts sandwich and hitting the sack, I asked Marge, the curly haired receptionist in cat's-eye glasses, to book the first flight for me from Boca to Moscow that would make one stopover at JFK the following morning and also to knock me up one hour later on the dot. Marge, all smiles and customer courtesy, thought it best to commit the instructions to paper.

Chapter Thirty-Five.

Later that afternoon, I got to Mrs. Whoever's place, parked my car in front of her Spanish colonial, and rang the doorbell. It also occurred to me that it wouldn't be such a terrible idea to have a gun on me and know how to use it. Just in case. Because at that point, I had no clue whom I had been dealing with for the past couple of weeks nor what that person was up to now.

"Who's that?" she asked, sounding irritated, her voice more muffled than usual.

I answered.

"Isn't it our day off, Mark?"

"It's an emergency, Mrs . . ." I paused for a second. "Teal. A double emergency, in fact."

"Wait. Let me get dressed. I was taking my postprandial nap."

"Post what?" The word seemed new, yet I think I'd heard it before.

She took her time getting dressed as I paced back and forth outside her door, deep in thought. I felt consumed with guilt about Tasha's passing, yet completely hollowed out—a weird in-between state akin to being submerged in slumber while staying alert at the same time.

At last, she opened the door. There was something off about her appearance. At first, I couldn't put my finger on it. Neatly coiffed as ever, dressed in a silk turquoise dress, wearing jewelry and cologne. Then it dawned on me: she had her thin prescription glasses on, not the shades that she wore customarily during our sessions, and her eyes, though as unseeing as usual, were not pale blue but light brown. It looked strange and unsettling, and I tried to blink it away, but chose not to comment. After all, I'd never seen her around that time of day. For all I knew, Boca's late afternoon light might have been playing tricks on my vision, imperfect to begin with, what with the long hours spent transcribing the BRA tapes.

"Have a seat, Mark. Or maybe you want to make us a nice fresh pot of coffee first? What's the emergency? You sound flustered." She seemed genuinely concerned.

"No coffee for me, thank you, Mrs... Teal. The huge emergency is my Moscow girlfriend passed away this morning."

"Oh! Oh no. So very sorry to hear that, Mark. Ah... I seem to recall you had plans to reunite with Dasha at some point?"

"Too late for that. Tasha."

"Tasha. Please accept my condolences, my dear young man. That is so very sad. Oh dear. Very sad. What happened?"

"Sepsis."

"Scepsis?"

"Sepsis."

"What's that? Isn't it blood poisoning?"

"It is."

"Horrible. Rare in this day and age, too. Well, maybe more rare here than... elsewhere. Terrible. So sorry to hear. One has to be strong. Words can mean only so much, I know. I had my share of family losses; Rosie... Rosie, they always told me, take heart. And I learned to do the best I could. It took time. Plenty of it. Sad, very sad. So, what is the other bit of bad news? You said double emergency. Bad news and more bad news? Can't get worse than this, can it?"

"Not worse. Weirder, maybe. Here goes," I began hyperventilating, as I think I already mentioned was my habit when I get excited or confrontational. "It appears that Greg Davis never had a younger sister, Mrs. Teal. Nor did he have an older sister. No mention of any siblings in the papers, older or younger, living or deceased, at the time of his disappearance. Care to comment?"

"Since when do you believe what you read in the papers, you gullible young man?"

"Since I don't know what to believe anymore! Why such a glaring omission?"

"Shoddy reporting. Otherwise, who do you suppose I am, Mark?"

"Your guess is as good as mine, Mrs. Teal. But then yours would probably be better educated."

"Oh? Oh, really? What do you say I pick up the phone and call the police and have you thrown out in a matter of minutes? Just giving you fair warning. Harassment, forcible entry, you name it."

"How so?"

"Today is not our business-as-usual day. You have no right to even be here. Let alone threaten me! I understand you lost your . . ."

"Wait. How am I threatening you?"

"Implying I'm not Rosalyn Teal? What do you call that? A false accusation?"

"It's an accusation, all right. Just how false, you might have to explain downtown. False identity, posing as the sister of a famous man? Let's talk it over peaceably if we can. Come to some mutual understanding?"

"Understanding with a blackmailer? You want to see my Florida driver's license?"

"Come on, I'm not a detective, Mrs. Teal. A blind person's driver's license, why would a research assistant need to see that?"

"I mean my Florida ID."

"Don't bother."

"What, then?"

"For starters, what happened to Mr. Davis? Were you involved in his disappearance? What is this wall-to-wall snow job?"

"My patience is at its limit, Mark. Too many questions. Unnecessary questions, venomous questions. You're hurting because of your friend's passing, but don't take it out on me!"

"Let's keep my friend out of this, shall we? a) What is your connection to Mr. Davis? b) What are the inconsistencies in his body of work? c) What part of your stories, if any, is true? And d) What did you say might give my project a whole new dementia? I mean, dimension, scratch dementia."

"You scratch it. But only if it itches, okay?!" my host suddenly yelled.

"What's that supposed to mean?" I raised my voice a notch, too.

"I said 'a whole new spin,' not dimension. I'm not senile, Mark. Just a little frail. You'll be too when you hit my age, mark my words. You realize that twenty years ago, all things being equal, you'd be in a bad way had you carried on like this in my residence? Really bad way. Black-and-blue way. Broken neck way, maybe."

"It is twenty years later, okay? Retroactive threats; how effective are they, exactly? I have a plane to catch tomorrow morning, Mrs. Whoever. And I'm bushed. And crushed by the news from Moscow. Not in the mood for tricks, that's for damn sure."

"Better hurry along, then. I'm really sorry for your loss, Mark. Sepia . . ."

"You already said that. I appreciate the sentiment. Now, back to our muttons. Are you in any way related to Mr. Davis?"

"Hmm, yes. You might say that. So?"

"So you are not the sister that he never had, are you?"

"He did have a sister," my interlocutor sighed. "Though I'm not her. I wish I were. Always did."

"I'm afraid I don't follow. What happened to her?"

"Pneumonia. Rosie caught it in her teens playing in the snow with her girlfriends that winter night a long time ago, which I told you about a few sessions back. The year they were dispatching ministers right and left. Six months before we left. Mother and Father cared for her the best they could, didn't spare any expenses, hired the best doctors. All for naught. She just could never get rid of her horrible whooping cough. Almost didn't pass muster at Ellis Island; not Chatterbox Ben as I told you, but her. So, much of what I shared about her life was true. Up until the Stanislavsky's actor's caper. Including it, actually. But nothing happened after that. Not to her, not with her. Other than her brief illness and untimely death at age twenty. She caught a bad cold watching the bungled kidnapping from across the street in the pouring rain. Her illness recurred, then exacerbated. A few days later, our beautiful Rosie expired. So much for the immortal dragonflies she so believed in as a child."

"Very sad. Sounds like a wonderful and delicate young woman. So, then, you would be . . . ?"

"I would. And I am. Her brother."

"What?! You don't look like anybody's brother if you ask me! Hairdo and all. How many brothers did she have anyway?!"

"Just one."

"Wait. So . . . one has gone missing. And?"

"I'm the missing one, Mark! And you are one clingy, annoying pest of an interviewer if I ever did see one. Not too quick on the uptake either!"

"So, your name is . . . ?"

"That's right." My interviewee slowly stood up from her armchair, then turned her back to me and gestured to help unzip her dress.

To say that I balked at the request is to say nothing. Gerontophilia is not my bag, never was. Vjollca was as far as I went on the road to milfdom. Plus, my deceased lover looked fifteen years younger than her actual age, which was early middle age. So I blushed deeply, broke into a sweat, and asked my host if he thought it was necessary.

"Only if you want to get to know me a little better, sonny boy," my interviewee whispered, turning his face to me and giving me a mischievous wink that almost made me puke on the carpeted living room floor.

"Come on, Mark," Mr. In-All-Probability-Davis continued. "I'm not trying to seduce you. Aren't we both a little too long in the tooth for this crazy remake of *The Graduate* Florida-style?"

So I helped him unzip his turquoise dress, which he got out of with the agility of a much younger person, then he carefully took off his well-coiffed wig and turquoise clip-on earrings and stared me right in the eye. Standing before me on veiny limpy legs was a grinning, rosy-cheeked, bespectacled, nonagenarian gentleman with little hair on his pale, flaky scalp. He wore tight lavender lacy panties and a matching padded bra over the yellow t-shirt that read "Florida Is for the Ageless." He also puckered his chapped lips and blew me a kiss, followed by a hearty giggle. A sight and a half to behold, a quick gender-defying striptease, an ill-fitting finale to our BRA sessions, which suddenly attained a new, literal meaning.

"Gregory Davis, pleased to make your acquaintance," he said, modestly cupping the bulge protruding from his panties with his left hand as he extended his right one for a handshake.

"Good to meet you too, Mr. Davis, finally," I muttered, shaking his withered hand. Though I was never into the whole drag scene, I must confess that the spectacle unfolding before me piqued my curiosity a bit, so I just kept staring at him unblinkingly as a hundred questions galloped through my mind.

"So why the masquerade, the blindness, the whole Houdini act, Mr. Davis? Who is it that you're hiding from?!" I raised my voice yet another notch, calling after my interviewee as he shuffled over to the bedroom only to reemerge from it minutes later wearing an emerald tracksuit and the same t-shirt sans the padded brassiere.

"Good question. Used to be IRS, IRS, and more IRS, sir. The fuckers got too nosy at some point. Started sending me snitches. Bugged my gazpacho twice, imagine that! That's what we called our best boy. Hot-wired the bidet at the Algonquin, the oldest trick in the book. Implicated me in all sorts of savagery short of cannibalism and rainmaking. Long story skirt, I mean short, now I just enjoy being my sister, period. Blind yet sighted. Being someone else can be a lot of fun, Mark," he responded as he shot me a stare with his very seeing light brown eyes. Was he wearing contacts before? Did it matter now? "And so the story I've been telling you was more about her. I don't really like to talk about myself anyway. I think I already told you that. Never did. Plus, at first, I had my suspicions about you, too. You passed the test, though. And I do apologize for taking you for a ride, a long and bumpy one at that. Not that the time you spent here went unremunerated for you. Or for me, for that matter."

"Okay, but . . . But what about the movies that were never made? Shouldn't you, of all people, know your filmography?! I mean, how do I present these cockamamy fabrications to my employer?"

"Ah, Mark. There's the rub-a-dub, as my late pal George Cukor would put it over a nightcap past midnight as we talked the 'Lubitsch Touch.' Those were no fabrications. At least, I believe they were not. That's where you come in without knocking. I may still be able to move about, albeit not without difficulty. And I still enjoy the use of my eyes . . . Yet certain things slip my mind, sometimes. They do. So yesterday night, after our spat, let's call it that and move forward—why dwell on unpleasantries?—I had to go back to my notes to check a few items. Guess what. A whole lot of movies, preparatory notes, and storyboards were missing from my archives. Gone. As if someone clean erased them. Imagine my surprise. Panic attack was what it was, really. Not that I'm that worried about legacy. Never have been. I'm a known filmmaker, notes or no notes, school curricula or otherwise. But I am also a sucker for order. Cause-and-effect disruption doesn't sit well with me. So. Since I also happen to have a small screening room here up in the attic, I climbed up there yesterday night, fired up my projector, and screened a few 16 mm films from my library. But . . . it was a bit of a challenge. Takes a steadier hand and a sharper pair of peepers. All I was able to check was just one title: *Bad Boy Rob*. Though the white duct tape label on the can was blank, I knew it was *Bad Boy* because films had been shelved alphabetically. Guess what. Not only was the tape blank, but the entire picture was blank, too! All ninety-four minutes of it!"

"Damage? After all, it's been a long time, Mr. Davis. Or maybe that fire?"

"I know how to store film, temperature and all, believe me, Mark. And there was no fire, remember?"

"Oh yes. Silly of this gullible interviewer. So what do you make of it, Mr. Davis?"

"This is for us to find out, Mark. Test my hunch. You thread, I deduce," said Greg Davis as he motioned me to follow him to the bedroom.

"What's the old sneaky geezer up to now?" I remember thinking as I watched him draw the curtains between his enormous dark oak armoire and mahogany king-sized bed. Behind the curtains was an eggshell-colored double door.

He pushed it open with effort and stepped inside. I couldn't help noticing that he was panting and wheezing more than when he was Mrs. Teal. But then, Mrs. Teal never really had to do much moving about, since all she did throughout our sessions was sit still in her armchair. It was me who was busy making coffee or fetching her mail when we heard the postman drop it in the mailbox outside her door. How come I never wondered how "Mrs. Teal" was able to read her mail is a whole different question. A possible answer again might be "gullible."

Chapter Thirty-Six.

After we climbed up the short flight of stairs and entered the cool semi-darkness of the attic, redone as a small screening room, Mr. Davis flicked the light switch on. I noticed a 16 mm optical Elmo projector with two take-up arms, which stood on the tall cream-colored Art Deco pedestal table with curved legs next to the attic window and across from it a small screen on the opposite wall. There were six wall shelves beside the projector, three of them stacked with thick black binders, some of their four-inch spines labeled, others blank. The remaining three lower shelves were lined with a good many tin cans and two devices were sitting at either end of each shelf. I assumed they had to do with monitoring the temperature and humidity in the room, though what they looked like were high-end miniature washer and dryer machines. Strange.

"Welcome to the Davis treasure trove," announced the film director, with a note of pride in his voice. "I had all my pictures transferred to 16 mm for storage efficiency when I got settled in my modest abode here."

"Double dupe-downs?" I thought the time was right to flash one of the five film processing terms I still remembered from grad school.

"You know your film, young fella," Greg Davis smiled. "Let's see some of mine now. Start from the end; see if it's a happy one." He reached for the last can on the shelf and handed it to me. "You can wake me up in the middle of the night and I'll know it by heart. This one here is *My Witness, My Neighbor, My Wife*. Go ahead, play the projectionist, Mark. Nothing like a steady hand when it comes to threading."

So I opened the hefty tin-plated can, extracted a 16 mm reel from it, put it on the supply arm, and, in less than a minute, threaded it through the gate and inserted the loose end into the take-up arm with the empty reel already in place.

"Once a film student, always a film student," I said, quite pleased with myself.

"Fire it up, Mark," commanded Mr. Davis as I briefly envisioned him in my mind's eye wearing director's boots on the set and fiercely bellowing "Action!" into a megaphone.

Only there was none on the screen. No action, no camera, just a palish-yellow beam coming from the projector for five minutes, interrupted by Mr. Davis's barely audible "cut" followed by "It's not in the can. Where is it, then?"

"Just as I thought, damn it all to hell," he mumbled, then shuffled over to the shelf and pulled another reel from it, the first one in the first row. "No label on this one either," he grumbled. "But I know for damn sure it should be *The Asphalt Cyclops*, the A's. For this one, I had Ron Silver, my screenwriter, rework an old Italian tale about a monk held captive by a giant. Only in my play, there's the thug's ring that the monk (an insurance agent in the updated version) puts on his finger and is thus bound to return to the one-eyed thug's headquarters in Red Hook . . . The insurance man can't take it off for the life of him, so he is forced to cut off his ring finger. But first, he takes out a dismemberment policy as the sole beneficiary . . . Okay, let's give it a spin. See how it's stood the test of time."

It had not. A repeat cycle revealed no Red Hook Cyclops, no insurance man, no finger with or without a ring—nothing. Except for a steady whirring of sprocket holes and the flickering palish-yellow light on the screen across the room.

"Following in the footsteps of Paul Sharits and the rest of the structural film gang?" I chuckled stupidly.

"What the fuck you blathering about?!" growled Greg Davis.

He clearly didn't know diddly-squat about the American avant-garde, nor did he appreciate my cheek.

"Sorry, Mr. Davis. No disrespect meant. It's been one heck of a day. And I have a morning flight to catch. Lots on my mind. Don't get upset, please."

"Apologies accepted," said Greg Davis hesitantly.

After a few more predictably false starts, Mr. Davis suggested we check out some films in labeled cans.

"That's how tests ought to be conducted," he explained. "You vary data to see if you arrive at similar results. Though I hope to God, we don't," he quickly added. Then he pulled from the shelf the rusty can with *A Flat* scribbled on the off-white tape pasted across its lid. I promptly removed the reel from it, threaded the film, and flipped the projector switch on. "The Roadster Studios present," the opening title said, "*A Flat.* Photoplay directed . . . by Gregory Davis. Play . . . by Gregory Davis. Cast: The Young Man . . . Gregory Davis. The Policeman . . . Rudyard Thornton. Camera . . . Norman Breuer."

The film started with the establishing shot of a deserted intersection with a lone figure of a mustachioed traffic cop standing bolt upright in the middle. Suddenly, out of nowhere, a roadster approached the intersection, raising billows of dust behind it. The cop halted the roadster, then motioned it to proceed, and the car passed him. Only to run over a small dark object on the road, presumably a beer bottle. The roadster got a flat and veered wildly over towards the shoulder. A young man in a straw hat got out of the car and examined the tire ruefully. Then he opened the trunk, took the air pump out, and rolled up his sleeves.

"Next!" Mr. Davis handed me a can labeled "A Noose Too Loose" and winked at me as if we shared an understanding that this part of the test would be a cinch. This time, a big man was walking his Scottish terrier at dusk by the reservoir in Central

Park. The dog was sluggish yet alert; a flock of ducks gliding on the water got his attention. Now, he was going crazy, pulling on the leash and barking but in a subdued, weary, tired dog way. His owner pulled on the leash: "Quiet, Janacek, quiet." Next scene: a clean-shaved rotund man in thick glasses fussed about his living room, pulled down the window curtains, cranked up an old-fashioned Radiola, and put a thick 78 rpm record on the spindle. A military march played as the Nazi, his eyes half-closed, tapped his thick fingers on the rolltop desk and nodded his head to the march's rhythm. A doorbell rang. He stopped the music and let in his sprightly and handsome girlfriend, who kissed him on both cheeks. He lifted her up and spun her around the room. She laughed infectiously and ruffled his thinning hair.

"What do you think?" said Mr. Davis as he motioned me to stop the projector.

"I like it," I said, "though I personally would have let the scumbag dangle thirty minutes into the movie! Plus, she is the spitting image of my late girlfriend. What gives?"

"So you know what happens?"

"I know my Davis, Mr. Davis," I answered coyly as I noticed him smile out of the corner of my eye.

"Oh, goodie," said the director and patted me on the shoulder. "But I was done with shorts by the mid-'20s. Stopped making them right after this one-hour baby." And with this, he handed me yet another reel.

The one-hour baby turned out very familiar. It opened with a fragile young girl tidying up the modest room, most likely a mansard: picking up the clothes strewn about the floor, holding the rumpled shirt to her chest, brushing the wide-brimmed hat that hangs on the wall. In the next scene, a young man in a similar hat approached a casino. The soft organ music from the previous scene gave way to the loud cacophony of the gambling den as the camera left the young man's headgear and soared up to reveal a row of hats sitting on a counter in front of a cloakroom attendant. Then, a pan alongside fedoras, top hats, and cabbie hats followed until the camera finally closed in on the withered attendant watching over the clients' hats. A pack of cards fanned out and folded again where the attendant's heart should've been. But it's not there: he is Play personified, cold, heartless, calculating. "Ah, to be at the right time in the right place! Isn't that what success is all about?" The intertitles flowed in and out of the frame like smoke from a hookah. The young man bet his last dollar on the wheel of luck. "Make your game . . . The game is made . . . Bets are closed!" cried out the effeminate bald croupier ecstatically—and the young man lost. Dejected, he stumbled out of the hall, ready to leave the gambling house. "Your hat! You forgot your hat!" the attendant called after him, contorting his lipless mouth. The young man took a few steps toward the attendant, who handed him his headgear and extended his hand. The young man made an apologetic gesture: no money for the tip, none, pardon me, sir.

In the next scene, we see the young man on the pier, staring off into the dark waters of the Atlantic Ocean. The ocean is merely suggested, too dark to see anything save for reflections of the distant lighthouse illuminating the young man's face intermittently. The images of his doting mother, his friend Eugene puffing on his eternal pipe, Pauline (the beautiful young lady from the opening scene), and finally, the gambling den's attendant, his face paler than death itself, float through his mind as he contemplates jumping off the pier. When lo! a simple melody played upon a solitary reed stops the young man in his tracks, compelling him to turn around and follow the tune coming from a tiny place by the side of the road. In the next scene, the young man is standing in front of the pawnbroker's shop, looking at the handwritten sign that says Open, then Closed, then Open again: not easy to tell in the darkness of the night.

The young man pulls his hat down and knocks on the door. No one answers, so he slowly opens it and takes a few cautious steps inside the sparsely lit room. To say its interior is cluttered would be an understatement. The place is chaotic, the way the primeval chaos might have looked had there been anyone to see it. But instead of chemical elements, the shop is filled with fragments of civilizations long gone or still extant. A hodge-podge of midsize Egyptian mummies, nineteenth-century prints of New York City's barely developed downtown; a shoddy painting of Theodore Roosevelt and his Rough Riders charging ahead through the San Juan Hills in Cuba; a bas-relief of Zeus above a small statue of Athena Pallada in her helmet, a staff in her hand and an owl perched upon her shoulder; WWI gas masks and dishpan hats, a Civil War cannon ball, a replica of Cleopatra's needle, the effigy of a yawning bear cub on hindlegs, a vase bearing Abraham Lincoln's portrait standing beside a bust of Benjamin Franklin, a poster-size daguerreotype of P. T. Barnum standing on Jumbo the Elephant's back underneath the American eagle wall plaque complete with banner, thirteen arrows held in its left talon and an olive branch in its right one; a reproduction of David Tenier's *Adam and Eve in Paradise,* the first man's hand reaching for the fruit his lady friend clutches to her groin, the couple's moment of tender friendship intruded upon by the serpent in a tree right next to a framed map that compares the expansion of the US slave states through the nineteenth century and the territories comprising the Pale of Settlement of the Russian Empire before 1914, a number of hand-woven tree of life Persian rugs, a Cherokee scalping knife which made the young man's hair stand on end, and other objects of art, craft, cartography, and worship too numerous for the viewer to take in or the writer to list.

Suddenly, a slouching figure in a dark coat appears behind the young man's back and taps him on the shoulder. Startled, the young man turns around. Before him is a centenarian, incidentally played by the thoroughly made-up yet uncannily recognizable Rudyard Thornton, the actor who portrayed the policeman in Davis's first short, *A Flat*. Only this time, there is obviously no ticket issued for sleeping behind the wheel, just a grave admonition uttered upon hearing the young man's five-intertitles-long account of his despair and grim plans to end it all in one fell swoop. "What's your hurry, young man!" the shopkeeper cries out, rolling his eyes, then succumbs to a protracted coughing fit. The young man pats him on the back as the shopkeeper nods appreciatively, then motions the visitor to stop, his coughing in check now. "Live a little, for Adam's sake. See how things play out." The young man shakes his head. "I have made up my mind. No turning back for me, sir." "Ah, the folly of youth!" the old man exclaims. "There's always a turning back. Look at what I have here. Maybe that will help you change your mind!" With this, the proprietor opens a glass cabinet, exposing a wild ass's skin stretched out like a map of terra incognita on its back wall. "I don't believe I will have any use for it where I'm headed. No need to keep warm in the undiscovered country from whence no traveler returns", says the young man, unable to hide the sadness upon his face. "Says who?" scoffs the old shopkeeper. "This magic skin will help you cross the chasm between 'To Will' and 'To Have Our Will.' 'To Will' consumes us, and 'To Have Our Will' destroys us. But the brain, that intermediary between the two, the brain alone can steep us in a perpetual calm, for it is through its agency that one is capable of living a life of moderation. Use it. The only way to lead your life. As I found out the hard way. Look," and the old man flips the skin over, exposing words written on its lining in Sanskrit, which the young man, scholar and polyglot that he is, has no trouble translating into English as presented by the intertitles: "Possessing me, thou shalt possess all things. But thy life is mine, for God has so willed it. Wish, and thy wishes shall be fulfilled; But measure thy desires according to the life that is in thee. This is thy life; with each wish, I must shrink even as thy own days. Wilt thou have me? Take me. God will harken unto thee. So be it!"

"Cut," ordered Greg Davis. "Still packs a punch, does it not?"

"And how!" I said, turning off the projector as the young man's wide-eyed close-up froze on the screen. "A powerful story's assured and inventive screen adaptation. I assume you penned the screenplay, too, Mr. Davis?"

"The skin play practically wrote itself," answered the director. "All I had to do was press the blank sheets to it, mimeograph style."

"Come again?"

"Let's return to the living room." Mr. Davis sounded tired but resolute. "The test is effectively complete. I thank you for lending a hand, Mark. My hunch is proven beyond a reasonable doubt. No doubt at all, as a matter of fact. Let me share something with you. You will likely find it puzzling and think your host is nutty as a fruitcake. I don't care. All I want to do for now is indulge your patience and ask you to suspend your disbelief." He was uttering these words haltingly, a can of film pressed to his chest with one hand, the other one clutching the railing as we took our time descending the stairs, and at last found ourselves in the dark living room. The time was 7:25 p.m. He flipped the lights on, shuffled across the room back to his armchair, and plopped down in it with a stifled breath of relief.

"What hunch is that, Mr. Davis? Seems I'm ready for everything, though not too much more of it," I said, pulling my chair closer to his and turning my tape recorder on.

"Turn that thing off now," the director said curtly. "Listen. Here comes the fun part. Maybe a windfall for you, too, like nobody's business. Maybe not. Up to you how you slice that pie."

"A windfall? I'm all ears, Mr. Davis," I turned the tape recorder off.

"You remember my train encounter with the officer gentleman who was traveling with us? The lieutenant I got into fisticuffs with and pushed off the train?"

"Sure do. Yuriy? One of the more vivid episodes of your epic. A figment of your imagination like so many others, I presume?"

"Figment, my foot. The luckiest thing that ever happened to me!"

"Not to him, apparently. No worries, though. Consider yourself exonerated. Water under the bridge. Three-quarters of a century of it, to be exact, Mr. Davis."

"Keep your exonerations to yourself, Mark! Listen to me. The soldier who accompanied the tsar's family to their final destination jumped off the speeding train on his own!" announced Mr. Davis while scoping the room as if expecting a standing ovation from an invisible audience. "I certainly didn't push him. He jumped into the night of his own volition. Or otherwise disappeared. I can't be entirely sure now . . . Rolled off into the night?"

"Mr. Davis, can I ask you a stupid question? Just don't get mad, please?"

"What?"

"You're not on some sort of meds, are you? And you didn't skip them on my account by any chance?"

"Don't be silly, Mark. I take all the meds I need. Vitamin supplements, too. Sometimes a nightcap. It has nothing to do with anything."

"Oh, good! So. Are you saying the lieutenant jumped to his death from the speeding train? And you don't mean some action scene from one of your films either? *A Train to Reno*?"

"Rolled off from the train window like a wheel, I'm telling you! Listen here, Mark. It may sound insane, but listen. What the sucker, though I shouldn't be calling him no names, what the passenger had in his *sac de voyage* was the wild ass's skin, the magic skin, the real deal with a capital D!"

At this point I started looking around furtively, thinking of a polite yet final way to make my exit. Pat the ever sleepy Honoré D. on his big brown head, thank my host for his time and entertainment, drive back to my hotel, try to get some shut-eye, drive to the airport first thing in the morning, take all the cash out of my Boca bank account on my way there, return the car to the rent-a-car place, and get on the plane to New York with the connecting flight to Moscow in time for the funeral of my dear departed bear girl, my golden-haired Tasha. And I didn't have to worry about flying the red-eye this time. I had the bread now. What I didn't have, though, was the time or the patience for bullshit dished out aplenty by a demented ex-filmmaker who'd spent the last ten years of his life in drag and apparent solitude. Nothing wrong with either, I thought to myself. I just have other things on my plate at the moment.

"Mr. Davis, I hate to be rude, but I'd better get going. So much on my mind, like you wouldn't believe. Finish packing, say goodbye to parents, haven't quite gotten to say hello yet, book a flight. Actually, scratch the flight. Marge, the hotel receptionist, did that. And yes, get some winter clothes. Here or at JFK. Winters in Moscow are very different from Boca, let me tell you. December in Moscow? Are you kidding me? 'Punishing' is the word I'm groping for."

"Listen to me, young man," Mr. Davis said, switching to a loud, hissing whisper. "The lady who saw the so-called lieutenant off in the city of Lemberg was a distant relation of Evelina Hanska, the Polish noblewoman that Balzac himself was married to once. It's public knowledge, okay? Less known is the fact that Balzac was in possession of the real magic skin. Don't ask me how he got a hold of it, but he did, and he bequeathed it to Pani Hanska shortly before he expired. How do you think one gets to write ninety novels by age fifty? Ninety, Mark! Yes, enormously gifted; yes, superbly prolific. Yes, wrote at night drinking industrial quantities of Turkish coffee. But ninety freaking novels, some of them masterpieces, no ifs or buts?! Ever thought of that?"

"Can't say I did 'cause I didn't," I confessed indifferently. "Never crossed my mind to do the math. Plus, I read just three, to be honest. Duly impressed by the scope and vitality, though bombastic and wordy is not my cup of tea."

"Never mind your tea, Mark! And while we're at it, ever thought of how I managed to make forty movies before Greg became Rosie?"

"What forty movies, Mr. Davis? Get real, please! You made no more than twenty! Period."

"Listen to me, and don't contradict a man thrice your age. The gent who shared our compartment happened to be a spirit, a demon, an ouroboros, his head temporarily out of his ass. Call him what you will, though I wouldn't bandy the D-word about in vain. But I wouldn't put that past him either. There was no fight, that's for damn sure! I made up the fight for my family right there on the spot. What fight? No fat lip or bleeding, either. It takes two, remember? You negotiate, you make deals. If you're lucky. Or unlucky. But you don't fight with his kind. A little chat in the corridor did take place. Chat is a misnomer, too. He didn't as much as move his lips. I certainly didn't utter a word. Yet I knew exactly what it was he was trying to impart. He said he forgave my outrageous display of disrespect but asked me to abstain from expectorations in the future. One misdirected spittle, he said, can cost one one's life. You don't go around spitting in a spirit's eye with impunity, he said—or anyone else's, for that matter. For if you do, he said, the Devil may take you one day. Or your kin. He also told me the skin in the patent leather *sac de voyage* was mine for the asking. Would make my life in the New World a whole lot easier and my career more rewarding, in more ways than one. That he was doing it for me because I was special. Just how special? Who the hell knows? And the trade I plied was special, too. Graven images were his domain, he said. And he knew for a fact, he said, that my input would be especially weighty and welcome, what with my little quirks, which he, a devious shapeshifter and con artist extraordinaire, had a soft spot for. And more significantly, I shouldn't ever blame him for our having to flee the country. Part of the perpetual process. He wasn't on anybody's side; that's ridiculous. Maybe there are no sides. It wouldn't behoove him to make a choice, even if there were one. He said his stock-in-trade was stirring things up when things got stale. Period. New wine in new wineskins to borrow a phrase from people he normally didn't like to borrow from, he said. And if history is to teach us anything, though it rarely does, pity the land whose Hebrews abandon her. And the damnedest thing is, embarrassing as it is to admit it even now, while he was talking to me, talking in a manner of speaking, I had a distinct sensation as if many hands, feet too, soft and flexible, were giving me a full-body, sensual, rub-down. Was I being caressed by a spirit of the lower world in an upright position on a speeding train to Romania, unless it was Belgium, as he was bestowing a present of shagreen upon me while giving me a history lesson? Is the transmission of knowledge inherently an act of seduction? Then he asked me not to put him in any of my future pictures directly (though he wasn't averse to allegories or symbolism), mentioned something about leaving the heavy-handed, on the nose treatment up to the mix (what mix?), and rolled out of the train window into the night."

"Very well, then. So your crossing the Atlantic was homicide-free after all," I observed coldly. "And you met one of the deputies of the Evil One or maybe the dude himself, or ouroboros, whatever that is, who didn't seem all that evil and a crackerjack masseur to boot. Then what happened?"

"Stop being condescending, for fuck's sake!" thundered Greg Davis and clenched his fists. "Yuriy Borisovich's lady friend who gave him the ass's skin didn't know shit about its power. Or her friend being the ouroboros. She knew from her ma or her grandma that the skin was special. And that was that. She didn't know Arabic and couldn't make out the inscription on the back. I did, and I could. Learned some when we were doing the Yiddish Scheherazade back in my shtetl. It wasn't a shtetl, I shouldn't be putting it down like that. But it was no Hollywood either, also a shtetl, if you ask me. Only more socialists running around back when I did a few pictures for Warner Brothers. Anyway, a few years after the encounter on the train, when I was down on my luck in New York, I rubbed the skin for the first time. To see what happens if you ask it to spot you a crisp C-note. Spot is the wrong word—you don't have to pay it back, you understand. I'll explain. The writing on the back of the skin said, 'The man who owns me will possess everything.' So I asked for a hundred, a tryout magic, a test. Guess what? I should have asked for a cool mil. Just as well, I didn't. Wouldn't have had the time to spend it before the big crash. The dough would have turned to dust in the blink of an eye. And it does shave off some time of your life for every wish it grants you. But the hundred I found in my breast pocket sure came in handy-dandy. It would probably be like five hundred dollars in today's money. So what if it made my life an hour shorter? Or maybe a few minutes, who knows? It's not like it sends you the billable hours after every session."

"Did it shrink much? I mean, the skin?" I asked stiffly, trying to play into the conversation the best I could, still far from being sold on the bizarre tale.

"Nah, not appreciably," said the director. "It shrinks the same regardless of how much money you ask for. Kind of a fixed rate deal. I also wondered what would happen when I asked for a movie favor working on my first biggie. Yep, the eponymous *Skin*. Shrank a bit more. Something funny about it philosophically: asking for the skin's help while scripting and shooting *The Skin*. Shrank quite a bit when I asked her to stop Mother from drinking herself to death. Then, a few '30s MGM musicals were financed with its help. Though I must say all the artistic decisions I made were magic-free. Except for *The Wild Skin* proper. I was timid; I needed help; I could use encouragement. Not much of it from then on. A human mind has all the magic it needs. Sounds corny, but it does."

"So, Mr. Davis. Let me get one thing straight here," I said to the old man as he grew silent, catching his breath. "If I am to believe your story, you have this ticking H-bomb on your hands way before the real H-bomb is even developed. And with its help, you could conceivably stop wars and the Holocaust, derail McCarthyism, prevent political assassinations, halt the escalation of Vietnam, what have you. Yet you choose to use it to finance musicals and fucking courtroom dramas? Aren't you missing the bigger picture? What is this fixation on popular entertainment?!"

"But Mark, listen, don't you think I tried?" My interlocutor sounded downhearted, perhaps for the first time during our sessions. "The thing is, it doesn't do the big picture. As I was quick to discover when I tried meddling in WWII and later in the Korean War. And let's not forget the Cuban crisis! It does only what immediately concerns its possessor. Period."

"Okay, I hear you, Mr. Davis. But I do believe what makes the bigger picture genuinely big is that it touches everyone, *including* the skin's possessor, does it not?"

"No. It doesn't work that way." Mr. Davis shook his head. "Only if its possessor is Jack Kennedy or McNamara. And I never did trust the government enough to let them in on my little secret here."

With this, he stood up from his armchair and lightly patted what I had assumed to be a small piece of loose upholstery covering its seat. Then he beckoned me to get a closer look. I obliged as he flipped the hide over, revealing the miniature Arabic script that embellished its lining. Then he uttered haughtily, as it probably befits the man who used to possess all things, or maybe still does, "Any further questions, young man?"

"You betcha," I said. "So what about the missing movies, Mr. Davis? The ones you claim to have made, but actually never did? What's that all about?"

"Ah, a very good question, Mark! A very good question indeed. No wonder you probably asked it five times already, though I had no good answer for you. Not until now, anyway. You see, what happened when McCarthyism struck full force, and investigations were shaking the army and the arts, when everyone and his uncle was called to testify before the committee, I had my moment of doubt. We all do sometimes, skin or no skin. What I thought to myself was: What if I don't have it in me to pull through the hard times? I'm an artist, after all, not a hero, Mark. In a word, I was afraid I'd cave in under pressure. So what I asked the skin to do for me was to erase all the movies I had directed since 1948 entirely. I was making about a picture a year back then, some casting a probing, not to say jaundiced, eye on the social ills besetting the nation, others pure fluff; though, one hopes, always staying this side of schlock. So what happened was all the movies that I made, all the colleagues that I worked with, all the creative talent and personnel involved, from screenwriters to assistant sound editors and best boys, and all the press and eventual references in textbooks were erased from the celluloid, public memory, history—without a trace. Gone with the wink. A bit of rewriting of Hollywood to save my good name and the names—and the lives—of others. A drop in the bucket, to be sure. But my very own drop. A safety valve. And it worked, too. Because the wish concerned first and foremost myself, the director, the man at the helm. But it ultimately saved the lives, careers, reputation, and freedom of hundreds of others."

"Wow," I mouthed, temporarily at a loss for words. "Wow. Mr. Davis, this is totally insane, and fascinating and unbelievable, though believe you, I do. What a beautiful and selfless thing to do! I mean four years of filmmaking at the peak of your productivity flushed down the toilet. Of course, I have no reason to doubt that you did this admirable, self-effacing deed... Though, come to think of it, *A Noose Too Loose* still wouldn't have been your last picture. Not according to your own account. Am I right?"

"True enough, dear Mark. True enough," sighed the old film director. "What happened, and here comes our grand finale, though hardly any fanfare will be called for—few raspberries and a fool's cap with bells for a prize would be more apropos... Anyhow, when I asked the skin here," and he patted the edge of it again like it was a sentient being which, for all I knew, it could very well have been, "when I asked it circa 1952 or '53 to erase all the movies from existence starting from 1948, either I didn't word my wish clearly (don't forget I was under enormous pressure what with testifying and blacklisting going on all around me), or maybe the skin didn't quite get it. Language is a tool open to interpretation and misinterpretation, as you well know. Math, by comparison, is not. However, I do believe I was articulate enough back then. Still had my own teeth, too. But what happened, and we just witnessed firsthand the multiple proofs of it up in the projection room, what happened was *all* the pictures I ever made since 1948 vanished for good. Not just the ones made between 1948 and 1953, as I hoped they would, but also the ones I kept making through the mid-'50s up until the mid-'70s. And that was the direct and unfortunate result of my garbled wish fulfilled ass-backwards or the skin being, well, a little thick. Or both. Too late to look for a scapegoat now. But what I realized while watching reels upon reels of blank footage up in the attic was that my pictures kept being regularly produced, only to vanish into thin air the moment I finished them. Without a trace: a blank in the audience's memory, no magazine write-ups, no box office. Nada. Void. Was this Yuriy aware ahead of time that that would happen? Did the fact that the skin destroyed the pictures I had been making play into his hand? Were my films undesirable at the highest—one is tempted to say the metaphysical—level of censorship at the time? Just thinking out loud, or maybe ranting out loud. Your guess is as good as mine . . ."

"Good Lord," I said, stupefied and feeling sorry for my host. "So all of this you realized just now as we tried to screen your films upstairs? That, frankly, I find hard to believe, Mr. Davis! Did you never bother to check how your films did at the box office or how the critics or public received them? What is this vacuum you imposed on yourself for years before your retirement?"

"Mark, but I never cared a jot about the press. I already told you that! I never cared to read the reviews. Trades or daily press, least of all the glossies. What's the use? I wanted to create, not to know which way the wind blew when my AD barked, "Quiet on the set!" and I yelled, "Action!" Out of sight, out of mind when the film's in the can; onto the next thing financed by the skin was my modus operandi as far back as I can recall. Jack, my accountant, and his firm handled my finances. Well, I thought they did anyway. As a matter of fact, when you started bugging me about inconsistencies and stuff, I got really pissed first. Then I went to my production notes and sketches, only to see a whole lot of them missing! And yes, I finally forced myself to start screening the pictures. All those years, up until the last one completed in 1976, I thought I was making movies for an audience, when, in fact, I was making them for myself alone. Not even that. It was a lot like drawing on the ocean's surface with a twig. Like that unexplained squiggle of an epigraph in *The Wild Ass's Skin*. Disappears right after you're finished with it. Took your confronting me in the most ridiculous, most bullying fashion—"

"I'm sorry, Mr. Davis. All I was trying—"

"—to actually bother checking. And then I thought back on how, coincidentally or not, I almost drowned in that Algonquin suite. I mean indoor snorkeling has never been my forte. The money all of a sudden becoming tight . . . IRS snooping around. Bills piling up. My wife, my dear and fragile Felicite passing on after a protracted illness. So one day, I just thought it best to say goodbye to it all. Well, not goodbye goodbye. Become someone else. Someone of the opposite gender, a soft lateral transformation, no cutting off your pecker. My pecker. Always got a kick out of dressing up like the fair sex anyway. So why not become someone I really cared for? Someone nipped in the bud. Someone I missed terribly. See if that eases the pain. But you already know all that . . ."

"Incredible. And incredibly sad. And touching and . . . I mean this and your skin wish. So much work, such great art. All perished!"

"Some great, some decent, some made just to stay in the game. At least now I get why I'm near forgotten. Haven't been in the public eye for one-quarter of a century. That will certainly do it!"

"But wait . . . Wait just a sec. Doesn't the skin work both ways, like at the end of your movie?"

"How do you mean?"

"I mean, you remember how at the end of *The Wild Ass's Skin* Raphael asks the shagreen to take back all the possessions it bestowed upon him, all the favors he was ever granted? And it does that, leaving him penniless and growing in size? I mean, the skin grows in size, while Raphael in the movie epilogue adds new wisdom and quite a few years to his life at the same time?"

"I don't know, Mark. Maybe it does, maybe it doesn't. I personally never tried it. It's just the ending I thought of—again, not without a little help from the skin—as we collaborated on the play, knocking around a few ideas . . ."

"Care to try now, Mr. Davis? I mean, what better time? What if life occasionally does imitate art? It wouldn't hurt either. I mean, if the skin indeed erased the movies made since 1948 until the mid-'70s, you could conceivably ask it to restore them, make them appear again. After all, they were really truly made. Made by you. Had everything to do with you."

"Are you saying?.."

"Precisely! Bring back two decades' worth of your work in film. Will put you right back on the map. Put some money in the bank, too. Think about it for a minute, Mr. Davis!"

"Hmm . . . No harm in trying, I suppose. Can't say easier said than done. Because saying amounts to the same thing as doing with this baby. To will and to have your will. Going back should be a no-brainer with her. Come to think, maybe you want to hop a ride, too. Eh, Mark?"

It was my turn to ask what the old man had in mind. He cleared his throat before responding, speaking slowly, giving weight to each word that issued from his lips.

"What I mean is I owe you one. Big time, Mark."

"How's that?"

"Simple," he continued in the same well-tempered yet solemn tone of voice. "If not for you, I wouldn't have gone to my notes to check just what sort of inconsistencies this Russkie weirdo was bugging me about. What was all this crap about there being not a trace anyplace of the stuff I positively recalled making? So, without your prodding, what with my memory not being what it used to be, I wouldn't have figured out what the skin did to me. Naughty, naughty girl," and he playfully slapped the shagreen sticking out from under his backside. I swear I could hear her purr softly back at him. Unless it was Mr. Davis breaking wind on the sly, it was hard to tell.

Then Mr. Davis stood up from the chair, leaned over the skin, and whispered to her, cajolingly annunciating every word like you would talk to a child or a headstrong lover: "Please bring back all the motion pictures that I ever made after *A Noose Too Loose.* I specifically refer to the ones that disappeared through your agency. Please bring them back on film, or video—any reproduction format!—including but not limited to soundtracks released and references made in other works of art, as well as people's memories, the press, and academe. But no changing my age, please, please! I don't want to get any younger, and there's not much room to get older. Respectfully." He concluded the request as if the skin was his girl Friday taking dictation, "Gregory Davis, American film director."

A split second later, he glanced at the lid of the can he had placed on the small coffee table next to his armchair. Beaming with delight, he held it up to my face. The off-white label that ran across it, previously blank, now featured the title "The Asphalt Cyc" scribbled on it. Actually, the title was in the slow process of being written by an invisible yet assured hand right before my eyes. Greg Davis opened the can after the title appeared on the label in its entirety, pulled the reel out, rolled off a few shiny coils of perforated celluloid, then handed them to me and asked me to describe what I saw. I discerned the words "Columbia Pictures Presents," the familiar figure of a draped lady with a torch in her right hand, followed by the title *The Asphalt Cyclops*. And that's precisely what I reported to my host.

"No need to check the rest, except maybe my bank account for some new direct deposits," said Mr. Davis, quite pleased with himself and apparently with the skin, too. For it was now visibly expanding in size until it became twice, then four times as large as it had been mere minutes before Mr. Davis articulated his wish. The skin was hanging freely from the chair's seat, touching the carpeted floor in front of it.

"Look at this baby playing it square," marveled Mr. Davis, rubbing his hands in delight. "She could have easily penalized me, treated the wish as a whole new one, and therefore gotten smaller. Uh-huh, not my fair lady!" he exclaimed, then turned to me abruptly. "Mark, my dear boy, once again, I don't know how to thank you for your help, prodding, perseverance. But thank you I must. And thank you I will."

I had never seen my host so ebullient, so determined. Getting to the bottom of things and finding the overflowing pot of gold down there would do it, I thought.

"Ah, don't even mention it, Mr. Davis. My five cents in the history of filmmaking." I smiled a smile of relief. "Not sure how to break it to my St. Pete's employer, though. But that's a whole different enchilada." I scratched my chin thick with a two-week-stubble beard. "The whole story is so fantastic! Inconceivable. I'm still trying to wrap my mind around it. Nothing like solid proof, just like you said . . ."

"I know," echoed the old man. "And you probably still can't believe your friend is gone, too . . . I feel for you, Mark. Believe me, I do."

"Appreciated, Mr. Davis. But . . ."—I heaved a sigh—"I do think I'd better push along. It's getting late. And I'm glad to have been of help. Really. Inadvertently, but still."

"Wait," said the film director. "Let's see if I can reciprocate. I'm ninety-six—no major wishes expected on this end. You've just lost your loved one. Let's use the skin to bring your girl back."

"What?!"

"You heard me, Mark."

"I'm not in the mood for joking, Mr. Davis!"

"I'm serious. As serious as a dead man, Mark. Plus, she's not even technically buried yet. Buried, you run into all sorts of issues. Tried to bring back Rosie a year after they laid her to rest in Washington cemetery. Not a pretty picture, believe you me. Had to put her right back in. For reasons both emotional and sanitary. 'Nuff said. Let the dead bury their dead."

"But . . . how do I bring Tasha back, buried or not? I'm no Savior, Mr. Davis. No fisher of men last I checked."

"That much I know, Mark. But correct me if I'm in error, what you do for work is restore computer stuff after it crashes?"

"That's right. Rollback procedures. So?"

"So use it for what really matters! For Pete's sake, do I have to spell it out for you? Roll up your sleeves and roll it right back. Go back and fix things before they crashed!"

I grew silent for a second, mulling his crazy suggestion over. The only sound heard in the room was the whir of the Casablanca fan blades above us cutting through the blue smoke, what blue smoke? Then I blurted out, "That would be the coolest thing, Mr. Davis. Way beyond cool, actually. If you let me borrow the skin, that is."

"Be my guest. And a responsible designated driver for my gal here. Go back to the point before things got out of control.

Pinpoint that point. How do I know they went haywire? Ah, I have my sources right at my fingertips, you know. Make it my coccyx." And he flashed me a whimsical smile as he patted the skin gently. "And after that reunion with your loved one, we'll figure out what to cook up next. Maybe do a movie to end all movies? Or to start them from scratch? What do you say?"

"I don't know how to thank you, Mr. Davis," I said after a brief pause. "Not sure it'll work, but it's the thought, however far out, that counts."

"About time you started calling me Greg. And do save your thanks till your mission is accomplished. Please!" With this, the old man handed me the skin, which, upon a closer look, was a beige piece of hide, thick and irregularly shaped and roughly the size and heft of a mid-sized half-full valise.

Part Three

THE ROLLBACK PROCEDURE

Chapter Thirty-Seven.

What's with the beard, Mr. Lincoln?

A work-in-progress, Mom, what?

You a tanner now? Not a car dealer?

Neither, Dad. What's a tanner?

A niner plus oner, don't you know anything? They squared with you, then?

Almost.

Almost? What's with the hide?

A little something for a Moscow friend.

It can barely fit in your bag!

It can. Just don't want to bunch it up.

Not enough for a *dublenka* there, wouldn't you say, Larissa?

A mini-*dublenka*?

Maybe.

They still do minis over there?

Some do.

Better put it in your carry-on, Marik, seriously. Airports are not that safe.

You should visit Moscow someday, Mom. Compare and contrast.

Thanks. But no thanks. What are you flying back for anyway? Bring a girl some hide? A shortage of beasts of burden in the land of perestroika?

Please, Mom.

Please what? You got us worried sick, you know that? You call in the middle of the night? You ask us to meet you at JFK? What the deuce is going on? Level with us, Mark!

What the deuce! You a Dickens fan now? Deuce, Pops?

Cut the crap, son. You came back and never told us? You kept calling your mother from Florida, pretending you were still in Moscow? What kind of crazy games are these? Are you a ten-year-old? A pathological liar? And now you're flying back? What, you miss random street violence that bad? A little sanity here for a change, please!

How can you afford it anyway? I don't get it. You almost got paid for your Cadillacs? Start saving for an apartment! Better to own than to rent. Be here now, hello? Enough with Russia. Be here, starting as of now.

Stop smirking like we drove all the way to JFK just to tickle your funny bone. Turn on the sound. Earth to Mark. A straight answer, por favor.

I met a girl, okay?

Yeah, we remember. So?

So she's got into a bit of hot water.

And?

I'm going back to help her out.

What kind of trouble?

Ah . . . existential?

Hmm, so you like her?

Yeah, I like her.

Can't live without her and all that?

Guess not. What is this, a pop quiz?

Go get her, then. Bring her over, what the deuce. But remember one thing, son. Any relationship is like a chair.

A chair? How is it like a chair?

It should rest on four legs, ideally. So as you don't wind up on your ass one day. Your partner has to be: a) not attached; b) capable of warmth and tenderness; c) located someplace near; d) free of a lethal health condition. Dixi.

Hmm. Doesn't sound like much of a challenge.

Really? Well, look at you hauling ass to the end of the world for a girl!

Told you she's in trouble. One leg needs fixing, is all.

The distance leg?

That too.

Not sure I follow. You said just one leg needed work, son?

And, of course, your art slut has all four legs going for her plus a little extra between them, right, Efim?

Larissa, will you spare us your crudeness and uncalled for vulgarity until our boy gets on the plane? Really!

Vulgar is what your art hag from the sticks is, not me! Vulgar and opportunistic. What's the attraction anyway? The torrents of spring between your Turgenev's girl's inner thighs?

That's it. I'm leaving! Safe journey, son. And do try to make the right personal choice. Someone in this family ought to, for a change!

Like hell you are!

You keep this travesty up, and I'm leaving. Enough is enough.

Will you stop it, you two? Save the blood sport for later! Listen. The reason I asked you to come here, besides missing you these three months, is because I have some cash for you. Lots of it, actually. Money's right here in the bag.

What? Now you are talking!

I am, right? Talking 250 grand plus change. Hard-earned, too. I thought it'd be safer with you than in my Boca bank. I mean, should there be any delays on my way back.

What delays? What the hell are you talking about?

Any reason you are concerned about your safe return that your father and I should be aware of?

No reason. The coup is squashed, dust settled. But . . .

But what?

Russia being Russia, you know. Rampant corruption. The twelve time zones. But hey, I'll be okay. Let's go sit down in the corner. I don't want to count the money in plain view.

250K and change! These guys did pay you plenty, Mark!

Took some doing.

I bet it did.

You wouldn't believe half of it, Dad.

Maybe I would, maybe I wouldn't.

Don't spend it all in one place, okay? Better yet, don't spend it at all.

You kidding? I'll put it in the bank for you this afternoon.

You do that, please. Or . . . actually ten percent of it I owe Uncle Shura Trotsky. Fair is fair.

Trotsky? Whatever. It's your money.

You got that right.

So. What is your girl's name, Mr. Bigshot?

I didn't tell you? Tasha.

Nice. All right. Hey. Bring this Tasha over, and we'll do a proper chuppah wedding, the whole nine yards. You have her picture?

A chuppah wedding! Her mother will be ecstatic. Here you go.

Cute. Very. A shayna goyishe punim. Wait. She looks like somebody. Somebody famous?

Let's see. Don't hog it, Efim. Doronina. The young Tatiana Doronina.

You think, Mom?

Absolutely. Only slimmer. And sadder. A spitting image otherwise. *Odno litso.*

I know, right?

A dead ringer of an older sister, the movie.

What movie?

What do you mean "What movie"? The one where she auditions for a college entrance exam and does her "Go to the theatre and die there if you care" monologue?

"If you can." I remember the monologue. Just couldn't think of the movie. Guys, listen. I hate to be rude . . . I could use some privacy before takeoff. I need to do some thinking. Plus, I'm a little nervous.

Your fifth flight in three months ... What nervous? Ought to be a cinch.

This is no ordinary trip. Not sure how to explain. But ... a lot is riding on it. No room for slipups.

Ah, you'll be fine. See you soon, sonny. Your friend, too. Let me know when you're coming back. I'll pick you up.

Thanks ... Okay, Mom. Gotta put that thinking cap on right now.

Wait just a minute. Listen, I don't want you to make any mistakes either, Marik.

What mistakes?

I mean, your going back.

I thought you were down with that?

When'd you meet this Tasha anyway? Two months ago? Three?

So?

Give it a year, what's your hurry? Get to know her. Takes almost that long for a baby to pop out.

We don't have a year, Mom. I gotta go, really. You want to stay a while? Just let me grab a table over there, and you look the other way. Watch the planes come in for a landing. Fun, huh?

A thrill a minute.

No peeking, okay?

Give me a break, Marik ...

And Mom gave me a look, puzzling and disapproving in equal measure, then shook her head as she turned towards the fingerprints-stained wall-to-wall window overlooking a few silver aircrafts glistering on the tarmac in the winter sun. It would have been so much nicer had her look been more comforting and reassuring instead. Because that was the last time I saw Mom's face, or she mine.

Chapter Thirty-Eight.

Once seated at the table across from the souvenir store, its name forming a palindrome not entirely familiar to me, I began jotting down a few lines of code in a palm-sized spiral notebook that said "Directorio" on its off-white glossy cover. I had purchased it for a dollar from an elderly street peddler in Buenos Aires, where I had vacationed a few years back. As for the idea, or the concept of my wish, it was simple enough: return to a safe place with someone I cared for before the shit hit the fan. And, importantly, if the safe place for some reason was not to my liking, if it was lacking in some way or another, then I thought of including a provision for an emergency exit: restore all the data, update all the system tables, as it were, to the pre-rollback state. Not in so many words, actually, in substantially fewer words, or rather, commands of the code that I whispered to the skin as I leaned over my partially open bag and reached inside it to gently rub the hide. If/then, if/then/else/abend, was it in its skeletal form. The gist of my wish reduced to the code that I thought needed no further elaboration. The thing is, before the wish gets formalized by the code, there's got to be a clear-minded, unequivocal human intent behind it—something the old Greg Davis found out the hard and roundabout way. Go to the safe haven with someone you care for. Abend if it's not all it's cracked up to be. I guess I should have specified "the value" of that someone special. I mean, named the name of the one I cared for, leaving nothing to chance. The whereabouts of the safe haven, before the weather got rough was also something I could have been more specific about.

Because the next thing I knew, it suddenly got dark around me, not pitch black, just very murky, a pink-beige velvety hue; wet was the tight space I found myself in, warm were my surroundings, not unpleasant in the least, except for the smell of urine, also not too sharp or offensive. The shifting lights outside the silky, gooey quarters I was in, the distant rumble of planes muffled to a barely audible droning, and the shriveled face of a bald little Genghis Khan look-alike sans the facial hair completed the picture. Was I watching a foreign movie? Had I seen it before?

"Take your thumb out of your mouth, young man, when you're spoken to!" Genghis Khan squeaked in English, not without authority, and gave me a little elbow nudge for extra emphasis. I thought it best to follow his orders. Why contradict a stranger in a confined and unfamiliar space?

"Who are you? Where am I?" I demanded, but softly, couldn't have possibly been thinking to myself because the shriveled manikin responded readily.

"Maybe if you stopped peeing all over me, we could have a normal fetus to fetus? What do you say?"

"Aha, um, that's who we are? A couple of embryos having a tête-à-tête? Tell me another! Whose womb is this, then?"

"Take a wild guess, Mark."

"No idea. Mom's?!"

"Bingo. Your mom's, that is. My future ex-mom-in-law's. What do you think?"

"Every boy's wet dream come true, I suppose. If it is true."

"Not your dream by any stretch?"

"Ah, not really."

"Famous first words. What are we doing here then?"

"We? Who are 'we' anyway? I don't recall having any siblings. Certainly no snotty twin."

"Welcome to the beta trans-world, bud."

"And . . . um, who might you be in that world, then?"

"Just told you—your future ex. Lilly's the name. Pleased to make your prenatal acquaintance."

"No fucking way!"

"Would I lie to you? We even look the same. Most folks do at this stage, anyways. And please, watch your language. Mixed company, you know. Plus, Mom's listening."

"Wait. I certainly had no plan to wind up here! Least of all with you by my side!"

"Be careful what you wish for, as the saying goes."

"Well, if you must know. I wished to get to someplace nice and quiet before the weather got rough. With someone I loved, mind you."

"Here we are. Quiet enough for you?"

"Not with you chewing my newly formed ear off, Lilly!"

"Face it, bud. You aren't over me. Never have been. I knew it. Just didn't expect it to last this long and way past your subsequent emcees. Including the current one. Me of all the dames. Flattering, I guess."

"Dames? Sounds plenty noir for a fetus."

"A very scantily clad fast-talking femme fatale awash in amniotic fluids? Nah, not me."

"Funny how articulate an unborn can be!"

"You ain't exactly tongue-tied either, hon. That's what being identical boils down to . . ."

"That what we are? Not even semi? Not that I'd know the difference."

"Who gives a flying monkey? The whole thing is beta, anyways. Beta be good."

"Funny, are you? An intrauterine comedy for an audience of one."

"So long as we don't *try* nothing funny. As in funny funny. Adult funny. You know, one thing might lead to another . . ."

"Oh no! No way I'm making it with my pseudo-twin inside my mom's belly. Ain't cool."

"The last thing on my mind. What's with you? Ow! Will you stop kicking?"

"You're imagining things!"

"*I'm* imagining things? See, it got darker. Larissa Semenovna must've put her hand on her belly. Must've felt us jostle. Must've sensed the discomfort."

"I think she got up. She is walking now. Wow, this boat sure rocks. What a feeling. Sit you down, Mother, rest you."

"Cut it out. Why do you think we fought so much, Marik? I mean, in the alpha world?"

"Search me, girl. Cause we loved each other too much? Just guessing. I was crazy for you, that's for damn sure. And you—you were enough for me. It is you who always wanted more. More than a standing ovulation from an audience of one, Lilechka."

"Ah, what's the use now . . ."

"What's the use? All things being equal, we stand to become brother and sister, like, in four weeks is what the use is. Who cares if it happens in the alpha or beta trans-world, in the new or the old country? We don't even know what year it is. Maybe there won't be any old or new country in the beta version. But then, who would want to develop a crush on one's twin sis? Not in our neck of the woods, aka Western civilization."

"Yeah, okay. But what if we are born into a different civilization? Plus, isn't it the case most of the time? Latent crushes on siblings?"

"Latent, maybe. Manifest, I don't think. Honestly, it's my first time in the altogether next to someone I had a huge falling out with. At least we don't share an umbilical cord. One less thing to haggle over."

"Exactly how many things do you see here to fight over anyway? The stage is bare, no props to speak of. And no religion, too. Welcome to paradise."

"Paradise? This ain't no paradise, Lilly. Not the way Dante had it. Nor a golden age or the Garden of Eden either. Just the inside of my mommy's tummy."

"There won't and can't ever be a paradise for you, friend. Better face it. I was being figurative. Facetious, too."

"How come?"

"Because. Because possessive is what you're all about. Jealous, too. Always have been. No sense of chronology or antecedence. Time is linear and unidirectional where we hail from. The laws of cause and effect are immutable. Effects follow causes unfailingly. For free will, try a different universe. In alpha-world, I had had a fling with your buddy Sashka *before* I met you. Something you were never able to forgive or forget. I never cheated on you. Ever. He and I fooled around before I knew you. Shoulda learned to deal with it instead of holding a grudge all along. It happened. It is irreversible."

"Not at this point in time, it is not. Not in this version of our lives, it did not. Not in this gestation period as you sit before me bowed down, looking at your knees, like some scaled-down version of Rodin's *Thinker* it is not!"

"What are you saying?"

"Things can be reversed!"

"Too late now."

"That's the thing! I'm in bidirectional mode, okay? I hit reverse. Rollback time, baby. Dragged you along to the wrong stop, unwittingly. I can drop you off at any time you want."

"Don't bother, Mark. I'm fine where I am. Nineteen ninety-three is okay with me."

"Suit yourself, girl. Say hello to Sashka if you chance upon him."

"Your friend's in Ukraine."

"Doing what?"

"This and that. Dismantling nuclear warheads for the US government, mostly. An iffy job, but someone's got to do it."

"What? Is he even qualified?"

"MS in engineering plus the languages. What else is there?"

"I don't know. The big picture?"

"Funny, you sound just like this dude I once bumped into in New York."

"What dude?"

"Arhi, short for Arrivederci."

"You know Arhi?"

"One-nighter, all-night-longer. You could say I do."

"When was that?"

"Hey, who cares? I was a single woman back then. Taken in by his talk of the big picture and dark good looks."

"What picture was that? I mean, according to Arhi?"

"According to Arhi, it keeps changing. Right now, it's 'Go East, young man' across the board. Before the East comes after you. Doesn't get any bigger. Ciao, Mark. Time to part ways for real and let Larissa Semenovna deal with beta-postpartum."

"So long. It looks like we'll never know which twin, by rights, was the evil one, girl." I smiled as I planted a brotherly kiss on Lilly's soft forehead gleaming in the pink-beige darkness.

EPILOGUE

A Luna Park in the Sun

Because, no, that won't do, before, now that's better, a funny thing happened on the way here a million years ago. Because "because" points to causality, and what we are after is antecedency. Funny as in strange, nothing lmao about it. Speaking of, as I pull my tail out of my mouth first time in many a moon, as I prepare to ruminate out loud for talking with your mouth full, things come out garbled, more garbled than is healthy for you, no room for misunderstandings, misconceptions, plenty of that going around anyway, what is happening to you before my eyes, beneath the sky up above festooned in stars as bright as diamonds, sure things are more scientific this day and age, ebony black and otherworldly beautiful from her pierced head to her pedicured toes is she, back from a brief stopover in the realm of the dead, both of you buck naked underneath your translucent tunics stitched together from thousands of resplendent dragonfly wings, leaning against the peach tree, I believe it is peach this time around, but don't quote me on that, botanist I'm not, extra-meaning is my field of competence, otherwise I just hear things about things, I speculate vis-à-vis speculations, on occasion I tamper with temptations though not as much as in the days of yore, and the tree looks a thousand years old, I can tell just hanging upside down from its branches thick as trunks.

Basking in the dazzling light, two to tango, only if you choose to, a question of balance before the fall or instead of it, no pressure either way, this time around, squinting, guarding your eyes against the sun, a multitude of suns, the lights up above, Fresnel, Tunsel, kickers concealed in the nearby trees, you name it, we've got it. The working title, circuitous like all the projects I take on, *The Making of the Making Of*, the lighting design, nothing elaborate yet serviceable, is to my liking too. I may be a mere AD, the final say is up to Mr. Helmer, who happens to be engaged otherwise, too much on His plate at the moment, some moment, some plate, yet I'm entitled to my opinions, just like the next guy, it's a free universe, at long last, thankfully. This early in the game, it is. No business like show business, love that tune, though the scene we've been prepping for feels more like a riff on "Across the Universe" with additional lyrics by Beckett, a musical quote or two from Stravinsky. How does it go again? A million suns shining like limitless undying love, or is it the other way around? A lovely tune, a profound sentiment.

"Where are we?" Tasha and I look up, puzzled, hesitant, disconcerted. "What, you a tree hugger?" My girlfriend puckers her lips, then flashes a tentative smile. "Wait. I know you," she says to Arhi. "You are that soldier who picked me up in the Patriarch's Ponds when I was little!"

"Wrong soldier, lady," Arhi demurs. "Yuriy Borisovich's the name, a stand-in for eternity's my game. Ouro-boros, get it? But enough about me. How do you want to play it this time, kiddos? It's your call at long last. Eat the fruit of the tree of knowledge and return to innocence? Or fornicate your way to extinction all over again? You don't have to answer now. Though lots depends on the opening shot, the opening move. And by the bye, let's see what you got left of that skin," Arhi says as he wipes his mouth with his tail and spits the pit out.

"What's it to you?" I inquire glumly.

"What's it to me?" Arhi bares his teeth. "You are funny. It's mine, after all! The skin off my back, literally. I shed it as a gift to humanity once in a blue moon. To the small deserving part of it, that is. Balzac, Gregory, your turn now. Then, of course, there were some folks before Balzac . . ."

"But why me?" I am taken aback yet produce the hankie-sized skin concealed within the folds of my iridescent tunic.

"Because you're qualified, *khlopchis'ko*. The right background, a decent person, I don't care what they say, hey hey hey. Passed the tests the Helmer threw your way, too."

"Not much left there, I'm afraid," I say as I hand Arhi the piece of hide.

"Smaller than a breadbox, bigger than a foreskin. Must have been one exhausting, skin-consuming ride for you guys. First, to that undiscovered country from whence your friend was lucky to escape. Then to our little oasis here."

"What is this place anyway?" asks Tasha tensely as she tries to get her e-cigarette going. "And why is Mark black all of a sudden?"

"Do you have to ask?" Arhi chuckles. "Elysium. Paradise. Heaven. A Luna Park and a zoo rolled into one. Nonsmoking laws apply, please. Wait till you see our outdoor menagerie. A garage for two hundred electric bumper Cadillacs for our mafia ride way over yonder. Call it what you will, kiddos. It's yours, run with it, tour the grounds, feed the animals. They are harmless, too. Oh, and you guys are black because the first couple was."

"Are you for real?!" says Tasha as she removes the cartridge from her cigarette.

"Hey, it's a no-brainer, I tell you. Check it out. If hell is other people," Arhi rattles on cheerfully, "like that pipe-puffing coffee fiend in the wrinkled cream-colored trench coat intimated one October night over a game of chess in a bistro, just off the, appropriately, Champs-Élysées, then paradise is your people. Or rather, non-people. You and Mark are the two non-people from now on. Cyborgs? Maybe. First cyborgs ever? For sure. Puppeteers before the Fall who are super-puppets themselves? Not unlikely. Of course, there's no 'now' now, so things can get a little tricky, come to think, though thinking ought to be the last thing on your mind from now on. You two are black and beautiful, and you, young lady, are about 80,000 years older than Mark. Not that you look a day over twenty-five! Still, the first gal ever was the ultimate milf, wouldn't you agree? Too tricky even for me to fathom. Geneticist, I am not. This place is best viewed as a generic matrix ring, a dummy, if you will. You know, the tree, the fruit, the slithering tempter dude, maybe it's time to say to death, 'Kaput'? Again, entirely up to you to take that bite. Or not. Señor G. D. wouldn't mind either way. A word of advice? Turn it into a working vacation. How does cultural climate coordination sit with you? Start with film. Not project by project coordination, mind you, but system by system. Look at Greg. Had his pie and ate it too, free of free market impediments and thanks to my skin. Now, you give it a spin. Try a couple of thousand years for size. We can get Pushkin to knock off a few screenplays, for starters. Say, a boxer and a bear boxing match interrupted by a cartoonish mafia hit, bullets flying everywhere, mid-career Tyutchev in VO, sky is the litmus. Huh, Tasha? You like? Be all that you can be. Be here now. See how you like it. I'm the one who's running this circus now, logistics and all. Someone has to. Call it the state before things went wrong. Or maybe, thanks to you, they never will. Have fun in the sun, why don't you. Because that's where we are. In a manner of speaking. A paradise in the sun, though it never gets over eighty-two Fahrenheit. The place where ideas are generated before their solar premieres and only then beamed down to Earth. What do you say, guys?" Arhi winks at me theatrically and proffers to Tasha a fuzzy peach, which he pulls off the branch above my head with a soft twanging sound.

"Why the hell not?" shrugs Tasha as she takes a big juicy bite, then offers the fruit to me, "You wanna?"

"Oh. So that's what it is?!" I laugh so hard I'm almost crying. "Are we back to good old good and evil?"

"Nah," replies Arhi. "The difference is you're doing it with G. D.'s consent this time. Not against his regulations. Part of the plan. You get a head start, there's more free will ahead. Tautological? But come to think, lots of things down below are, too. Knowledge of good and evil doesn't imply you'll know the difference. Because there ain't much. Didn't we already cover that in Moscow, dude?"

"I suppose we did, dude," I smile again and shrug my shoulders as I bite into the peach.

"Just a convenient way of saying 'everything.' Good, evil, the gray area, the whole kit and kaboodle. Time to revise old Bill's adage: it's not the world that is the stage, but the stage that is the world. Has always been. Same difference? I beg to differ. Because the stage came first. Then, the chicken. Then they come home to roost. But you—you just do your thing and try not to trip over yourself. And please don't put me in your projects, kids. Leave it up to the mix, you hear?"

"Here we go again." I blink as I take Tasha by the hand and give her a light squeeze; I haven't seen my girl in forever. "I had no idea what Greg meant when he quoted you saying that. And I still don't. What mix?"

"Mick Jagger and Mick Bulgakov. The Micks. Can't be too direct in portraying yours truly—bad luck. You know the gents who brought you "Sympathy for the Devil" and *The Master and Margarita*, starring you know who. Hello? Anybody home?"

And as Arhi's question fell on two pairs of deaf ears, and the two blank stares of the newly minted first couple reigned over the opening shot of the movie to start all movies, our friend the Bad One could clearly see that my lady love and I finally and irrevocably found ourselves entirely bereft of all cultural references past and present and—hello, are you even alive there?

***

"Hello?!"

Marge, the curly haired receptionist's rapping on the door, woke me from my deep sleep. "You don't want me to use the master key now, do you, Mr. Mark? You asked me to knock you up in an hour? You are fifteen minutes late! We don't offer snooze service here. We are just three stars, you know!"

"Thank you. Thank you, Marge. No need to use the master key. Or raise your voice."

"How else am I supposed to . . ."

"Thank you, Marge. I got it."

I did. I was sitting on my bed, wide awake and fully dressed, staring at the rolled-up shagreen on top of the small pillow next to me, unable to fathom how and when it got there. Not after a heart-to-heart with my ex inside of my mother, a moment in the sun with the black and beautiful Tasha, and having eaten of the permitted fruit in the Luna Park called Heaven. Instead, I turned on the overhead lights in my room, pulled down the venetian blinds that had seen better days, spread out the skin on the bed in front of me, leaned over it, and began rubbing its rough surface gently but firmly, intoning that I wanted to be next to Tasha in Moscow on the late afternoon in December the moment her father abandoned her at the Patriarch's Ponds in the falling snow. I repeated these words like a fool, rubbing the shrinking skin before me until there remained nothing left to rub.

New York City–Brooklyn
2018–2024

Acknowledgments

In a somewhat different format, chapters from the book were published in *Abandon Journal* and *Articulation, online almanac.* The author would like to extend his gratitude to the following people: Frank London, jazzman and klezmer musician, for suggesting the book's title; Mark Lipovetsky, literature and culture scholar, for referring me to Peter Sloterdijk's study *Critique of Cynical Reason* as well as sharing his insights into the book's main character whose name should not be invoked in vain; Andrei Codrescu, novelist and poet, for weighing in on an early draft of the novel; Marina Gorbis, futurist, for bringing to my attention Western consultants' role in unleashing the forces that turned post-Soviet Russia into the kleptocracy it is today; Alexander Ilichevsky, novelist, for sharing his views on the relation between the universe's expansion and entropy; Anna Katsnelson, literature professor and writer, for her editorial input into an earlier draft of the novel; Lily Balasanova, artist, Ilya Bernshteyn, publisher, and Timur Mukanov, musician, for filling the author in on Moscow toponymy; Maxim D. Shrayer, scholar and writer, for reminding the author that less can be more and welcoming the book to the Immigrant Worlds & Texts series.

Heartfelt thanks are also due to Dame S. for making the publication of this book possible.

For the description of Moss Hart's first visit to Times Square, I am indebted to his book *Act One: An Autobiography,* while the exchange between Dimitri Tiomkin and David Selznick derives from Otto Friedrich's study *City of Nets: A Portrait of Hollywood in the 1940s.*

And, of course, Honoré de Balzac's *La Peau de Chagrin,* Mikhail Bulgakov's *The Master and Margarita* and the Rolling Stones' "Sympathy for the Devil" informed some of the book's thematic preoccupations.

www.ingramcontent.com/pod-product-compliance
Lightning Source LLC
La Vergne TN
LVHW100514110826
845146LV00002B/631

9798897830206